Children
of the Jedi

Also by Barbara Hambly

Time of the Dark
The Walls of Air
The Armies of Daylight

Dragonsbane

The Ladies of Mandrigyn
The Witches of Wenshar
Dark Hand of Magic

The Silent Tower
The Silicon Mage
Dog-Wizard

Stranger at the Wedding

The Rainbow Abyss
The Magicians of Night

Bride of the Rat-God

Those Who Hunt the Night

Search the Seven Hills

Star Trek novels:
Ishmael
Ghost Walker
Crossroad

Children
of the Jedi

Barbara Hambly

B A N T A M   B O O K S
New York   Toronto   London   Sydney   Auckland

CHILDREN OF THE JEDI
A Bantam Spectra Book / May 1995

SPECTRA and the portrayal of a boxed "s" are trademarks of
Bantam Books, a division of Bantam Doubleday Dell Publishing
Group, Inc.

Library of Congress Cataloging-in-Publication Data

Hambly, Barbara.
Children of the Jedi / Barbara Hambly.
p.   cm. — (Star wars)
ISBN 0-553-08930-7
I. Title.   II. Series: Star wars (Bantam Books (Firm) :
Unnumbered)
PS3558.A4215C48   1995
813'.54—dc20   95-5214
                              CIP

Published simultaneously in the United States and Canada

Bantam Books are published by Bantam Books, a division of Bantam
Doubleday Dell Publishing Group, Inc. Its trademark, consisting of the
words "Bantam Books" and the portrayal of a rooster, is Registered in
U.S. Patent and Trademark Office and in other countries. Marca
Registrada. Bantam Books, 1540 Broadway, New York, New York
10036.

PRINTED IN THE UNITED STATES OF AMERICA

BVG   0 9 8 7 6 5 4 3 2 1

For
Anne

Chapter 1

Poisoned rain speared from an acid sky. The hunter scuttled, stumbled a dozen yards before throwing himself under shelter again. A building, he thought—hoped—though for a second's blinding terror the curved shape lifted, writhing, into a toothed maw of terror from which darkness flowed out like the vomited stench of rotting bones. Serpents—tentacles—twisting arms reached down for him with what he would have sworn were tiny cobalt-blue hands . . . but the burning rain was searing holes in his flesh, so he closed his eyes and flung himself among them. Then for a clear moment his mind registered that they were blue-flowered vines.

Though the stink of his own flesh charring still choked his nostrils and the fire scorched his hands, when he looked down at them his hands were whole, untouched. Realities shuffled in his mind like cards in a deck. Should those hands be stripped away to bone? Or should they sport a half dozen rings of andurite stone and a thin scrim of engine grease around the nails?

In what reality were those fingers limber, and where did he get the notion a moment later that they were twisted like blighted roots and adorned with hooked nails like a rancor's claws?

He didn't know. The sane times were fewer and fewer; it was hard to remember from one to the next.

Prey. Quarry. There was someone he had to find.

He had been a hunter all those years in shrieking darkness. He had killed, torn, eaten of bleeding flesh. Now he had to find . . . He had to find . . .

Why did he think the one he sought would be in this . . . this place that kept changing from toothed screaming rock mouths to graceful walls, curving buildings, vine-curtained towers—and then falling back again to nightmares, as all things always fell back?

He fumbled in the pocket of his coverall and found the dirty sheet of yellow-green flimsiplast on which someone—himself?—had written:

HAN SOLO
ITHOR
THE TIME OF MEETING

"Have you seen it before?"

Leaning one shoulder on the curved oval of the window, Han Solo shook his head. "I went to one of the Meetings out in deepspace, halfway from the Pits of Plooma to the Galactic Rim," he said. "All I cared about was sneaking in under the Ithorians' detection screens, handing off about a hundred kilos of rock ivory to Grambo the Worrt and getting out of there before the Imperials caught up with me, and it was still the most . . . I dunno." He made a small gesture, slightly embarrassed, as if she'd caught him out in a sentimental deed of kindness. " 'Impressive' isn't the right word."

No. Leia Organa Solo rose from the comm terminal to join her husband, the white silk of her tabard billowing in her wake in a single flawless line. "Impressive" to the smuggler he'd been in those days, navigationally if nothing else: She'd seen the Ithorian star herds gather, the city-huge ships maneuvering among one another's deflector fields with the living ease of a school of shining fish. Linking without any more hesitation than the fingers of the right hand have about linking with the fingers of the left.

But this today was more than that.

Watching the Meeting here, above the green jungles of Ithor itself, the only word that came to her mind was "Force-full": alive with, drenched in, moving to the breath of the Force.

And beautiful beyond words.

The high, thick masses of raincloud were breaking. Slanting torrents of light played on the jungle canopy only meters below the lowest-riding cities, sparkled on the stone and plaster and marble, the dozen shades of yellows and pinks and ochers of the buildings, the flashing, angled reflections of the antigrav generators and the tasseled gardens of blueleaf, tremmin, fiddleheaded bull-ferns. Bridges stretched from city to city, dozens of linked antigrav platforms on which thin streams of Ithorians could be seen moving, flowerlike in their brilliant robes. Banners of crimson and lapis fluttered like sails, and every carved balcony, every mast and stairway and stabilizer, even the wicker harvest baskets dangling like roots beneath the vast aerial islands were thick with Ithorians.

"You?" Han asked.

Leia looked up quickly at the man by her side. Here above the endless jungles of Bafforr trees the warm air was fresh, sweet with breezes and wondrous with the scents of greenness and flowers. Ithorian residences were open, like the airy skeletons of coral; she and Han stood surrounded by flowers and light.

"When I was little—five, maybe six years old—Father came to the Time of Meeting here to represent the Imperial Senate," she said. "He thought it was something I should see."

She was silent a moment, remembering that puppyfat child with pearls twined in her thick braids; remembering the smiling man whom she'd never ceased to think of as her father. Kindly, when it sometimes didn't pay to be kind; wise in the days when even the greatest wisdom didn't suffice. Bail Organa, the last Prince of the House of Alderaan.

Han put his arm around her shoulders. "And here you are."

She smiled wryly, touched the pearls braided in her long chestnut hair. "Here I am."

Behind her the comm terminal whistled, signaling the receipt of the daily reports from Coruscant. Leia glanced at the water clock with its bobbing amazement of glass spheres and trickling fountains, and figured she'd have time to at least see what was happening in the New Republic's capital. Even when embarked on a diplomatic tour that was three-quarters vacation, as Chief of State she could never quite release her finger from the Republic's pulse. From bitter experience she had learned that small anomalies could be the forerunners of disaster.

Or, she thought—scrolling through the capsule summaries of reports, items of interest, minor events—they could be small anomalies.

"So how'd the Dreadnaughts do in last night's game?" Han went to the wardrobe to don his jacket of sober dark-green wool. It fit close, its crimson-and-white piping emphasizing the width of his shoulders, the slight ranginess of his body, suggesting power and sleekness without being military. From the corner of her eye Leia saw him pose a little in front of the mirror, and carefully tucked away her smile.

"You think Intelligence is going to put the smashball scores ahead of interplanetary crises and the latest movements of the Imperial warlords?" She was already flipping through to the end, where Intelligence usually put them.

"Sure," said Solo cheerfully. "They don't have any money riding on interplanetary crises."

"The Infuriated Savages beat them nine to two."

"The Infuriated . . . ! The Infuriated Savages are a bunch of pantywaists!"

"Had a bet with Lando on the Dreadnaughts?" She grinned across at him, then frowned, seeing the small item directly above the scores. "Stinna Draesinge Sha was assassinated."

"Who?"

"She used to teach at the Magrody Institute—she was one of Nasdra Magrody's pupils. She was Cray Mingla's teacher."

"Luke's student Cray?" Han came over to her side. "The blonde with the legs?"

Leia elbowed him hard in the ribs. " 'The blonde with the legs' happens to be the most brilliant innovator in artificial intelligence to come along in the past decade."

He reached down past her shoulder to key for secondary information. "Well, Cray's still a blonde and she's still got legs. . . . That's weird."

"That anybody would assassinate a retired theoretician in droid programming?"

"That anybody would hire Phlygas Grynne to assassinate a retired theoretician." He'd flipped the highlight bar down to *Suspected Perpetrator*. "Phlygas Grynne's one of the top assassins in the Core Worlds. He gets a hundred thousand credits a hit. Who'd hate a programmer that much?"

Leia pushed her chair away and rose, the chance words catching her like an accidental blow. "Depends on what she programmed."

Han straightened up, but said nothing, seeing the change in her eyes.

"Her name wasn't on any of the lists," he said as Leia walked, with the careful appearance of casualness, to the wardrobe mirror to put on her earrings.

"She was one of Magrody's pupils."

"So were about a hundred and fifty other people," Han pointed out gently. He could feel the tension radiating from her like gamma rays from a black hole. "Nasdra Magrody happened to be teaching at a time when the Emperor was building the Death Star. He and his pupils were the best around. Who else was Palpatine gonna hire?"

"They're still saying I was behind Magrody's disappearance, you know." Leia turned to face him, her mouth flexed in a line of bitter irony. "Not to my face, of course," she added, seeing *Who says?* spring to her husband's lips and hot anger to his eyes. "Don't you think I have to make it my business to know what people whisper? Since that was back before I held any power in the Alliance they say I got my 'smuggler friends' to kill him and his family and hide the bodies so they were never found."

"People always say that about rulers." Han's voice was rough with anger, seeing the pain behind the armor of her calm. "It was true about Palpatine."

Leia said nothing—her eyes returned for a moment to the mirror, to readjust the hang of her tabard, the braided loops of her hair. As she moved toward the doorway Han caught her arms, turning her to face him, small and slender and beautiful and not quite thirty: the Rebel Princess who'd turned into the leader of the New Republic.

He didn't know what he wanted to say to her, or could say to her to ease the weight of what he saw behind her eyes. So he only brought her to him and kissed her, much more gently than he had first meant to do.

"The awful thing is," said Leia softly, "that a day doesn't go by that I don't think about doing it."

She half turned in his grip, her lips set in that cold expression that he knew hid pain she could not show even to him. The years of enforced self-reliance, of not giving way in front of anyone, had left their mark on her.

"I have the lists. I know who worked on the Death Star, who Palpatine hired in his think tanks, who taught at the Omwat orbital training center—and I know they're out of the Republic's jurisdiction. But I also know how easy it would be for me to juggle credits and Treasury funds and hire people like Phlygas Grynne or Dannik Jericho or any of those 'smuggler friends' they talk about to find these people and just . . . make them disappear. Without a trial. No questions asked. No possibility of release on a technicality. Just because *I* know they're guilty. Because *I* want it so."

She sighed, and some of the pain eased from her face as she met his eyes again. "Luke talks about the power that lies in the dark side. The Force isn't the only thing that has a dark side, Han. And the tricky thing about the dark side is that it's so easy to use—and it gets you what you think you want."

She leaned close and kissed him again, thanking him. Outside the movement of wind filled the sky with light and the sound of chimes.

Leia smiled. "We're on."

The herds ingathered. Cities themselves, they linked and joined to form one great shining city of bright stone, dark wood, flashing glass, exuberant with greenery. Segmented bridges stretched like welcoming hands to join clan platform to clan platform, house float to house float. Balloons, gliders, kites skated the air between the platforms; arborals, tree skimmers, the gaudy fauna of the jungle's top canopy clambered insouciantly up the harvest baskets from the trees below, chattering and whistling on trees and balconies while the Ithorians made their way to the *Cloud-Mother*'s central square.

The *Cloud-Mother*—the herd best known for its hospitals and glass manufacturing—had been voted the site of the reception of the Republic's representatives, mostly because it had the best guest facilities and the largest shuttleport, though it was also true that it was one of the most beautiful of the herds. Leia had the impression, as she stepped out into the clear, burning sunlight of the top platform of the Meeting Hall's steps, that the huge square before her was a garden, packed with brilliant silks, wreaths of flowers, from which emerged a forest of wide, leathery necks and gentle eyes.

An ululation of applause and welcome rippled from the crowd, like the song of a million birds at morning. Ithorians waved scarves and flowers, not rapidly but in long, swooping curves. To human eyes they appeared ungainly, sometimes frightening, but here in their home they had a weird, graceful beauty. Leia lifted her hands in greeting, and beside her she saw Han raise his arm to wave. Behind them, solemnly, the three-year-old twins, Jacen and Jaina, released their nurse Winter's hands to do the same; the toddler, Anakin, only stood, holding Jaina's hand and gazing about him with round eyes. The leaders of the herds stepped from the crowd, over a dozen of them, ranging in height anywhere from two to three meters and in color from darkest jungle green to the bright yellows of a pellata bird. Atop the broad necks, the T-shaped heads with their wide-separated eyes had an air of gentle wisdom.

"Your Excellency." Umwaw Moolis, Ithorian liaison to the Senate, dipped her neck and spread her long arms in a graceful gesture of submission and respect. "In the name of the herds of Ithor, welcome to the Time of Meeting. General Solo—Master Skywalker . . ."

Leia had almost forgotten that Luke would be present, too; he must have come out onto the platform behind her. But there he was, inclining his head in response to the greeting. Her brother seemed to wear an inner silence like a cloak these days, a haunted stillness, the burden of being a Jedi and the roads that it had caused him to travel. Only when he smiled did she see again the flustered, sandy-haired farmboy who'd blasted his way into the detention cell on the Death Star in his borrowed shining white armor and said *Oh . . . er . . . I'm Luke Skywalker. . . .*

In the shadows of the Meeting Hall's columned porch, Leia could just glimpse the others who'd come with them to the diplomatic reception: Chewbacca the Wookiee, Han's copilot, mechanic, and closest friend from his smuggling days, two meters plus of reddish fur well brushed for the occasion; the golden gleam of the protocol droid C-3PO; and the smaller, chunkier shape of his astromech counterpart, R2-D2.

All those battles, thought Leia, turning back to the Ithorian delegation. All those stars and planets, whose names, sometimes, she could scarcely recall, though in nightmares she felt again the ice and heat and terror. . . . And yet, after all the danger and fear, the Republic was alive. Growing in spite of the warlords of the fragmented Empire, the satraps of the old regime, the planets that tasted liberty and wanted total independence from all federation. Here in the clear glory of the sunlight, the utter peace of this alien world, it was impossible to feel that they would not succeed.

She saw Luke move, swing around as if at some sound, scanning the two-level arcades that flanked the Meeting Hall, and she felt at the same moment the terrible sense of danger . . .

"Solo!"

The voice was a raw scream.

"Solo!"

The man sprang from the arcade's upper balcony with the unthinking speed of an animal, landed halfway up the steps, and raced toward them, arms outstretched. Ithorians staggered, taken by surprise, as he shoved his way between them; then they fell back from him in shock and fear. Leia had an impression of eyes rolling in madness, flecks of spittle flying from his dirty beard, even as she thought, *He isn't armed,* and realized in the next second that this was one to whom that fact meant nothing.

The Ithorian herd leaders closed on the man, but their reflexes were the reflexes of a thousand generations of herbivores. The attacker was within a foot of Han as Luke stepped forward, with no appearance of haste or effort, and caught the claw-fingered hand, flipping the man in a neat circle and laying him without violence on the pavement. Han, who'd stepped back a pace to give Luke room to throw, now moved back in, helping to pin the attacker to the ground.

It was like trying to hold down a frenzied rancor. There was something hideously animal in the way the man bucked and heaved, throwing the combined strength of Han and Luke nearly off him, screaming like a mad thing as Chewbacca and the Ithorians closed in.

"Kill you! Kill you!" The man's broken, filthy hands flailed, grabbing at Han as the Wookiee and Ithorians dragged him from the ground. "Going to kill you all! Solo! *Solo!*"

His voice scaled up into a hideous scream as one of the herd's physicians, loping from the Meeting Hall in a billow of purple robes, slapped the man on the side of the neck with an infuser. The man gasped, mouth gaping, sucking air, eyes staring in lunatic pain. Then he sagged back unconscious into a dozen restraining arms.

Leia's first reaction was to reach Han—the intervening two meters of platform were suddenly a virtual stockade of towering, gesticulating

Ithorians, chattering like some impossibly beautiful orchestra whose players have all suddenly been dosed with brain-jagger or yarrock. Umwaw Moolis was in her way. "Your Excellency, never in the history of this herd, of this world, have we been subjected to such an attack . . ."

It was all she could do not to push her aside.

Luke, she was interested to note, had gone straight for the arcade from which the man had come, springing from platform to balcony and scanning the colonnade and the square beyond.

The children!

Leia forced her way through the crowd to the doorway.

Winter was gone. See-Threepio toddled forth from the shadows with his slightly awkward mechanical walk and caught her arm.

"Winter has taken Jacen, Jaina, and Anakin back to their nursery, Your Excellency," he reported. "She stayed only long enough to point out to them that General Solo was completely unhurt. Perhaps it would be advisable for you and General Solo to go there and reassure them at the first convenient opportunity."

"Are they guarded?" Han could look after himself . . . for one awful moment the hairy, convulsed face of the madman returned to her, reaching for the children . . .

"Chewbacca has gone with them."

"Thank you, Threepio."

"Can't see any further danger." Luke appeared at her side in a swirl of black cloak, light-brown hair ruffled where he'd pushed back the hood, his face—scarred from a long-ago encounter with an ice creature on Hoth —unreadable as usual, but his blue eyes seeming to see everything. "Kids all right?"

"They're in the nursery. Chewbacca's with them." She looked around. Han was still standing where he had been, in the midst of a hooting, waving crowd of Ithorians, staring at the shadowed door through which the attacker had been taken. He was nodding and even making some kind of reply to the herd leaders, who were assuring him that such things never happened, but Leia could tell he wasn't really hearing them.

She and Luke edged their way to him.

"You all right?"

Han nodded, but gave them only a glance. Leia had seen him less upset by full-scale artillery ambushes with Imperial starfighter support.

"That can't have been anything like a planned attempt." Luke fol-

lowed his gaze to the door. "When he starts to come out of the tranquil-
izer I'll see if I can go into his mind a little, pick up who he is—"

"I know who he is," said Han.

Brother and sister regarded him in surprise.

"If that wasn't a ghost," said Han, "and it might have been . . . I'd
say it was about fifty percent of my old buddy Drub McKumb."

Chapter 2

"Children." The man lashed to the diagnostic bed mumbled the word as if lips, tongue, and palate were swollen and numb. Blue eyes stared blankly up from an eroded moonscape of wrinkled flesh. Above the padded table, small monitor screens traced jewel-bright patterns of color. The central one, Leia could see, indicated that the smuggler was in no physical pain—with that much gylocal in him he couldn't possibly be—but the right-hand monitor showed a jangled horror of reds and yellows, as if all the nightmares in the galaxy held shrieking revel in his frontal lobe.

"Children," he muttered again. "They hid the children in the well."

Leia glanced across at her husband. In his hazel eyes she saw the reflection, not of the emaciated creature who lay before them in the ripped green plastene coverall of a long-distance cargo hauler, but the fat, blustering planet-hopper captain he'd known years ago.

The Healing House of the *Cloud-Mother* was a dim place, rank with plants like all the herd and bathed in soft blue-green light. Tomla El, chief healer of the herd, was small for an Ithorian and like the lights of the place also a soft blue-green, so that in his purple robe he seemed only a shadow and a voice as he considered the monitors and spoke to Luke at his side.

"I am unsure that going into his mind would profit you, Master

Skywalker." He blinked his round golden eyes at the frenzied right-hand
screen. "He's under as much gylocal and hypnocane as we dare adminis-
ter. The brain has been severely damaged, and his whole system is full of
repeated massive doses of yarrock."

"Yarrock?" said Luke, startled.

"Sure explains him being off his rocker," commented Han. "I haven't
seen Drub in seven or eight years, but back when I knew him he wouldn't
even sniff dontworry, much less go in for that caliber of hallucinogen."

"Oddly enough," said the Healer, "I don't think his condition is
attributable to the drug. Judging by his autonomic responses, I believe the
yarrock acted as a depressant to the mental activity, permitting brief
periods of lucidity. These were found in his pockets."

He produced a half dozen scraps of flimsiplast, stained and filthy and
creased. Han and Leia stepped close to look over Luke's shoulders as he
unfolded them.

HAN SOLO
ITHOR
THE TIME OF MEETING
BELIA'S BOSOM—SULLUST—BAY 58
SMELLY SAINT—YETOOM NA UUN—BAY 12
FARGEDNIM P'TAAN

"P'taan's a medium-big drug dealer on Yetoom." Solo rubbed unconsciously at the scar on his chin, as if contact with it reminded him of his
own rough-and-tumble contraband days. "If Drub was on yarrock he
could have got it from him, provided he'd found some way to make
himself a millionaire in the past seven years. And you'd have to *be* a
millionaire to take enough of that stuff to give yourself that kind of
damage."

He shook his head, and looked again at the starved body on the table,
the filthy, clawlike nails.

"I take it the *Smelly Saint* and *Belia's Bosom* are ships?" Leia's eyes
were still on the nightmare readouts above the bed.

"The *Saint* runs ripoff copy agri-droids out of the Kimm systems,
sometimes slaves from the Senex Sector. Makes sense. Yetoom's on the
edge of the Senex."

He shook his head again, staring down at what was left of the man he had known. "He used to be bigger than the three of us put together; I kidded him about being Jabba the Hutt's younger, cuter brother."

"Children," whispered McKumb again, and tears leaked from his staring eyes. "They hid the children down the well. Plett's Well." His head jerked, spastic, face contorting with pain. "Han . . . Kill you. Kill you all. Got to tell Han. They're there . . ."

"Got to tell Han," repeated Luke softly. "That doesn't sound like a threat."

"Plett's Well. . . ." Leia wondered why the name tugged on her mind, what it reminded her of . . .

What voice had said it, and who had hushed the speaker at the sound of those words?

"He's definitely suffering from severe and prolonged malnutrition," said Tomla El, surveying the line of numbers on the bottommost readout screen. "How long since you saw him last, General Solo?"

"Eight years, nine years," said Han. "Before the fighting on Hoth. I ran across him on Ord Mantell—he was the one who told me Jabba the Hutt had major money on my head. I never heard of anything called Plett's Well."

"Plettwell." Drub McKumb spoke in an almost natural tone, turning his head toward Leia, who stood nearest, though his eyes, momentarily calm, seemed to see something or someone other than her. "Get to Solo, honey. Tell him. I can't. All the children were down the well. They're gathering . . ." He flinched, and the right-hand screen scorched to blood; his body spasmed, twisting up into a heaving arc.

"Kill them!" he screamed. "Stop them!"

Tomla El moved forward swiftly, slapping another patch of gylocal to the row already on the man's neck. McKumb's eyes slipped closed as the raw color of the monitor faded and darkened.

"Children," he whispered again. "The children of the Jedi."

The brain-wave patterns of the left-hand monitor dipped and eased as he sank into sleep, but those on the right continued to flare as he slid into dreams from which he could not be waked.

"Plettwell." Dr. Cray Mingla spoke the word as if tasting it, turning it over like a circuit board of unfamiliar make to look at all sides. At the same time her long, exquisitely manicured fingers stirred through the little heap of debris retrieved from Drub McKumb's pockets—credit papers, broken ampoules, and tiny packets of black plastene coated with fusty-smelling yarrock residue, and half a dozen pieces of old-fashioned jewelry: a pendant of three opals, a bracelet, and four earrings which did not match, their intricate lacings of bronze wire and dancing pearls crusted thick with pinkish gold mineral salts. Her straight brows, darker than the winter-sun silk of her upswept hair, tweaked down over the bridge of her nose, and Leia, on the opposite side of the Guest House's dining table, heard again the name in her mind.

Plett's Well, someone—her father?—had said . . . When?

"My mother," said Cray after a time. "I think my mother talked about it." She looked hesitantly over at Luke, standing in silence near the door. "She and my great-aunt fought about it, I think. I was very little, but I remember my great-aunt slapping her, telling her never to speak of it. . . . But she had jewelry like that."

As she spoke of her childhood, her uncertainty broke through the careful perfection of her beauty, and Luke remembered she was only twenty-six, a few years younger than himself. She scraped at the mineral deposits on an earring with a lacquered pink thumbnail. Oxydized sulfur and antimony, Tomla El had identified it, mixed with trace minerals and mud.

"My aunts had some, too," said Leia thoughtfully. "Aunt Rouge, Aunt Celly, and Aunt Tia . . . Father's sisters." Her mouth flickered into a wry quirk at the memory of those three redoubtable dowagers. "They never stopped trying to turn me into what they called a Proper Princess—and marry me off to some brainless twerp from one of the other ancient ruling Houses. . . ."

"Like Isolder?" Han named the hereditary Prince of the Hapes Consortium—and Leia's erstwhile suitor—and Leia made a face at him where he stood next to Luke in the dining room doorway.

"But they had jewelry like this," Leia went on after a moment. "It's Old Republic bronze, the strapwork and the iridescent wash."

"He must have started out with pockets full of the stuff," remarked Han, "if he's been buying yarrock with it along the way."

Leia reached across the table to touch her own earrings, which she'd discarded the moment she was out of public view: sleekly modern disks of silver, polished and chaste. "Maybe forty, fifty years old? They don't make anything like that now."

Cray nodded, being well up on every nuance of fashion. Even in the laboratories and lecture rooms of the Magrody Institute she was impeccably turned out, a tall, slim young woman—*the blonde with the legs,* Leia remembered Han's description, slightly envious of her elegant height, which made it possible for her to carry off fashions that Leia, a good eighteen centimeters shorter, knew were out of the question for herself. Only when actually engaged in the rigors of Jedi training on Yavin had Leia ever actually seen Cray without makeup and jewelry, and even then the young scientist managed—Leia reflected enviously—to look gorgeous.

"What did your mother say about it?" asked Luke in his quiet voice. "Why didn't your aunt want her to talk about it?"

Cray shook her head, and Luke turned to the golden protocol droid who had joined them in the dining room, his stubby astromech counterpart at his side.

"Ring any bells with you, Threepio?"

"I'm sorry to say it does not, sir," replied the droid.

"It was a fortress."

They all turned, startled, to look at the man—or the thing that had once been a man—standing beside Cray's chair.

The ambassadorial receptions were over. The ceremonial tours of the various herds, the luncheons, teas, flower viewings, and the descent to tour the jungle floor had all been accomplished, albeit with larger and more heavily armed parties than had been previously planned. Cray and her fiancé, Nichos Marr—two of Luke's most recent students at the Jedi Academy on Yavin who had accompanied Luke to Ithor to consult with Tomla El—had been asked to do service as bodyguards, extending their Jedi-trained senses through the brightly dressed, friendly crowds. With night's gentle cloaking of the floating megalopolis, they had returned with the Presidential party to the privacy of the Guest Houses, the first chance Leia had had all day to speak to Cray Mingla in private about the assassination of Stinna Draesinge Sha . . . the inconspicuous theoretician who had studied with the people who had helped design the Death Star.

Though Leia's news of the assassination had shocked her, Cray had had little to tell about her former teacher. Draesinge, like Nasdra Magrody himself, had been almost completely apolitical, seeking knowledge for the sake of knowledge . . . like the physicist Qwi Xux, thought Leia bitterly, to whom Magrody had taught the principles of artificial

intelligence in Moff Tarkin's orbital accelerated learning center above the
hostage planet of Omwat.

Only afterward had Cray asked about Drub McKumb.

Beyond the suite's lacy translucent groves of arches and windows, the
warm night was alive with colored lights and snatches of music as, all over
the joined flotilla of the herds, clans and families entertained and rejoiced.
Above their heads in the pendant networks of the ceiling, baskets of solar
globes shed their warm light on the little group: Leia still in her formal
gown of green-and-gold-worked vine-silk and her white tabard, Han in
his sharply tailored military trousers, though the first thing he'd done
upon returning to the Guest House had been to get rid of the jacket; Luke
a shadow in his black Jedi cloak.

"Artoo ran a cross-check of Plett's Well and Plettwell through the
master computer bank on the herd ship *Tree of Tarintha,* the largest on the
planet," Threepio diffidently informed the room at large. "No referent
was found."

"As a child . . ." Nichos paused, collecting his thoughts, a mannerism Luke noticed now because it was something his student almost never
did anymore. He caught the way Cray glanced back at the man—or
former man—to whom she was still officially betrothed; saw the way she
watched him. Searching, Luke knew, for those other mannerisms, the way
he used to put his hand to his forehead when he was thinking . . .
hunting vainly for the small human gestures of knotting his brows, shutting his eyes . . .

The face was still that of the young man who had come to Yavin over
a year ago, asking to be tested for adeptness in the Force. The technicians
of the biomedical institute on Coruscant had saved that much. They'd
duplicated his hands as well. Luke recognized the scar on the little finger
of the right one, which Nichos had gotten the first time he'd tried maneuvering an edged weapon with the Force. They fitted perfectly into the
droid body Cray had designed when Nichos had been diagnosed with the
first signs of Quannot's Syndrome, as if Nichos—the Nichos Luke had
known, the Nichos Cray had loved—were simply wearing smooth, form-
fitted armor of brushed pewter-gray steel, exquisitely articulated, every
joint and stress point filled in with metal-meshed plastoid as fine as vine-
silk, so that not a strut, not a wire, not a cable showed to remind anyone
that this was a droid.

But the face was perfectly smooth, without expression. All the musculature was mimicked there, with an accuracy never before achieved in prosthetics. Nichos—though he tried to remember, knowing that his expressionlessness disturbed Cray—usually forgot to use them. He was expressionless now, his mind delving back through every fragment of digitalized memory, searching for some forgotten thread.

"I was there," he said at length. "I remember running up and down corridors, hallways cut in the rocks. Someone had . . . had raised a mental barrier, an illusion of dread, to keep us out of some of them—had used the Force to do it. The kretch would eat us, someone said, the kretch would eat us. . . . But we'd dare each other. The older kids—Lagan Ismaren and Hoddas . . . Hoddag? . . . Umgil, I think their names were—said we were looking for Plett's Well."

"What was the kretch?" asked Cray, into the silence that followed.

"I don't know," said Nichos. Once he would have shrugged. "Something that ate kids, I guess."

"Someone raised a mental barrier with the Force to keep you out of tunnels where you weren't supposed to go?" Leia leaned forward, the earring still in her hand.

"I think so, yes," said Nichos slowly. "Or used the Force to . . . to instill an aversion in us. I didn't think anything of it at the time but looking back . . . it was the power of the Force."

"You have to try that with Jace and Jainy," remarked Han, and Chewbacca, sitting heretofore silent on his other side, groaned in assent.

"How old were you?" asked Luke. "Do you remember any other names?" Beside him, Artoo whirred softly as he recorded data.

Nichos's blue eyes—artificials, but they duplicated the originals exactly—stared blankly in front of him for a few moments. A living man would probably have closed them. Cray looked aside.

"Brigantes," he said after a moment. "Ustu. She was a Ho'Din, almost two meters tall and the loveliest pale green. . . . A woman—girl—named Margolis looked after us. I was extremely young."

"Margolis was my mother's name," said Cray softly.

There was another silence.

"The children of the Jedi," Luke whispered.

"A—a colony of them? A group?" Leia shivered, wondering why that sounded so familiar.

"My mother . . ." Cray hesitated, smoothed back a tendril of ivory-pale hair with one long-fingered hand. "My great-aunt was always watching my mother, criticizing her. Later I put together that my mother's mother had been a Knight and Aunt Sophra was afraid Mother—or I— would show signs of sensitivity to the Force as well. Mother never did. I told you about that when Nichos first brought me to Yavin, Luke."

Luke nodded, remembering. Remembering Nichos's shining grin, *The most brilliant AI programmer at the Magrody Institute—and strong in the Force as well.*

"Like Uncle Owen," he said softly. "The worst yelling-at I ever got in my life was the one time I . . . I guess I found something using the Force. Aunt Beru had lost the little screwdriver she used to fix her mending stitcher. I shut my eyes and said, 'It's under the couch.' I don't know how I knew that. Uncle Owen claimed he punished me because the only way I could have known was if I'd put it there myself, but now I think he knew it was the Force, and *that's* why he was mad."

He shrugged. "I must have been about six. I sure never did that again. I didn't even remember it until I was with Yoda on Dagobah."

"Yes," said Cray. "Aunt Sophra was like that with Mother. And I must have picked it up, because until Nichos and I talked about it, it . . . it never even occurred to me I might be sensitive to the Force."

Nichos remembered to smile, and put his hand on her shoulder. Luke knew they'd even got the body temperature right, in the hands and face at least.

"*They hid the children down the well,*" said Leia softly. "Do you think when . . . when Vader and the Emperor started hunting down and killing the Jedi, some of the Knights . . . I don't know, smuggled their spouses and children to some place of safety? Did you talk to Drub about the Jedi, Han? About the Force?"

"I don't remember much about the conversation," admitted Han. "Especially not after we got drinking. But I remember telling him about Luke, and about Old Ben. Drub wouldn't let it get in the way of business, but he always did want to see the Rebels win." He shrugged, embarrassed. "He was kind of a romantic."

Leia hid a smile and her own private reflections about smugglers who let the Rebellion interfere with their business, and returned her gaze to Luke. "They must have been scattered later," she said. "But if there was a group of the families of the Jedi hiding out in Plett's Well, or Plettwell . . . they might have left records of where they went. And who they were."

She picked up the earring again, turning it to the light. "You say Yetoom's on the edge of the Senex Sector. Sullust is between Yetoom and here. Most of the credit papers here are Sullustan . . . What would the *Smelly Saint*'s range be?"

"It's a light stock freighter, like the *Falcon*," said Han thoughtfully, glancing at Chewbacca for confirmation. The Wookiee nodded. "It's got deepspace capabilities, but most small-time smugglers don't go more than about twenty parsecs to a jump. Since there's nothing much below or above the ecliptic around there, that would put his point of origin somewhere in the Senex or Juvex Sector, or in the Ninth Quadrant, say, between the Greeb-Streebling Cluster and the Noopiths."

"That's a lot of territory," said Leia thoughtfully. "It's broken up, too —Imperial holdouts and little two-planet confederacies; Admiral Thrawn never made much headway with the Ancient Houses that rule in the Senex Sector, but we haven't, either. I know the House Vandron runs slave farms on Karfeddion, and the House Garonnin gets most of its revenue from strip-mining asteroids under pretty scary conditions—even back in the old days there were always questions in the Senate about Rights of Sentience in those areas."

"It doesn't sound like someplace that would be easy to search for word of the Jedi," said Cray.

"No place will be easy," said Leia. "Because we can jump from one hyperspace point to another, we forget how much distance—how many thousands of light-years—lie between one inhabited system and the next. People can hide anywhere, or be hidden anywhere. All it takes is for one line, one collection of phosphor dots, to get dropped out of a computer somewhere, and they're lost. Completely. Forever. You can't really search."

"Surely there're backup records somewhere." Cray looked uneasy at the concept of such possibilities for loose ends. Leia gathered that with Luke's teaching, Cray wasn't as firmly wedded as she had once been to the principle that all things were ultimately controllable by intelligence, but she had a long way to go. She looked over at Luke. "Have you tried to go into McKumb's mind?"

Luke nodded, flinching from the memory. Whether because of the yarrock, or the brain damage, or from some other cause, he had encountered none of the normal human barriers that prevent invasion by telepathic force, but neither had he found in the old smuggler's mind anything for his own seeking thoughts to link to, nothing to ask, to see. Only a burning chaos of pain, through which hideous shapes came slamming: rending monstrosities, scalding streams of acid, noise that beat and hammered in his ears, and fire that suffocated him. He'd come to shaking all over, Tomla El holding him up and gazing at him in deep concern, fractions of a second after he'd tried to go in.

"Could you go into mine?" asked Nichos. "I only remember what a child would see, but at least you could narrow down your field of search. I was human then," he added, and remembered again to smile. "And at the time, I was able to touch the Force."

Only Cray and Leia accompanied Luke and Nichos down the curving sweeps of narrow stairs and across the small rear garden to the suite Cray and Nichos shared. Though Han and Luke were both fairly certain now that Drub McKumb's intent had been warning rather than assassination, Han was unwilling to assume that they knew everything he'd been trying to say. So he and Chewbacca remained in the Presidential Guest House near the children, with Artoo-Detoo hooked into a printer spilling out starcharts and calculations concerning the Senex Sector and See-Threepio standing happily on the balcony comparing the elaborate Ithorian herd ceremonials taking place in the square below to his internal records of what they were supposed to be.

"We knew that he'd—at least temporarily—lose his ability to use the Force when he was . . . was transferred." Cray spoke quickly, with a slight brittleness in her voice, as if admitting that a contingency had been expected would somehow give her power over it. She glanced ahead at Nichos and Luke, walking side by side, the tall, silvery shape of the onetime student almost dwarfing Luke's black-cloaked slightness. The terrace outside the Guest Quarters faced away from the dances in the square, and their passing footfalls sounded loud on the elaborate lapis and gold of the starmap pavement.

"I know Luke and Kyp Durron, and some of the others who studied the Holocron, think the Force is completely a function of organic life, but I don't see how that can be necessarily so. It isn't like he's a construct, like Threepio or Artoo. Nichos is as alive as you or I." She kept her head up, her voice brisk, but by the light of the sun-globes half hidden in the branches of their parent trees, Leia saw the telltale silvery gleam of suppressed tears in the younger woman's eyes.

"Right now I'm working on crunching and cubing hypersmall micros, in order to duplicate what can be reconstructed in X-rays from the brains of the other students in the Academy. The good thing about what I've done with Nichos's brain is that the information can be transferred to more efficient processors as I improve and fine-tune the design." She touched her hair again, as a cover for a quick brush at the corners of her delicately colored eyelids. Hers was a perfection that would admit neither grief nor doubt.

"He's only been in that body for—what, six months?" Leia hated herself for holding out a comfort that in her heart she suspected was false. Quite sincerely, she added, "It's a miracle he's alive at all."

Cray nodded once, briefly, taking no credit as they passed through a vestibule of lacy air walls and stalactites, like a sea cave festooned with flowers. "And he wouldn't be, if it weren't for some of the research Stinna Draesinge Sha did on captured Ssi-ruuk wreckage. On transferring the . . . the actual person, not just a data print . . . into an artificial construct. She was very hopeful about the work with Nichos, very helpful. She said the Ssi-ruuk entechment process would have fascinated Magrody —*her* teacher—and he would almost certainly have come up with better answers than she did about the relationship of organic and artificial intelligences, but he'd—uh—gone by that time. She . . ."

She shook her head. "I can't imagine who would have wanted to hurt her."

She was quiet again as they entered the pleasant, grottolike central chamber of her suite and Nichos took a seat at the table, with Luke opposite him under the dim pinkish light of the few sun-globes embedded in the translucent network of the low ceiling. A sinuous divan shaped for human contours nestled in a niche; Leia and Cray settled on it, Leia reaching up to unhook another sun-globe's cover, to shed soft pinkish light around them.

Cray went on, low enough not to be heard by the men at the table, "I was just glad that when Nichos . . . when they diagnosed him . . ." She shied from any mention of those memories. "I was glad I was able to keep him alive. That he had enough training in the Force to . . . to detach himself from his . . . his organic body. And analyzing how to transmit Force skills to an inorganic sentience will only be a matter of time. Some of Magrody's researches were pointing in that direction before he . . ."

Again she bit back the word "disappeared," and Leia knew she, too, had heard the stories. The whispers. The rumors that she, Leia Organa Solo, had used her "smuggler friends" to take revenge on the man who had taught Qwi Xux, Ohran Keldor, Bevel Lemelisk, and the other designers of the Death Star.

Going into Nichos's mind was one of the strangest things Luke had done. When he used the Force to probe someone's thoughts or dreams, they most often came to him as images, as if he were recalling or dreaming about something he himself had seen long ago. Sometimes the images took the form of sounds—voices—and, very occasionally, a sense of heat or cold. Eyes closed, Luke sank now into the light trance of listening, searching. He was aware of Nichos's mind, open and receptive to his as the meditations of the Jedi taught . . . aware of the personality of the young man who had come to him with such ability in the Force, with such open-hearted determination to use it responsibly and correctly.

Luke had had far more powerful students, but—though Nichos was Luke's elder by a number of years—seldom a more teachable one.

Under Luke's grip, Nichos's hands felt warm—like his own prosthetic, heated by minute subcutaneous circuitry to exactly body temperature, so that those who touched them might not be disconcerted. Luke was aware that Cray and Leia had fallen silent, was aware of their breathing, and of the faint, wonderful drift of songs floating on the night air from the city's thousand parties and balls.

He was briefly aware, as he sank deeper into his probing trance, that Nichos did not breathe.

He had wondered a little, on their way across the plaza, whether he'd be able to do this at all; whether, in fact, Nichos *was* the man he had known, the man who had come to Yavin to find him, saying, *I think I have the powers you seek* . . .

Cray Mingla, for all her relative youth, was one of the leading experts on artificial intelligence programming in the galaxy. She was in addition an apprentice Jedi herself, aware of the interaction of the Force, the body, the mind, and all of ambient life. She had followed Nasdra Magrody's teachings, trying to close the gap between artificially constructed intelligence and the workings of the organic brain; had even studied what could be known of the technology of the forbidden Ssi-ruuk, seeking to learn what the essence of human personality, human energy, actually *was*.

But he still hadn't known whether this was Nichos Marr, or only a droid programmed with everything the man had known.

The memory was there. A child's memory, as Nichos had said: dark tunnels twisting through rock seams, and a dense, damp heat; in other places bitter cold. Snowstorms howling across empty wastes of ice and black rock; caves of ice, and below them caldera of sullenly smoking mud. Crystalline cliffs flashing blue in a dim twilight of a heatless sun; thick jungles; banks of ferns shoulder-deep around streams and pools that steamed in the weird sharpness of the air.

A woman singing.

> *"Children playing in the field of flowers,*
> *The Queen's on her way to the King's three towers . . ."*

He remembered that song, so far back he couldn't even recall whose voice he'd heard singing it.

But he was aware of those memories as if he'd read them somewhere. *Snowstorms howling across empty wastes . . .* was a string of words in his mind unattached to the sear of the ice-wind he himself recalled from Hoth; he knew the streams had steamed near the glaciers without seeing either water or ice.

All the words of the old song were there—the tune, too, in standard musical notation, he supposed. But no memory of the voice that had sung them, any more than he had himself.

Only a darkness, eerily, heartbreakingly empty.

> *"The Queen had a hunt-bird and the Queen had a lark,*
> *The Queen had a songbird that sang in the dark.*
> *The King said I'll hang you from the big black tree*
> *If your birds don't bring three wishes to me. . . ."*

Then it hit him. Breathtaking, terrifying, a sense of cold horror and a stinging almost-sound that lanced through his brain like a splinter of frozen steel. He saw, for one instant, the massive cliffs of ice glittering like volcanic glass in iron twilight and below them the beveled and faceted jewel face of a shallow antigrav dome closing in all the valley beneath.

Lights shone dimly through steaming mists, trees thick with blossom and fruit, gardens like enchanted ships suspended in the air . . .

A ruined tower, standing dark against the face of the dark cliff.

And something else. Some image, some shock . . . a wave of darkness that spread outward, reaching, searching, calling in all directions. A wave that chilled him, then folded in on itself before he could identify it, like a black flower growing backward into a deadly seed that vanished . . .

And he was gasping, fully conscious once more and feeling the startled flinch of Nichos's hands under his.

"What is it?" he demanded at once, as Cray sprang up and strode across the room.

"Nic . . ."

The silvery man regarded him inquiringly. He'd felt Nichos's hands flail away from his, and Nichos was looking at them in some surprise.

"You convulsed." Cray was kneeling by the chair, already checking the row of gauges on Nichos's chest.

"What happened?" asked Luke. "What did you feel?"

"Nothing." Nichos shook his head, a fraction of a second too late to be natural. "I mean, I have no recollection of any untoward sensation at all. I felt Luke's hands over mine, and then I was out of the trance and my hands had moved away from his."

"Did you see anything?" Leia had come to stand at his other side. Cray was still checking gauges, though she knew their ranges by heart.

"I think it has to be Belsavis." Luke rubbed his temples; the ache in them was different from the throbbing that sometimes developed when he'd used the Force to probe deeply against resistance, or to listen for something far beyond human hearing. "I saw an antigrav-supported light-amplification dome of some kind over a volcanic rift valley; Belsavis is the only place I know of that has one like that."

"But the dome was only built a dozen years ago," objected Cray. "If Nichos was there as a child . . ."

Luke hesitated, wondering where that image had come from. Why he felt shaken, shocked . . . why he felt there was some part of the vision he had already forgotten. "No, it fits with other things as well," he said. "The tunnels he remembers could have been geothermic vents; I think the rift valleys were all jungle before the fruit-packing companies moved in."

He glanced quickly at Cray, at the way her hands rested on Nichos's shoulders, her gaze on his face . . .

No visual, no aural, no olfactory memories at all. Only that neutral knowledge of what had been.

The sense of something forgotten tugged at his mind, but when he reached for it, it evaporated like light on water.

"Belsavis is on the edge of the Senex Sector, too," he went on after a moment. "So it's within striking distance of Yetoom. What's the name of the valley where they built the dome? Do you know, Cray?"

"There's two or three domed volcanic valleys in the glaciers," said Cray, seeing Leia's inquiring frown. "The domes are standard light-amp with apex-mounted antigrav systems to take the stress. Brathflen Corporation built the first one twelve or fourteen years ago over Plawal . . ."

She paused, as if hearing the word for the first time. "Plawal."

"Plettwell," said Leia. "Plett's Well."

"How long have colonies been there?"

Leia shook her head. "We'll ask Artoo. At least twenty-five or thirty years. The Ninth Quadrant's pretty isolated; the systems there are far apart. It would be the ideal place for the Jedi Knights to hide their families, once they knew the Emperor was out to destroy them."

She straightened, the folds of her tabard falling into shimmering sculpture about her. "*They hid the children in the well,*" she repeated. "And after that they scattered, and didn't even remember who they were."

Leia frowned, a diplomat again. "Belsavis is an independent ally of the Republic," she said. "They keep pretty tight security there because of the vine-coffee and vine-silk, but they should let me in to have a look at their records. Han and I can get the *Falcon* from Coruscant and be back before we were due home from the Time of Meeting. It's supposed to be beautiful there," she added thoughtfully. "I wonder if the children—"

"No!" Luke caught her sleeve, as if to physically stop her from taking her children; both Leia and Cray regarded him in surprise. "Don't take them anywhere near that place!"

The next moment he wondered why he'd spoken, wondered what it was that he feared.

But all that remained was a sense of something wrong, something evil —some vision of blackness folding itself away into hiding . . .

He shook his head. "Anyway, if there's folks like Drub McKumb there, it's not someplace you want to take the kids."

"No," said Leia softly, seeing again—as Luke saw—the groaning figure strapped to the diagnostic bed, the jarring reds and yellows of agony on the monitor screens. "We'll be careful," she said quietly. "But we'll find them, Luke. Or we'll find where they went."

The muted radiance of the sun-globes caught the flicker of her robes as she passed beneath the pillars and out into the luminous velvet of the Ithorian night.

Chapter 3

Tatooine.

The iron cold of the desert night; the way the darkness smelled when the wind died. Luke lay staring at the low adobe arch of the ceiling of his room, barely visible in the small glow of the gauges on the courtyard moisture condenser just outside his window . . .

Small, comforting clicks and whirrings came from the household machinery: Aunt Beru's yogurt maker, the hydroponics plant Uncle Owen had set up last year, the hum of the security fence . . .

Why did the night feel so silent?

Why did his chest hurt with a terror, a sense of some malevolent enormity moving slowly through the dark?

He rose from his bed, taking his blanket to wrap around his shoulders. The stairs were tall for his short legs, the night air biting on his fingers. The desert smell made his nostrils itch, prickled on the skin of his face and lips.

He was very young.

At the top of the steps, above the sunken court of the farmstead, the desert lay utterly still. Huge stars stared from the absolute black of the sky with the wide-open glare of mad things, deeply and personally aware of the child pattering across the sands to the point just clear of the fence's field—even in those days, he knew that to a centimeter.

He stared out across the long wastes of dune and salt pan and harsh, pebbled reg, formless in the dark and without movement.

There was danger out there. Danger vast and terrible, moving stealthily toward the isolated house.

Luke woke.

His open eyes gazed at the lofty arcs of resin and pendants woven with patterns of glass vines. Latticed flowers curtained the windows and the sun-globes among the courtyard trees made shadow-lace on the wall. Though it was deep in the night, still the music of the feasting, of hundreds of weddings and joyous dances of reunion and celebration wafted on the air thick with the green scents of the jungle below, with the honey and spice and vanilla of a dozen varieties of night-blossoming plant.

Tatooine.

Why did he dream about his childhood home? Why about that night, the night he'd waked to that silence more in his heart than in the night, knowing that something was coming?

In that case it had been the Sand People, the Tusken Raiders. He'd gotten too near the fence and tripped one of the small alarms. Uncle Owen had just come out looking for him when the first, far-off groaning of the banthas was heard. If Luke hadn't wakened when he had, the first anybody would have known would have been when the Sand People attacked the fence.

Why did he feel that huge silence, that approaching evil, tonight?

What had he sensed in that split second when his mind was open, reaching for the memories stored in Nichos's electronic brain?

Luke got out of bed, gathered the sheet around his body as he had in the childhood he'd just experienced, and walked to the window.

All was stillness in the courtyard, save for the whisper of an unseen fountain, the night conversation of trees. A bird warbled a few notes . . .

The Queen had a songbird that sang in the dark. . . .

Han and Leia were gone. They had used Drub McKumb's attack as an excuse, arguing concern for the safety of their children, and this the Ithorian herd leaders had understood. Of course their visit must be cut short, they must return to Coruscant in the face of possibly unpredictable attacks. Drub McKumb himself remained, under the care of Tomla El, sunk deep in his muttering dreams.

Artoo-Detoo had gone with them. His greater computing capacity would be needed more where they were going, Luke knew. And See-Threepio, fussy and particular as he was, was needed here, for the strange and difficult task that had brought Luke to Ithor in the first place: A droid communicator and translator was needed, to work with Cray Mingla and the Ithorian healers in integrating Nichos Marr back to being the man he once had been.

But it was Artoo whom Luke needed now.

Another thought came to him.

Hitching the sheet up over his shoulders, he padded to the doorway. See-Threepio, seated in the empty dining room of the Guest House, switched on the moment Luke crossed the threshold, the glow of eyes springing up like round yellow moons in the dark. Luke gestured, shook his head. "No, Threepio, it's okay."

"Is there something I can do for you, Master Luke?"

"Not right now. Thanks."

The protocol droid settled back into his chair, but Luke was aware, as he descended the few steps to the outer door and crossed the terrace in the violet dark, that Threepio did not switch himself back off. For a droid, Threepio had a very human nosiness.

Like See-Threepio, Nichos Marr sat in the outer room of the suite to which Cray had been assigned, in the power-down mode that was the droid equivalent of rest. Like Threepio, at the sound of Luke's almost noiseless tread he turned his head, aware of his presence.

"Luke?" Cray had equipped him with the most sensitive vocal modulators, and the word was calibrated to a whisper no louder than the rustle of the blueleafs massed outside the windows. He rose, and crossed to where Luke stood, the dull silver of his arms and shoulders a phantom gleam in the stray flickers of light. "What is it?"

"I don't know." They retreated to the small dining area where Luke had earlier probed his mind, and Luke stretched up to pin back a corner of the lamp-sheathe, letting a slim triangle of butter-colored light fall on the purple of the vulwood tabletop. "A dream. A premonition, maybe." It was on his lips to ask, *Do you dream?* but he remembered the ghastly, imageless darkness in Nichos's mind, and didn't. He wasn't sure if his pupil was aware of the difference in his human perception and knowledge, aware of just exactly what he'd lost when his consciousness, his self, had been transferred.

"How aware are you of the computerized side of your being?" he asked instead.

A man would have knit his brows, pressed his thumb to his lips, scratched his ear . . . something. Nichos answered with a droid's promptness, "I am aware that it exists. If you were to ask me the square root of pi or the ratio of length to frequency of light waves I would be able to tell you without hesitation."

"Can you generate random numbers?"

"Of course."

Of course.

"When I probed your mind, read your memories of that childhood planet, I felt a . . . a disturbance. As if something were reaching out, searching . . . Something evil, something . . ." Saying it out loud, he knew now what he'd felt. "Something conscious. Could you place yourself in a receptive trance, as if meditating on the Force, open your mind to it, and . . . generate random numbers? Random coordinates? I'll get you a stylopad, there's one connected to the terminal here. You were trained as a Jedi," Luke went on, leaning against the table and looking up into those cobalt-blue, artificial eyes. "You know the . . . the feeling, the taste, the heft and hand, of the Force, even though you can't use it now. I need to find this . . . this disturbance. This wave of darkness that I felt. Can you do this?"

Abruptly Nichos smiled, and it was the smile of the man Luke had known. "I haven't the slightest idea," he said. "But we can certainly try."

In the morning Luke excused himself from the expedition Tomla El had organized with Nichos and Cray to the Falls of Dessiar, one of the places on Ithor most renowned for its beauty and peace. When they left he sought out Umwaw Moolis, and the tall herd leader listened gravely to his less than logical request and promised to put matters in train to fulfill it. Then Luke descended to the House of the Healers, where Drub McKumb lay, sedated far beyond pain but with all the perceptions of agony and nightmare still howling in his mind.

"Kill you!" He heaved himself at the restraints, blue eyes glaring furiously as he groped and scrabbled at Luke with his clawed hands. "It's all poison! I see you! I see the dark light all around you! You're him!

You're him!" His back bent like a bow; the sound of his shrieking was like something being ground out of him by an infernal mangle.

Luke had been through the darkest places of the universe and of his own mind, had done and experienced greater evil than perhaps any man had known on the road the Force had dragged him . . . Still, it was hard not to turn away.

"We even tried yarrock on him last night," explained the Healer in charge, a slightly built Ithorian beautifully tabby-striped green and yellow under her simple tabard of purple linen. "But apparently the earlier doses that brought him enough lucidity to reach here from his point of origin oversensitized his system. We'll try again in four or five days."

Luke gazed down into the contorted, grimacing face.

"As you can see," the Healer said, "the internal perception of pain and fear is slowly lessening. It's down to ninety-three percent of what it was when he was first brought in. Not much, I know, but something."

"Him! *Him! HIM!*" Foam spattered the old man's stained gray beard.

Who?

"I wouldn't advise attempting any kind of mindlink until it's at least down to fifty percent, Master Skywalker."

"No," said Luke softly.

Kill you all. And: *They are gathering . . .*

"Do you have recordings of everything he's said?"

"Oh, yes." The big coppery eyes blinked assent. "The transcript is available through the monitor cubicle down the hall. We could make nothing of them. Perhaps they will mean something to you."

They didn't. Luke listened to them all, the incoherent groans and screams, the chewed fragments of words that could be only guessed at, and now and again the clear disjointed cries: "Solo! Solo! Can you hear me? Children . . . Evil . . . Gathering here . . . Kill you all!"

Punctuation is everything, thought Luke wryly, removing the jack from his ear. *Is that one thought or three? Or only the bleeding seepage of his dreams?*

From a pocket at his belt he took the strip of hardcopy that the stylopad had extruded early that morning under Nichos's rapid generation of random numbers, and, clipped to it, the readout he'd had from the herd's central computer a few hours later. What it meant he didn't know,

but the fact that it quite clearly meant *something* was intensely disquiet-
ing.

Feet passed in the corridor, the sharp click of Cray's exquisite but
intensely impractical shoes, and he smiled to himself. Even on an expedition to the jungles, Cray could be counted upon to dress fashionably if she
could. He heard her voice, its usual brisk sharpness honed to the brittleness he'd heard in it more and more in the past six months . . .

"It's really just a matter of finding a way to quadruple the sensitivity
of the chips to achieve a pattern, instead of a linear, generator." She was
the expert, Luke knew—his own knowledge of droid programming and
droid minds started and ended with how to talk Threepio out of his more
impractical ideas for the care of Han and Leia's children . . . But his
sense, his perception of the slight shifts of feeling audible in the human
voice, picked up the desperate note of one trying to convince herself, of a
rear-guard action against doubt and unwanted certainty and too little
sleep.

"Hayvlin Vesell of the Technomic Research Foundation spoke in an
article of going back to the old xylen-based chips, because of the finer
divisibility of information possible. When I return to the Institute—"

"That's what I'm trying to impress on you, Dr. Mingla—Cray."
Tomla El's voice was a murmuring concert of woodwinds. "This may not
be possible no matter how finely you partition the information. The answer may be that there is no answer. Nichos may simply not be capable of
human affect."

"Oh, I think you're wrong about that." She'd gained back the smooth
control in her voice. She might have been speaking to a professional
colleague about programmatic languages. "Certainly a great deal more
work needs to be done before we can dismiss the possibility. I'm told also
that in experiments with accelerated learning, at a certain number of
multiples of human learning capacity, tremendous breakthroughs can oc-
cur. I've signed up for another accelerator course, this one in informational patterning dynamics . . ."

Her voice faded down the corridor. *A great deal more work,* thought
Luke, hurting for her, pressing his hand to his brow. It was Cray's answer
to everything. With sufficient effort, sufficient maneuvering, any problem
could be surmounted, no matter what the cost to herself.

And the cost to herself, he knew, had been devastating.

He remembered the weeks after Nichos had been diagnosed with the inexplicable degenerative decay of the nervous system: remembered Cray turning up for her training every morning after nights spent with the learning accelerator therapies she'd had shipped to Yavin, brittle, exhausted, not telling him or anyone that she was forcing herself through hypnosis and drug therapies to absorb the farthest frontiers of her chosen field in order to know enough, to learn enough, to save the man she loved before it was too late. After Nichos was hospitalized he remembered those terrible nights of going to the medcenter on Coruscant, while day after day Cray bullied and hurried her suppliers, sweated sleepless over her designs, racing the disease while Nichos's body weakened and melted away before their eyes.

Cray had worked a miracle. She had saved the life of the man she loved.

After a fashion.

A man who could recall the complete text of that old childhood song but had no sense—neither joy nor sorrow nor nostalgia—of what it meant to him.

"Luke?"

He'd heard the light, soft step in the corridor, and with it the very faint mechanical hum of Threepio's servos. The two of them—the golden droid and the pewter-gray one with the man's pale face—stood in the doorway.

"Did the random numbers I generated turn out to mean something?"

Faint water stains marked the silvery arm and shoulder on his left side, as if he'd stood close to the Falls. Luke wondered how the experience of that beauty, shared with the woman he loved, had registered in his memory banks.

"They're coordinates, all right." Luke touched the hardcopy that lay on the cubicle's small desk before him. "They're the coordinates for the Moonflower Nebula, out on the Outer Rim, past the K Seven Forty-nine System. There's nothing out there, never has been, but . . . I've made arrangements with Umwaw Moolis to lend me a ship. I just think it needs to be checked out."

One of Luke's hardest lessons concerning the use of the Force had been to abandon mechanical, provable realities and trust his hunches. These days people generally didn't ask questions of the man who had destroyed the Sun Crusher.

"Will I be accompanying you, Master Luke?"

"Of course you'll be accompanying him, Threepio." Nichos stepped back a half pace to regard the protocol droid. "As will I. And Cray, too, I hope." He turned his head, and Luke heard, a moment before he saw her come into the lights of the cubicle doorway, Cray's quick-tapping footfalls in the hall.

"You hope what?" She put her arm around Nichos's waist, smiled up at him almost the way she used to, though Luke observed the almost infinitesimal pause before he draped an arm around her shoulders in return. As Luke had known she would be, Cray was beautifully turned out in a gown of black and white, carefully made up, a bright scarf wound in her flaxen hair.

"That you'll be coming to the Moonflower Nebula with Luke and Threepio to investigate this . . . whatever it is. This hunch he has."

"Oh, but I . . ." She stopped herself from saying something—probably, Luke guessed, from protesting that she had to continue Nichos's rehabilitation and rehumanization therapies with Tomla El. He saw her visibly rein herself in, and look at him again with concern in her face. "What, Luke? Nichos told me this morning about the random number field."

"It may be nothing." Luke rose from the little table, switched off the monitor, and shoved the hardcopy back into the pouch on his belt. "The two of you came here to work—to help you, Nichos. It's not—"

"You had work of your own to do back on Yavin." Cray met his eyes gravely, her brown gaze almost on level with his own. "Yet you came here with us."

"You don't know what's out there, Luke." Nichos put a hand on Luke's arm. "Between the warlords and Grand Admiral wannabes of the various parts of the Imperial Fleet, and whatever Princes of the Ancient Houses in the Senex Sector who think they can grab a piece of power . . . they're coming up with new things all the time. Request Umwaw Moolis to get you a bigger ship."

The Outer Rim. Many years ago Luke had described his homeworld of Tatooine—one of the worlds in that very sparsely settled and marginally habitable region of the galaxy—as the point that was farthest from the bright center of the universe, with considerable accuracy. He had since visited places beside which Tatooine looked like Coruscant during Carnival Week, but his original definition would still hold up . . . and the same could be said for most of the rest of the Outer Rim as well.

Swollen crimson suns circled by frozen balls of methane and ammonia. Hot-burning blue stars whose light and heat crisped their planets to cinders. Pulsars whose orbiting worlds alternately froze and melted and clusters so filled with ambient radiation as to cook out any possibility of life on whatever bodies weren't torn apart by the conflicting gravitational fields.

Everywhere in the galaxy were a lot of empty planets, balls of rock and metals too expensive to exploit because of heat, or gravity, or radiation, or proximity to strange hazards like gas cauldrons or fluctuating anomalies. As Leia had said to Cray, distances in space were vast, and it was easy to lose or forget about whole systems, whole sectors, if there was no reason to go there. In the Outer Rim, the Empire had never bothered much with local law.

The armored explorer-cruiser *Huntbird* the Ithorians had lent to Luke came out of hyperspace a healthy distance from the luminous zone of dust and ionized gases listed on the starcharts as the Moonflower Nebula.

"Are you sure that's what the random coordinates were for?" asked Cray doubtfully, studying the readouts of all information on the area on the three screens immediately beneath the bridge's main viewport. "It isn't even listed in the Registry. Might the coordinates have been for System K Seven Forty-nine, for instance? That's only a few parsecs away, and at least there's a planet there—Pzob . . ." She read off the screen. "Human-habitable and temperate . . . the Empire could have had a base there, though there's none listed."

"It's habitable," agreed Luke, tapping through instructions on the keypad with one hand and keeping an eye on the changing images on the central screen as he spoke. "But it was colonized way, *way* back in the days by Gamorreans, goodness only knows how or why. Anybody wanting a permanent base there would have had to spend a fortune in security."

"A most unpleasant people, Gamorreans," agreed Threepio primly from the bench seat he shared with Nichos in the passenger area of the bridge. "They were difficult enough to deal with in the entourage of Jabba the Hutt. . . . Procedures programs for visiting Gamorr consist of a single line: DO NOT VISIT GAMORR. Really!"

"I don't know . . ." Luke studied the viewscreen ahead of them. The reflective veils of dust picked up the light of surrounding stars, and glowed from within to indicate that somewhere in that vastness two or three stars were concealed, their rays diffused by the all-encompassing gases so that almost nothing could be seen. "Readings show a lot of rocks in there."

He touched a switch, and a schematic manifested itself on one of the small screens. On it the zone was thickly speckled with what looked like grains of sand and pebbles held in uneasy random suspension.

"Asteroid field," he said. "Looks like all sizes. Usual iron-nickel composition. May be a belt going all around one of the stars in there . . . I wonder if the Empire ever did any mining?"

"It would cost a fortune, wouldn't it?" asked Nichos, getting up to step close and look down over their shoulders.

Luke flipped through screen after screen, studying mass readings, spectrographic analyses, local gravitational fields, while all the time the glowing, shifting wall of light drew nearer, so bright that its soft colors streamed from the viewscreen over the faces of those grouped around the console. "It would help if I knew what I was looking for. Whoa, looks like we got something in there . . ."

He accelerated gently into the first outstringers of the veils of light. Colors swirled and drifted, chunks of rock the size of office blocks on Coruscant floating suddenly out of dustbanks and sandbars of brilliance, so that Luke had to maneuver slowly among them. "There we go." He toggled a switch, and before them they made out the shape of a cold gray worldlet, seemingly embedded in veils of chilly whites and greens, pitted with holes in which old crane arms and landing cradles could be seen.

"A base of some kind," said Luke. "Probably mining, but it looks like scavengers have been at it for scrap and whatever parts they could float away."

"I'm surprised anybody bothered." Cray peered around his arm for a better view. "Can we get a readout on the rocks around us? With all the interference we're getting from the magnetic and ion fields of the dust cover, this would be a swell place to hide."

"I'm not picking up anything, but that doesn't mean there's nothing here." Luke thumbed the viewer to show a couple of the larger rocks, in the nine-kilometer range, but ionization from the nebula's electrical fields blanked anything much out of visual range. "Let's have a look around."

Cray continued to flip through the readouts and specs while Luke guided the *Huntbird* through the glowing mazes of veils, light, and stones. Few pilots would even venture into asteroid fields—the appearance of languid drift was an unsafe illusion to bank on. Even Luke was wary of them. Most of the asteroids were the size of the vessel or larger, too big to be shuffled away by the deflectors. The ship's mere movement was sufficient to cause gravitational ripples and swirls in the uneasy equilibrium of the field. The field itself was enormous, the fritzed-out sensor pickup showing more and more rocks. *Almost certainly a planetary belt,* thought Luke. It would take days to explore it in even the most cursory fashion.

And yet . . .

Every instinct he possessed told him there was something there. Or near there, and one look at the readouts told him there wasn't *anything* near there but there. They passed close to a massive ball of rock, almost sixty kilometers through, and under the shadows of its flank Luke glimpsed more holes and the remains of a self-erecting dome. Another installation, a big one this time. Clearly deserted, but . . .

Why two mines?

Or were mines what they were?

"They have any readings for mining activity in this area?"

Nichos, who had quietly taken his place at the computer station, tapped the keyboard for a moment, then said, "There're no observation posts anywhere in this sector. Funny," he added. "No records of any mining having gone on anywhere near here at all."

"Can you pick up any antimatter trails?" asked Luke, steering the *Huntbird* around a tight mass of large asteroids that had drifted into one another's gravitational proximity and now clung together, bumping and scraping with the silent, stupid clumsiness of ex-spouses at a party. "Hyperdust? Any sign of ships coming through here at all?"

"Trails would dissipate in a few weeks," Cray reminded him, checking anyway. "Nothing. Drat this interference. We—"

"*Shields!*" yelled Luke, slamming his hand on the deflectors and wondering—in the same split second that something impacted with the explorer like the crushing fist of some vengeful demon—if he was crazy . . .

Purple-white light rammed through the viewport with an almost physical force, leaving blindness and the sickening jolt of the gravity going out. Light again, as a second plasma bolt smashed the ship in the same instant that Luke swung the helm. He smelled burning insulation and heard a sizzle, then Cray's cursing. She had a startling line of profanity for someone that proper and controlled. As his eyes readjusted he saw that most of the board in front of him was black.

"Where are they coming from?" The readouts weren't telling him.

"Sector two, back behind—"

"There!"

Luke had already begun to whip the vessel into another yaw, hoping his impression was correct that that area wasn't occupied by an asteroid, and from the tail of his eye saw the white sword of light stab out from an enormous asteroid that had, until seconds ago, indeed been in their rear.

"Get a fix on it!"

"Look out!"

"Oh, dear!" That was Threepio, as the Internal Systems Console to his right exploded into a geyser of sparks. Luke barely noticed, for the next plasma bolt splintered a meteorite and showered the ship with several thousand superheated cannonballs.

"There's nothing on the surface!" yelled Cray over the crackle of shorting wires. "No domes, no emplacements, I can't even see gunports . . ." He wondered that she could see anything in the nebula's weird, shadowless light. "There's holes all over the thing—"

"Watch it!" Luke spun the vessel, whipped behind another hunk of rock and ice, praying he wasn't diving straight into the attacker's gunsights. Except for size, every asteroid in the field looked almost exactly like every other asteroid, and unless it was actually shooting at them it was nearly impossible to tell on which of the half dozen one-to-two-kilometer rocks immediately visible in the universe of glowing dust the guns were situated. The asteroid behind which the *Huntbird* had ducked took a terrible hit, only its size preventing it from splintering as the smaller one had; it blocked the attackers from view.

"I've got a fix . . ."

"It'll be inaccurate in two seconds." Luke ran a hasty systems check. He was peripherally aware of the dig of his safety harness into his shoulders and hips; if internal gravity was failing probably heat and air were out, too. "We're getting out of here."

"Aft starboard sensors blind," reported Nichos, hanging on to the safety handle by the crippled data console. His feet were off the floor. "Deflectors one-third power . . ."

Luke maneuvered carefully along the line of sight behind the shielding asteroid, fighting the helm's drift to port, which told him the stabilizer was out. He didn't even have to key the readout to know the vessel wouldn't make hyperspace. "How far to Pzob?"

"Three or four hours at top sublight," reported Cray. She sounded grim but not scared, though this was her first time under fire. Good, Luke thought, for a young woman who'd gone straight from the schoolroom to the lecture room with no stops in between. "That's just guessing. I've got a helm bearing but I can't get an exact distance."

"Our sublight engines seem to be okay," said Luke. "We'll be on emergency oxygen and we'll probably be pretty cold by the time we get there. Threepio, I hope you know Gamorrean."

Threepio said, "Oh, dear."

"Course seems to be clear all around." Cray toggled through the setting a second time, though the navicomp screen was fritzing in and out of focus. If they lost that, thought Luke, they were *really* down a hole.

No further shots from the asteroid base. Nevertheless his scalp prickled, and he laid the course for the longest line of sight he could to keep the asteroid between him and where he figured the base was.

"Right," he said softly. "Let's make hyperdust."

The *Huntbird* had just started to move when a bolt of ionized plasma hit the shielding asteroid like the hammer of Death. Rocks, energy, heat slammed into the explorer vessel like monstrous shrapnel. Luke felt the safety harness that held him tear loose with the violence of the impact: Cray screamed, and he was grabbed by darkness.

Chapter 4

Luke came to long enough to throw up, not a pleasant occurrence in zero-g. Two See-Threepios unhooked him from the safety harness in which he floated and steered him—with surprising nimbleness for a droid who always seemed so carefully balanced—out of the small cubicle and into what he thought was the aft crew room before he passed out once more.

The Force, he thought. *Got to use the Force.*

Why?

Because your lungs have stopped working.

It took an astonishing amount of concentration to inhale again, and it hurt a lot more than he'd thought it would. A little later he wondered if he could use the Force to do something about the crazed bantha that seemed to be trapped inside his skull and trying to ram its way out.

It occurred to him the next time he came to—the cold woke him, that time—that he probably had a concussion.

"Luke," said Cray, and now she sounded scared. "Luke, you've got to wake up!"

He knew she was probably right.

The Force, he thought again. Cilghal, his Calamarian student, had taught him enough about the specific physiological mechanism of concussions that he knew exactly where to bring the Force to bear, though it was a little like trying to take off a glove one-handed. His lungs felt as if he'd inhaled a sand drill and neglected to turn it off. No wonder breathing hadn't been a lot of fun.

Increased blood flow to the capillaries to clear the impurities. Accelerated healing to the cells of that rioting squadron of drunken Gamorreans that had formerly been his brain.

Opening his eyes, he worked on consolidating both Crays into the single individual he was pretty sure they were.

"Where are we?"

"Coming up on the K Seven Forty-nine System." She had a huge bruise on the side of her face, the makeup that had been on her eyes streaked black with the residue of tears of pain. She wore a yellow thermal suit over her clothing, the cowl pushed back and her pale hair floating loose around her face. "We've picked up a signal."

Luke breathed deep—at the cost of a certain amount of nausea—and worked on channeling the Force to the center of the worst pain and dizziness in his head. He couldn't remember how good a pilot Nichos was, but he knew Cray had no experience in it at all. If they were going to make Pzob alive he'd better be in shape to take the ship down.

"I thought there was nothing out here. From Pzob?"

"K Seven Forty-nine Three, yes."

Luke had completely stopped cussing at petty misfortunes round about the time he'd lost his right hand—after he'd realized he'd aborted and imperiled his own training as a Jedi, betrayed his Master, and put himself in deadly danger of succumbing to the dark side *for no purpose whatsoever,* his perspective on minor annoyances had changed. He only sighed now, letting his worry run off, and asked, "Imperial?" If the base in the asteroid field was an Imperial one it stood to reason.

"The data section of the computer's out," said Cray. "I've got the navicomp back on line from the backups but that took every coupling that wasn't burned out by that last power surge. Can you recognize Imperial signals by internal code?"

"Some of them." He reached over—carefully—to strip free the straps that held a silvery thermal blanket around him, while Cray unfastened the restraining straps that held him in place. He was, he saw, in the aft crew

room as he'd thought. The lighting came from a single emergency
glowpanel in the ceiling, but it was sufficient to enable him to see his
breath.

"Here you are, Master Luke." Threepio floated across to him from
the lockers on the opposite wall, holding out a t-suit and an oxygen filter
mask. "I'm *so* gratified to see you conscious and well."

"That's a matter of opinion." Even the small movement necessary to
get himself into the t-suit made him queasy, and despite all the channeling
of healing he could do, his head still throbbed agonizingly. He took the
filter mask and glanced inquiringly at Cray.

"The coolant lines ruptured. We got a mask on you as fast as we could
but there was a while there we thought you were a goner."

He touched the back of his head, and was immediately sorry. Whatever he'd struck—or whatever flying debris had struck him—had raised a
lump approximately the size of the smaller of Coruscant's moons.

"I salvaged as much of the battle readouts as I could." Cray slipped
on her own filter mask and followed him across the crew room to the
door. "There are some stills, a little footage that I can't get to run, and a
half dozen computer extrapolations of what I think are the site of the
attack, but the system's too damaged for me to get any kind of clear
picture of which asteroid it is. When we make port and I can salvage the
data I'll be able to tell you more." She pushed aside a drifting logpad and
a couple of spare filter masks as they entered the short hallway. Though
spacegoing vessels as a rule kept to a minimum objects that weren't
strapped or magnetized down, there were always some: comlinks, stylos,
coffee mugs, logpads, empty drink bubbles, and data wafers.

The bridge was even colder than the crew room, and murky with
pinkish coolant gas. Nichos had lashed himself to the safety bolts on the
edge of the main console itself; the chair Luke had been sitting in was tied
to a handhold on the far wall, having been ripped loose from its moorings
by the impact that had torn Luke out of its harness. The lights had gone
completely in here, and only the chalky starlight from the main viewport
illuminated the room. Feral red or blinking amber power lights glinted
like strange jewels in reflection from the silvery droid's arms and back.

"The signal we're picking up from Pzob isn't strong enough to reach
into the Moonflower Nebula," reported Nichos, as Luke pulled himself
close with a floating remnant of the safety-harness strap. "Look familiar?"

Luke checked the readout on the single screen left functional. "Not any Imperial signal I've ever seen," he said. "Which doesn't mean that whoever's sending it isn't allied with one or another of the warlords." It was odd, and a little disconcerting, to see Nichos without either mask or t-suit in what was rapidly becoming a frozen and depressurized coffin.

"The Gamorrean colonists?" suggested Cray. "Or smugglers, maybe?"

"The Gamorreans haven't stopped fighting each other long enough to set up a technological base of any kind on any planet where they've settled," said Luke doubtfully. "It might be smugglers—which doesn't mean *they* won't be allied with Harrsk or Teradoc or some other Imperial wannabe, or with one of the big smuggler gangs for that matter. But at this point," he added, toggling the readout back to the navicomputer and marveling a little that Cray had gotten the thing workable at all, "we don't have any choice."

Massive, porcine, primitive, and belligerent, Gamorreans will live and thrive wherever there is soil fertile enough to farm, sufficient game to hunt, and rocks to throw at one another, but given their preference they will take forested country, if possible where mushrooms grow. The woods surrounding the four- or five-acre fire scar in which Luke put the *Huntbird* down were monumental, dense, thick, old, and hugely tall, like the rain forests of Ithor but heavier, and the shadowed, brooding silence beneath their leathery leaves made Luke profoundly uneasy.

"The base should be in that direction," he said, sitting down rather quickly on the steps of the explorer's emergency exit—the boarding ramp was inoperational—and pointing off in the direction of the lately risen orange sun. Despite all the energy of the Force that he could summon he felt giddy and ill, and though his lungs were healing rapidly he was still short of breath. "It's not very far; the energy readings don't look big enough for power fences or heavy weaponry."

"Wouldn't they need power fences at least if there are Gamorreans in the area?" Like Luke, Cray had stripped out of her t-suit; her deft fingers were rapidly rebraiding her hair even as she spoke. *Quite a trick without a mirror,* thought Luke, a little amused. But Cray could manage it if anyone could.

"The Gamorreans may not have colonized this continent," he pointed out. Wind stirred at the long grass, dark blue-green, like all the vegetation in this amber-lit world, but far from being unsettling the slight goldenness of the light gave everything a deep sense of sunset peace. A flock of tiny bipeds—red and yellow, and no higher than Luke's knee—fled, startled from behind a fallen tree trunk, and went whistling and chirping away toward the eaves of the woods.

"For that matter, we may find a colony from some other race altogether. The reports on this world haven't been updated in fifty years."

"We have the engine hatches open, Master Luke." Threepio and Nichos appeared at the top of the steps, the gold and silver metals of their bodies dented and streaked with oil. They, too, had taken a beating in the battle with the asteroid. "Most of the coolant gas has now dissipated into the atmosphere."

The impact of the last plasma bolt and the shattered asteroid had jammed the hatches into the engine compartment; in addition to the intermittent waves of dizziness that still plagued him, Luke had thought it wiser to let the droids, who needed no breath masks, use their greater strength to force the doors while the humans made a quick reconnaissance of the outside.

The engine itself was a complete mess.

"We'll need about thirty meters of number eight cabling, and a dozen data couplers," said Luke half an hour later, sliding gingerly out of an access hatch in the darkened engine room. Even the glowpanels had gone out here, the claustrophobic chamber illuminated by a string of emergency worklights wired to a Scale-10 battery from the emergency kit. "The rest of it I think I can patch."

I'd better be able to patch, he reflected grimly. Leia's words about how easy it was to get lost between inhabited worlds reverberated unnervingly in his mind.

Cray withdrew her head from the innards of the navicomp. "I'll need couplers and some twelve-mil flat cable . . . you okay, Luke?" For he'd tried to stand, only to sink back, gray-faced and sweating, against the soot-stained bulkhead.

Luke concentrated the Force in his body, on his brain chemistry and the pinched capillaries of his lungs: relaxing, accelerating repair and regrowth. He felt very tired. "I'll be fine." *Please don't let there be hostile smugglers at that base,* he thought, trying desperately to gather the strength he'd need. *Or some kind of secret base of one of the warlords. Or a hidden mine worked by slaves. Or the concealed research station of some nefarious power we've never even heard of . . .*

If there was any trouble—even the smallest fight—he didn't think he could cope with it.

Cray had never seen real action, real trouble. Threepio wasn't designed for it, and Nichos . . .

Whatever happened, he had to get back with word that there was definitely something hiding in the Moonflower Nebula. Something dangerous.

"Luke?"

He realized he'd almost blacked out again. Cray was kneeling in front of him—two Crays, dark eyes filled with concern. The accumulated heat of the engines still lingered in this compartment, but even that couldn't account for the suffocating sensation he felt, hot and stifled, though his hands and feet were cold.

Capillaries. Recovery. Healing.

"Why don't you let Nichos and me go investigate that signal?"

He took a deep breath and wished he hadn't. "I think you may need help there."

Of course, harmless people—good, helpful people—*did* inhabit unknown bases on remote planets. *Please let it be that . . .*

The bad feeling he'd sensed, the knowledge of darkness advancing, didn't leave him.

"The sooner we can get a message out, the better," the young woman pointed out. "Whatever's out in the nebula, we can't risk letting the Imperial warlords find it, and that risk grows every hour. I can scope out the settlement or camp or whatever it is, ask for the parts we need, and send out a distress signal while you rest a little, then start the patching part of the job as soon as you feel up to it. All right?"

Luke's head was swimming. He rested it against the bulkhead behind him, fighting for breath. *Not all right,* he thought. *Not if there's any kind of danger in that camp or in the woods around it.*

The spark-charred units, the ruptured hoses dangling like dead limbs, the opened hatches of the compression accelerator and gyro-grav systems, all seemed to be swaying gently, as if the ship were floating on deep water, and the hardrock miners in his skull had resumed their thermal blasting operations again. The thought of getting to his feet, of walking the two or three kilometers to the site of the signal, gave him a sinking feeling inside. *I can do it,* he told himself grimly. *With the help of the Force . . .*

"I think you'll need me there."

He held out his hand, shut his teeth hard against nausea as Cray helped him to his feet. She eased him through the hatch, helped him down the steep, ladderlike steps. "What makes you so sure there'll be trouble?"

"I don't know," said Luke softly. "But I can feel trouble of some kind. There's something . . ."

They stepped through the hatchway onto the bridge, turned, and found themselves staring down the muzzle of a blaster rifle held by a white-armored Imperial stormtrooper.

Luke's hand shut around Cray's wrist as she went for her blaster. "Cray, no!" The trooper tensed—Luke raised his hands, showing them empty. After a moment Cray did likewise. If he went for his lightsaber, Luke thought, the man might still catch them both in the rifle blast, and there was no way of knowing how many others were in the rest of the ship.

From the faceless white helmet a buzzing voice demanded, "State your name and business."

Cray and Luke stepped back a pace, backs pressed to the wall. Dizziness hit Luke again—he tried to control it, tried to summon enough of the Force to pull the man's rifle from him if he needed to do it, but suspected it was more than he could manage.

"We're traders," he said. "We're lost, our ship was damaged . . ."

Blackness closed on his vision and he felt his knees buckle. Cray tried to steady him—the stormtrooper sprang forward, dropped his rifle, and caught his arm.

"You're hurt," said the stormtrooper, helping him to sit and kneeling beside him. Nichos and Threepio, hands full of patching materials, appeared from the storeroom hatchway and stared in surprise as the stormtrooper pulled off his helmet, revealing a kindly, much-lined black face surrounded by a grizzled popcorn halo of hair and beard.

"Oh, you poor folks, you look like you've had an awful time," said the man. "You come on over to my camp, I'll get you something to eat and a cup of tea."

Bereft of his gleaming armor, Triv Pothman proved to be a trim, strongly built man in his mid-fifties—"Though I admit the damp's getting to me and I'm not so quick as I used to be." He gestured to the racks of armor along the curved inner wall of his shelter, a low, white, self-erecting dome patched all over outside with black and salmon-colored lichens, rain-streaked and covered with the dirt of years. Second-growth trees, suckers, and vines surrounded what had been a clearing of Imperial military regulation size all around, though most of the sheds and shelters, and the long-dead posts of the security fence, lay buried now under tangles of vines.

"Forty-five of us, there were." There was something akin to pride in his voice. "Forty-five of us, and I'm the only one left. The Gamorreans got the rest, mostly, except for that giant fight between the Commander and Killium Neb and his friends over . . . Well, that was a long time ago, and it cost some good men their lives." He shook his head regretfully, and poured water from a bearing housing hung over the fire into a spouted pot of painted terra-cotta. The smell of healing herbs filled the vine-hung dome.

"And there they all are." He gestured to the helmets. "For all the good it ever did them."

The old unit medkit was far more complete than what had been on board the *Huntbird* even before the impact had scattered and smashed half the vessels in the explorer craft's sick bay. Pothman had dosed Luke with another two ampoules of antishock—in addition to what Cray had given him right after the final blast—and had hooked him for half an hour to a therapeutic respirator that still, for a miracle, worked. Looking around over the edge of the breath mask that covered his lower face, Luke was deeply grateful. From his days as a pilot in the Rebel fleet he knew too well that once you got injured, unless you got medical help soon you were going to keep on getting injured as you became less and less able to protect yourself.

Though he never, he reflected with a certain wry amusement, thought he'd be so glad that the Empire took good care to equip its stormtroopers with the best.

A feathered lizard, turquoise as palomella blossoms, appeared between the looped-back curtains of the dome's doorway, chittered and spread its mane, and Pothman tweaked a chunk of crust from one of the brown rolls he'd taken from his oven in honor of his guests, and tossed it. The lizard minced forward on delicate little feet, picked up the bread, and nibbled, watching the gray-haired hermit all the while with black jewels of eyes.

"Sure is good to see human beings again." Pothman offered the plate of rolls and honey to Cray, who sat beside Luke on the edge of Pothman's bunk. He winked at her. "Sure is good to see a nice-looking young lady."

Cray drew herself up and started to retort that she wasn't a nice-looking young lady, she held a full professorship at the Magrody Institute, but Luke moved his hand just enough to touch her arm.

The stormtrooper had already turned back to survey the helmets along the wall. They were of an older style than Luke had known, longer in the face to allow for the earlier configuration of respirators, with a dark band of sensors above the eyes.

"They *would* go on fighting the Gamorreans," Pothman sighed. "That was like sending them out invitations to tea, of course. They'll miss their dinners to have a fight." His grin was very white in his beard. " 'Course in those days I was quite a fighter myself."

"You've held the Gamorreans off by yourself all this time?" Luke carefully removed the respirator mask from his face, breathed deep, tasting the sweetness of the air. It still made him dizzy, but no longer hurt so much. It should hold him, he thought—he hoped—until they reached civilization again. He turned his head to survey the wide room, the simple clay dishes on the shelf, the traps wrought of reptile sinew and engine strapping, the monofilament fishing lines that had patently started life as part of standard Imperial equipment. A loom reared up near the door, constructed of various grades of engine pipe, with several yards of home-spun woven on it.

"Oh, gracious, no." Pothman handed him a cup of tea: herbal, spicy, warm, and, Luke sensed, healing. Luke had seen no kiln and wondered where he'd gotten the dishes, and the thread on the loom. Out of his white armor, Pothman wore soft-dyed green and brown clothing, embroidered on breast and sleeves and hem with meticulously accurate renderings of the local flowers and reptiles.

"I got caught early on. They took all the rifles and blasters, you see, and they needed somebody to fix them. But after the power cells died they didn't bother keeping an eye on me. I figure the Emperor forgot the mission a long time ago. You ever hear what happened to it?"

"Mission?" Luke sat up a little and sipped the tea, and did his best to look innocent, something he'd always been good at.

"The *Eye of Palpatine.*" Pothman opened an equipment locker, brought out a utility pack, and started loading it with wire, cables, couplers, backup data wafers, tools. "That was the name of the mission. Scuttlebutt said there were about two companies of troopers in it, but scattered, so nobody would know, nobody would guess. They put us on the most out-of-the-way planets they could find, to be picked up in the biggest, most dangerous, most secret vessel of them all, a supership, a dreadnaught, a battlemoon . . . One the enemy wouldn't see coming until it was too late."

"What enemy?" asked Luke softly.

There was stillness again, save for the rustling of the trees outside, and the faint clunketing of Pothman's much-mended machinery, a sound that brought back to Luke his childhood on Tatooine.

Pothman was silent, his back to them, looking down at the utility pack on the chest lid before him. "We didn't know," he said at last. "We weren't told. At the time I thought it was . . . Well, it was my duty. Now . . ." He turned back, his face troubled.

"I suppose something went wrong. Somebody found out after all, though everyone said that was impossible, since the Emperor was the only one that knew. After we'd been here nearly a year I got to wondering if maybe the Emperor himself had forgotten. When I saw your ship come over I sort of hoped he'd finally remembered—that he'd sent scouts to see what was left." His big hands toyed wistfully with the straps.

"But if it wasn't the Emperor who sent you out, you see, I know enough to know that whoever screwed up and scrapped the mission, nobody's going to want to be reminded it ever existed. Which means I might be sort of an embarrassment."

He slung the pack over his shoulder, and came to stand next to the tidy bunk where Luke lay on the silvery survival blankets and feather quilts. "My signal isn't strong enough to reach anybody, not way out here. But if we can get your engines fixed, you think maybe you might just drop me in some out-of-the-way place where they might not find me? It's nice to see human faces again. I was the company armorer; I know everything's changed in all this time, but I can still work pretty good with my hands, and I've learned to be a fair cook. I can find work. It's been a long time."

No bargaining, thought Luke wonderingly. No *Take me off this rock or you won't get so much as a screwdriver out of me. Everything freely offered, expecting nothing in return.*

"It's been a long time," he said gently. "The Emperor's dead, Triv. The Empire's in pieces. We can take you back to your home, or wherever you want; in the New Republic, or to some port where you can get a flight into the Core Systems, or any other place you want to go."

"We're doomed." See-Threepio turned from the gauges of the slowly filling oxygen tanks to where Nichos, knee-deep in the meadow's dark grass, was carefully daubing sealant on the Spatch-Cote repairs. The outer hull had been holed in a dozen places. Though the space between outer and inner hulls had been automatically filled with emergency foam and Nichos had done a quick patch job on the inner hull during the long flight to Pzob, if they were going to stand any chance of a hyperspace jump the outer had to be tight.

"Master Luke and Dr. Mingla have almost certainly walked into a trap!" The golden robot gestured with the hand not holding the round, bulky Spatch-Cote extruder. "A stormtrooper like that has to be ground support for whatever base is out in the asteroid field! I warned them. Standard Imperial bases house at least three companies. More, in isolated locales such as this! What can they do against five hundred and forty shock troops, with Master Luke injured as badly as he is? Plus tracker droids, interrogators, surveillance equipment, automated traps!"

"Power readings weren't high enough for anything like that," pointed out Nichos, switching off the intake valve on the tank.

"Of course a hidden base would alter its power readings!" surmised Threepio despairingly. "We'll be disassembled, cannibalized for scrap, sent to the sandmines of Neelgaimon or the orbital factories around Ryloon! If they're short of parts here we'll be—"

"I will be." Nichos took the extruder from Threepio and walked along the battered white side of the *Huntbird,* probing at other dents. "It would not be logical for them to destroy you. I, however . . ."

When with Luke or Cray, or his other friends at the Academy on Yavin, he had made an attempt to use the facial expressions programmed into the hair-fine complexities of his memory, but Threepio had noticed that when around droids, Nichos no longer bothered. There was no sadness, either in his blue eyes or in his voice.

"You—and Artoo-Detoo—are programmed, designed, for specific purposes, he to repair and understand machinery, you to understand and interpret language and culture. I am only programmed to be myself, to reproduce exactly all the knowledge, all the instincts, all the memories of a single, specific human brain, the experiences of a single human life. When you come right down to it, this is of no use to anyone."

Threepio was silent. He understood that Nichos expected no reply, for conversation among droids tends to be largely informational with few social amenities. Yet, as when speaking with a human, he felt it incumbent on him to disagree if nothing else. But he also knew that Nichos was absolutely correct.

"So you see," the not-quite-man went on, "if, as you say, Luke and Cray have walked into a trap and you and I are destined for capture as well, of the two of us I am probably the only one actually doomed. I think the metal here looks a little thin in the dent." He returned the spatch gun to the protocol droid's intricately mechanized hand.

Artoo-Detoo—or any other droid of Threepio's wide acquaintance—would not have been able to make such a pronouncement without reference to an interechoic micrometer. Threepio had observed, however, that humans were not only willing to "eyeball" such measurements, but frequently did so quite accurately, something that logically they should not have been able to do.

He was still trying to align probabilities about what that made Nichos when a voice called, "Threepio!" from across the meadow, and he turned, thankfully, to see Dr. Mingla, Master Luke—mercifully on his feet again and not floating on the damaged antigrav sled on which they'd taken him from the ship—and the strange, solitary stormtrooper who had stolen onto the ship while he and Nichos were in the storage hold. The man had dispensed with his armor and blaster, and carried instead a bow and arrows, his clothing of the coarse vegetable-fiber weave typical of primitive cultures.

Which meant there *were* local tribes, probably Gamorreans, all of them hostile, who would delight in tearing apart both droids and the ship itself for scrap metal.

They were doomed.

The Gamorreans made their appearance long before the engines were even halfway to liftoff capability. Luke was dimly aware of them, through the exhausted pounding in his head, mostly as a sense of time running out, a sense of someone trying to tell him something. But between channeling the Force to his own healing and the dizziness that still remained whenever he moved too quickly, it was hard to understand. He was lying on his back under one of the bridge consoles, pin-checking wires to see which were still capable of taking power. He laid the pin down, closed his eyes, and relaxed, letting the images come to his mind of clumsy, weirdly stealthy forms moving through the slate-dark shadows of monster trees.

"Company coming." He slid—carefully—out from under, and made his way as quickly as he could to where Cray and Nichos were repairing the stabilizer through the portside emergency hatch.

He could see Cray had already sensed something, too.

"Batten it," said Luke. "Get in the ship."

An arrow shattered against the hull inches from his face. He wheeled, the whole world seeming to jerk under him, sent a lance of blaster fire into the woods to make them keep their heads down, and scrambled back through the hatch as the first band broke cover.

Gamorreans on the whole, seen against a backdrop of more civilized worlds, generally appear clumsy and slow. This is at least partially a function of their stupidity: They don't understand much of what goes on around them, and tend to knock things over when they're not calculating how to use them as weapons in the happy event of a fight breaking out. In the woods of a primitive world with which they were familiar, the huge, muscle-bound bodies moved with terrifying speed, and in the drooling porcine faces showed neither intelligence nor the need for it.

They saw what they wanted, and they attacked.

Axes and stones splintered on the hatch as it slammed shut. Luke stumbled, dizzy, and Cray and Nichos seized his arms, half dragged him up the emergency gangway and onto the bridge, where Triv Pothman was leaning forward across the main console to peer through the glassine viewport at the attackers hammering the ship's sides.

"That's the Gakfedd tribe," reported the local expert equably. "See the big guy there? That's Ugbuz. Alpha male."

A huge boar Gamorrean was pounding the hatch cover with an ax made of a hunk of stained blast shielding strapped to a hardwood shaft the size of Luke's leg. His helmet was covered with plumes and bits of dried leather, which Luke realized a moment later were the ears of other Gamorreans.

"That one there with the necklace of microchips is Krok, junior husband to Ugbuz's wife, Bullyak. If I know Bullyak, she's watching from the woods . . ."

"You know them?" said Cray, startled.

Pothman smiled. "Of course, lovely lady." He still held the gauge and snip-welder he'd been using when Luke had gone down to warn the others. "I was slave in their village for the better part of two years. In a minute we'll see . . . Yep, there they are."

A second band had emerged from the trees on the opposite edge of the great clearing, equally dirty, drooling, shaggy, clothed in spiked armor wrought half of bright-colored reptile leather, half of scrap metal clearly scavenged or stolen from the Imperial base that for thirty years now had rotted in the woods.

"The Klaggs," said Pothman. "Look, back in the trees . . . That's Mugshub, their matriarch. Like Bullyak, making sure they don't damage anything of value in their enthusiasm. And besides . . ." He made a close-fisted mime of a manly muscle-flex. "Fighting just wouldn't be fighting unless the girls were along to watch."

The new band of Gamorreans fell upon those already pounding on the side of the ship. Ugbuz and the other boars of the Gakfedd tribe turned on the newcomers and in instants a full-fledged battle ensued. "The Klaggs held me prisoner for most of a year as well, after I escaped from the Gakfedds," said Pothman pleasantly. "Horrible people, all of them."

The five occupants of the ship—Luke, Pothman, Cray, Nichos, and Threepio—lined up along the console, looking down through the front viewport at the melee outside.

"We can go back to fixing the engines now," said Pothman after a few moments. "There's no way they can break into the ship, but they'll be fighting each other until it's too dark to see, at which time we can break out the lights and finish work outside."

"They can't see well in the dark?" asked Cray. Outside, Ugbuz picked up a smaller boar by the scruff and seat and heaved him at the rest, ignoring the shower of darts and rocks that fell around him like grimy rain.

Pothman looked surprised. "It'll be suppertime."

Shadow fell across the meadow.

Cloud, Luke thought. Then he realized it wasn't.

It was a ship.

Gleaming, massive, gray as hypothermic death, it descended like a steel flower under its five outspread antigrav reflectors. Imperial without a doubt, though Luke had seen nothing like it anywhere: It was far too large, too sleek, for a smuggler craft. Short legs unfurled from the lander's underside, and the grass of the meadow swirled around the crude hide boots of the Gamorreans as they stopped, lowered their weapons, stared.

"The Emperor." Pothman's face was filled with awe and a sort of terrified confusion, as if he weren't quite sure what he should feel. "He didn't forget."

The lander touched ground, the displaced air and gravitational currents joggling the *Huntbird,* fifty meters away. The tall central column of the unmarked craft, bigger than a fodder barn for a herd of banthas, settled a little, the movement reminiscent of some huge insect gathering itself together. White arc lights beneath the shelter of the antigravs flared on, automated vid pickups swiveled silently, triangulating on the silent horde of watching Gamorreans. Then the round column of the base rotated, and wide doors hissed smoothly open. A ramp reached forth, extended to the ground.

With a howl of delight audible even in the explorer's bridge, all the Gamorreans in the meadow piled up the ramp, weapons upraised, and foamed into the lander like a dirty and violent tidal race.

"Get the repairs finished," said Luke softly. "I've got a bad feeling about this."

The doors remained open. The vid pickups turned, recalibrating on the smaller ship. A moment's silence. Then the *Huntbird*'s intercom crackled to life. "Exit your ship," commanded a cold male voice. "Escape is futile. Survivors will be considered in sympathy with Rebel forces."

"It's a recording," said Luke, still watching the lander's open door. "Is there—"

"Exit your ship. In sixty seconds vaporization cycle will be initiated. Escape is futile. Exit. . . . ."

Cray, Luke, and Pothman traded one look, then headed for the hatch. "I'll take the center," panted Luke, gritting his teeth as the deck seemed to lurch under his feet. "You go left, Cray; Triv, head right." Luke wondered just how exactly he was going to elude whatever was going to come out of that lander, let alone give any help whatsoever to his companions. "Threepio, Nichos, get clear of the ship and head for the woods. We'll rendezvous at Pothman's base, it's two kilometers west of here. . . ."

He saw the lander's autocannons turn, half hidden by the protective petals of the antigrav, as he and his companions were halfway down the emergency ladder. He yelled, "Jump!" and threw himself off, falling the three meters to the long grass as white stunbeams seared noisily off the *Huntbird*'s sides. The impact with the ground was almost as bad as being hit with a beam. For a moment he couldn't breathe, couldn't see . . . but even in that moment he was rolling, dodging, trying to collect enough of his concentration to concentrate the Force—any quantity of the Force —on clearing his spinning head.

"Do not attempt escape." The hateful metal voice clanked through his swirling consciousness like an automated dream. "Mutineers and evaders will be considered in violation of the Capital Powers Act. Do not attempt escape. . . ."

His vision cleared and he saw Pothman running, zigzagging in the long grass. One shot from the autocannon puffed dirt and shredded stems on the black man's heels; a second caught him square between the shoulder blades. Luke hit the ground again and rolled to avoid a similar blast. From the tail of his eye he saw Cray do the same.

The Force. Got to use the Force . . .

Silent and evil, like silvery bubbles, tracker droids drifted from the open door of the lander.

They paused for a moment at the top of the ramp, round and gleaming, the small searchbeams clustered at their apexes moving, shifting, actinic beams stabbing around them, crisscrossing in the rich dim sunlight as they established bearings. Sensors turned like obscene antennae—Luke saw the round lenses on their equators iris open and shut, vile, all-seeing eyes.

Steel pincers and grippers unfurled from beneath them like insect feet, jellyfish tentacles, dangling as they drifted. With medium but inexorable speed, they floated down the ramp.

Concentrate the Force on body temperature, thought Luke. *Lower it, slow the heart rate, anything to fox their signals . . .*

Nichos, with far more agility than average for human-form droids, was running for the woods. Threepio, not designed for headlong flight, hastened determinedly after him. The trackers ignored them both.

"Do not attempt escape. Mutineers and evaders . . ."

Forty meters away, Cray rose to her knees behind a fallen log and got off a perfect shot, burning away the nest of sensors on the tracker homing in on where she lay. Luke shut his teeth on a cry of *"Don't . . ."* knowing that it didn't matter if she gave away her position. The trackers knew her position.

As the injured machine whirled, lurched, sensor lights stabbing and swiveling wildly to reorient, a second tracker spun in midair and caught Cray hard with a stunbolt, dropping her like a dead thing in the long grass.

Luke flattened, felt for his blaster, fighting to keep his vision single as the image of two of the floating droids divided into four, hovering over Cray's fallen body, reaching down with glittering, jointed limbs. Halfway to the clearing's edge, Nichos halted.

"Cray!"

His cry was a living man's cry of despair.

A shadow fell over Luke. He knew what it was even as he rolled to face it, turned on the ground, summoned all the Force, all his will and concentration, for a single shot.

White light blinded his eyes and he heard the oily soft chitter of steel limbs unfurling toward him as he pressed the trigger.

It was the last thing he recalled.

Chapter 5

"The children of the Jedi." Jevax, Chief Person of Plawal, slowed his steps on the hairpin switchbacks of the red-black rock stairs, deep-set green eyes taking on a faraway expression as he gazed out into the still rainbow mists that shut them in. The steps were cut straight into the coarse, faintly sparkling rock of the little valley's cliffs, but whoever had done that cutting had had either limited facilities or a paranoid streak about the original inhabitants of the valley floor. Leia could touch the rock to her right, and the railing of stripped shalaman wood on her left, without extending her arms more than a dozen centimeters from her sides, and by the look of the wood the railing was fairly new. Beyond it lay fog, darkened by blurs that she knew were the tops of trees.

"Yes," said Jevax softly. "Yes, they were here."

He returned his concentration to the climb, pushing through overhanging branches bearded with sweetberry vines and holding them politely back for Leia, Han, and finally Chewbacca to follow. In the steam-chamber atmosphere of the Plawal Rift, trees grew from the smallest juts and irregularities in the succession of "benches"—natural rock platforms or ledges that led up to the sheer wall of the cliffs themselves. Dark leaves mixed with trailing gray curtains of moss that hung over the rock face, jeweled with speckled bowvines and blood-red sweetberry fruit.

Leia shifted her shoulders under the baggy white linen of her shirt. The sticky heat was far worse than Ithor, the humidity gruesome, though at least up at this, the higher end of the valley, the unpleasant sulfur tang that managed to get past the processing plants lower down was almost hidden under the heavy green sweetness of the leaves. Looking up, it was impossible to believe that a hundred and fifty meters over her head, iron winds scoured glaciers deeper than the towers of most cities.

Looking up, in fact, it was impossible to see anything except green, and more green: galaxies of starbloom, riotous armies of orchids, fruits of every color, shape, composition, and degree of ripeness, all blurred and softened and hidden by the omnipresent density of the mist.

"Do you remember them?" On the way to Belsavis she'd looked up statistics about the original population. The Mluki were adolescent at seven, old at thirty. With his long white hair elaborately braided into crests down his back and arms, Jevax would have been a child when the Jedi left.

"Not clearly." Jevax, small among his peers, was still taller than Han, and would have been taller yet had his natural posture been straight instead of inclined slightly forward, long arms almost touching his bowed knees. He wore a great deal of jewelry, silver and iridescent blue shell-work imported from Eriadu, mostly in the form of earrings. His sarong-like breeches were printed in dark purple and black. Like nearly everyone in Plawal, he wore black rubber injecto-kit shoes of the kind manufactured on Sullust and sold by the freighterload in every corner of the galaxy, incongruous on the slumped, hairy, primitive form. The shoes had bright orange latches.

"It was years, you see, before any of us remembered the Jedi had been here at all."

. "That quiet, hunh?"

Leia reached back to give Han a shove. "They blotted your minds, didn't they?"

"I think they must have." Jevax led them around another corner and up another knee-breaking screw of stairs. Trees and promontories of rock overhung the way, and Leia could see Chewbacca gazing up approvingly at the possibilities for defensive ambush. The mists shredded away around them, the pallid daylight almost blinding after the ghostly dimness of the rift floor. Matte-gray cutouts of plants showed a cliff edge overhead, the tallest of the benches that graded up in the narrow end of what had originally been a small volcanic crevasse.

"I can't recall them doing so, of course," went on Jevax, rubbing his head in rueful amusement. "Nor could my mother. I was only three." He smiled at the recollection. "Funny, looking back. For ten or twelve years nobody remembered them at *all*—though it's quite clear from examining the ruins of Plett's House that he'd been living here for some seventy years before the other Jedi brought their spouses and children here to hide. Lately a few people have remembered: small things, memories that don't seem to fit with what we all thought we knew. But it's as if . . ."

He shook his head, searching for a way to explain. "It's as if for years we just didn't think about our past."

"I know people who run their lives that way," remarked Han. He didn't add—though he could have, Leia thought—that for a good percentage of his life he'd been one of them.

"Well, it isn't that we didn't have plenty of present and future to think about," the Chief Person went on. "The Jedi, bless their spirits, saw to that."

The last turn of the stair took them above the level of the mist. As if they had stepped through a trapdoor, the atmosphere was clear and noticeably warmer. Strange small winds stirred at Leia's hair, rustled the gray-stemmed trees that grew like a stalky curtain along the cliff's edge. To her left and below lay a mingled sea of green and gray, trees like islands amid vaporous billows, bright-winged birds and insects flitting between them in the wan and shivery light.

Leia looked up, and gasped.

"The Jedi," said Jevax, with shy pride, "were responsible for that, we think."

From the black rock of the ribbed volcanic cliffs sprang girders, supporting in their turn the webbed weight of durasteel with columns as thick as a man was high. Graceful as birds, the girders soared out over the nothingness of mist and flowers, every crystalline facet of the intricate plex roof they carried beveled and angled, designed to catch and multiply the smallest gleams of the weak sun's light.

Scrims of mist flowed like streams among the hanging garden beds that depended from the lacework of transparisteel vaults and domes, pendant gondolas as big as houses, some high in the swift-shifting streams of mist just under the plex, others lowered on cables nearly to the level of the broken turret of the stumpy stone tower that stood on the lava bench that Jevax and his party had just achieved: all that remained of the citadel of the Jedi.

"That's quite an engineering job for a bunch of folks who just ran around the galaxy with swords." Han as usual was determined not to be impressed.

"In running around the galaxy with swords," said Jevax, smiling and tugging on the end of one white braid, "I assume they encountered and befriended not only reliable engineers, but those trading corporations who were both interested in the exotic fruits and vegetable fibers our unique climatic conditions produce, and honest enough not to completely exploit the natives of this and the other volcanic rift valleys on the planet. The first representatives of Brathflen Corporation made their appearance, to the best of my calculations, within a year of the Jedis' departure. Galactic Exotics started development of shalaman and podon orchards here very soon after that. They joined with Imperial Exports to dome the valley, mostly because of a plan designed by—I believe—the Jedi Master Plett himself, to grow vine-coffee and vine-silk on the adjustable platforms beneath the dome."

He pointed upward. A large gondola, trailing festoons of pale, green-striped foliage, glided silently along one of the myriad tracks that followed the girders, halted under the center of the dome, and lowered itself with graceful ease a good ten meters. In doing so it put itself level with another hanging bed, from which tiny figures threw out a portable bridge made of a single line of chain ladder, and a second cable for handhold before they scrambled insouciantly across.

"Both plants depend on short-cycle temperature swings of thirty degrees or more. Few environments can sustain them, and those that can are seldom habitable enough to make the investment worthwhile. Those aerial plantations support a good thirty percent of our total economy."

Leia refrained from saying that a quantity of vine-silk sufficient to make a decent dress would cost enough to support a good thirty percent of *any* planet's total economy. Which was why Han's gift to her of a gown and tabard of the stuff a short time ago had reduced her to speechlessness. Her friend Winter had picked them out. Han still had a weakness for clothing completely unsuited to the Chief of State, and had learned not to trust his own judgment on things to be worn in public.

Chewie, gazing upward, yowled appreciatively. Leia remembered her unnerving adventures on the Wookiee's home planet of Kashyyyk and shivered.

"So you think they arranged commercial development of the planet as a . . . a kind of thank-you?"

"Well . . ." Jevax led the way toward the broken walls and half-ruined buildings that formed a clotted line where the bench joined the rise of the cliff behind it. "Brathflen, Galactic, and Imperial/Republic are the only three corporations with completely clean records as far as treatment of the local populations goes. Given the number of other companies operating in the Core Worlds, it can't be a coincidence that they were the three who got the coordinates for this planet."

The bench—the last giant step of rock at the end of the valley—was less than thirty meters wide, running back in an uneven triangle into the sheerness of the cliffs. A jungle-covered slope of debris blunted the inner point of the triangle, before which rose the tower, its front wall broken out to reveal two stone floors and the remains of two more, reduced to little better than ledges around the tower's inner wall. What looked as if it might have been a curtain wall lay about fifteen meters out from that, more or less halfway between the point of the triangle and the edge of the bench. It had been shattered in a dozen places, as if some huge creature had taken bites out of the stonework. Another curtain wall, reduced to a chain of dark rubble, skirted the edge of the bench itself, punctuated with trees, and between them lay a lush, rather unkempt lawn pitted with old blast craters in which thickets of lipana grew around small, silvery rain pools.

"How many of them stayed here?" asked Leia, making quick mental calculations and feeling a sort of shock of surprise and disappointment.

"It can't have been very many, that's for sure." Han surveyed the narrow space of the inner courtyard, hands on hips and a slight frown between his brows. "Not unless they were *real* friendly."

"They may have had perishable dwellings—tree houses or brush huts —on the lower bench where the MuniCenter now stands, or on the valley floor," said Jevax. "Though before the dome was built the valley was intermittently subject to cold—nothing like the cold up on the surface, of course. And I suspect that if they'd stayed in the houses of the villagers, more people would have remembered."

He gestured with a long arm to the roofless buildings, the tower whose every open floor and window embrasure, like the cliff behind it, sported its own pendant garden of fern, spider plant, Wookiee-beard, and sweetberry vine. "As far as I know, this is all there ever was."

"This can't have been more than Plett's original laboratory," objected Leia. "You couldn't fit ten families into this place."

"You obviously haven't been in a tenement in Kiskin," muttered Han. He walked through the broken gateway to the inner court and stepped through a gap in the wall of the single square building left standing roofless against the cliff at the foot of the tower. "So Plett was here first?"

"He was a botanist and a savant," said Jevax. "A Jedi Master of great age, we've heard; a Ho'Din from the planet Moltok. We've deduced by the growth of the lichens at the foot of the walls that he built this place about a hundred years ago, and since many of the plants that grow in the valley have been genetically tailored to our climate of geothermic heat and low light—even to the microclimates of high acidity down in the more active lower end of the valley—we assume he was an ecologist and scientist of considerable skill. Legends say he could talk to birds and animals as well, and send away the storms that periodically swept down even into the valleys. Some of this we know from the original inhabitants of the other rifts, of Wutz and Bot-Un, where, apparently, their memories were not tampered with."

"Meaning that the Jedi didn't stay there." Leia gazed around her at the square of heavy lava-block walls, over a meter thick and the hue of old blood. Despite the fortresslike appearance of the place, Plett's House was filled with the most profound sense of peace she had ever encountered.

Good people lived here, she thought, not knowing why the sense of it filled her so strongly, like the scent of forgotten flowers. *Power, and love like a sun's light.* She closed her eyes, overwhelmed with the impression that, if she listened hard enough, she could hear the voices of children playing.

"Exactly," she heard Jevax say, his voice diminishing as he and Han walked around the chamber's inner wall. "We think Plett originally chose this place not only because of the singular climate of the rift valleys, but because the glacial winds and extreme atmospheric conditions on the surface make landing any kind of spacecraft extremely difficult, and any kind of signals or sensors almost impossible."

"Yeah, tell me about it." Han had had some scary minutes bringing the *Millennium Falcon* down the tightest guidance beam he'd encountered in years and into a vertical hundred-meter landing silo bored straight into the rock, virtually blind.

"What about the tunnels?" Leia opened her eyes.

Jevax turned, raising his white shelf of brow. Han, who'd been inspecting one of the line of keyhole-shaped openings in the wall—doors or windows, though if they were doors they were so narrow only someone as slight as Luke or Leia could have slipped through—looked surprised at the question.

"That's just it, Your Excellency," said Jevax. "There *are* no tunnels. No 'secret crypts,' in spite of the rumors. Every few months someone comes up with a new theory and makes a search, and believe me, nobody has ever found a thing."

A sleek, small, green mammal Leia didn't recognize ran along the top of the wall; a yellow manollium perched in one of the window arches and fluffed its feathers, regarding the intruders into its domain with bright ruby eyes. The manollium must have come in with the Ithorians of Brathflen Corporation, she thought automatically. She'd seen hundreds of them already and she and Han had arrived only that morning.

"*They hid the children down the well,*" she repeated softly. "Nichos mentioned tunnels—I assumed McKumb meant there were crypts of some kind under Plett's Citadel. I suppose that's the 'well' in question?" She nodded toward the heavy disk of durasteel, sunk into the stone of the floor.

"One of them," said Jevax. "All of these rift valleys were called wells at one time, because of the hot springs. This . . ." He gestured up toward the green-hung dome visible high above the roofless walls, the town hidden within the mist, the varying microclimates of hot springs, warm springs, and mud pots that ranged up and down the vent; the towering dark cliffs with their suspended volutes of fern and orchid, the trailing banners of mist, ". . . this is *all* Plett's Well."

He led the way through the empty doorway—of the same keyhole shape as the windows, a characteristic of the old lava-block houses that clustered in what had been the original town at the foot of the bench at the high end of the valley—and out into the courtyard again. Gorgeous, filmy-winged insects blossomed up from the grass around them as if the warm earth itself had hurled handfuls of celebratory confetti.

Leia said, "But the rumors persist."

The heavy-browed, simian face widened into another smile. "Your

Excellency, for all its beauty, Plawal is a very dull place. The central library, the municipal archives, and all the city services rent space from the computer system that Brathflen, Galactic, Imperial/Republic, and Kuat teamed up to install twelve years ago, and there's very little room for new entertainment. Those people who don't have families to keep them interested have only work in the canneries or the silk-packing plants, and the bars along Spaceport Row. Of course they'd like to think there are secret crypts under the only ruins in the town that aren't being used for the foundations of perfectly ordinary Sorosub prefab housing. One has to do something."

He gestured around him again, the gluey breezes stirring the silky white fur of his long arms. "You're perfectly welcome to remain and search if you wish. I warn you, people have gone over the place with sensors of every variety. Research facilities in the archives won't be available until eighteen hundred hours—which is when the packing houses shut down their systems for the night—but after that, come down to the MuniCenter and I'll give you whatever help you wish rooting around in the records."

From a pocket of his utility belt he produced three laminated wafers, and held them out to Han, Leia, and Chewbacca. "These will open any room in the MuniCenter, the spaceport, the city garages, or the elevators that lead up the shafts from the spaceport and out onto the surface of the glacier, though I strongly advise that you get me or someone else local to go with you if you want to go out onto the ice for any reason. Will you care to walk back to the MuniCenter with me, or do you want to stay here awhile? The only decent café in town is the Bubbling Mud, by the way, off Brandifert Court."

"We'll stay awhile, thanks," said Han doubtfully.

"One more thing." Leia held up a finger; the Chief Person turned politely back. "Have you ever seen this man before?"

The holo cube of McKumb, taken while he was asleep, showed a slack, shut-eyed, skeletally thin face not much like the ruddy pot roast of a man Han had known, but it would have to do. Drub McKumb, like Han himself, had been in a business that discouraged accurate portraiture.

Jevax tilted his head, the white bar of brow curving in the middle with his frown. "I don't think so," he said. "You can try it in Port Records this evening, though if the man were a smuggler there would be no record of

him. During the last decade or so of the Empire we had quite a problem
with smugglers—the Imperial Governor kept only a small staff of tariff
police. Lately even that's slacked off."

"I'll check Port Records." Leia returned the cube to her pocket.
"Thank you, Jevax. Thank you for all your help."

"Thank *you*, Your Excellency, General Solo." The Mluki's ugly face
brightened into another grin. "You've spared me an entire afternoon at
the Computer-Time Reapportionment Board—a gift more valued than
glitterstim." And he strolled off through the somber green grass,
wreathed in bright insects, all his earrings twinkling in the pallid light.

Chewie growled softly.

"You're right," said Han quietly. "I think he was lying."

"Or someone lied to him."

Han nodded toward the curving bites taken out of the inner wall. "If
Imperials had meant business there wouldn't be a wall standing," he said.
"This looks like two or three carriers and a bunch of TIEs, tops. All the
way out here with no assault wing? No destroyers? If they knew the Jedi
were here, there'd be nothing but a hole in the ground. All right, all
right," he added at Chewbacca's gruff rumble, "so this place *is* a hole in
the ground. You know what I mean. If they didn't mean business, why
attack at all?"

Leia shook her head, still looking around her at the broken walls, the
small kitchen wing, the few rooms that could have been workshops. Still
haunted by that sense of vanished happiness, that deep, silent aura of rest.

"I've never dealt with an implanted belief," she said after a time.
"Luke has. He says they can go pretty deep. For all we know, the Jedi
implanted their own children—Nichos, and Cray's mother—with beliefs
after they left, to keep them from being traced. The damage looks bad
enough that these people would have needed *some* outside help right after
it was over. Turning it over to an Ithorian corporation at least kept it from
being exploited by some relative of the Emperor's, once everyone knew it
was here. But even if they did that—even if they implanted everybody in
the village with the belief that there never were crypts—the Jedi were
gone by the time the corporations arrived. Maybe the Ithorians who run
Brathflen treat the inhabitants of their commercial worlds decently, but I
can't see them—and I *certainly* can't see the Twi'leks who run Galactic—
passing up rumors of secret crypts. You notice how Jevax sort of skipped

over the part about rumors 'persisting.' 'Every few months' doesn't sound like something that gets put out of the way by a sensor check. There's got to be something else going on."

As they spoke they worked their way back into the triangle of the ruins, where the tower poked domeward under the massive, graceful spring of the girders and beetling outcrops of the cliff leaned inward, garlanded with hanging tapestries of flowers. Beds of vine-coffee hung above the remains of Plett's House, like obese and gaudy hoverbirds, the trailing ends of the vines only a dozen meters above the highest peak of the tower itself. Beyond them Leia could see the dome through the fragments of mists, and was surprised at how dark the sky appeared overhead.

In an inner room, one of a line cut into the cliff itself, a pipe tapped into a warm spring deep in the rock. Up at this end of the valley the water emerged from the earth little warmer than a truly hot bath, and without the sulfurous stink of the scalding springs lower down. The opening was crusted with pink and yellow deposits of sinter. Leia broke off a fragment, turned it over in her fingers. "Look familiar?"

"So much for there not being any crypts," said Han cynically.

"It doesn't mean the jewelry in Drub's pocket came out of a crypt near this particular spring. Even a source with the same combination of sulfur and antimony could have a number of outlets."

"You take a whole lot of convincing."

Leia grinned at him. "I deal with politicians all day."

"Yeah . . ." Han glanced toward the wrecked gate through which Jevax had passed. "I think you just got to deal with another one."

In one of the cliff-cut rooms Chewbacca found an old ladder, which they dragged up after them, floor by floor, to climb the remains of the tower, Leia picking her way carefully through the broken-out doorways, the thick embrasures of what had been windows, the curve of the broken stair. From the highest room the view out over the valley was breathtaking, mist filling the land like swirling water in a dark basin, the white or green plastic roofs of the packing plants rising through on the far end like a floe of bizarrely regimented icebergs where the greater heat stirred the fogs at the dark cliff's base.

Above them, the gondola beds of vine-coffee moved along their tracks, homegoing boats headed for the small wooden wasp's nest of the Supply Station, curtained in vines like everything else, clinging to the cliff.

From the far end of the broken remains of the tower floor, Leia gazed down at the miniature ecosystem of the rift, a steaming jungle snuggled in the midst of some of the most vicious icefields in the galaxy, fed by the heat of the planet's core.

What had the place been like, she wondered, when they'd been here, those children whose shrill voices she could almost hear? Those families whose wisdom and love had soaked, it seemed, into the very stone of the walls?

Intermittently colder, without the dome, she thought—necessitating the building of the rock houses of the old town over the hot springs. Wilder jungles near the warm vents, bare tundra perhaps away from them . . .

Why had the Jedi Master Plett come here in the first place, deliberately seeking a world where none could easily follow? Who had convinced him to offer sanctuary, and how?

A pair of strong arms circled her waist from behind. Han said nothing, just gazed out past her, and Leia leaned back into his strength, closing her eyes and letting her mind drift.

To Ithor, green and graceful and busy.

To the curious, meaningless death of a woman in the Senex Sector, killed by a man too expensive for the job.

To the fact, relayed to her that morning, that the head of the House Vandron, in whose territory the crime had taken place, was obstructing any investigation of Draesinge's death.

To Drub McKumb.

They hid the children down the well . . .

The voices of the children floated up to her. They were playing in the big, square room below; she saw them darting among the heavy tables of shalaman wood set along the inner wall, a whole pack of them: mostly human, but including an Ithorian, Wookiees, a Twi'lek, Bith . . . A woman repairing a half-dissected sterilizer at one of the tables called out an indulgent warning to one toddler who'd ventured too near the bronze, flower-shaped grille that screened the well in the floor's center, though the grille's openings were too small to admit anything except the smallest of the toys with which they played. Steam floated up through the openings, warming the room, as did the dim sunlight magnified by the angled crystalplex set in each keyhole window. A dark-haired man played a red-lacquered mandolin. Pittins of every color that pittins came in dozed on the windowsills or tracked the occasional myrmin across the floor.

The door in the rear wall opened, and an old Ho'Din came in, two and a half meters tall and graceful in his black cloak of Jedi mastership, his flowerlike headstalks faded with age. Calm seemed to flow from him, and a deep sense—such as she sometimes felt from Luke—of vast strength bought at a terrible price.

She opened her eyes.

The roofless chamber below her at the base of the tower was empty, full of shadows as the feeble daylight waned.

There was no door in the rear wall.

"They sealed it somehow." Han passed his palms along the smooth dark stone where the rear wall of Plett's House had been cut into the rock of the cliff. "Even the best patch jobs will leave a join, but this is watertight."

"It was about here, though." Leia half closed her eyes again, recapturing the scene. There was a kind of pain in the memory, a sense of having lost or mislaid something treasured, a long time ago.

The happiness she had felt rising from that room? The peace of being loved unconditionally, which had dissolved in searing laser violence when someone on the Death Star had thrown a final switch?

Looking at the man beside her, she wondered if Han had ever known that kind of peace, that sense of belonging, in his childhood.

Chewie growled a query; Han gave it some thought. "Yeah, I think we've still got the echolocator—if Lando didn't borrow it the last time he flew the *Falcon* for some cockamamie treasure-hunting scheme."

"I wouldn't bet on even an echolocator finding the tunnel that Master came out of," said Leia. She turned to survey the empty chamber once again. "The Jedi . . ." She hesitated, thinking about the things Luke had taught her, the things the old Jedi Vima-Da-Boda had said. "If the Jedi could cover their tracks to the extent of having everybody in the valley just forget they'd ever been there *in the face of some pretty severe bomb damage,* I don't think an echolocator's going to do us a lot of good."

"I think you're right." Han caressed the stone again, as if he half believed it was illusion rather than technology that concealed it. And perhaps, thought Leia, it was. "But at least now we know two things."

"Two things?"

"That there was an entrance here," said Han grimly, ". . . and that it wasn't the entrance Drub used."

Chapter 6

The Jedi Knights had murdered his family.

A band of them had descended on the town where he'd grown up, summoning fog by the power of the Force in the dead of night and moving through it in cold and shadow, wraiths of power and silence with eyes glowing green as marshfire in the dark. He'd fled, gasping, the icy pressure of their minds clutching at his, trying to cripple him and bring him back. He'd lain in the trees outside of town . . .

(trees?)

. . . and seen them line up the women, laughing at their screams as they pulled their babies from their arms and sliced them to pieces with their lightsabers. He'd seen cauterized stumps lying on the ground, heard the shrieks that had echoed in the bitter night air. The Jedi had sought him, hunting him in speeders, whooping derisively while he fled over rocks and mud and streams . . .

(mud and streams? I was raised in the desert.)

. . . and then turned back, to slaughter the children. He'd seen his younger brother and sister . . .

(What brother?)

. . . cut down while they pleaded for their lives . . .

Who made this up?

It was true. Every word of it was true.

Or something very like it was true, anyway.

Luke shut his mind, breathed deep through the pain that remained in his chest and lungs. He gathered the Force to him, let the knowledge run off him like water from oiled armor. The memories were like those in Nichos's mind, he realized. Words, sometimes powerful words, but absolutely without images. Words that said they were the truth, that felt like the truth . . .

His head ached. His body ached. His concentration wavered, darkened, and the feeling of betrayal, the bruised and savaged ache in his heart, returned. The Jedi *had* betrayed him.

He spiraled back into darkness.

Lying on Han's bunk in the *Millennium Falcon* with the bandaged stump of his right arm a blaze of agony underneath the painkiller Lando had given him, and worse than that agony the knowledge that Ben had lied to him. Ben had lied: It was Darth Vader who had spoken the truth.

Yes, revenge, voices whispered. *Take your revenge for that.*

For a moment he was twenty-one again, his soul a bleeding pulp of betrayal.

Why did you lie, Ben?

Looking back, he knew exactly why Ben had lied. At eighteen, the knowledge that his father still lived, still existed in some form, no matter how changed, would have drawn him to that father as only an orphan could have been drawn . . . would have drawn him to the dark side. At eighteen, he would not have had the experience, the technical strength, to resist. Ben had known that.

The Force flickered in him, like a single flame on a windy night.

"Luke?"

Revenge on the Jedi, on their harlots and their brats. Burn and kill as they burned and killed your parents . . .

The image in his mind was of seared skeletons in the sand outside the demolished wreck of the only home he'd ever known. The stink of burning plastic, the desert heat hammering his head less terrible than the oily heat of the flames. The emptiness in his heart was a dry well plunging lightless to the center of the world.

That farm in the desert hadn't been much of a belonging-place, but it had been all he'd ever had.

When he'd gone back to Tatooine to rescue Han from Jabba the Hutt, he had returned to that ruined farmstead on the edge of the Dune Sea. Nobody had taken up the land. Jawas had looted what was left of the house, probably as soon as the ashes cooled. The rooms around the sunken courtyard had collapsed. The whole place was only a crumbling subsidence, half filled with sand.

The markers he'd put on the graves of the people who'd been parents to him had been stolen, too.

Uncle Owen had given his whole life to the farm. It was as if he had never existed at all.

"Luke?"

He blinked. It wasn't a good idea.

"Luke, are you all right?"

"Oh, please, Master Luke, try to remember who you are! The situation is quite desperate!"

He opened his eyes. The whole room performed one slow, deliberate loop-the-loop and Luke tightened his grip on the sides of the bunk in which he lay to keep from falling out, but at least Nichos and See-Threepio, standing over him, didn't try to clone duplicates of themselves, and the pain in his chest was far less than it had been. He felt deeply, profoundly tired.

Beyond Nichos and Threepio he could see the shut door of the small cell in which he lay: brightly illuminated, comfortable, with three other bunks and a couple of lockers and drawers. Clean, cold, and with an air of being barely lived in, except for his own black flight suit hanging in one locker, his lightsaber on a dresser top, and the black cloak of a Jedi spread like a blanket across one of the other bunks.

Luke raised his arm and saw that he was wearing the olive-gray undress uniform of an Imperial stormtrooper.

The Jedi killed . . .

The Jedi killed . . .

He took a deep breath, summoned all of the Force away from the healing of his body—Nichos and Threepio immediately split into two again—and directed it inward on those memories like a cleansing light.

The voices in his mind yattered on for a bit, then scoured away.

He woke up again, weak and shaken. He couldn't have been unconscious for more than a few moments because Threepio was still explaining . . .

". . . said that there was nothing wrong with you and you'd only malinger if you went to sick bay! We didn't know what to do . . ."

"We're going to shell Plawal," said Luke.

Both his companions looked at him in alarm. "We *know* that, Master Luke!"

Luke sat up, catching at Threepio's arm as a wave of nausea swept over him; Nichos said, "We've been hyperjumping to half a dozen planets along the Outer Rim where the Empire hid its shock troops for this mission thirty years ago. The lander went down on Tatooine, Bradden, I don't know where-all. Everything's automated: landers, pickup, indoctrination . . ."

"Indoctrination?" said Luke. Another image came, distant and blurred through the ache in his head: a semicircular chamber heaped with unconscious Gamorreans, weapons still in their hands and the tiny, gray, parasitic morrts that clung to them even into battle beginning to recover from the stunrays and skitter nervously over the bodies. Two huge silvery droids of the old G-40 single-function type were moving among the bodies, pulling the Gamorreans to their feet—which G-40s could do with terrifying ease—and giving each an injection, then shoving them into the white metal coffins of single-man indoctrination booths that ranged along the curved back wall of the room.

He touched his forehead. A small circle of slightly roughened skin remained where the cerebral feed had been hooked in. The same thing, he realized, must have been done to him.

"Where are we?" He got up—carefully—and fastened his lightsaber to his belt as they stepped through the door, into a corridor smelling of metal, chemicals, and cleaning solution. The walls were medium gray under smooth, even light; the deck underfoot vibrated with the faint hum of subspace cruising speeds. A boxy MSE-15 droid glided by, cleaning the floor.

"On the ship," said Threepio. "The . . . the dreadnaught. The battlemoon Trooper Pothman spoke of. The giant vessel masked as an asteroid that fired on us. The *Eye of Palpatine.*"

The *Eye of Palpatine.* The name rang familiar in Luke's mind. The voices had told him all about it in that long, hazy spell of memories that were not his own. Somehow he knew the dimensions of the ship, huge, more vast than even the biggest of the Super Star Destroyers, bigger than a torpedo sphere, with firepower to waste a planet.

Of course, he thought. It had been built back before the Death Star, when the Imperial Fleet still thought bigger was better.

"It wasn't a base on that asteroid, Master Luke," explained Threepio. "That asteroid *was* the ship, firing at us with an automatic gunnery computer . . ."

"Are you sure?" Luke could have sworn it had been a living hand on the guns. No computer had that kind of timing.

"Absolutely," said Nichos. "Nobody can get up into the gun decks. And there's nobody on board who can handle weaponry—not this kind of weaponry, anyway."

"Nobody . . . ," said Luke. And then, "They're picking up troops . . ." He stopped himself, remembering the overgrown base in the forest, the forty-five helmets staring emptily from the wall. "Don't tell me there were still troops waiting."

They stepped into the troop deck's main mess hall. Ten or twelve enormous, white, furry bipeds were clustered nervously around the food slots, pulling out plates and swiftly sucking up everything smaller than bite-size through short, muscular probosci set under their four blinking black eyes. Several of them carried weapons—mostly legs wrenched off tables and chairs, it looked like—so Luke guessed they had to be at least semisentient.

There was a noise from the doors at the opposite end of the long room. The armed bipeds turned, raising their weapons. Seven tripodal creatures wandered in, baglike body masses swaying weirdly down from the central girdle of bone supported by the long legs, the tentacles between the hip joints dangling loose. Eyestalks rising above the body mass wavered with a motion that even Luke could tell was disoriented.

Two of the furry bipeds reached into the food slots and gathered as many plates and bowls as they could carry, and, guarded by one of their chair-leg-bearing mates, crossed cautiously to the newcomers. The larger of the two fuzzies raised a paw, hooted something in soft, unintelligible crooning, and, when the tripods made no response whatsoever, held out the plates.

The tripods extruded feeding tubes from among the eyestalks and ate. Some of them reached confusedly up with the tentacles to take the plates. The white furries remaining by the food slots wheeped and muffed to one another. The taller of the food bearers reached out with a curious gentleness and touched—patted—the nearest tripod in a gesture Luke knew at once was reassurance.

"That'll be enough of that, trooper!" The room's third set of sliding doors *hurshed* open, and a gang of about fifteen Gamorreans strode in. Some of them had wedged themselves into pieces of the largest storm-trooper fatigues obtainable by cutting out the sleeves, or had fastened chunks of the shiny white armor onto their arms and chests with silver engine tape. Others wore naval trooper helmets, and others still had the short-faced white stormtrooper helmets perched on top of their heads like hats. Ugbuz, in the lead, had donned a scuttle-shaped black gunner's helmet, and under it his warty, snouted face looked surprisingly sinister. All were armed to the tusks with blasters, forcepikes, axes, and bows.

"The man's malingering! Everyone had a physical before signing up. That's Fleet regulations, and there's no excuse for this kind of thing! Too many damned malingerers on this ship!"

Ugbuz snapped his fingers. Another Gamorrean—Krok, Luke thought—headed for the food slots and coffee machines with the heavy, rolling stride typical of the race while Ugbuz and the others took seats at a table. Luke saw that Cray and Triv Pothman were among them.

Dim memories crowded back from the past several days. He remembered eating, sleeping, sometimes trying to convince his commanding officer to let him go to sick bay when the pain and dizziness got too bad . . . practicing occasionally in the ship's gunnery range, though his head ached too much for him to shoot well . . . with other stormtroopers.

In his memory they were all human.

The white fluffies moved back a little to let the Gamorrean stormtrooper get coffee for himself and his mates, scratched their heads and made cooing noises as they watched the group around the table with puzzled unease. They, too, bore the fading singe marks of a cerebral feed, and Luke deduced that the indoctrination had taken on some species more firmly than on others. One of the tripods stumbled vaguely toward the stormtrooper table; it got too close and Triv Pothman swatted the thing with a vicious backhand, sending it stumbling among the chairs. The aging savant had shaved, and his face wore the hard expression of careless arrogance with which Luke was familiar among the troopers of the Empire: an utter sureness of position, the knowledge that whatever deeds he might commit, they would be sanctioned by those above.

The same look was on Cray's face.

Luke understood. He had felt like that himself for the past several days.

He sighed, and picked his way between the tables toward them, wondering if he could channel the healing of the Force sufficiently at this point to lead Cray out of her indoctrination. His head ached and every limb felt weighted, but the pounding nausea of the earlier stages of the concussion was gone. In a pinch, he thought, he could rally enough concentration, enough power of the Force, to touch the Force within her.

The Gamorreans—or at least the Gakfedd tribe of them—were obviously born to be stormtroopers. They seemed to have made themselves thoroughly at home: The floor of the mess hall was littered with plastic plates, bowls, and coffee cups, rising to a drift almost a meter deep near the food slots themselves. MSE droids moved over and around the mess like foraging vermin, but were mechanically unable to pick up the dishes and return them to the drop slots that would take them back to the automated kitchens. Near one of the several sets of sliding doors, a stolid SP-80 droid was methodically washing a spatter of foodstains off the wall.

"Captain." Luke saluted Ugbuz—who returned the gesture with military briskness—then took a seat next to Cray.

"Luke." Her greeting was casual, buddy-to-buddy. She'd cut off her hair—or Ugbuz, in his persona of a stormtrooper officer, had made her cut it. The centimeter-long bristle lay close and fine against her scalp. Without makeup, and in the olive-gray uniform only slightly too large for her tall frame, she looked like a gawky teenage boy.

"Pull up a chair, pal, rest your bones. You figure the jump this morning was our last pickup? Get us some coffee, you," she added, with barely a glance in the direction of the two droids. "You want any, Triv?"

"I *want* some coffee." The elderly man grinned. "But I guess I'll have to settle for that gondar sweat those machines are puttin' out."

Cray laughed, easy and rough. It was the first time Luke had seen her laugh in months—oddly enough, the first time he'd ever seen her this relaxed. "You on rotation for the holo tapes, Luke?" she asked. "I dunno who stocked the library on this crate. Nuthin' later than—"

"I need to talk to you, Cray." Luke nodded toward the open door to the hallway from which he'd come. "In private."

She frowned, her dark eyes a little concerned, though it was clear to him that she saw him as a fellow trooper. She probably remembered after

a fashion that they'd been friends for some time, the same way she remembered her name was Cray Mingla, but probably didn't think much about
it. Luke knew that at the height of the Emperor's power the Imperial
troopers had been highly motivated and fanatically loyal, but this depth of
indoctrination was something he'd never before encountered. An experiment that hadn't been followed up? Something in use for this mission
alone because of its intense secrecy?

He took a deep breath and wondered how much of his present dizziness and disorientation was the lingering effect of the concussion, and
how much a side effect of a too massive indoctrinal shock. He would need
all the Force he could summon to break Cray out of this . . .

Cray got to her feet and trailed after Luke toward the doorway,
casually kicking aside plates and an MSE as she went. Even her walk was a
man's walk, adopted unconsciously, the way the Gamorreans seemed to
have acquired Basic speech. Threepio and Nichos followed unobtrusively,
and Luke let his hand slide down to loosen his blaster in its holster,
thumbing the setting down to mildest stun.

He never got the chance to use it.

He and Cray paused to let the white furries, still clutching their
makeshift weapons, amble out of the door ahead of them. "I dunno what
the service is comin' to," muttered Cray, shaking her head. "Look at that.
Gettin' recruits from all over the damn place. They'll be takin' festerin'
aliens next." The tripods continued to wander aimlessly around the mess
hall, bumping occasionally into furniture or tripping over the MSEs.
Clearly the indoctrination that had worked so thoroughly on the Gamorreans had left them—whatever they were—totally bewildered. *Where
would you put the cranial wires on them, anyway?* wondered Luke.

Then the doorway across the room swished violently open and a voice
yelled, "Get 'em, men!"

It was the rival Gamorrean tribe of the Klaggs.

Ugbuz and his Gakfedds upended tables, dropped behind them as
blaster bolts blazed and spattered wildly around the room. The Klaggs,
too, wore bits of stormtrooper gear, engine-taped to their homespun and
leather, and cried orders and oaths in Basic. Cray swore and hauled up a
table into a makeshift barrier, blazing away in return with no regard for
the deadly ricochets bouncing and zapping crazily in all directions; her
first bolt caught a Klagg on his chest armor, hurling him back among his
fellows as the others of his tribe ducked, ran, zigzagged into the room,

firing as they went. Some were armed with blaster carbines and semiautos, others with slugthrowers, forcepikes, and axes. Their aim was universally awful.

The two Gamorrean tribes clashed in thick waves of metal, flesh, and garbage, and began to beat and tear one another as if taking up the battle outside the *Huntbird* exactly where they'd left off. Cray screamed, "Scum-eating mutineers! Captain!" and plunged into the fray before Luke could stop her.

"Cray!" Luke ran two steps after her, the deck seeming to lurch beneath his feet, and collided with two frantic tripods that couldn't seem to locate the door three meters in front of them. With a roar one of the Klaggs bore down on him, swinging an ax. Luke ducked and nearly fell, shoved the tripods toward the door, caught up a chair, and deflected the ax; the Klagg struck him aside and plunged after the defenseless tripods. It caught one of them by the leg, the poor thing screaming and flailing with its tentacles. It took all the Force Luke could summon just to get back to his feet, forget about levitating anything—he grabbed the chair again and swung it, slamming the Gamorrean full force in the back, then whipped his lightsaber free and planted himself in the doorway as the tripods fled wailing into the corridor.

The Gamorrean hurled a table at him, which Luke bisected, then struck at him with an ax at the same moment a ricocheting blaster bolt caught Luke glancingly on the shoulder. Either the blaster was turned fairly low or its power cell was nearly exhausted, but the jolt of it knocked him, gasping and confused, to the floor. He rolled, his vision blurring, blacking. Cut at the Gamorrean, who'd been joined by a friend, also wielding an ax—*double vision?* Luke wondered cloudily, but he took off one assailant's arm and tried to get to his feet and out the door. He couldn't—his head was swimming too badly for him to figure out why—and he could only slash upward at his remaining assailant, cleaving in half the table that slammed down on him before it could crush his bones.

The cold sick weakness of shock and the sensation of something being wrong with the gravity . . .

Then the Klaggs were gone, leaving a shambles of blood and broken furniture. Luke stayed conscious just long enough to switch off his light-saber.

Pain brought him to as if someone had drenched his left leg with acid. He cried out, clutching at the greasy mess of blankets on which he lay, and someone slapped him hard enough to slam him back down, breathless and dizzy and almost nauseated with pain.

"Shouldn't you get something from sick bay for that?"

Ugbuz's voice.

And in reply a vicious, squealing snuffle, and warm drool spattered down onto Luke's face and bare chest. More pain, as someone jerked tight a bandage around his left leg.

Not a bandage, he thought, identifying another sound, the slick, shrill searing noise of engine tape being pulled off a roll. A familiar sound. If it weren't for engine tape the Rebellion would have collapsed in its first year.

Cold air on his thigh, his knee, his foot. And rough, clawed hands taping a splint onto his leg.

The wrench of it made him cry out again and Ugbuz said, "Suck it up, trooper."

Luke wondered about the incidence of Imperial officers being killed from behind by friendly fire. He opened his eyes.

He was in a hut. *A HUT?* The ceiling, only a meter or two above his head, was made of plastic piping roofed with pieces of stormtrooper armor and mess hall plates held together with wire and engine tape. Glowrods dangled from the piping rafters, their trailing wires plugged into a backpack-size Scale-20 power cell in the corner, providing the only illumination. Beyond the doorway, curtained with a silver t-blanket on which the words PROPERTY OF IMPERIAL NAVY were clearly visible, could be seen the vague gray steel walls of some larger space, a gym or a cargo hold. Ugbuz stood in the doorway, arms folded, looking down at him where he lay on a bed made of dirty blankets, and above him—taping the splints to his leg—knelt the enormous, vicious-looking Gamorrean sow whom Pothman had pointed out to him as Bullyak, head female of the Gakfedd tribe.

"Now, I'll have no malingering in my unit, mister," grunted Ugbuz, when Bullyak turned away. "We've had some losses, and we've had some injured, but those mutineers aren't going to interfere with our mission." He thrust a metal flask at Luke. The fumes alone would have dropped a bantha in its tracks. Luke shook his head. "Drink it! I don't trust a man who won't drink."

Luke put it to his lips but didn't let the alcohol go any farther than that. Even that movement throbbed hideously in his leg. It took all the disciplines he had learned, all his control of the Force within his own body, to put the pain aside.

The ax, he thought. The Klaggs who'd attacked him had both carried axes. Had one struck him in the final melee? He didn't recall, but remembered not being able to get up.

His head hurt, too. For the first time the desperate importance of getting injuries seen to immediately was brought home to him—he'd be even less able, now, to protect himself, and it was quite obvious that he'd have more need to do so.

Why was the great hold around them dark?

"What about Trooper Mingla, sir? Skinny blond kid?"

Ugbuz's tiny eyes squinted harder at him in the gloom of the hut. "Friend of yours?"

Luke nodded.

"Missing. Festering mutineers. Two men killed, three missing. Sons of sows. We'll get 'em."

Bullyak squealed something angrily at him, her long, gray-green braids swinging heavily over the gelid, bitten flesh of her six enormous breasts. Morrts were blood parasites, gray, finger-size, and furry; one of them was even now, Luke could see, fixed on Ugbuz's neck, and another was crawling up Bullyak's braid. The pinny glitter of their eyes flickered all around the hut, in the corners, in the rafters. The blankets stank of them.

Slowly, agonizingly, he tried to get to his feet.

Bullyak snarled something at him, and thrust a stick into his hand. It had clearly started life as a pole arm of some weapon brought from Pzob, six feet of knobbed and hand-smoothed wood. His trouser leg had been slit from halfway down his thigh, to let her dress the wound. Even if he'd been able to stand the thought of putting weight on that leg he knew it wouldn't bear him. She'd wrapped his left foot in rags, having cut off the blood-soaked boot. Rather to his surprise, his lightsaber was hooked to his belt.

The sow shoved him in the direction of the door, with a violence that nearly had him on the floor again.

"She says get yourself some coffee," said Ugbuz, with an officer's hearty cheer. "You'll heal up fine."

"Master Luke!"

Luke looked around. Two dozen huts had been erected, ranged around the walls of what looked like a cargo hold. Doors, pieces of metal paneling, plastic and corrugated crate sides had gone into their construction, as well as blankets, bits of armor, mess hall plates, wire, cable, pipe, and the ubiquitous engine tape. More plates and coffee cups littered the metal decking, and the place had a faint, garbagy smell in spite of the best efforts of the MSEs buzzing and puttering around the open square in the center. There were few Gamorreans in sight.

In the dark, open doorway of the vast chamber, Threepio stood waiting. Had he been programmed to do so he'd have wrung his hands.

Slowly, every step an acid jolt of suppressed agony, Luke limped the fifteen meters that separated them. Threepio made a move as if he would have come through the door to help him, but seemed to think better of it.

"I'm terribly sorry, Master Luke," apologized the droid. "But the Gamorreans don't permit droids in their village. The SP Eighties have tried repeatedly to dismantle the huts and put the pieces away in their proper places and . . . well . . ."

Luke leaned against the wall and laughed in spite of himself. "Thanks, Threepio," he said. "Thanks for following this far."

"Of course, Master Luke!" The protocol droid sounded shocked that there would have been any question of it. "After that dreadful fracas in the mess hall . . ."

"Did you see what happened to Cray? Ugbuz says she's missing . . ."

"She was carried away by the Klagg tribe. They seem to regard the Gakfedds as mutineers, and vice versa. Nichos went after them. She was putting up a good fight, but I'm afraid she was no match for them, sir." He clanked softly along at Luke's side as Luke started to walk again, limping down the corridor and grimly blocking his mind against the pain in his leg. Simply keeping the agony at bay took enormous amounts of his concentration, far more than he'd channeled against the effects of his concussion. He had to find sick bay, and fast. At least with so obvious an injury Ugbuz couldn't argue that he was merely malingering.

"Any idea where they're headquartered?"

"I'm afraid not, sir. Captain Ugbuz has sent out scouts to locate their stronghold, so it's quite clear he has no idea either."

"They shouldn't be too hard to find." Luke was checking every door they passed, mostly cargo holds in this part of the ship. Owing to the *Eye's* configuration as an asteroid the ship possessed long stretches of hallway unbroken by doorways; the lights were on here, gleaming coldly off the gray metal walls. Here and there a plastic plate or coffee cup from the mess hall made a bright spot in the monochrome, and once they passed a tripod, wandering vaguely through the hall gazing around with its three thick-lashed green eyes.

"I'm not so sure of that, sir. The SP Eighty cleaner droids were very diligent about scrubbing all trace of their trail from the walls and floors."

Luke stopped, and leaned back against the wall, his head swimming. *Did other Jedi Masters have to go through this?*

"What happened here?" He opened his eyes again. The stretch of hallway before them was dark, as the Gakfedds' village hold and the area around it had been, the glowpanels of the ceiling dead for easily a hundred meters in front of them. A hatch cover had been ripped loose halfway down and wires and cables trailed out into the hall like the entrails of a gutted beast. As he limped nearer Luke smelled a familiar odor, faint and distant now, but distinctive . . . "*Jawas?*"

If Threepio had possessed lungs he would have heaved a long-suffering sigh. "I'm afraid so, sir. It appears that on such planets where the Empire posted troops to be picked up for this mission thirty years ago, the automated landers collected whatever sentient beings they could find."

"Oh, great," sighed Luke, bending carefully to study the frame of the gutted hatch. It was grubby with small handprints. He wondered how many of the meter-tall, brown-robed scavengers the lander had picked up on Tatooine.

"Those were Talz we saw in the mess hall, from Alzoc Three. I have not been very far afield, Master Luke, but I know there are also Affytechans from Dom-Bradden aboard, and the Maker only knows what else besides!"

"Great," said Luke again, limping on. "So in order to blow up the ship before it reaches Plawal I'm going to have to find the troop transports and somehow get everybody on board. I suppose I could always tell the Gamorreans it's orders, but . . ." He hesitated, remembering the vicious skill of the ship's gunner, the one Threepio insisted did not exist. Whatever else might be automated on the *Eye of Palpatine,* there might very well be one member of the original mission crew still on board.

"Here. This looks like what we're after."

They had traversed the blacked-out section of corridor to the lighted area beyond. A small office on the right had clearly belonged to a super-cargo or quartermaster; a black wall-mounted desk bore a large, curved keyboard, and the staring onyx darkness of a monitor screen gazed gravely down above. Luke sank gratefully into the leather padding of the chair—*definitely a quartermaster,* he thought—propped his staff against the desk, and flipped the on toggle.

"Let's see if we can talk this thing into giving us some idea of how much time we have, before we do anything else."

He typed in **Mission status request.** It was a common enough command, involving no classified information, but even knowing when the *Eye* was expected to reach Plawal would tell him how urgently he had to move.

- **Mission time consonant with the objectives of the Will**

"Hunh?"
Luke typed in **Menu.**

- **The Will requests objective of this information**

Orientation, typed Luke.

- **Current status aligned with timetable of the Will. No fur-ther information necessary**

"They really didn't want to risk anyone outside finding out about their mission, did they?" murmured Luke. The screen grayed and swam before his eyes, and he drew the Force to him, wearily clearing, strengthening the slowly healing tissues of the brain.

Sick bay, he thought tiredly. *Right after this, sick bay . . .*

"When did the last lander come aboard, Threepio?"

"Yesterday, I believe. Those were the Talz."

Luke considered. "If they're trying to avoid suspicion, it makes sense that they'd lie low for a day or two, maybe longer, before making another hyperspace jump. Maybe a lot longer, depending on who they think was watching them thirty years ago."

Ben Kenobi, almost certainly. Bail Organa. Mon Mothma. Those

who'd watched the rise of Palpatine to supreme power, the birth of the
New Order, first with suspicion, then with growing alarm.

"The ship's certainly big enough to keep a couple of companies
comfortable for a while."

Schematic.

A deck plan appeared; Luke identified the big cargo hold without
trouble, and the quartermaster's office where he now sat. A readout in the
corner flagged this as Deck 12. He keyed the command for the deck
above, and the one above that, noting the irregular shapes of the decks.
Sick bay was two decks below. The decks were huge, but presumably
after two or three days Ugbuz wouldn't be sending scouts for rival tribes
on his own deck.

The computer refused to display the schematic for Deck 9.

Keying down, Luke could only get displays for Decks 10 through 13.

Total schematic.

- The Will requests the objective of this information

Location of alien life forms.

- All things are within parameters defined by the Will.
  There are no unauthorized life forms aboard

"Oh, there aren't, hunh?" Again Luke keyed in Total schematic.

- The Will requests the objective of this information

Damage control.

- The Will is in control. The Will ascertains no damage in
  any area

All the lights browned out and the pale-blue letters of the monitor shrank
into a tiny dot and blinked away. From the blackness of the corridor
outside came the shrill chitter of Jawa voices, the scrabble of fleeing feet.

Luke sighed. "I've got a bad feeling about this."

Chapter 7

Sick bay was dark, silent, and cold.

"*Drat* those Jawas, sir!" cried Threepio.

Luke Skywalker had dealt successfully with battling a clone of himself, with being enslaved by the Emperor and the dark side, with wholesale slaughter and the destruction of worlds.

A good deal of Han Solo's vocabulary did come to mind.

"Come on," he sighed. "Let's see what we can manage."

"These were quite decent early Too-One-Bees, sir," remarked Threepio, holding aloft one of the few emergency glowrods left in the rifled emergency locker on the wall. "But of course the reason they are independently powered in modern ships, instead of hardwired into place, is painfully obvious here."

"Painfully," thought Luke, leaning against the self-conforming plastene of the diagnostic bed, was certainly the appropriate word for this occasion.

All the cabinets had been frozen shut when the Jawas had pulled the main wall hatch in search of wire and components. Though none of the diagnostics worked, Luke was fairly certain—by the way his left foot moved, and by the excruciating pain that shot up the back of his thigh whenever he put the slightest weight on it—that one or more tendons had been severed, which meant that even discounting the near certainty of infection, until he could get to a genuine medical facility he would be seriously lame. Simply keeping traumatic shock at bay took all the healing power of the Force that he could muster, and even that, he knew, couldn't last long.

In addition to ripping free coverplates and hatches to get at the machinery within, the Jawas had carried off portions of the autodocs, taken the power cores out of the X-ray and E-scan machines, and tried to remove the temperature regulator from the bacta tank, with the result that the tank itself had leaked half its contents onto the floor in a gigantic sticky pool.

So much for the possibility of standard regenerative therapy.

Luke caught one of the horde of MSE droids that were faithfully attempting the herculean task of cleaning up the mess, pulled its power core, and used its wiring to short the locks on the cupboards. The dispensary was stocked with huge quantities of gylocal, a horrifically powerful pain-blocker/stimulant that would allow a warrior to go on fighting long after shock would have felled and killed him—Luke turned the black boxes of ampoules over in his hand and remarked, "They sure expected a fight, didn't they?" He put them back. Gylocal decomposed after about ten years in storage, separating into its original—and highly toxic—components. Even if the stuff had been fresh Luke wasn't sure what the effect of the drug would be on his ability to wield the Force.

Less heroic measures were available in the form of nyex, which made many people—and Luke knew from past experience he was among them —drowsy, and the nonnarcotic painkiller perigen. He planted a perigen patch on his thigh just above the knee and immediately felt the pain lessen. It wouldn't heal the damage and he'd still be lame, and perigen lacked the mild stimulant included in gylocal, but at least the debilitating stress of fighting the agony would be eased. In the absence of bacta-tank therapy to accelerate the healing of his concussion—and Luke knew he was already over the worst of its effects—the simple reorientive comaren would deal with the last of the symptoms.

At least there was plenty of that.

More worrying was the fact that most of the antibiotics and all the synthflesh on the ship had completely decomposed with age.

In a locker in one of the labs next door he found a regular trooper's gray coverall whose baggy shape would fit over the taped and splinted dressing on his leg. Changing into it, Luke filled the pockets with all the comaren and perigen he could locate, and wired half a dozen glowrods to the end of his staff.

"Okay, Threepio," he said, as he belted his lightsaber once more around his waist and carefully used his staff to lever himself up from the self-conforming chair where he'd sat to change. "Let's see about finding Cray in this place."

In the dark corridors around sick bay, Talz—as Threepio identified them—fled from them like enormous white powder puffs; from the pitch-black maws of holds and wards, little quadrangles of eyes glittered out at him in the bobbing reflection of the glowrods. Luke halted two or three times, and had Threepio translate for him, "I am your friend. I will not harm you, nor lead anyone here to harm you." But none of the great, soft aliens returned a sound.

"The Empire used them for work in the mines on Alzoc Three," said Luke, as he and Threepio headed toward the lighted areas visible far down the corridor. "Alzoc wasn't even *entered* in the galactic registry. The Senate found a mention of it a couple of years ago in secret corporate files. Nobody knew what was going on there. They were lied to, betrayed . . . no wonder they learned to distrust anything humanoid. I wonder what happened to the stormtroopers who waited on their planet to be picked up?"

Beside the lift he surprised a group of Talz in the process of feeding a band of ten or twelve tripods, setting down big mess-hall basins on the floor, one of water, one of a horrible mixture of porridge, milk, and fish stew, which the tripods knelt to devour eagerly. The Talz themselves took one look at Luke and Threepio and fled. Within minutes a dozen MSEs and two SP-80s appeared, determined to clean up what they obviously considered mess. The tripods moved back in confusion, watching helplessly as the MSEs slurped up what was left of both water and food—cutting in to do so behind Luke's back when he tried to shoo them away—and the SP-80s made valiant but futile attempts to bend down far enough to pick up the basins themselves.

"I have nothing but respect for the entire Single-Purpose series, Master Luke," said Threepio, reaching down to hand the basin to the older and blockier droid. "Truly the core of droid operations. But they are so *limited.*"

Threepio could provide no identification or linguistic information on the tripods, and even his translational analog function couldn't arrive at a complete understanding of their speech. Luke could only gather that they were People and they came from the World and they were looking for a way to go back there.

"You and me both, pal," sighed Luke, as the spindly forms wove away down the corridor, still hunting for the right door to go through that would open onto home.

At least the lift still worked, though with the Jawas at large it was anybody's guess how long that would last. The dirty little creatures were born scroungers and thieves, especially of metal, wire, and technology. Only four lighted buttons glowed beside the lift door: 10, 11, 12, 13. Up on Deck 12 again the lights were still on, the air clean and circulating. An occasional plate or coffee cup littered the corridors, and cast-off pieces of stormtrooper armor amply indicated a Gamorrean presence, but as Threepio had said, the SP-80 cleaners and the little black boxlike MSEs had meticulously wiped out any evidence of whatever trail the invading Klaggs had left.

They came around a corner and Luke stopped, startled, to find the corridor in front of them dotted with what looked, at first glance, like blubbery, putty-colored mushrooms; a meter to a meter and a half tall, lumpy, and smelling strongly like vanilla. A second glance showed him that they had arms and legs, though he could see no sensory organs whatsoever. Threepio said, "Good Heavens! Kitonaks! They weren't here yesterday."

He walked forward among them.

Luke followed. There were thirty at least in the corridor, more, he saw, in the rec room that opened to the right. He touched one and found it room temperature, though with a suspicion of greater heat deep within. Under huge folds of fat many of them showed round, open holes in what were probably their heads, and, peering within, Luke identified two tongues and three rows of small, cone-shaped teeth.

"What are they doing?" Several bore abrasions and what looked like knife wounds that had bled, clotted, and were on their way to healing, apparently unnoticed.

"Waiting for Chooba slugs to crawl up into their mouths," replied the droid. "It's how they feed."

"Nice work if you can get it." Luke reflected that at some point an expedition to the mess hall sounded in order, though it would call for a certain amount of caution. "They look pretty safe for now."

"Oh, they are, Master Luke." Threepio clanked briskly among the weird forest of still shapes. "They're among the toughest species in the galaxy. Kitonaks have been known to go without food for weeks, sometimes months, with no ill effects."

"Well, unless those landers picked up Chooba slugs in mistake for stormtroopers," commented Luke, glancing back over his shoulder at them, "they're going to have to."

Where the lights failed and the corridors became dim-lit caverns illuminated only by the reflected glow of glowpanels in the lighted areas or an occasional bleary yellow worklamp, they found the corpse of an Affytechan, the gaudy vegetable people of Dom-Bradden. MSEs crawled over it like greedy insects, trying vainly to clean a mess beyond their small capacities; ichor congealed on the floor for meters in all directions and the smell of its rotting sugars lay thick and nauseating in the air. Luke was silent, aware again of the dangers of this not quite empty ship.

A scream echoed down the darkened corridor from the direction of the Gakfedd village in the cargo hold. Luke swung around, listening; then started toward the sound at a limping, staggering run. Its queer and almost metallic timbre told him it was a Jawa, terrified and in agony. He knew long before he reached the hold what he'd find, and in spite of what he knew about Jawas, the hair on his head prickled with fury.

The Gamorrean stormtroopers had gotten a shredder from someplace, and were holding a Jawa by the wrists above it, lowering it feet first into the whirling blades. There were four or five of them, including Ugbuz, all howling with laughter as they dipped their wretched little captive up and down.

From the threshold of the giant chamber, Luke reached out with the Force and swatted the shredder away with such violence that it spattered to pieces on the wall ten meters away. Krok—who was holding the Jawa—hurled the miserable little clump of rags and filth aside and whirled, roaring a curse; Ugbuz brought his blaster carbine to bear. Luke, hobbling toward them between the huts, impatiently ripped the carbine from the Gamorrean's hands while he was still meters away, sending it spinning, and did the same a moment later to another trooper's ax. Torture of anything fired in him a white and scalding rage. Krok launched himself at him with his huge hands outstretched, and Luke levitated him as if he'd been a hundred and seventy-five kilos of bagged rocks, and held him for a moment two meters above the floor, staring at him with cold blue eyes.

Then, carelessly almost, he threw him aside, and turned to face Ugbuz.

"What's the meaning of this, trooper?" demanded the Gamorrean furiously. "That was a Rebel saboteur, out to thwart our mission! We caught him with that . . ." He gestured furiously to the bundle of wires and computer chips, torn ends trailing, that lay near where the shredder had been.

Luke met the Gamorrean's eyes with a chilled and icy stare before which, after a moment, the piggy gaze dropped. Sullenly, almost, Ugbuz demanded, "Who the hell do you think you are?"

"It isn't who I *think* I am," said Luke softly, stepping close. "It's who I *am.*" He lowered his voice to exclude the others, and spoke for Ugbuz's ears alone. "Major Calrissian, special services. 229811-B." He gave the serial number of the *Millennium Falcon*'s engine block. "Intelligence."

Had it been possible for Ugbuz's eyes to widen they would have; as it was his hairy ears shifted forward in awe and respect. He threw a quick glance over his shoulder to where the Jawa had been thrown. Though Krok had slung the Jawa with sufficient force to have surely broken all its bones, it was no longer there—Jawas being endowed with the ratlike ability to take almost any amount of physical punishment and still slither away through the first unwatched crack the moment they were no longer actually restrained.

Luke laid a hand on the stormtrooper captain's arm. Both his fury and the exertion of using the Force had left him trembling, almost nauseated, sweat icy on his face, but he kept his voice soft, projecting into it all his Jedi power. "It's all right," he said. "You did as you thought best and it was clever work capturing it. But it was acting under my orders, infiltrating the Rebels. There was no actual damage done. You did right to protect the mission, and I'll see your name shows up in commendations to the Ubiqtorate, but after this . . . let me interrogate prisoners."

"Yes, sir." For a moment a thoroughly Gamorrean expression of disappointment crossed Ugbuz's tusked face. Then he was Captain Ugbuz of the Imperial Service again. He saluted.

"You did well, Captain," said Luke, and used the Force to subtly project into Ugbuz's mind the pleased warmth that surety of approval brings.

"Thank you, sir." The pseudostormtrooper saluted again and lumbered over to pick up his blaster carbine, stopping once or twice to look over his shoulder at Luke, who limped away in the direction of the door, leaning heavily on his light-clustered staff.

"Very good, Master Luke," said Threepio softly when Luke, weak with exhaustion, reached the door once more. "Though I must say, you really ought to find some way to discourage those Jawas from further depredations on the fabric of this vessel if we are not to all perish of cold and suffocation. They seem to have no idea of the damage they're causing to their own environment."

"Well, they wouldn't be the first," Luke remarked, leaning against the wall. He felt drained and beaten, his head aching in spite of the comaren. If in immediate danger of death by freezing, he doubted he could have summoned enough of the Force to light so much as a candle.

"If you'll come this way, sir," said the droid, "I believe I have found a partial schematic of the ship."

The schematic of Decks 10 through 13 was etched onto four crystalplex panels in what was probably the office of the physical plant manager, showing the locations of lifts and gangways, power lines marked in red and water trunks—shower facilities, coolant lines, fire-control sprinklers —in blue. The asymmetry of the ship's form made it difficult to remember. From the outside, Luke recalled, the asteroid was more bean-shaped than round, so the higher decks would be smaller, and grouped aft. From the location of coolant trunks, Luke deduced that the main power cores that fed the reactors, the computer core, and the guns were located aft as well.

His request for a full schematic from the office computer was greeted with a demand for an authorization code, and tinkering with all the various standard Imperial codes he knew or had been told by Cray only got him **Current status of all departments consonant with the timetable and objectives of the Will.**

The Will, he thought. The core program. The central, coordinating plan. The thing that regulated everything in the ship, from the temperature of the mess-hall coffee to the nearly human targeting of the defensive guns . . .

Nearly human? Luke wasn't sure anymore about that.

The thing that knew when the jump to hyperspace would be, that would take them to Belsavis. That knew what the battle plan was for destroying that undefended town.

Without human knowledge, he thought. Therefore, there was no one who could have been forced, or coerced, or coaxed, to talk, had they been captured. Only the Will.

He went back to studying the schematics it *would* show.

"They've got to keep the lines to the fuel tanks and the power chargers short," he explained, limping along the corridor again a few minutes later with Threepio clanking softly at his side. "That means all the main hangars are going to be in one area, or at most two—port and starboard. Now sick bay is portside on Deck Ten, and next to that a series of decontamination chambers, so I'm betting that big rectangular chamber that's unmarked on the Deck Ten schematic is the hangar where the lander came in."

So it proved. The lander's engines were dead and nothing Luke could do could revive them—"Well, why not? They fulfilled their purpose"— and in any case, there was no way of manual steering or controls. The G-40 droids stood silent and dead, one already half dismantled by Jawas who couldn't carry it off. The silvery, bubble-shaped trackers were nowhere to be seen.

By judicious manipulation of the controls on a service lift—using, again, the power core and wiring of a somewhat indignant MSE—Luke managed to freeze the lift car between Decks 10 and 9 and to get the doors open at least somewhat. While Threepio fretted and predicted doom in the Deck 10 hangar, Luke attached a hundred feet of emergency cable from a locker around one of the lander's legs and scrambled, with considerable difficulty, down through the lift car and into the hangar immediately below on Deck 9.

The lights were out there, the bay a vast, silent cavern illumined only by the blanched glow of the starlight beyond the magnetic field that protected the atmosphere of the hold. Through the huge bay doors, rimmed around with the rock of the concealing asteroid in which the *Eye* had been built, Luke could stare into the endless black vistas of the void. A handful of asteroids had been brought along with the *Eye* when it made its hyperspace jumps to pick up its long-vanished personnel—probably for cover, Luke thought—and a few of these drifted aimlessly in the middle distance, like bleached hunks of bone.

The shadowy bay itself was designed to accommodate a single medium-size launch, by the look of it. Cables from the power cell dangled from the ceiling and directional markings indicated where the vessel would stand, in the center of the bay, nose pointing toward the starry darkness that lay beyond the magnetic shield. But there was no launch there.

Instead, to one side of the hangar, a charred and battered Y-wing craft stood. The empty vastness of the hangar picked up the echoes of Luke's staff as he crossed the floor to it, and shadows twitched restlessly as he held up his staff with its glowrods to look at the open cockpit above his head.

A two-seater. Luke couldn't see well from where he stood, but he thought that the pressure hookups from both stations had been used.

"It explains what happened." Luke sank gratefully into one of the white plastic mess-hall chairs and accepted the plate Threepio handed him: reconstituted and radiation-packed, maybe, and bearing only nominal resemblance to actual dewback steak and creamed topatoes, but close enough. In spite of the perigen Luke's leg felt as if it were about to fall off at the hip—which, Luke reflected, in its current state didn't sound like such a bad idea—and he was so tired he ached, but he had a sense of matters being at least partially in hand.

"What happened when?" inquired Threepio.

"What happened thirty years ago. As Triv told us, the *Eye of Palpatine* —the whole Belsavis mission—was set up to be a secret, a secret even from the Jedi Knights. That's why they automated everything. So there would be no leaks.

"But there was a leak, Threepio. Somebody found out."

A sound from the doorway made him turn his head. Four or five tripods wandered through the mess-hall door, beautiful with their shadings of turquoises and pinks, their long yellow fur around the hips and tentacles. Luke got to his feet, leaning painfully on his staff, and limped to the water spigot near the food slots. The pile of discarded plates along that wall was nearly a meter high; Luke selected the deepest bowl he could find, filled it with water, and carried it over to the tripods, having learned that even setting it on a table wouldn't work. Threepio, at Luke's orders, followed with a couple of dishes of porridge, which the poor

befuddled creatures accepted gratefully, dipping long snouts in and slurp-
ing deeply.

"Somebody found out," Luke continued as he worked, "and came to
the Moonflower Nebula. Their Y-wing got shot to pieces by the
autodefenses—which are the closest thing to human I've ever seen—but
they made it in. They disabled the *Eye*'s triggering mechanism—probably
disabled whatever slaved signal-relay stations they could find, so no signal
could come in to start the mission. Then they took the launch from the
hangar, and fled."

"One could only wish," said Threepio, "that they had disabled the
autodefenses as well."

"Maybe they couldn't," said Luke. The tripods began to move off,
hooning and muttering vaguely among themselves, and Luke and
Threepio started back to the table where Luke had been.

"According to the power cell readings in the hangar, that bay is just
above the fighter berths where the short-range fliers—the ground sup-
ports and the escorts, TIEs according to the power consumption graphs
—are docked. If the mission involved a ground assault—and it has to
have, if they were picking up stormtroopers—there have to be assault
shuttles somewhere, probably on the upper decks in this same area, but
they wouldn't have been any good either in deep space. They have to have
taken the launch."

"I see," replied the droid. He was silent a moment, holding Luke's
staff and offering his arm to help him down into the chair. "But if the
signal relay was destroyed, what started it up again?" he asked. "After
thirty years?"

A horrible cacophony of shouts sounded in the corridor outside.
Luke swung to his feet, outdistancing Threepio as he limped to the door.
Through the grunting, shrieking, bellowing, he could hear the heavy thun-
der of feet.

It was a member of the Klagg tribe. Luke recognized it instantly, for
the Klaggs had all been wearing helmets and armor from regular navy
troopers rather than stormtroopers, bucket-shaped helmets and gray
breastplates instead of the familiar white. Wherever their headquarters
was, it was obviously close to different armories than the Gakfedds'.
However, Luke scarcely needed this observation, since the Klagg was in
full and terrified flight from fifteen Gakfedds, howling, waving axes and
forcepikes, brandishing blasters and carbines, and occasionally letting off

a shot that ricocheted wild and lethal along the corridors like a red-hot hornet.

Luke said, "Come on!"

"I beg your pardon?"

"He'll be heading back to his home territory!"

Luke crossed the mess hall to the opposite doors, knowing that the corridor down which the Gakfedds chased their prey led nowhere and the Klagg would have to double back. Sure enough, moments later Luke heard behind him in the corridor the thudding crash of a single set of feet, the snuffling, slobbering pant of the fugitive Klagg. He led Threepio into a laundry drop room to let the Klagg hasten by without seeing them, then stepped out again, following, listening. The Gakfedds seemed to have lost their prey, the echoes of their shouting ringing from corridors nearby, but Luke, listening ahead, could trail quite easily the solitary Klagg's gasping breath and lumbering feet. Gamorreans weren't runners. With the use of both his legs Luke could have outdistanced any Gamorrean ever littered, and even leaning on a staff he had little trouble keeping up.

As he had half suspected, half deduced, the Klagg was heading aft.

"They found some way to get above the crew decks," he murmured to Threepio as they crossed through chamber after chamber of armories, looted weapons holds, stores whose bins and crates had been broken to disgorge uniforms, boots, belts, and blast armor on the floors and down the halls. "Listen. He's doubling back on his steps. He knows he has to get a level up."

He halted, looking cautiously around a corner. The Gamorrean stood in an open lift car, prodding angrily at the buttons there, obviously wanting one that read higher than 13 and not finding it. A moment later the pseudotrooper stepped out of the car again, looking around him, hairy ears swiveling as he listened, breathing clearly audible in the silence. There was an expression *sweating like a Gamorrean,* and Luke understood it now. The creature's body glistened and he could smell it from where he stood.

The Gamorrean lumbered on.

"Is he lost, Master Luke?" Threepio could gear his voder down to the faintest hum of almost-inaudibility.

"Looks like. Or the Gakfedds are cutting off the way he came down."

There was a rumble of shouts, coming closer. The Klagg increased his speed to a clumsy trot. He was still easy to keep up with, through corridors bright with the hard cold light of glowpanels, or dark where the Jawas had looted the wiring. His ears kept swinging backward—Luke wondered how acute they were, and if he could pick up the faint scrape and click of the staff, and the soft creak of Threepio's joints.

There was a black door, double-blast-sealed and surmounted with a crimson light. The Gamorrean jabbed at the switch, with no result, then pulled out a blaster and shot the whole mechanism. The door jarred a little in its socket, and a voice said, "Entry to upper levels in this area is unauthorized. Security measures are in force."

The Gamorrean ripped loose the coverplate on the manual hatch by main force, and worked the dogged wheel within. Far down the corridor Luke heard renewed clamor, and knew the Gakfedds had heard the computer's voice:

"Entry to upper levels in this area is unauthorized. Security measures are in force. Maximum measures will be taken."

The red light began to blink.

The door opened to reveal a gangway. Black metal steps, gray walls, a checkering of pale squares of opalescent light set in a curious, asymmetrical almost-pattern that seemed at once impersonal and queerly sinister.

"Maximum measures will be taken. Maximum measures will be taken. Maximum . . ."

"There's the stinking mutineer swine!"

As Ugbuz and his troopers appeared from a cross-corridor twenty meters away, the Klagg plunged up the gangway.

Watching it, Luke reflected—in the part of his mind not stunned with horror—that it was very like the Empire to design a "security measure" that wouldn't take effect until the violator was too far into the gangway to turn back.

The Gamorrean raced up five or ten steps before the lightning started, thin, vicious fingers of it stabbing out from the walls, playing over the creature's body like a delicate, skeletal spider torturing its prey. The Gamorrean screamed, fell, his big body spasming, flopping on the black metal of the stairs. The pursuing Gakfedds skidded to a halt at the door, staring up in momentary shock.

Then they began to laugh.

Ugbuz let out a bellow of mirth, pointing as the Klagg's flesh blistered and blood poured from a thousand pinholes drilled by the lightning. The others whooped, doubled over, slapping their thighs and one another's shoulders in genuine amusement. Luke shrank back into the cross-corridor where he and Threepio stood, sickened. The Klagg, impossibly, was still trying to get to his feet, still trying to ascend the stairs, slipping in blood now, charring to death as he moved.

Gamorreans were tough. And the Klagg, quite clearly, considered the sizzling nightmare of the gangway a preferable fate to what the Gakfedds would do.

Luke turned away, almost ill, and headed back toward the mess hall. He could hear the Gakfedds' laughter a long way down the hall.

Armories, naval (regular)—search

• Purpose of this information?

Inventory control

• All inventory consonant with the parameters and intentions of the Will

"Master Luke?"
Schematic search—water piping

• Purpose of this information?

"Master Luke, it's getting quite late."
Emergency maintenance

• All maintenance proceeding in accordance with the intent and timetable of the Will

"You lying wad of synapses, you've got lighting blacked out over half your crew decks and computers down everywhere you look."

"Master Luke, the longer you remain this far from the Gakfedd village, the greater your danger from a retaliatory Klagg raid. There haven't even been Talz, or tripods, in this sector for . . ."

Luke raised his head. He was sitting at a terminal in the quartermaster's office, the entrance to a small complex of workshops and storage rooms. The long corridor leading to the mess hall's starboard entrance was visible through the open door. Visible past Threepio's shoulder, that is. The protocol droid was standing nervously in the doorway, glancing out with the frequency of a Coruscant stockbroker on the scout for a hovercar after a lunchtime meeting. If Threepio hadn't had an internal chronometer, thought Luke, he'd be looking at a watch every ten seconds.

He said, "They have Cray."

Torturing the Jawa had been petty viciousness, like children tormenting an injured animal. The Klagg had been an enemy. And the Klagg would see Cray as an enemy of theirs.

Especially, he thought, after the death of their mate in the gangway wired with that evil opalescent grid.

Wearily, he typed:

Sysshell

• Purpose of this information?

Sysview

• Purpose of this information?

Revsys

• Purpose of this . . .

"The purpose of this information is to make you cough up something besides the fact that the Will is in charge of everything and everything is perfect," muttered Luke through his teeth. His head ached again—his whole body felt as if he'd fallen down a flight of stairs, and in spite of the perigen patch on his leg there was a suspicious, grinding inflammation deep inside that made him wonder how long he could summon the Force to battle infection in the torn flesh. "And if I have to go through every Imperial code and slicer Cray and Han and Ghent ever taught me I'll do it."

"I do wish Artoo were here, sir," said Threepio, clanking diffidently to his side. "He's much better at talking to these supercomputers than I.

Why, back when we were with Captain Antilles, we . . . Oh! Shoo, you nasty little thing!"

Luke knew it was a Jawa even before he turned. Anyone who'd had even the smallest experience with Jawas knew when one had entered an enclosed space.

"No, it's okay, Threepio." After seeing the Klagg's death, Luke had considerably more sympathy for the Jawas. He frowned, puzzled, as he swiveled his chair, for Jawas generally avoided contact with other races, particularly on this ship.

"What do you want, little guy?"

It was the Jawa he'd saved that morning. How he knew this he couldn't say, because with their all-envelopingly ragged brown robes, grubby gloves, and faces invisible in the shadows of their hoods, it was almost impossible to tell one from another. But somehow he was sure of it.

"Master." The slangy, squeaky patois of the desert was almost unintelligible. One filthy little hand reached out to touch the lightsaber at Luke's belt.

He put his own hand guardingly over it, but sensed no real desire to steal. " 'Fraid that's mine, pal."

The Jawa stepped back, silent. Then it reached into its robes. "For you."

It held out another lightsaber.

Chapter 8

There was a technique to trolling the bars along Spaceport Row for information. Leia recognized it at once as a variation of what she herself did at diplomatic receptions: more an attitude than any specific set of questions, a kind of easy friendliness compounded of genuine interest in other people's lives, an almost limitless tolerance for meaningless trivia, a finely honed mental garbage filter, and the acceptance—artificial, if necessary—that there wasn't anything else one had to do that afternoon.

She enjoyed watching Han work. Clothed in a dress that he'd picked out for her, of the "not-to-diplomatic-events" variety, she lounged on barstools consuming drinks with paper spaceships in them and listened to him trade trivialities with various barkeeps, watching game transmissions in the seemingly depthless black boxes in the corners—in eight years of close association with Han Solo she had acquired a vivid working knowledge of the rules and strategies of smashball—listening to extremely bad music and getting into marginal conversations with packers, stokers, small-time traders, and smaller-time hustlers and bums. Even in the Core Worlds most people didn't recognize Leia or Han if they didn't know them or know who they were. To ninety percent of the species in the galaxy, all members of other races looked alike anyway, and most humans wouldn't have recognized the Senators from their own planets.

There was something to be said, Leia reflected, for the planets still ruled by the Ancient Houses. On Alderaan, everyone had known her: grocery clerks and subspace mechanics had studied the home lives of the House Organa on a day-to-day basis over the tabvids, watched them marry and divorce and squabble over property settlements and put their children through private academies, tsk'ed over the unsuitable attachments of Cousin Nial and recalled that long-ago scandal that had broken off Aunt Tia's engagement to . . . What had his name been? . . . from House Vandron.

Her onetime suitor Isolder had told her it was the same in the Hapes Consortium, whose ruling House had been in power for centuries.

Here they were just a lanky man with a scar on his chin and a smuggler's habit of watching the doors, and a cinnabar-haired woman in a dress that Aunt Rouge would have locked her in her room before permitting her to wear in public.

Leia listened, with increasing respect, to Han discussing puttie, which had to be the most boring sport in the entire Universe, for thirty minutes with a wizened Durosian before bringing up the subject of the local action. She didn't quite know how he'd come to the conclusion that this was the bar where such a question might be asked.

The reward was that the Durosian—whose name was Oso Nim—remembered Drub McKumb, and recalled his disappearance six years ago. "You sure he didn't just skin out ahead of trouble?" asked Han, and the aged one shook her head.

"Fester it, no. Skin out how, without his ship? Thing musta sat in the impound for ten months, with every tramp skipper and planet hopper that came through trying to bribe the yard captain to let 'em strip parts. Finally sold the whole shebang to a bunch of Rodians for gate fees." She chuckled, displaying several rows of tiny, sharp, brown teeth. "First-timers, they were. Took off with a load of cut-rate silk trying to run the tariff barriers into the Core Worlds and got themselves blistered out of existence first revenue cutter they met. Waste of a good ship, not to speak of all that silk."

She shook her head regretfully. The Smoking Jets, like every other bar on the Row, consisted of three prefab white plastene room units fixed together and opened into a single long chamber, mounted on a broken foundation of some older rock structure and cantilevered awkwardly to fit. The factories on Sullust turned out interlocking room units by the millions and there wasn't a commercial colony from Elrood to the Outer Rim that didn't have at least some buildings—towns, even—that consisted entirely of three-by-three white cubes.

Down in this part of town, near the segment of the cliff where the Port Offices formed a kind of gateway into the tunnels that led to the docking silos themselves, most of the room units had been fixed—with varying accuracy—to the heavy walls and keyhole arches of the older structures, where steam from the hot springs in the foundations still drifted forth through broken pillars and colonnades. Most of the dwelling-houses so built, Leia had noticed—including the one in which she and Han were staying—had been decorated and added to with native hangings of woven grass, bright cloth, trained trellisworks of vines, to minimize their undeniable resemblance to packing crates.

No such care had been lavished on the Smoking Jets.

"And nobody tried to figure out what happened to Drub?" Leia signaled the barkeep to refill Oso Nim's glass.

"Bzzz." The Durosian made a dismissive noise and a gesture reminiscent of scaring flies. "A million things can happen to a man on the game, sweetie. Even in a backwater hole like this one. It's sometimes six months before his friends figure out he hasn't disappeared on purpose, ship or no ship."

"And was it six months before his friends went looking?" asked Han.

Oso Nim cackled and gave him a sidelong glance from iridescent orange eyes. "In six months, you know where your friends are going to be? Drub's mate and crew said he'd been on about crypts under the old ruin at the top of the town and went pokin' themselves, but fester it, there's no crypts! People been looking for them crypts for years, and all they found was solid rock. Smuggler tunnels, sure, there's smuggler tunnels all over this damn town, but crypts? Solid rock is all Drub's mate and crew found, same as others before 'em."

"And what," asked Han, taking the bottle from the barkeep and repairing the old Durosian's depredations on her glass, "were others before 'em looking for?"

He spoke low, under the tinny audio of the holo box above the bar where the final game of the series between Lafra and Gathus was in process; she laughed heartily. "Oh, you're a friend of his, after all these years, sweetie? His long-lost brother?" Durosians generally don't laugh, and in the face of the wholesale horror of lines, teeth, halitosis, and flashing eyes, Leia could understand why other races might discourage them from doing so.

"Hey, Chatty!" she called to a human in a purple-splotched coverall with a packer's stained and bandaged fingers. "Here's old Drub Mc-Kumb's long-lost brother, come searching for his bones at last!"

"What, you think there's secret crypts down under Plett's House, too?" Chatty was if anything more wrinkled and decrepit than Oso Nim, though, looking at him, Leia realized he wasn't much older than Han. "Secret tunnels filled with jewels?"

Han made an I-didn't-say-it gesture, and Chatty winked. One of his eyes was a replacement, the cheap kind manufactured on Sullust with a yellowing plastic cornea.

"If there's jewels in them crypts, why ain't Bran Kemple richer, hunh? Why's he playin' penny-ante stakes smuggling coffee and running card games over at the Jungle Lust?"

"Bran Kemple's the town boss?" Han raised his eyebrows in genuine surprise. "I thought it was Nubblyk the Slyte."

"What hole you been hidin' in for the past eight years, Sugar-drawers?" laughed the Durosian, and Chatty took the bottle from Han's hand and poured himself a glass, courteously offering Leia a refill as well. Leia, thoroughly amused, refrained from remarking that people who'd been living at the bottom of a volcanic vent for decades had no business accusing others of hiding in holes. "The Slyte pulled his stakes out eight, nine years ago. Whole scene's gone to pieces since then."

"Gone to pieces," Chatty agreed, nursing Han's bottle mournfully. "Hot rockets, boy!" he yelled furiously, his attention suddenly riveted by the activities of twenty-five skaters on the planet Lafra, "you call that festering shooting? For a million credits a year I'll festering join your festering team and lose your games for you, you stupid sons of slime devils!"

"You sure the Slyte actually pulled his own stakes?" Leia leaned her elbows on the bar and looked innocent and fascinated.

The Durosian grinned and pinched her cheek with fingers like mummified knotgrass. "Your girlfriend catches on quick, Angelpants. The Slyte was a clever old bug. If he was goin' snoopin' around where he had no business, *he* wouldn't come in here half drunk like Mubbin the Whiphid did, carryin' on about how he'd found a big secret about Plett's House, or like old Drub with his 'calculations.' Oh, I don't doubt there's somethin' up at those ruins the high-ups around here don't want people snoopin' with. Maybe enough to load dim-cells like Mubbin or Drub or what's-his-name, that Wookiee who worked as a mechanic for Galactic . . . enough to load them into an outbound ship."

She shook her head, polished off another glass, took the bottle from Chatty, and tilted it, regarding with profound sadness the few remaining drops that trickled into her glass.

"Well, whatever it is, it ain't worth it, so why put yourself in trouble, I say." She shrugged. "Maybe Drub just fell down a repair shaft in some orchard someplace and the kretch ate him."

"Kretch?" said Leia sharply.

The orange eyes glittered in unholy amusement. "How long you been in town, Pretty-Eyes? You'll see the kretch mighty quick. As for old Drub, what was it to him what the high-ups are hidin', long as there was no money in it? And you can be sure there wasn't, else the big corporations'd be sellin'."

She smiled beatifically as Leia signaled and another bottle materialized on the stain-repellant lexoplast of the bar. "Why, thank you, darling . . ." She nodded toward Han and leaned forward to whisper confidentially, "You're way too good for the likes of him."

"I know," whispered Leia, and Oso Nim cackled with delight.

She saddened again, and tossed off another drink. "Well, the whole scene's turned to garbage now anyway. Pity, 'cause eight, ten years ago this place was really movin'. You'd get twelve, fourteen ships a week in on the sly, goods slippin' in under the ice, and this place was as jammed at noon as it was at midnight, maybe more. The Slyte was one who knew how to run things. Since he left it's all turned into nerf-feed."

Odd, thought Leia, as she sought out the Smoking Jets' plumbing facilities a little while later. As far as she could ascertain from Oso Nim's increasingly foggy conversation (Han had ordered still another blue glass bottle, and Chatty was absorbed in the second half of the doubleheader), Nubblyk the Slyte had departed, the "game"—i.e., smuggling—had drastically declined, and Mubbin the Whiphid, a friend of Drub McKumb's, had vanished, all in the same year . . . the year after Palpatine's death and the breakup of the Empire. A year later—when Drub McKumb had returned to Belsavis—he'd vanished, too.

Her aunt Rouge's housekeeper had frequently observed, *Just because you keep soap in the pantry doesn't make it food.*

The temporal proximity of the events could have been coincidence. And yet . . .

With every possible inch of arable ground in the volcanic rift given over to cash crops, lots in town were small and buildings like the cantina —and the older stone house upon which it was built—were squinched right to the property lines, leaving no room for sanitary accommodations aboveground. An old-fashioned manual hinged door at one end of the bar bore the universal symbols, and behind it a thoroughly insalubrious stair plunged by the light of a minimum-strength glowpanel into the grotty obscurity of the foundations. Though most of the warm springs over which the old houses had been built had been diverted long ago, the heat belowground was even worse than above, the air held a lingering whiff of some sour gas and the dense black-red stone of the walls was patched with a crop of molds and fungus that made Leia glad she hadn't ordered a salad off the cantina's small food menu. At the far end of the narrow passageway something moved, and Leia, nervously activating the small glowrod that hung at her belt, got her first look at what had to be a kretch.

It was half again as long as her hand, possibly the width of three fingers together, and the color of a scab. Two sets of jaws—one above the other—were large enough that even at a distance of five meters she could see the serrated teeth, and the barbed grabbers on the tail. It lunged at her with a motion something between a hop and a dash, and Leia, who knew better than to fire a blaster in the closed space, scooped up the chunk of stone used as a doorstop at the top of the steps and hurled it at the thing in a reflex of panic and horror.

The stone cracked squarely on the thing's jointed back, rolled off as the kretch spasmed, quivered, and then hauled itself swiftly to vanish between the pipes that ran along the wall. As Leia edged nervously down to retrieve the stone she could see the brown stain it left, and smell a kind of sweet nastiness, like fruit in the final stages of decomposition.

She checked out the repellent little cubicle at the end of the passageway very carefully with the light before entering and afterward hurried her steps along the passage to return to the bar above.

The kretch would eat us . . .

If those were the kretch, she thought, she was *not* looking forward to encountering them in the crypts where the Jedi children had once dared each other to hunt for Plett's Well . . . provided they could find the crypts at all.

"Just because you keep soap in the pantry doesn't make it food," agreed Han thoughtfully, as they walked through the drifting glitters of mist on their way back to the house Jevax had arranged for them. "But it's no accident you keep it close to where you wash the dishes."

She nodded, accepting that train of logic, then grinned. "And what do you know about washing dishes . . . *Angelpants?*"

"When you spend three quarters of your life bumming around the galaxy, Your Highness-ness, believe me, you end up loading a lot of dishwashers and even washing dishes by hand." He hooked his hands in his belt, but Leia knew he was watching everything around them to the limits of his senses. The eternal vapors of Plawal were unnerving. Thickest down at the far end of the valley where the true hot springs bubbled forth, even here, where the land lay low around the warm springs, visibility was down to a few meters. Even up on the raised streets that skirted the orchards, scenes had a tendency to appear and disappear like isolated tableaux: fruit trees jeweled with orchids, up which sweetberry and bowvine had been trained so that every branch hung heavy with two or three different varieties of fruit; thousands of tiny bridges spanning the faintly steaming pools and streams whose fern-choked verges swarmed with salamanders and frogs; yellow, green, or sea-blue pittins dozing on the thrusting knees of shalaman and aphor trees or hunting insects in the grass; automated watch-critters crouched at the bases of the more expensive trees, beady eyes of green or amber gleaming eerily through the mists. Lava-block walls loomed unexpectedly out of the shifting vapors, topped by the sleek white plastic of the prefabs; ramps of wood or plastic ascending to the doors from street level, lined with pots of imported red plastic or local terra-cotta, lush with berries, slochans, lipanas.

Beautiful . . . But Leia was extremely conscious of the fact that visibility was down to two meters or less.

"So what's this about smuggler tunnels?"

"Back when I was in the game," said Han, "I never made it out here

—too close to the Senex Sector—but I knew there were at least a dozen landing pads out on the ice. Judging by the number of people in the bars who're still in the game, I'd be surprised if there's more than one or maybe two still operational. Now, according to Lando, what's left of the Empire hasn't changed its tariffs and the export duties *here* haven't changed any . . . gone up, if anything. Which means that nine years ago, *something* dried up."

"Right about a year after the Battle of Endor."

Han nodded. "Something you might want to keep in mind when you go through the town records—now that old Jevax has had time to pick out the parts that might tell you anything."

"You know, Han . . ." Leia paused at the top of the wooden ramp that climbed the high, broken stone of their house's foundations to the wide front door. "That's the first thing that drew me to you. The childlike innocence of your heart."

He caught her arm, grinning; she tried to duck away to open the door but he pinned her, a hand on either side of her shoulders, their eyes laughing into one another's, his body warm against hers. "You want to see how innocent I can be?"

She reached to touch the scar on his chin. "I know how innocent you are," she said, meaning it, and their lips met, isolated in the still cloak of the mist.

Only the padding footfalls on the ramp broke them apart, and the soft whirring of servos. They stepped back from each other in time to see Chewbacca's tall form materialize out of the pearlescent shimmer of the air, trailed a moment later by Artoo. The glittering colors of the mist were darkening as the dome-magnified sunlight waned. Between the gray trees of the orchards that stretched downhill from the back of the house, the twilight was growing thick.

"Find anything?"

As they passed through the front door Chewbacca shrugged eloquently and groaned. He'd pursued his own investigation of the local scene in places that left the smell of strange smokes in his fur, and had learned, he said, very little. Very little was going on. One of the smuggler pads out on the glacier was still in operation sometimes, though there were fewer and fewer pilots looking to make the difficult run in through the Corridor. A couple of ships were buying vine-silk on the cheap— mostly grade-two skimmings from the factories. A couple of dealers running in yarrock, ryll, and various sorts of frontal-lobe candy for the old buzz-brains living in the grubby shacks and lean-tos behind Spaceport Row. Bran Kemple was evidently the only person selling it on a regular basis. Everybody said *Not like the old days.* You could make more money packing brandifert if you didn't mind purple fingers.

"I'm going to take Artoo with me to the MuniCenter, if you don't mind." Inside the house Leia hunted out a dark green-and-violet tunic slightly more respectable than the garment she'd worn to go touring the bars of the Row—she owned underwear more respectable than that particular outfit, for that matter—and more comfortable shoes. "You find anything from public access while we were up at Plett's House, Artoo?"

The astromech trundled obediently over to the small monitor-printer setup in the corner and extruded a comm plug, and the printer began to chatter. Han crossed the room to see. "Export figures for all seven main packing plants for the past week," he reported with a grave nod. "Mmmm . . . oh, now we've got employee health figures . . . fuel intake of all vessels for the past week . . . Better and better. Wow, here's a hot item! Repair costs for malfunctions of mechanical fruit pickers amortized over the past ten years. Leia, I don't know if my heart can take this . . ."

She rapped him on the arm with the back of her knuckles. "Don't tease Artoo . . . That's very thorough of you, Artoo, you did a good job. You always do."

The droid beeped. Past the bedroom's line of floor-length windows and the narrow stone terrace beyond, darkness had settled, the lights that dotted the orchards below the house making raveled blurs of brightness in the mist. The house was one of the few in Plawal to consist mostly of the original stone—only the kitchen and half the living room were prefab —but had been remodeled in the past few years, the old keyhole windows replaced by modern crystalplex with sliding metal shutters to cut out the orchard lights. It was environment-controlled, too, after a fashion—better than the Smoking Jets, anyway. An ironic refinement, thought Leia, for a planet whose surface temperature averaged in the minus fifties.

Like most houses in the old town it was built over a small warm-spring site, and though the spring had been diverted to warm the orchard, the basement floor still produced errant wisps of steam. Leia wondered with a sudden qualm of disgust if kretch lurked there.

"You'll be okay here?" She paused on her way to the door.

"I'll have a go at calling Mara Jade. She may know where those landing pads were, and something about why Nubblyk the Slyte left." He made a show of checking his pockets. "And I know I picked up a card in the bar for order-in dancing girls."

"Just make them sweep up the confetti when they're done."

They kissed again, and Leia strode down the ramp to street level, Artoo trundling in her wake. It had grown dark. Silver-winged moths fluttered crazily around the lamps; pittins and mooklas hunted frogs beneath the bridges. The world smelled of sweet growing things, of grass and fruit—fruit bred specially, calculatedly, to make the inhabitants of this rift, this world, wealthy and competitive in the galactic markets. In the darkness among the trees, luminous insects flickered like fairy candles.

A paradise, thought Leia.

If you didn't know about the kretch underneath it.

If you didn't know about Drub McKumb's voice screaming, *Kill you all . . . going to kill you all . . .*

They're gathering . . .

If you didn't know that occasionally someone who followed up unsubstantiated rumors about the tunnels beneath Plett's House would vanish without a trace.

In a market square among the sleek white prefabs, the dark huddle of old stone walls, barrow men and vendors were striking their awnings, folding up their wares amid the final desultory shoppers of the day. Above the market the MuniCenter reared on the first of the low benches above the town, only its lights visible as a blurred galaxy in the dark fog. The sloping path toward it wound among the orchards, and because of the multitude of hot springs that came out of the valley's point there the fog was thick, the sodium arc lights with their unreal white glare edged a few leaves with light and left all else swallowed by the night. Now and then a mechanical tree feeder would stalk momentarily into view, unnervingly like a huge metal spider with its half dozen long, jointed arms, its blind turrets and proboscislike squirters, rows and rings of yellow lights outlining it like shining crowns and bracelets of jewels.

Unlighted, silent, not quite ruined enough, Plett's House rose invisible in the dark behind. Leia remembered the vision she'd seen there, the deep sense of silent peace. Remembered the voices of the children, and old Ho'Din, beautiful with his pale-green skin against the black Jedi cloak; remembered his haunted eyes.

She remembered also the urgency in Luke's voice when he'd told her not to bring the children to this paradise of a place.

Had she brought them, she wondered, what would they have seen?

Abruptly, Artoo-Detoo, who had been following her along the path, made a right-angle turn and trundled off into the foggy darkness to her right. Leia turned, startled: "Artoo?" She could hear the crash of his heavy cylindrical body in the foliage, the furious *yik-yik-yik* of the guard-critters around the trees, the startled whoops of night birds.

"Artoo!"

His treads left deep marks in the soft grass. Leia followed, pushing at the leaves, wet fern slapping at her boots, pulling out her glowrod and holding it before her where the darkness grew dense away from the lights. "Artoo, what is it?"

The ground dipped sharply beneath her feet. She heard Artoo's startled tweet, the crash of something falling. Branches caught at her hair, slithered damply across her face as she hurried forward.

The little astromech droid had come to a stop at the base of a wall, pressed against it and still trying vainly to go forward. Leia could hear the whirr of his servos, the grind of his treads in the soft ground. She flashed the light swiftly to the right and left but saw nothing, only the dark of the enclosing foliage, barely visible through the dense mists, the bob of fire-bugs among the sweet-scented trees. "Artoo, stop!" she ordered. "Stop!"

The whirring of the gears halted.

"Back up."

He was mired. "Hold it," said Leia, and after another careful scout around with her light, she took from her boot the small knife she carried and cut branches—making sure they bore no fruit—to lay in the deep tread marks on the muddy ground. "Back up."

The droid obeyed.

"Artoo, what is it? What happened?"

Luke was better at understanding the little droid than she was, though she could interpret some of his odd beeps and warbles. But the reply he made was a quick, almost perfunctory double gleep, telling her nothing.

"Well, let's not stand around here in the dark." Something about the way the vine-hung boughs with their ghostly orchids seemed to bend close unnerved her, even in this safe and well-patrolled paradise. A sharp rustle in the darkness made her nearly jump out of her skin, but it was only a tree feeder, pausing to lower its hoselike proboscis to the roots of a shalaman tree and pump forth a measured dose of rank-smelling organic goo before picking its careful way back among the trees.

"Let's see if we can get back to the path."

It wasn't easy, between the dark and the mushy unevenness of the ground. Artoo's base was weighted to give him maximum stability, but though he was better than he looked on rough terrain he wasn't perfect, and the base weight would make it, if not impossible, at least backbreaking, for Leia to right him should he unbalance. It took a half hour of muddy searching, stumbling over tree roots and getting yikked at by watch-critters in the dark, along the bed of a steaming volcanic stream before they found a sufficiently gentle incline and a clearing among the ferns that let her see the path again.

Just for a moment, Leia looked up and saw someone standing at the top of the slope, under the yellow blur of the light.

She thought, *What's* she *doing here?*

And then wondered why, as the woman turned from the light and walked quickly away down the path . . .

Why had she thought that? It wasn't anyone she knew.

Was it?

Schoolfriend? Her age looked about right, so far as Leia could tell at that distance and behind the blurring of intervening fog. But somehow she couldn't picture that slim, childlike body in the white-and-blue uniform of the Alderaan Select Academy for Young Ladies. She was sure she'd never seen that chained ocean of rain-straight, coal-black hair plaited in a schoolgirl's braids. That let out the possibility of her being the daughter of an Alderaan noble altogether, since they'd all gone to the same school . . .

Someone from the Senate? It rang a bell, but she'd been the youngest Senator herself at the age of eighteen, and there had been no one near her age there, certainly no girls. A Senator's daughter? Wife? Someone she had met at one of those endless diplomatic receptions on Coruscant? Someone seen across the room at the Emperor's levee?

HERE?

She regained the path as quickly as she could, but steadying Artoo over the bumpy roots took her whole effort and attention. When she reached the top of the slope and looked quickly down the path, the woman was gone.

Chapter 9

See-Threepio didn't like the idea. "You can't trust those Jawas, Master Luke! There has to be a gangway somewhere . . ."

Luke contemplated the hatch cover the Jawa had removed from the wall in one of the laundry drop rooms, the dark shaft full of wiring and cables that lay beyond. A ladder of durasteel staples emerged from the silent well of blackness below, vanished up into the lightless chimney above. He thought about the physical effort involved in hitching himself up those rungs, without use of his left leg, one rung at a time, compared with what the mental effort would cost him to use the Force to levitate. The choice wasn't pleasant.

Neither were the memories of the Klagg stormtrooper's death.

"I'll be all right," he said quietly.

"But *all* the gangways can't be wired!" protested the droid. "I don't like the idea of you going alone. Can't you wait a little, sleep on this? If you'll forgive my saying so, sir, you look as if you would greatly benefit from some sleep. Though I never use it myself, I'm told that humans . . ."

Luke grinned, touched by Threepio's concern. "I'll get some sleep

when I get back," he promised. In the dark of the shaft above he heard
the rat-rustle of the Jawa's robes halt, an interrogatory piping squeal,
"Master?"

"If I don't track this down now I may not get another chance." He
made a quick check of the power cell of the glowrods taped to his staff,
then slung the wire loop he'd taped on the staff's upper end over his
shoulder, balancing carefully on his good leg with his hands against the
hatchway's narrow sides. "I'll be all right," he said again.

He knew Threepio didn't believe him, of course.

He ducked his head through the hatch, reached over the narrow shaft
to seize the rungs, and hopped across. Even that small movement caught
his leg with a flash of pain that left him breathless, despite all the healing,
all the strength of the Force he could summon. He glanced down at the
seemingly bottomless plunge of the shaft, and thought, *I'll need to save my
strength.*

"Be careful, Master Luke . . ." The droid's voice floated up after
him in the dark.

In the crazy, bobbing dimness of the glowrods slung to his back, the
Jawa was barely visible, a dark, scrambling figure like a robed insect
skittering up the ladder now far over his head. Bundled trunk lines of
cable and wire brushed Luke's shoulders as he hitched himself laboriously
in the Jawa's wake, hoses like glistening black esophagi and thinner lines
of rubbery insulated fiber-optic coax crowding close, as if he were indeed
ascending the alimentary canal of some monstrous beast. The Jawa
paused every now and then to finger the cabling in a way that made Luke
extremely nervous. Who could tell what systems depended on that particular hunk of wire?

Here and there orange worklights burned dim above closed hatch-
ways—dogged shut on the inside, he observed, and equipped with the
dark boxes of magnetic seals. Elsewhere he climbed in darkness, lit only
by the glowrods on his staff. The tube smelled fusty, of lubricants and
insulation and now, overwhelmingly, of Jawa, but it lacked the characteristic, slightly greasy smell of air recycled countless times through the noses
and lungs of a living crew. Even with the vessel's current bizarre populations, it would be long before it acquired that smell.

Longer than they'd be aboard.

Longer than this weird mission would last.

What started it up again?

Threepio had put his intricately jointed metal finger on the crux of the problem, the galling root of Luke's anxious dreams.

The *Eye of Palpatine* had been wrought in secret for a secret purpose, a mission that had been thwarted. It had lain sleeping in its remote screen of spinning asteroids in the heart of the Moonflower Nebula for thirty years, while the New Order that had planned that mission, armed the ship's guns, programmed the Will's single-minded control, had risen to power and then cracked apart under the weight of its own callousness, monomania, and greed.

The stormtroopers stationed on half a dozen remote worlds of the Rim had grown old and died.

Palpatine himself had died, at his own dark pupil's hand.

So why had the Will awakened?

Luke shivered, wondering whether it was simply his own apprehension for the safety of those on Belsavis—for Han and Leia and Chewie— that cast a shadow on his heart, or whether the shadow was of something else, some separate entity whose power he had sensed moving like a dianoga underwater through the darker regions of the Force.

The tube topped out in a thick-barred metal grille painted garish, warning yellow and black. Affixed to it—in case anyone should miss the point—was a sign: ENCLISION GRID. NO FURTHER ASCENT. DANGER.

Beyond the bars, Luke could just distinguish a lateral repair conduit, through which the cables of the ascending shaft continued like runners of some thick-fleshed, ugly vine. The walls of the conduit gleamed with the asymmetrical pattern of opaline squares, each square a deadly laser port, waiting in the dark.

Just beneath the metal safety bars, a ring of dirty fingerprints around an open hatchway showed clearly which course the Jawa had taken.

Luke dragged himself through, into light only marginally brighter than that of the worklamps in the shaft.

It was the gun room. Rank after rank of consoles picked up the moving firebug of his glowrods from the shadows of soot-colored metal walls. Screen after screen, large and small, regarded him with dead obsidian eyes.

In the center of the chamber a ceiling panel had been removed, and a barred grille like the one that had blocked further ascent in the repair shaft lay propped in a corner. Holding the staff with its glowing end aloft, Luke could see that the shaft rose upward, where the bundled pipes and hoses, finger-fat power lines and the wide ribbon-cables of computer couplers, flowed aloft in a static river from half a dozen lateral conduits to some central locus above. Yellow and black banded the lower half meter or so of the shaft, but there was no sign, no written warning. Only the small, baleful glare of red power lights, and above them, the opal glister of the enclision grid, spiraling eerily into darkness.

A tug on his belt caught his attention. Luke put down his hand protectively as the Jawa pawed at the lightsaber that hung at his belt—the second lightsaber, the one it had brought him. After a moment's hesitation Luke yielded it, and the Jawa ran to a spot directly under the open shaft. It set the weapon on the floor, considered it for a moment, then moved it a few centimeters and changed the angle, clearly re-creating the exact position in which it had been found.

Luke hobbled to stand over it, and looked up. The shaft gaped above him, a narrow chimney breathing death.

It led to the heart of the ship. There were too many power lines, too many bundles of fiber-optic cables, too many heavy-duty coolant pipes for it to lead anywhere but to the computer core.

Luke stooped, carefully balancing on his staff, and picked up the lightsaber, then straightened and gazed up into that darkness again.

He understood.

Someone had ascended that shaft, thirty years ago.

There had been two of them who'd made it onto the ship in the battered Y-wing he'd found. One had taken the launch and left, probably arguing that reinforcements should be sought.

The other had known, or guessed, that there might not be time before the ship jumped to hyperspace to start its mission: that the risk was too great, the stakes too high, to permit the luxury of getting out of there alive. And that other had remained, to attempt to disarm the Will.

The deadly enclision grid seemed to grin, like pale, waiting teeth.

"I'm sorry," said Luke, very softly, to that waiting column of shadow. "I wish I could have been here to help you."

She would have needed help.

He turned the weapon in his hand, knowing instinctively that it had been a woman who made it, who wielded it. A woman with large hands and a long reach, to judge by the weapon's proportions. . . . Yoda had told him that the old Jedi Masters could learn quite startling things about a Knight just by examining the lightsaber whose making was a Jedi's final test.

Around the rim of the handgrip someone had taken the time to inlay a thin line of bronze *tsaelke,* the long-necked, graceful cetaceans of Chad III's deep oceans.

Still more quietly, he said, "I wish I could have known you."

He clipped the lightsaber to his belt, and began to hunt for the way this woman—his colleague and fellow Jedi—had gotten into the gun room.

There was only one entrance, straight into a turbolift, which refused to respond to Luke's touch on the summoning button, but at a guess it was the way she had used. With a little effort he could short the doors into opening, he knew. From there he'd have access to the decks below, either via rope—which could be liberated from a storeroom—or via levitation, if he wanted to risk that great a drain on his limited strength. He wondered if the Force could be used—as it sometimes could—to hold off the blue lightning-threads of the enclision grid long enough for him to get up the shaft to the ship's computer core.

The thought of trying it turned him cold.

Once in the core, it should be fairly simple to trigger an overload, to destroy the *Eye of Palpatine* as it should have been destroyed thirty years ago . . .

And hadn't been.

He remembered the Klagg's screams as it bled and charred to agonizing death in the gangway.

The Jedi who had ascended that shaft had lived long enough to damage the ship's activation trigger, dying up in the core while the Will itself had been left alive. Because she hadn't been quite strong enough? Quite experienced enough?

Or was the enclision grid something not even the strength of a Master could outlast?

A dirty little hand closed around his sleeve. "Not good, not good." The Jawa tried to pull him in the direction of the repair shaft that led downward again. It pointed up at the dark square in the ceiling. "Bad. Die a lot."

Die a lot. Luke thought about the Jawas, and the filthy, rival, feuding villages of the Klaggs and the Gakfedds, reestablishing here the patterns of their homeworld in terms of what they now thought they were. About the Kitonaks in the rec room, waiting patiently for their Chooba slugs to crawl into their mouths, and the dead Affytechan on the floor, and the Talz guarding each other's backs—against whom?—as they took water to the tripods.

Destroying the ship, he understood, was going to be the easy part.

See-Threepio was sitting in front of the comm screen in the quartermaster's office, a long flex of cable plugged into the droid at the back of his cranium and a tone of serious annoyance in his voice as he said, "You silly machine, you've got enclaves of alien life forms all over you, what do you mean, 'No life forms alien to the intent of the Will?' What about a trace on Galactic Registry Standard 011-733-800-022?"

Luke leaned one shoulder against the jamb of the doorway, aware that there was no more need for Threepio to address the Will aloud than there was for the droid to use human speech to communicate with Artoo-Detoo. But Threepio was programmed to interface with civilized life forms, to *think* like a civilized life form. And one of the marks of nearly every civilization Luke had ever encountered had been chattiness.

Threepio was chatty.

"What do you mean there are no life forms of that Registry number on board? You have seventy-six Gamorreans in residence!"

"I already tried that, Threepio." Luke stepped into the room, his entire body aching from the compensation of walking with the staff, the unaccustomed, agonizingly repeated set of movements involved in dragging himself up the ladder rungs by the strength of his arms.

Threepio turned in his chair—another unnecessary human mannerism, for his audio receptors would have picked up, and identified, Luke's footsteps and breathing eighteen meters down the hall.

"According to the Will, there are no aliens on this ship," said Luke, with a kind of wry weariness. "According to the Will, concentrations of bodies with internal temperatures of a hundred and five degrees— Gamorrean normal—don't exist, either. Or those with temperatures of a hundred and ten, or one-six, or eighty-three, which means there aren't any

Jawas, Kitonaks, or Affytechans around. But I have found a way to get up
onto the upper decks without—"

From the speaker on the wall on Luke's right a triple chime sounded,
and green lights flared in the onyx void of a ten-centimeter in-ship comm
screen above the desk. "Attention, all personnel," said a musical contralto
voice. "Attention, all personnel. Tomorrow at thirteen hundred hours an
Internal Security Hearing will be broadcast on all ship's channels. Tomorrow at thirteen hundred hours an Internal Security Hearing will be broadcast on all ship's channels."

The screen sprang to unexpected life. Within it Luke saw the image of
Cray, her hands bound, her mouth sealed shut with silver engine tape, her
dark eyes wide and scared and furious, being held between two ludi-
crously uniformed Gamorrean troopers, Klaggs by their helmets.

"Observation of this hearing is mandatory for all personnel. Refusal
or avoidance of observation will be construed as sympathy with the ill
intentions of the subject."

After the first shocked second Luke focused his attention on the
background, the texture and color of the walls behind Cray and her
guards—darker than those in the crew decks and not as cleanly finished—
the relative lowness of the ceilings, the visible beams, bolts, and conduits.
A corner of a makeshift hut intruded on the scene, part of a packing box
with SOROSUB IMPORTS DIVISION stenciled on it and a roof made of what
looked like a survival tarp. *Klagg village,* he thought.

Nichos stood by the hut, a restraining bolt riveted to his chest and
wretched, haunted horror in his eyes.

"All personnel with evidence to lay against the subject are requested
to speak to their division Surveillance Representative as soon as possible.
Neglect in this matter, when discovered, will be construed as sympathy
with the ill intentions of the subject."

Cray jerked her arm against the Gamorrean's grasp, kicked hard at
his shin. The Klagg half turned and struck her hard enough to have
knocked her down had he and the other guard not kept hold of her arms;
her face and the shoulder visible through her torn uniform tunic bore
other bruises already. Luke saw the look of agony Nichos cast in her
direction, but the droid-man made no move, no effort, of either help or
comfort.

He couldn't, Luke knew, because of the restraining bolt.

The guards were half carrying the nearly unconscious Cray out of vid range when the vid itself went dark. Nichos remained where he was, his eyes the only living part of his motionless face.

"Sorry, son, but we've had orders." Ugbuz folded his heavy arms and regarded Luke with a gaze that was hard as flint and not a bit sorry. The Gakfedd chief nodded to himself, as if savoring the orders, or the feeling of having had them, an eerily human gesture that made the hair on Luke's neck prickle.

"Yeah, I know we have to get them Klagg sons of sows . . ." The phrase came out all as one word, a leftover fragment from the part of Ugbuz that was still a Gakfedd, ". . . but we have orders to find the Rebel saboteurs before they wreck the ship."

His eyes narrowed, hard and yellow and vicious, studying Luke, as if he remembered it was Luke who had stopped them from torturing the Jawa.

Luke extended the power of the Force, focused it with the small gesture of his hand. "Yet it's vital that we find the Klagg stronghold immediately."

It was like trying to grasp one-handed a wet stone twice the diameter of his grip. He could see it in Ugbuz's eyes. He wasn't trying to influence the Gamorrean, but the strength of the Will.

"Sure, sure it's vital, Klagg sons of sows, but we have orders to find the Rebel saboteurs before they wreck the ship."

It was a programmed loop. Luke knew he wouldn't be able to get past it. Not with his body shaky from exhaustion, his mind aching from the effort to keep trauma and infection at bay. The big boar's brow furrowed suspiciously. "Now you tell me again why you had us let that saboteur go?"

Before Luke could answer there was a clamor of voices from the edge of the village. Ugbuz spun, jaw coming forward and drool stringing from his heavy tusks. "Got some!" he bellowed, yanked his blaster from the holster at his hip, and dashed for the dark rectangle of doorway into the corridor. From the huts all around the cavernous hold other Gakfedds came running, pulling on helmets and picking up axes, laser carbines, vibro-weapons, and blasters—two of them had gotten ion cannons from somewhere and one had a portable missile launcher.

"I do see their point, Master Luke." Threepio creaked briskly after him as he followed, much more slowly, in Ugbuz's wake. "We've already lost the lighting in almost all of Deck Eleven and it's getting more and more difficult to locate a computer terminal in working order. If the Jawas are not stopped they will eventually jeopardize the life support of the vessel itself."

As they passed the largest hut the matriarch Bullyak emerged, huge arms folded between her first and second sets of breasts, grimy braids framing a face replete with warts, morrt bites, suspicion, and disgust. She squealed something irritably, and spat voluminously on the floor. Threepio inclined his body in a little half bow and replied, "I quite agree, Madame. I agree absolutely. Jawas are no fit combat for a true boar. She's quite annoyed," he explained to Luke.

"I guessed."

When they reached the shaft in the laundry drop, Luke said, "I'll levitate you as far as the first hatchway onto Deck Fourteen. I'll take Deck Fifteen. We know the Klagg was trying to go up the gangway when he was killed, so we know their village is above us. Look for any sign of the Klaggs—footprints, blood, torn clothing . . ." By this time Luke knew the Gamorreans were as likely to fight within the tribe as outside it.

"I shall certainly try, sir," replied the droid humbly. "But with the SP-80s doing their duty in cleaning the floors and walls, tracking won't be easy."

"Do the best you can." Luke reflected that this would have been easier if Cray had been in her right senses—her true identity—when she'd been carried off. "Look also for the kind of walls we saw in the background of the video announcement. The tarp and the crate in that hut have to have come from Mission Stores. Make a note if you see anything similar. Also storerooms for regular navy trooper equipment, as opposed to stormtroopers. I'll be back to get you down the shaft again at twenty-two hundred."

When he reached Deck 15, Luke found that Threepio was only too right about the SP-80s and their unflagging mission to keep the *Eye of Palpatine* spotless. He found half a dozen plates and cups from the mess hall—polished clean by the MSEs but lying where they had been dropped —but no further evidence of where the Klaggs might have trodden. It was going to be a task, he realized, of laboriously quartering the decks one by one, looking for physical signs of the Klaggs and trying to pick up some trace, some whisper, of recognizable mental resonance from Cray.

And Threepio wouldn't even be able to do that.

A crippled man and a protocol droid. Luke leaned momentarily against the wall, trying not to think about the bruises on Cray's face, the way her body had snapped against the guards' brutal grip. Trying not to think about the look in Nichos's eyes.

Thirteen hundred hours tomorrow.

He limped on. The Klagg had been trying to go up. The walls on this deck—or in this section of this deck, which seemed to house the repair installations for the TIE fighters—were darker than those of the crew quarters below, the ceilings lower, but without the metal beams he'd seen in the vid transmission.

A hangar? he wondered. *Storage hold?* A corridor stretched to his left, pitch dark. Far down it he heard the scrabble of feet, saw the yellow rat-gleam of Jawa eyes. They were eating the ship to pieces. No wonder the Will had ordered Ugbuz to exterminate them. But he had the suspicion that whatever the result of the Jawa depredations, it would only kill the living crew. Nothing the Jawas could do—no damage or death of those aboard—would prevent the battlemoon's jump to hyperspace, when it thought nobody was looking. It would have no effect on its capacity to blow the city of Plawal—and probably the other settlements on Belsavis for good measure—to powder and mud.

He'd seen what the Empire had left of Coruscant, of Mon Calamari, of the Atravis Systems. He'd felt the screaming outcry of the Force, like the ripping apart of organs within his own body, when Carida had gone up.

To prevent that, he thought, he would go up the enclision grid himself, to make his own attempt at destroying this monster's mechanical heart.

Luke tried a door, and when it refused to open limped down the corridor, testing another, and another, until he found one that responded to his command. There was light in that area of the ship, and the air, though chemical, had the slightly ozoneous smell of new, clean oxygen that hadn't been passed around a hundred sets of lungs. He found another messroom coffee cup on the floor, but no sign of the Klaggs. No trace of Cray's consciousness.

It was difficult to keep his bearings, difficult to quarter the ship accurately, because of the closed blast doors on some passageways. He was forced repeatedly to circle through offices, laundry drops, lounges, counting turnings and open doors as he went. As a desert boy he'd learned early to orient himself with the most ephemeral of landmarks, and his training as a Jedi had sharpened and heightened this ability to an almost preternatural degree, but there were miles of corridor, hundreds of identical doors. SP-80s patiently made their rounds along the wall panels, removing already invisible smudges and stains, so there was no sense in marking his way physically with chalk or engine oil. MSEs scurried on their automated errands, as undistinguished from one another as the carefully cloned bepps grown in Bith hydroponics tanks: Luke had heard the expression "as alike as bepps" all his life without ever meeting anyone who actually enjoyed eating the precise, six-centimeter-square, pale-pink, nutritionally balanced and absolutely flavorless cubes.

Down a darkened hall a square of white light lay against a wall. Shadows passed across it, and Luke's quick hearing picked up the mutter of voices. Dragging himself along on a crutch, silence was out of the question, but he moved slowly, keeping his distance, extending his senses to listen, to pick out the words . . .

Then he relaxed. Though they were saying things like "All gunnery ports cleared, Commander," and "Incoming reports on status of scouts, sir," the lisping musicality of the voices—several octaves higher than those of human children—let him know that he'd just stumbled on an enclave of Affytechans.

The room was some kind of operations systems node, more likely connected to the ship's recycling and water-pumping lines than to its weaponry. Not that it mattered to the Affytechans. The gorgeous inhabitants of Dom-Bradden—petaled, tasseled, tufted, and fluttering with hundreds of tendrils and shoots—were bent over the circuit tracers and inventory processors, tapping the responseless keyboards and gazing into the blank screens with the intensity of Imperial guards on a mission from Palpatine himself.

And perhaps they thought they were. Luke had never been quite able to tell about the Affytechans.

Did they know, he wondered, leaning in the doorway, that the levers weren't moving, the knobs weren't turning? That the screens before them were dead as wet slate? "Prepare to launch TIE fighters, Lieutenant," sang out the obvious commander, a frilled purple thing with haloes of white fur outlining the yellow exuberance of its stamens, and the lieutenant—sixteen shades of oranges, yellows, and reds and big around as a barrel—gripped levers in its talons and produced an amazing oratorio of sound effects, none of which had the slightest relation to any mechanical noise Luke had ever heard.

As far as Luke had been able to ascertain, the Affytechans, unlike the Gamorreans, sought to harm no one. Their consciousness, if they had any, was wholly sunk into the dreams of the Imperial Space Service, not divided between dream and reality.

"They're firing on us, Captain!" cried a beautiful thing of yellow and blue. "Plasma torpedoes coming in on port deflector shields!"

Three or four others made what they clearly fancied were explosion noises—rumblings like thunder and shrill cries—and everyone in the room staggered wildly from one side of the chamber to the other as if the ship had taken a massive hit, waving their flaps and petals and shedding white and gold pollen like clouds of luminous dust.

"Return fire! Return fire! Yes?" The captain's lacy sensors turned like a breeze-tossed meadow in Luke's direction as Luke hobbled over to it and saluted.

"Major Calrissian, Special Services. 22911-B. Where are they holding the Rebel saboteur they caught?"

"In the detention area of Deck Six, of course!" cried the captain, out of at least six mouths in exquisite harmony. "I have no time for questions like that! My men are being slaughtered!"

Its vast, flinging gesture took in the doorway behind it. Luke touched the opener and saw, to his shock and horror, in the small lounge that lay behind, the dismembered bodies of four or five Affytechans scattered over tables, chairs, desks. Someone had activated the fire-prevention sprinkler in the ceiling, turning the nozzles so that a spray of fine, rather metallic-smelling mist rained down over everything on the room, pattering wetly on the puddled floor. Amid the pools the torn-off limbs and ripped-out nervous systems were sprouting, thin yellow pendules already bending under the swollen weight of a rainbow of fleshy bulbs.

"Captain, the hyperdrive can't take much more of this!" exclaimed someone who was obviously standing in for the ship's engineer, and a gunnery officer added, "More Rebel fighters coming in, sir! A-formation, starboard ten o'clock!" Everyone leaped to the dead consoles and began making important-sounding beeps and twitters.

Luke limped thoughtfully out into the corridor again.

Deck 6. Far below them—and the Klagg had definitely been trying to go up. Still . . .

Would the Klaggs have done that kind of damage to the Affytechans?

It was a possibility, thought Luke, trying a door, then doubling through a storage area (still no open ceiling beams) and down a viewing gallery above an empty hangar deck. The pieces hadn't looked charred so much as cut and torn. How *did* blaster fire react on the soft, silklike vegetable flesh?

He paused at a juncture, trying to get his bearings. Another door refused to open—one that he had the vague sensation *had* been open before—sending him back down a cross-corridor, through a laundry drop, along a passage that ended in another shut blast door.

I've been this way, thought Luke. He knew he had. And that door had been . . .

He stopped, his scalp prickling.

He smelled Sand People.

Idiot, he thought, as his whole body turned cold. *If the landers picked up Jawas from Tatooine you should have known there was a chance they'd pick up Sand People—Tusken Raiders—there as well.*

They'd been in this corridor not more than a few minutes ago. The air circulators hadn't yet cleared their smell. It meant they could be behind him, tall rag-wrapped shapes like brutally vicious scarecrows mummified in sand, crouched in one of the dark cabins, listening for his dragging footfalls behind one of those many doors the Gamorreans, or the Affytechans, or the Jawas had forced open . . .

Tusken rifles were mostly basement specials, tinkered by illegal manufacturers in Mos Eisley and sold to the Raiders by unscrupulous middlemen. Inaccurate, dirty-firing, but even a near miss in corridors like these could be fatal.

He could still smell them. The circulators should have cleared away the whiff of their dirt-colored wrappings had they been just passing through.

He moved back the way he'd come, stretching his senses for the smallest trace. Around the corner he'd last turned, he thought he heard the faint scratch of metal on metal. At the same moment, movement in the corridor crossing ahead of him caught his eye. A Mouse-droid zooming up the hallway stopped, as if its registers identified something ahead of it out of Luke's sight around the corner. Abruptly it reversed itself, backing full speed in panic.

Luke flung himself toward the nearest room as a searing blast of rifle fire scorched paneling all around him. The Sand People knew their ambush was blown; he heard their almost silent footfalls in the hall as he slammed over the manual on the doors, dashed across the room—it was a communal lounge of some kind, with a visi-reader and a coffee spigot— and through the door on the other side. A cabin, two bunks, like the one he'd come back to consciousness in. Two bunks and one door. Gaffe sticks and makeshift rams pounded on the door of the lounge and he tried another door, a laundry drop like the one from which the Jawa had led him into the repair shaft.

The panel that led to the repair shaft wouldn't budge. Luke heard the crashing of the lounge door being broken in, the wild, blistering rake of saturation fire into the lounge, the visi-reader exploding and the hiss of bursting fire-system pipes . . . He'd never get a chance to bring his lightsaber into play. The blast of the Force that he directed against the wall hatch dented it, but the dog-bolts on the other side held. He remembered seeing, on other hatches in the shafts, the black boxes of magnetic locks.

The door heaved, shook. There was a splintering crash, another harsh zatter as the lock was subjected to rifle fire, and the door opened a slot. Blaster fire roared through, raking the small area of the room accessible through the slit, but it was only the smallest of rooms. Ricochets bounced and sizzled wildly against the walls, and Luke flattened into a corner, trying to summon enough of the Force to keep from getting fried by strays. To an extent he could keep the spattering randomness of them off him, but once the Sand People got the doors open enough to crisp the room wholesale . . .

The Force. If he could use the Force to blow the doors off *outward,* to hurl himself through in a flying levitation, it might buy him a few seconds . . .

He knew that was absurd but was summoning his strength, his energy, to try it anyway when a faint clanging noise by his right foot drew his attention.

The repair shaft coverplate had fallen neatly inward.

Luke ducked through, pushed the panel back into place behind him
—it *had* been dogged, and there was a lock mechanism on it, too—and
latched it again with the bolts alone, which even without the lock should
hold against Sand People. The worklights still burned dimly here, a
grudging ocher glow that faded around him as he climbed down, leaving
only the faint light of the glowrods on his staff.

At the next level down he paused, resting his forehead against the
panel and stretching out his senses through the metal and into the room
beyond. He heard no sound, so dogged back the latches and, holding on
to the handgrips within the shaft, swung himself back and away from the
hatch and summoned the Force, like a violent kick of kinetic energy, from
the outside of the panel, smashing it in despite the magnetic lock.

The metal buckled, twisting against the outer latches, sufficiently for
Luke to work it free. He slipped through into a dim-lit storage area on
Deck 14.

Threepio was waiting for him in the laundry drop. "I was able to find
nothing, Master Luke, nothing," moaned the droid. "Dr. Mingla is
doomed, I know she is."

In the corridor outside, the lights were out. Those in the laundry
room dropped to the grimy yellow glow of the emergency batteries in
which Threepio's eyes shone like headlamps.

"And at the rate the Jawas are stealing wire and solenoids from this
vessel," added Threepio tartly, "we're *all* doomed."

"Well, nobody's doomed yet." Luke eased himself down against the
wall and stretched out his splinted leg, which had begun to throb in spite
of all the concentration, all the Jedi healing techniques he could summon.
He pulled open the engine-taped flap in the leg of his coverall and affixed
another perigen patch to his thigh. The analgesic compound lowered the
pain but did nothing for his utter weariness. He wondered if he could
force his own alertness to sustain a search of the Deck 6 Detention Block,
or whether he would miss some subtle clue from sheer exhaustion.

We're talking about Gamorreans here, he reflected. *How subtle can
they be?*

Though his every instinct told him to look on the upper decks for
Cray, he knew he couldn't neglect even the possibility of a lead. It did
make a kind of sense.

He took a deep breath. "You willing to search the next deck up,

Threepio? I can levitate you as far as the opening on Deck . . . I think it's Seventeen." He leaned through the open hatch and looked. The next opening looked at least two levels above the Deck 15 hatch.

"Very well, sir. But I do suggest, Master Luke, that you get some rest. And permit me to re-dress that wound on your leg. According to my perception of your vital signs—"

"I'll get some rest when I get back from Deck Six. Really," he added into Threepio's pregnant silence. "We just . . . I get the feeling we don't have a lot of time." His bones hurt at the thought of climbing down all those levels—one foot down with his whole weight supported on his arms, then move his arms to the next rung to take his whole weight again . . .

But his escape from the Sand People had convinced him that he was right in not expending his concentration and possibly dissipating his ability to focus the Force in self-levitation.

He had no idea when he'd need everything he could summon. Or how long he'd have to last on what little strength he had.

It was difficult enough, he found, raising Threepio all those levels— some ten or twelve meters—and pushing back the hatchway panel so that the droid could scramble through. "Do be careful, Master Luke," called Threepio's voice down the shaft.

Luke grinned. Aunt Beru used to call after him to take his poncho when he'd take the landspeeder out into the Dune Sea, never guessing that he was going hunting womp rats and that if anything went wrong, getting chilled without his poncho was going to be the least of his worries.

His grin faded as he looked down the blackness of the shaft. Most of the lighting was gone, only small, faded squares of brightness showing where hatches had been removed by Jawas using this route between decks. He slung his staff around his shoulder again.

Eight levels. One aching rung at a time.

Another thought made him stop and turn back to look around the dim chamber behind him.

Everywhere he had traversed in this vessel, he had known—felt—the malignant intelligence of the Will: keeping track of him, monitoring his footfalls, his heartbeats, the temperature of his body. His vital signs, as Threepio monitored them, though without the protocol droid's fussy protectiveness. He was almost certain it was the Will that had closed some of those doors on the deck above, guiding him toward the Sand People's ambush. For the first time, he had the oddest feeling that it wasn't the Will alone observing him.

It certainly hadn't been the Will that had undone the inner lock on that repair-tube hatch.

Or had it been? Had that only served the intent of the Will?

He didn't know. Nevertheless, before he swung himself back into the shaft for the long crawl down, he said quietly, "Thank you. Thank you for helping me."

And I'll feel like the President of the Galactic Society of Village Idiots if it was just a ruse to put me off my guard.

He eased himself off the floor and into the hatch and thence down into darkness.

Chapter 10

"C'mon, Chewie, didn't you hear the man say this afternoon there was nothing up here?" Han Solo flashed the beam of his light around the silent darkness of Plett's House. It was a much stronger beam than Leia's glowrod, a smuggler's actinic luminator. Something scuttled in a corner, invisible in the Stygian mist that curtained the ruined house, and Solo smelled a dirty sweetness, like rotting fruit.

Chewbacca produced a hoarse, disapproving groan.

"What, you gonna let a little bug scare you?" The luminator beam found the dull circle of the metal well cover. "Probably lots of 'em down there." Han knelt beside the cover and unslung his utility kit from his shoulder. Overhead, the lights of the hanging gardens sparkled distantly through the mists.

Han had put two calls through to Mara Jade on the Holonet transceiver, but neither had been picked up. His attempt to reach Leia at the municipal archives had failed as well. They said she had not yet arrived, which struck him as not like Leia, though between fog and darkness it was possible she'd taken a wrong turning and gotten lost in an orchard somewhere. Whatever might lurk in the reputedly nonexistent tunnels beneath Plett's House, it was difficult to imagine any genuine danger befalling anyone aboveground in this sleepy, mist-bound Garden of Delight. He'd contacted Winter on subspace, said hello to Anakin and talked briefly to Jacen and Jaina, who'd kept trying to put their hands through the holo field, clearly unaware that their father wasn't in the room with them. But when the call was over and silence returned to the borrowed house, he knew what the trouble was.

He wanted to go back to Plett's House and look around.

He thought he knew how to get into the crypts.

Like Drub McKumb, he reflected wryly, he, too, had his "calculations."

Chewbacca handed him the bundle he'd brought up from the *Millennium Falcon*'s locker—a Scale-3 antigrav generator, and a couple of backpack power cells. Solo set the generator on the well cover and flipped the magnetic catches, only to discover that the cover wasn't durasteel as he'd thought, but some kind of nonferrous metal. Interesting, considering the price differential between ferrous and nonferrous. There were no handles, either.

"Well, I guess we do this the hard way." He took a small drill from the utility kit, and hooked it into the power cell. It occurred to him to wonder who exactly had put the cover in place, and how long it had been there. By the dirt in the cracks, at least a couple of years, but Leia had mentioned that in her vision of former years the well had been guarded by open grillework, not a solid slab. Probably for reasons of warmth.

By the light of Chewbacca's torch he fastened bolts to the cover, affixed the antigrav. He couldn't guess how deep the air column of the well was—at least a hundred meters, he calculated from the combined height of the benches that rose above the valley floor. A Scale-3 was good for most jobs of this size, and in the event it lifted the cover easily. The metal slab was beveled inward, and thicker than one would expect, sitting easily in the shaped lip of the well.

Warm steam murky with sulfur sighed up around the cover as it lifted, and wisps of it trailed around the feet of the intruders as they guided the cover out of the way, but whatever lay at the bottom of Plett's Well was a warm spring, not a hot one. By the glow of the luminator, when Han held it down the shaft, thick pillows of moss and lichen could be seen on the glistening dark stone. Mingled with the sulfur and the acrid whiff of chlorine came the smell of rotting fruit.

Chewie growled.

"So it stinks," said Han. "So does the *Falcon*'s engine room when we blow a duct."

As he'd thought, there were handholds cut into the rock. The irregularities of the shaft itself, and the dense blocks and pits of shadow they created, hid everything beyond the first few meters, and ghostly drifts of steam threw back the light. Solo fixed a loop of safety line around the stone upright between two of the keyhole windows and clipped the other end to his belt. Chewie ran a double loop of the line around his waist.

"Right," muttered Solo and clipped the luminator to the front of his vest. "So let's see what all the fuss is about."

They hid the children down the well.

Solo almost missed the door that led into the passageway, set in the wall of the shaft where the shadows seemed to cross no matter where the light was coming from. The heat grew thicker as they descended, and with it the dirty, sweetish smell. He was aware of wet, crawly movement among the lichen and mineral deposits on the rock. But below the level of the passageway's entrance, the handholds were choked shut with moss. The difference was noticeable enough to send him searching up the shaft again, probing at each shadow around and behind him with his light.

"There." He shone the light on the walls of the tunnel as he and Chewbacca ducked through the low, oval mouth. The Wookiee shook himself uncomfortably, his coarse, tobacco-colored fur black-wet and pointy with moisture. The luminator beam played across old scarring in the walls, places where the moss on the floor had been gouged and regrown.

"Somebody was here, all right, and a lot less than thirty years ago." Han bent, and picked something out of the moss.

In the beam of his flash it glinted dirty yellowish, the size of his thumbnail, with a quality to it at once matte and glittery. Dark lines intricately stitched its surface.

"Xylen," he said. "A memory chip—if old Plett was the hot-stuff botanist everybody says he was the place would have been stuffed with sequencers and tanks and what-all else. No wonder people came around to strip it." He unhooked the safety line from his belt, letting it dangle back in front of the tunnel's mouth. "What's the price of xylen on the open market these days, Chewie?"

The Wookiee disclaimed specialized expertise in commodities, but Han knew at least that the xylen backing of that single old-fashioned chip would at least have paid for the dress Leia had worn that afternoon several times over. He slipped it into his pocket.

"No wonder Nubblyk kept it a secret." The luminator's beam picked out the uneven contours of the dripping walls, the low arch of the moss-grown ceiling. Something black and shiny and the size of Han's foot slithered and fled through the moss to vanish down the throat of the passageway. Han flinched involuntarily and Chewie, bent to keep his head from brushing the ceiling, ran a nervous paw over the back of his mane, as if he suspected that something had detached itself from the moss above him and was crawling in his fur.

He growled a question.

"Dunno," said Han. "The only thing that could have killed off the trade in chips—and whatever else they could pull out of the old machinery—is if they'd cleared the place out. That would have been the year after the Battle of Endor, by what they were saying in the bars." Rags of mist flickered around his bootheels as he led the way down a short incline into the tunnel that stretched away into the dark.

Another interrogative rumble.

"Yeah, Drub worked for him as a runner. But the Slyte kept a tight rein on things. My guess is nobody but him knew where the entrance to this place was. And there might have been more than one. Damn," he added, as they came to the top of a steeply zigzagging ramp. "Talk about a place that's bigger on the inside than on the outside."

The tunnel climbed, following the network of old volcanic passages and underground riverbeds that eventually opened into the great chasm of the Plawal Rift itself. At the top of the ramp a short tunnel pierced the rock, only to be blocked at the far end: "That's where the door Leia saw went into the House, I bet." They backtracked, followed the main tunnel, Chewie grumbling as he shifted his bowcaster and blaster rifle to a more comfortable position on his shoulders.

"Yeah, here we are. This vent probably runs straight out under the ice."

They followed the scratched marks on the floor to a wide cavern, crossed a narrow wooden bridge above a cleft from which steam and the acrid breath of subterranean gases rose in a suffocating wall. The rocks beyond, where the tunnel widened into a vast, uneven space of darkness, were coated with wrinkled, labyrinthine mazes of paste-white sinter formations, the floor pitted with long-dead fumaroles and slashed by steaming streams nearly choked in strangely tinted mineral deposits. Flat wormlike white tentacles groped from one of the fumaroles, clutching toward their feet, but when Han and Chewbacca drew away in alarm subsided again with a bubbly slurp.

At the far end of the cave a room had been cut in the rock, littered with plastic boxes and the small, flat packets smugglers used to store goods in when they shoved them behind hull panels or under floor sections. Most of them were chewed and mauled; a small kretch, no longer than Han's thumb, skittered away from the track of his light.

"Gold wire." Han nudged the plastic litter with his boot toe, then knelt to retrieve something metallic that twinkled dirty-bright in the light. It was kinked and twisted, having been straightened out from its original configuration and bundled for storage. Mineral deposits clung thickly to it, pinkish gold in the beam of the light. "Utility grade."

He flashed the beam over the room's two other doorways, which led, one to a stair, one to a tunnel beyond. The low ceilings were toothy with stalactites and furred with hairlike deposits of sodium and silica. Lichen glimmered in threads of blue, green, and crimson on the walls, and serpents of mist coiled across the floor.

"Let's see what else we got."

Hot, acrid breezes stirred Solo's sweat-drenched hair and the Wookiee's fur as they moved on into the vent system. Streams of water dripped through the formations on the walls, and the darkness was choking with sulfur and kretch smell. In another room cut from the tunnel wall Han's light glinted on a jumble of metal casings and circuit boards, flashed in the empty glass eyes of an old APD-40 droid's cylindrical head.

"When'd they quit making APDs, Chewie?" Han hunkered to turn the boards over in his hand. All the chips had been pried out, the power cells removed.

The Wookiee guessed the Clone Wars, but didn't come into the room. He remained in the low-beamed rectangle of the doorway, listening back along the blackness of the tunnel, to the echo chamber of the last cave. Han could hear only the distant rushing of water somewhere, but knew his friend's ears were far sharper than his own.

"Yeah, I thought that myself. They switched to the C Three series because the APDs used gold wire and xylen points. This's an old model, too." He flashed the light around the litter of split casings and looted boards. "Must be six, eight droids' worth of junk here. This was what they were after, all right."

In the next room along the corridor they found the jewels.

"What the . . . ?"

Han's light threw rainbows from the three boxes ranged along the wall, bright colors springing back to salt the low ceiling in fire. He stooped, brought up dirty, crusted earrings, chains, pectorals, pendants . . .

Chewie growled a remark, held up a plastic packing crate, half filled with xylen chips.

Their eyes met, baffled.

"That doesn't make any sense." Han ran his fingers through the chips. They were jumbled together with electronic salvage, gold wire, power cells, selenium . . . "There must be three quarters of a million credits in this room." He shone his light through the inner doorway, and the gleam passed over the hard angles of machinery, dark screens, the smooth curved arms of processors and pumps. "This stuff hasn't been touched. I can't see Nubblyk just walking away and—"

Chewie held up his paw, head turning toward the outer door, and made a sign to kill the light.

Silence and utter darkness. The far-off *hursh* of water echoed in the low groinings of the ceiling. A horrible scratching, and the dirty-sweet kretch smell, made Han fight to thrust from his mind the awful fantasy of a dozen of the things climbing his boots the minute the light was out.

He picked his cautious way to where he knew Chewie stood still in the entrance. His outstretched hand met fur. Had his companion been human he would have whispered his name to avoid a knife between his ribs, but the Wookiee would know his smell. Chewie did not growl, but under his fingers Han felt the fur of his friend's arm lift and prickle.

There was definitely something in the corridor.

Stray, hot wind down the tunnels brought a feral stink that almost made Han gag. Whatever it was, for that amount of smell it was *big*.

Then a scream, the scratch of claws; Han yelled *"Light!"* to warn Chewbacca and threw the full-force beam directly at the source of the sound. It flared diamond hard in yellow beast-eyes, slashing brown teeth. Chewie's blaster bolt went wild and spattered, ricocheting crazily in the narrow space while the creature threw itself on the Wookiee, howling and ripping in a mass of filthy, mold-covered hair.

There was no question of a second shot, and Han plunged in with his knife, stabbing at the creature's back as it bore Chewbacca to the floor. It screamed, writhed in Chewie's grip, slashed at Han, and the dropped luminator caught movement in the dark. Other things were running, eyes blazing, the uneven ceiling suddenly echoing with screams.

Han twisted loose from the first attacker as it slumped, grabbed the luminator and Chewbacca's dropped rifle, and the Wookiee rolled to his feet, leaped over the corpse, and pelted away into the dark. Han dashed behind him, firing back, the bolt hissing from wall to wall and showing like lightning the shambling, filthy things on their heels.

"Back that way!"

Chewie only roared, long legs taking him far ahead down the twisting rock of the tunnel. The luminator beam leaped crazily over mold-covered walls, bounced across doorways yawning into blind dark of dead-end rooms, transformed stalagmites in the great cavern into attackers and old vent holes and lava formations into bottomless pits. They scrambled, slipping in the thin mud of the floor, toward the dark cleft of the entry to the tunnel back toward the well . . .

The beam caught the glint of something in the tunnel, rounded and shiny, like black jewelry or the scales of some monstrous thing. Something like wet cobblestones that suddenly seemed to carpet the tunnel—walls, ceiling, and floor. Something that hadn't been there before.

Kretch.

The tunnel leading back toward the well was choked with them.

For one moment Han and Chewie stood aghast, staring at the nightmare seethe of insectile bodies that filled the passageway nearly twenty centimeters thick. Then, as if a plug had been pulled, the river of kretch flowed out.

Han screamed something entirely inadequate to the occasion and plunged away to his left into the lumpy ruin of old lava formations and sullenly steaming craterlets, Chewie at his heels and all the legions of darkness shrieking behind.

"Got to find a way back," panted Han desperately, as frail sinter and twisted crystal crunched underfoot and the patches of glowing lichen throbbed and stirred like rainbow embers at their passage. The air down here burned with volatile gases and the stench of sulfur, chewing at the lungs, and the baking heat made Han gasp. "Back to the vaults . . . maybe this way . . ."

More screams, and two black forms sprang suddenly into the glare of the luminator where it fell on the sloped side of an old debris cone rising up before them.

"On second thought, let's go this way—"

Chewie caught his arm, stopping him, and roared a challenge into the darkness ahead of them.

A challenge was screamed in return.

Han said, "Great." He raised the light, flashing the beam across the round, smooth terraces of what had been superheated mud pits, now cooled to dance floors of garishly colored hardpan still ringed with the traces of final bubbles—and there they were.

Three of them, maybe four . . . one running, a couple crawling on all fours.

He swung the flash, the white light splashing over finger-thin columns of rising smoke from a vent to their left, a wilderness of steaming caldera below them where the ground fell farther, picked up the eyes of the things scuffling, shambling, running toward them from behind: eyes and hands and the crude weapons they carried.

Chewbacca fired a bowcaster bolt that went through the chest of something that looked as if it had once been a flat-headed Carosite—it kept on coming, crawling, leaving a broad, bloody smear in its wake. Han opened fire with his blaster at the second group and missed, a huge scar ripping in the mud of the old pits, and from somewhere close by there was a rumble, the ground jarring slightly underfoot and loosened rock showering them from the dark above.

"This way!" he yelled, and swept the light again, picking up, far off in the darkness, what looked like human artifacts: a raised path among the dead caldera, a barely seen trace of stairs, and, at the top of a low black rise, outlined in the jeweled glow of colored lichen, a circle of stone pillars.

"We can pick 'em off the path!"

The second group of attackers was already halfway to the head of the path. Han leaned into his dash, the Wookiee loping ahead of him on his longer legs, their original attackers a feral pack not four meters behind. The first of the new group reached the path at the same moment as

Chewbacca, slashing at the Wookiee with a metal bar stolen from some ancient workshop. Chewbacca fired his bowcaster and the impact knocked the attacker backward into an old mud pit, filled with what Han had at first taken for a pale, delicate formation of curled and cranial-looking sinter or limestone.

As the attacker—a Mluki, he looked as if he had been, before madness and neglect had turned him into a screaming beast—went sprawling into the pit, the limestone formation came alive, a sudden heaving of rippling membranes, thrashing layers of fleshy, carnivorous mold. The Mluki, bleeding already from Chewbacca's energy bolt, rolled over and tried to get up, tried to run, but the thing in the pit gripped it with tentacles like elastic white snakes, dragging it down . . .

The whitish membranes, like a heaving flower or a mass of writhing tripe, slowly turned red, a color that spread among the membranes to the edges of the pit.

Han and Chewie fled past, the path narrowing among crater after crater filled with the carnivorous pit-mold, which rippled furiously and reached for their feet with snakelike tentacles. Behind in the darkness more shrieks resounded, but Han dared not look back to see what other creatures were emerging from the darkness in pursuit.

At the top of the path, in the circle of pillars, was a well.

A low curb surrounded the ten-foot hole. Below, Han could hear the rushing of water, feel the relative coolness of the rising air damp on his burned face. By the white glow of the luminator he could see the things shambling up the path behind them, mouths open and shrieking from hairy, scarred, madness-twisted faces. Some still wore the rags of what had been clothing, and waved makeshift knives and clubs. Some had been human.

Their eyes were crazed blanks. Drub McKumb's eyes.

They were coming fast. What had been a Gotal got too close to the edge of the path and was seized by a tentacle from the pit-mold alongside; the others didn't even look back as it was dragged screaming into a mountain of shuddering membranes. Chewbacca's first shot with the blaster rifle took out a hirsute skeleton that had been a Whiphid; his second missed and blew half-cooled mud from a minor crater like an explosion of steaming goo over everything in sight. The ground shook again, like a sullen warning. Flame sprang up from the mud pits and hot liquid began to creep out in glowing trickles.

None of the attackers even noticed.

Even with both of them shooting, Han knew, they'd never hit them all before they were overwhelmed.

There was no path down from the mound.

"Down the well!"

Chewie roared in protest.

"Down the well! There's a way out, that water's flowing, I can hear it . . ."

Whether the way out included space to breathe was problematical, of course.

A horrible Devaronian fell on Chewbacca, its arm already torn off by blaster fire, rending at him with a chunk of broken steel. Chewbacca flung it back into the others, fired another blast to cover them while Han sprang up on the well curb and flashed the light down at the water.

Five meters or so. As he'd thought, it wasn't a well so much as a shaft into an underground stream.

He stepped off the edge and dropped.

The water was hot, just below scalding—only contrast with air super-heated by the surrounding rock had made the updraft feel cool—and the current vicious. Han clung to the worn stone of the low arch in the well's side until he heard Chewbacca's heavy splash and reassuring growl. Then the water tore his grip free, swirled him along in utter blackness, pounding him against rock, pelting like a millrace to smash him breathless on some unseen obstacle.

Bars. There were bars across the stream's course.

Water slammed into his face, and he felt/heard the splash of something else striking the bars. He groped and felt the reassuring touch of soaked fur.

Chewbacca congratulated him on the excellence of his escape arrangements.

"Don't get smart on me, Chewie, I got us out of the cave, didn't I?" As he spoke he felt for a foothold, a handhold, anything he could find in the bars, stretched and felt his way up along the corroded metal. The bars ended in a slit in the rock ceiling a half meter above the surface of the water, a slit into which he could barely fit his hand. As he worked his fingers in, they brushed something leggy and chitinous that moved sharply, and he jerked his hand back with a cry of disgust. "Let's try down the other way."

Taking a deep breath, he turned over, climbed down the bars. They went deep, deep, the current crushing his body against them, always more blackness, always more water . . .

What was he going to do if they went deeper than he could climb on a single breath?

The thought made him panic, drag himself down and farther down.

Rock. And a space of about thirty centimeters, gouged in the bottom of the streambed by the vicious race of water over the years.

He snaked his body through, climbed desperately, wondering what he'd do if he became disoriented, climbed sideways, climbed down again, got swept away by the current that was dragging him, clutching him, sweeping him on into blackness.

He thought, *I may not survive this one.*

His head broke water just as he thought he couldn't hold his breath another second. He felt weak, sickened, but at least he could hook his arms through the spaces between the bars and not rely on the dwindling strength of his hands. "Down at the bottom," he gasped. "*Way* down."

The water ripped him away.

Han and Chewbacca lay for a long time on the grass beside the warm spring, gasping for air like half-drowned vermin belched from some Coruscant sewer. Far off, a dim gold low-power light marked where a path lay. Phosphor bugs played like truant diamonds among the trees. The smell of bowvine fruit and damp grass almost drowned the faint, putrid whiff of sulfur from the stream. Skreekers and peepers made a tiny bass line under the warbling of a nightbird in the orchard.

Han rolled over, threw up a considerable quantity of water, and said, "I'm getting too old for this."

Chewbacca concurred.

At least they wouldn't catch cold, Han reflected. The river that ran from Plett's Well was hotter than bathwater and the air around it not much cooler. Vapor wraiths surrounded them from the hotter springs that came to the surface lower in the orchard, piped from the cellars of the ancient houses. He wondered if they'd get into much trouble just falling asleep where they were.

But he recalled something about what had happened in the crypts, and decided that might not be such a good idea.

With considerable effort, and some misgivings, he propped himself up on his elbows.

"You notice something about our pals back in the crypts, Chewie?"

The Wookiee's sardonic reply made Han wonder why some people said the species had no sense of humor.

"When the second and third and fourth batches showed up," said Han quietly, "they knew where to find us."

Chewie was silent. For certain species of cave apes—perhaps even for Wookiees—this would have been no oddity. Smell, and echolocation, were highly developed in races and species used to the dark.

But these, Han had seen, were not members of those races and species, unless you counted the Gotal, who had been one of the first batch of attackers. They were, he suspected, exactly what Drub McKumb had been: smugglers, or friends of smugglers, who had heard the rumors about the crypts that weren't supposed to exist, who had their "calculations." Who had gone seeking the source of the xylen chips and gold wire that had formed the basis of Nubblyk the Slyte's brief wealth, and had found . . . what?

"C'mon, Chewie," he said tiredly. "Let's get home."

Chapter 11

Watching Cray's face, Luke tried to ascertain whether she had remembered who she was, whether she was still under the influence of the Will's programming.

From the small image in the section lounge vidscreen, it wasn't easy to tell. Bruises marked her cheeks and chin and her shoulder, visible through a tear in her tunic; her pale hair was stiff with sweat and grime. But her eyes, as two Klagg boars pulled her the length of the displayed chamber to the small black podium of the Justice Station, were desperate, hard with fury and frustration.

"Soap-lovin' Klagg!" howled Ugbuz, standing by the table at Luke's side. "Prissy-butt!" "Flower-nose!" "Cabbage-eater!" yelled the other Gakfedds, clustered close around the vidscreen in the dim confines of the lounge.

Though disheveled and exhausted, aside from her bruises Cray looked unhurt. In his utterly fruitless search of the Detention Block on Deck 6, Luke had been haunted by the dread that the Will had implanted in the Klaggs the notion that as a Rebel saboteur, Cray had to be interrogated, and this nightmare had kept him combing the corridors around the Main Block for several additional hours until he'd made certain that Cray

had never been there, the Klaggs had never been there, and all the interrogator droids remained in their original places, still hooked to their chargers on the walls.

He'd disconnected them and pulled whatever wiring he could reach.

Though ultimately reassuring, the search had been far from pleasant,
and, knowing the Gamorreans, Luke was aware that it was perfectly
possible they'd preferred to dispense with the interrogator droids and do
it themselves.

It didn't look as if they had, though.

Ugbuz poked Luke in the ribs with an elbow like a battering ram and
pointed to the fat white Klagg boar standing next to the Justice Station's
cold black viewscreen. "Kinfarg," he explained in an undertone. "Captain
of the stinkin' Klagg sons of sows." He added commentary on Captain
Kinfarg's personal habits, which Luke suspected were purely speculative.
The Gakfedds jeered and catcalled as Kinfarg swaggered up the aisle to
take his position next to the podium, but when he began to speak they fell
silent, as if by magic.

"What made you turn against your vow to the Imperial Service and
join the Rebels, Trooper Mingla?"

Cray straightened up. Luke wondered where Nichos was—the cam-
eras were focused solely on the Justice Station—and whether he was in
the room with her, still held to inactivity by his restraining bolt.

"It has yet to be established that I have done anything of the sort,
Commander Kinfarg."

The Gakfedds around Luke hooted and whistled derisively, except
for those engaged in trying to prevent the half dozen Talz and the small
herd of tripods from escaping the section lounge in which they sat.

"You stupid yammerheads, you *gotta* watch this!" Krok was growl-
ing. "It's the *Will*!"

The Talz scratched their heads, wuffled a little, and tried the other
door, with much the same results. The tripods just wandered dazedly
around, bumping now and then into the furniture or into the stolid ranks
of the forty-five Kitonaks whom the Gamorreans had carried laboriously
in, standing them like squashy, yeast-colored statues in the rear half of the
lounge.

The Gakfedds at least were taking the Will's orders that everyone
watch very seriously.

Presumably, thought Luke, the Affytechans were gathered around a screen in some other lounge. There was a good chance they'd forgotten to switch that screen *on,* of course, but to the Affytechans it wouldn't matter.

"That will now be established," Kinfarg said to Cray. It was still strange beyond words to hear excellent, if colloquial and a little slurred, Basic coming out of those bestial, snouted faces.

Behind him on the black podium screen, green letters rippled to life.

- You are a known associate of other Rebel spies and saboteurs
- You have assisted saboteurs on this vessel in damaging the fabric of this vessel and thus jeopardizing its mission
- You have attempted violence against officers of this vessel in the course of their rightful duties
- You were seen attempting to damage weaponry and landing vessels necessary to the completion of this mission

"That's a lie!" cried Cray furiously. "It's all lies! Show me one piece of evidence . . ."

- You are a known associate of other Rebel spies and saboteurs
  1. Your name was given by Rebel spies taken in a raid on Algarian
  2. Holograms and retina prints given by the government of Bespin after a Rebel raid match yours
  3. You were taken prisoner in a raid on a group of known dissidents and troublemakers on board this vessel

"That's a complete and absolute falsehood!" Cray was almost in tears of fury. "Not a single one of those allegations is correct, nor are they backed up with evidence—"

"Shut up, trooper!" Kinfarg struck her again, with the same casual violence as before, though Cray saw it coming and rolled with it this time. " 'Course there's evidence. Wouldn't be in the computer without evidence."

"I insist that the evidence be presented!"

Luke closed his eyes. He knew what was coming.

When he opened them again he saw that the Justice Station's screen had blandly displayed a screenwide and infinitesimally tiny reproduction of forms, reports, finger- and retina-print dupes, and tiny holo screens of Cray's image and the images of various "Rebels" talking in minute, tinny voices about Cray's involvement in Rebel activities.

"A computer simulation isn't evidence!" Cray shouted. "I can program a simulation like that with my eyes shut! I demand that counsel be provided for me—"

"You kidding, trooper?" demanded Kinfarg. He'd cut the face out of a white stormtrooper helmet and wore the cranium of it on the back of his head, the face on his chest like a bizarre skull mask. The effect was, against all probability, chilling. "No decent counsel's so disloyal he'd defend a known Rebel. What you want us to do?" He chuckled thickly. "Get a Rebel to come and defend you?"

The Justice Station's screen wiped. Then green lines of letters flickered into being:

- "All military offensives shall be considered under law as states of emergency, and subject to the emergency military powers act of the Senate."

  Senatorial Amendment
  to Constitutions of
  New Order
  Decree 77-92465-001

- "Without necessary capital powers it is considered impossible to maintain the stability of the New Order and the security of the greatest number of civilizations in the galaxy."

  Capital Powers Act
  Preface, Section II

"What am I supposed to do?" retorted Cray furiously. "Fall on my knees and confess?"

- Standing confession will suffice

"Like hell I will, you rusted-out pile of scrap!"

Luke wanted to leave, but knew he could not, even if the Gakfedds would let him. He had come not only to make sure Cray was still alive and more or less well, but to observe the background for clues, to look for whatever hints he could find as to where the Klaggs might be. Apprehension turned him cold as the Justice Station's screen flashed the new message,

- In view of the prisoner's intransigence, sentencing will take place tomorrow at 1200 hours. All personnel are required to assemble to view sentencing. Absence from viewing lounge will be construed as sympathy with the ill intentions of the prisoner.

The screen went dark.

"Find out anything?" Luke leaned his shoulder against the wall, watching the stolid, bronze-colored SP-80 plod a few meters down the corridor and resume its sponging of the walls in a new spot.

Had C-3PO possessed lungs, he would have produced a martyr's sigh. "Master Luke, I did try. Indeed I did. And far be it from me to disparage the programming of Single-Purpose units, because what they do, they do admirably well. But as I said, they are limited."

"Is there any way we can change their programming?" Luke scratched his cheek; he was beginning to get the fair, almost invisible brown stubble of a beard, itchy in the scars the snow creature had long ago left. "Program them to seek out Gamorreans—by the smell probably —rather than spots on the walls?"

"I expect when they attempted to wash the Gamorreans they found their functioning would cease in short order," reflected Threepio. "And we're already surrounded by Gamorreans."

"Not if we went up to Deck Eighteen or higher," said Luke. Threepio's search of Deck 17 had yielded him no more than Luke's investigation of the Detention Block and its vicinity, though Threepio, like Luke, had encountered many blast shields and doors that simply would not open. Luke wondered if these concealed classified areas, or if the Will was trying to herd Threepio as it had herded him. "Could you program an SP to find Gamorreans on one of those decks, so that we could simply follow it? Can their long-range sensors be extended that far?"

"Of course," replied the droid. "That's brilliant, Master Luke! Absolutely brilliant! It would take a minimum of—"

"You!"

Luke spun. Ugbuz stood behind him, drool dripping from his heavy snout, staring at him with flinty suspicion in his gaze.

"You're the friend of that Rebel saboteur, aren't you?"

Luke's fingers traced the small circle of focus, gathering the Force to his soft voice. "No," he said quietly. "That was somebody else. I never was near her."

Ugbuz frowned, as if trying to match two pieces of a jigsaw puzzle in his mind. "Oh." He turned and started back for the door of the lounge— the Talz were wandering out, wuffing to one another and shaking their soft white heads, heading en masse for the mess hall a few doors down. Then he turned back.

"But you was the kid who stopped us questioning that saboteur?"

"No," said Luke, drawing the Force about him, projecting it into Ugbuz's limited—and rather divided—mind. He found that even this small and simple exercise was difficult under the effects of pain and fatigue. "That was someone else also."

"Oh." Ugbuz's frown deepened. "The Will says there's something going on on this ship."

"There is," Luke agreed. "But none of it has anything to do with me."

"Oh. Okay." He disappeared back into the lounge, but in the doorway Luke saw him turn and glance back over his shoulder as if puzzling about edges that did not match.

Just what I needed, thought Luke. *Something else to worry about.*

"Let's go," he said softly. "I want to reprogram one of the SPs on Deck Eighteen, and there's something else I want to try up on Deck Fifteen."

"Great galaxies, Captain, there's hundreds of them!" The Affytechan second-in-command swung away from the blank screen—they were in the central lounge of Deck 15 this time, bent intently over the dead consoles of games and visi-readers—and fluttered all its tendrils and ramifications in horror. "They were lying in wait for us behind every asteroid in the field!"

"Gunnery! What's our status?" It was a different captain, ligulate, delicious pink grading into magenta, and extravagant with stalks and tassels. The former captain was in charge of a glitterball console at the far end of the lounge.

"Down to fifty percent, Captain," reported a tubulate mass of azure and periwinkle. "But we've still got enough juice to make 'em think twice!"

"That's the spirit, men!" cried the captain. "We'll have 'em yelling for their mothers before we're through. Can I help you?" The captain's lacy florets all turned in Luke's direction as Luke and Threepio approached the two chairs, piled one atop the other, which constituted the makeshift bridge.

"Major Calrissian, Special Services." Luke saluted, a gesture the captain returned smartly. Though all the screens and consoles were dead—including, Luke suspected, the main viewer on which the Affytechans had supposedly watched Cray's trial—at least the lights still worked. Luke couldn't be sure, but he thought there were more Affytechans than there had been before.

"New assignment, sir, which supersedes all previous orders." As Luke spoke he collected the Force, projected it into the mind—if there was a mind—within that mass of color and fluff.

"There's been a minor malfunction of the schematics library. Sabotage, we think. Nothing to worry about, but we need to know the location and status of all transport craft on board. It's a tough assignment—dangerous." Luke made his face grave. "I'd hesitate passing it on to inexperienced men, but you . . . Well, you're the best we have. Think you can handle it?"

The captain sprang down from his chair, a good meter and a half to the floor, and returned Luke's salute again. Whatever creatures the Affytechans relied upon for cross-pollination, they clearly found some rather strange enzymes appealing; the Affytechans, especially when they moved quickly, gave off an amazing galaxy of stenches, acrid, ammoniac, or gluily musky. In the damaged air-conditioning of the Deck 15 lounge the effect was overpowering.

"You can count on us, Major. Men . . ."

The Affytechans abandoned the battle midmaneuver and lined up in the center of the lounge, standing at rigid attention while their captain outlined the assignment and gave them a pep talk worthy of the great general Hyndis Raithal herself.

"It never ceases to amaze me, sir," said Threepio, as the exuberant crew streamed out of the lounge, "the ingenuity of the human species. Say what she will—and I certainly intend no criticism of either Dr. Mingla or her preceptors—I have never yet encountered a droid program capable of the kind of lateral thinking one sees in human beings."

"Let's hope not," said Luke quietly. "Because a droid program—an artificial intelligence—is exactly what we're up against in this ship."

They walked in silence for a time toward the laundry drop where the repair shaft rose to take them to Deck 18. While waiting for Cray's trial Threepio had changed the dressings of the ax wound on Luke's leg, and though the infection seemed to be contained, Luke thought the pain was getting worse again.

"I have observed, sir," Threepio said after a time, "that since Nichos's . . . transformation"—it was extremely rare for Threepio to hesitate over a word—"he and I have a great deal more in common than we ever did when he was . . . as he was before. He was always a pleasant and likable human being, but now he is much less humanly unpredictable, if you will pardon me for expressing a purely subjective opinion based on incomplete data. I can only trust and hope that Dr. Mingla finds this a benefit."

Trust and hope, thought Luke. Grammatical constructs programmed into Threepio's language to make it more human . . . but he knew that the pessimistic droid did not, in fact, either trust or hope anything. He wondered if Nichos did, anymore.

"Come on," he said quietly. "Let's find an SP and see if you can convince it to become a tracker."

Luke had been surrounded by droids all his life, had grown up with them on his uncle's farm. As Threepio said, they were excellent at what they were, but unlike humans what they were not, they were *not,* one hundred percent. And Cray, wherever she was, was finding this out in the cruelest possible way.

He only hoped he could reach her in time.

The area of Deck 18 immediately surrounding the laundry drop to which the repair shaft led them was high-ceilinged, almost twice the height of other decks. The walls were of the same dark gray Luke had seen in the background of both the Klagg village and the Justice Chamber. A short distance beyond the laundry drop, the corridors were utterly lightless; hatches and wall panels gaped open, spewing cables and wires like the entrails of gutted beasts. Luke didn't need to see the dirty fingermarks all around them to guess who was responsible.

An SP-80 was doggedly removing the fingermarks. It didn't pause when Luke flipped open the coverplate in its side and plugged in the comm cable from the droid in the back of Threepio's cranium. Over the course of the years back on Tatooine Uncle Owen had owned at least five different SPs that Luke could remember, and by the time he was fourteen Luke had been able to break down, clean, repair, refit, and reassemble one in four hours. Reprogramming from a translator droid that already had access to biocodes and serial indexes was candy.

The SP plodded off down the corridor almost before Luke had the cable out of it; he had to pace it to shut the coverplate. It still held its cleaner arm and vacuum absorption pad straight out in front of it, and for some reason Luke was reminded of the Kitonaks, patiently waiting for Chooba slugs to crawl to them across thousands of light-years of hyperspace and into their open mouths.

"Does it scent the Klaggs on this deck, d'you think?" asked Luke softly, limping in the SP's slow wake with Threepio clicking along at his side. "Or would it pick them up on the downdraft from a gangway?"

"Oh, the sensory mechanism of a cleaner SP is quite capable of detecting grease molecules in a concentration of less than ten thousand per square centimeter, in an area of a quarter of a square centimeter, at a distance of a hundred meters or more."

"Biggs's mother could do that," remarked Luke.

Threepio was silent for a moment. "With all due respect to Mrs. Biggs, sir, I understand that even if a human is born with an exceptional olfactory center in the brain, it requires a Magrody implant and extensive childhood training to develop such a skill, though among the Chadra-Fan and the Ortolans such abilities are quite commonplace."

"Joke," said Luke gravely. "That was a joke."

"Ah," said Threepio. "Indeed."

The SP halted before a closed blast shield that blocked the hall. Luke stepped forward and palmed the opener, without result. "Really, Master Luke, there are times when I almost agree with Ugbuz's attitude toward

the Jawas," said Threepio, as the SP's four small sensor pits curved and
shifted this way and that and streams of yellow numbers fidgeted across
its readout. Then it turned, with great deliberation, backtracked to a
cross-corridor a few meters behind them, turned right, and continued
through the maze of shut doors and dark, cavernous storage hulls.

Luke said nothing, but the hair on his nape prickled with the sensation of being watched, observed from the darkness. Jawas? He might not
have an SP-80's olfactory detectors but he'd know if Jawas were around.
Ditto for Sand People.

This was something else.

Another blast door. The SP recalibrated, changed course, through a
holding area filled with gutted packing containers whose contents—regular navy helmets, coveralls, gray-green half-armor, and blankets—strewed
the floor. Pieces of the containers themselves were gone; Luke noted that
those that remained were labeled SOROSUB IMPORTS. The walls here were
dark in the bobbing light of Luke's staff, and looked unfinished, with
rafters stretching bare overhead and bolt ends glinting in the shadows.
The door into a repair bay stood open. Luke glanced back over his
shoulder and saw that the corridor entrance, through which they had
come moments before, was shut now.

The Will, he thought. *It's herding us. Pushing us the way it wants us to
go.*

Clanking softly, the SP-80 turned down a long corridor on the starboard side of the ship. Though no damage by Jawas was evident, the
lights were gone here, too, and as he and Threepio drew farther from the
lighted area and the reflections of its glow got dimmer and dimmer, Luke
sensed ever more strongly the presence of an unknown, watching entity.
He kept as close to Threepio as he could, matching his halting stride to
the droid's and making sure there was never a space between them when
they passed under the periodic blast doors.

The SP-80 turned a corner. A stair led up into pitchy night. Luke
heard the *hiss-whirr-tap* of its short legs negotiating the stairs of a gangway
and extended his arm sharply to stop Threepio from following it, feeling
only the horrible inner prickling sensation of a trap.

He held out his staff with its dimly shining glowrods toward the
square opening of the stairs. The light was flung back by dim strips of
opalescent material, thick and thin alternating in a strange not-quite-
pattern, vanishing upward into the dark.

Luke looked up. The ceiling of the gangway was dotted with the cold pearly squares of the more usual form of enclision grid.

The SP ascended, unharmed, out of his sight.

"Good heavens." Threepio stepped closer to the door. "It's definitely some sort of enclision grid, sir. But obviously deactivated. Possibly the Jawas—"

"No." Luke leaned against the wall, his leg beginning to throb burningly as the first relief of the perigen wore off. "No, the Will wouldn't have herded us to a gangway that was disabled. It's just waiting until we're too far up to turn back."

Slowly, the heavy, mechanical stride of the SP droid faded. In the darkness, the weight of the ship seemed to press on them, waiting for them to follow it up the wired stair. Luke hurried his stride as much as he could to get back to the area of the lights.

The Affytechans were waiting for them down in the bright, warm lighting of Deck 15, like an ambulatory garden of enormous and slightly pixilated flowers. "We've located the transport craft, sir," said the captain —the post seemed to have shifted to a stalky tubulate of blue and white. "Two Beta-class Telgorns with a capacity of a hundred and twenty apiece, in the Deck Sixteen portside landing bays." It saluted him smartly. "Dr. Breen here has been working on getting the schematics program repaired."

The former orange-and-yellow captain saluted as well. "Simple transposition of numbers, sir. Probably due to operator error. Easily fixed."

Dr. Breen?

"This way, sir."

"Even if you *are* able to pilot one, or both, transport craft, sir," protested Threepio hesitantly, "however will you prevent the defenses of the *Eye of Palpatine* itself from destroying them, as they destroyed our scout craft? You said yourself they had an almost human targeting capability. And for that matter, how in the galaxy are you going to get the Klaggs and the Gakfedds into the craft to take them off the ship? Or the Kitonaks?"

A little to Luke's surprise, they passed a small group of the stumpy, putty-colored aliens, shambling along the corridor at the top of the communicating gangway to Deck 16 with excruciating slowness, conversing in their soft, rambling burble of rumbles and whistles. Luke couldn't imagine coaxing the torpid creatures into the shuttlecraft or making them stay there once they'd arrived. And as for rounding up the tripods, or the Jawas . . .

"I don't know." He wondered how he'd managed to get himself elected savior to this ship of fools. "But if I'm going to destroy the ship before it attacks Belsavis, Threepio, I've got to get them off it somehow. I can't leave them. Not even the Jawas. Not even the—"

They turned a corner and Luke halted, shocked. The corridor before them, low-ceilinged and slung with the heavy barrels of one of the ship's main water-circ trunks, was strewn with the hacked and dismembered bodies of Affytechans. Ichor and sap smeared the walls and floor with pungent, sticky streams of green and yellow, speckled with spilled pollen and floating seed. Hacked limbs and trunks were scattered in a ghastly rainbow, as if someone had overturned a clothes basket of gaudy silks. Mouse-droids swarmed, and the whole corridor reeked of the Affytechans' sour, pungent musk.

The blue-and-white captain and his followers kept walking through the carnage as if there were nothing there. "You were right about making sure of the location of the transport, Major," the captain was saying. It stepped over most of the torso of what had been the magenta captain in the laundry room. "I've always liked the Beta-class Telgorn transport. Two or three of those, plus an escort of Blastboats, should take care of any minor trouble no matter what—"

Luke spun, ducked, and had his lightsaber in hand and bladed as the weighted end of a gaffe stick nearly took his head off. The four Sand People who'd sprung from the pump station behind him fell on him, howling. Luke slashed the first one clean through the body, shoulder to hip, and took the hands off a second as it was bringing its rifle to bear. Threepio bleated, "Master Luke! Master Luke!" as he was knocked over in the fray and lay against the wall where he'd been kicked. "Switch off!" Luke yelled and dropped the blade a split second before a third Tusken fired its blaster at him, the bolt whining off the concentrated core of laser light.

He lunged through a doorway, hitting the closer, which refused to work. The Sand People, joined by two more with others audible in full cry in the corridors beyond, sprang after. Luke levitated a worktable and hurled it at them, scrambled across the room to the opposite door and hit the opener—that, too, refused to work.

Luke cursed, ducked a roaring blaze of blaster fire and levitated the worktable to throw at them again. Someone else fired a blaster and the bolt whined sharply as it ricocheted around the room—it was a long shot and frequently didn't work, but Luke reached out with his mind and flicked the ricochet into the door mechanism, exploding it in a sizzle of sparks. The door jerked up about half a meter and Luke rolled under it, dragging his staff through after him and scrambling to his feet, limping and staggering away.

He seemed to be in the heart of the Sand People's hunting territory. Two more sprang at him, from opposite sides, pressing him back into a corner. He sliced and parried, flattened against the walls for support, then fled again, falling, rising, dragging himself painfully down the dark length of a corridor, while on either side ahead of him doors hissed shut and the hoarse, baying yowl of the Sand People echoed against the walls all around.

He flung himself around a corner and jerked back just in time to avoid being cut in half by a blast door smashing down; fled back, half recognizing the lights of what looked like a laundry drop, which would have a repair shaft behind it, only to have the room's door slam shut when he was a few meters away. He decapitated another Tusken that leaped on him from the open black doorway of what looked like a lounge, scrambled over the body and fled through, throwing himself, rolling, just in time to avoid being shut into that room by its suddenly activated door.

The corridor in which he found himself was very dark. Tiny orange worklights made a thin trail along one side of the ceiling. Gasping for breath, Luke dragged himself to his feet, leaned trembling on his staff, his leg hurting as if the ax that had smashed it were slamming again with each beat of his heart.

The Will, he thought. The lightsaber weighed heavy in his hand, unbladed but ready at a second's notice. It was only a matter of time before it steered him into another wired gangway, or back to the arms of the Sand People.

Their yowling broke out again, close by; a lot of them, by the sound. Luke scanned the corridor. Shut doors. No vents. No cover.

Then, halfway down, a door opened.

It didn't hiss and spring, as doors did. The laborious creaking was more characteristic of someone turning the manual crank. It cracked a jagged line of grimy orange emergency light perhaps thirty centimeters wide, and stopped.

Luke glanced at the blast wall that sealed one end of the corridor, the darkness at the other end, shrieking with the cries of the approaching Sand People. Between them himself, breathless, lamed, a sitting target . . .

And that uneven line of orange light.

And the sense of waiting that seemed to press on him from the darkness like the dense watchfulness of some unseen mind.

Yet strangely he felt no sense of dread.

He stepped closer. Through the opening he could see the blank-eyed dark consoles of one of the lower-level gunnery chambers, the semicircles of consoles, the glistening dark levers and somber shadow.

Silence now, but he knew, could feel, the Sand People coming near.

In that silence, very faintly, he thought he heard the almost-whispered thread of melody:

*"The Queen had a hunt-bird and the Queen had a lark,
The Queen had a songbird that sang in the dark. . . ."*

Luke glanced back over his shoulder at the darkness, then stepped, very quickly, through the door.

It slid shut.

For some moments the only sound that came to his ears was his own breathing, steadying as he caught his wind. Shadow clustered thick around him, hid the far end of the long room like an obscuring curtain. Then, dimly, on the other side of the door, the scratch of metal on metal, the swift-moving whisper of feet.

Luke braced his body against the nearest console and held his light-saber ready, still unilluminated, in his hand.

Dim with the muffling of the walls, he heard the harsh *gronch* of their voices, the crash of gaffe sticks against the other doors along the hall. Six of them at least. If the door before him were to open again he could probably kill two or three, but shooting through the door at him they'd have him. He looked around at the dark chamber. Even the chairs were bolted down.

The door in front of him rattled under blows, but held.

If the Will wanted it to open, something else prevented it from doing anything about it.

It occurred to Luke that the Will had effectively imprisoned him here. All it needed to do was not open the gun room door again—ever.

The silence returned, lengthened. The pain in Luke's leg increased, the deep internal burning of infection unmistakable now. Keeping his senses stretched, his mind forced to attention on the corridor, he opened the patch in the leg of his coverall and affixed a new dose of perigen, though his supply was running perilously low. Anything to keep the pain at bay, to free his concentration for the use of the Force. Exhaustion and perigen-suppressed fever made him dizzy. He realized it had been some time since he'd eaten or slept, and his hand, when he straightened up to lean on his staff again, trembled.

After a very long time, the door opened, again that narrow crack, again that labored, dragging motion, as if against the strength of the Will.

Luke listened, breathed, sending his senses out. Far off he could still smell the stench of the dead Affytechans, but no whiff of the Sand People. Aching, he limped toward the door, lightsaber still in hand.

Movement caught his eye. He startled, swinging around, but it was only his own reflection in the dark mirror of the nearest monitor screen. It stared back at him, scarred face, fair hair, the stained gray coverall of a Star Fleet mechanic.

And beside it, behind it, just past his shoulder, he saw another face. A woman's face, young, framed in a cloud of smoky brown hair like a thick-leaved tree in summer, the gray eyes looking into his.

He swung around sharply, but of course there was no one there.

Chapter 12

"What? Who is it?"

Leia prodded her husband's shoulder. "I told you you should have waited for her to call back." She turned back to the holo image of the woman in the field, fiery hair tousled, green eyes blinking into the dim glow of the lights on her end of the transmission. She wore a gold chain around her neck and a shirt Leia recognized as belonging to Lando Calrissian. "Mara, I'm sorry . . ."

"No, it's all right." Mara Jade rubbed her eyes with a quick gesture, and that seemed to take care of any residual sleepiness, as if she'd clicked off a switch. "I must look like one of the Nightsisters of Dathomir. What time is it where you are? What's up? Is there a problem?"

"We don't know, exactly," said Han. He shoved back the towel from his still damp hair. "We know we got a problem but we're not sure what it means. What can you tell us about Belsavis?"

"Ah." Mara settled back in the white leather of her chair, which shifted around her like a flower, drew up her long legs, and folded her hands around her knees. Her eyes narrowed, as if she watched something scrolling past on some inner readout screen: thought, memory, surmise.

"Belsavis," she said thoughtfully. "You find out what was there that the Empire thought was so important?"

"You mean the children of the Jedi?" asked Leia.

"Is that what it was?" Her dark brows lifted, then she thought about it, and a corner of her lip curved down, wry and speculative. "Makes sense. The file on it was closed when I started working for the Emperor, you see. Closed and sealed behind six kinds of security locks."

She shrugged. "Well, closed files always have the same effect on me. But in this case even when I broke into it I couldn't find out anything except that at the end of the Clone Wars there'd been some kind of secret mission whose target was one of the rift valleys on Belsavis. Security was so heavy that even the people who worked on it didn't know what was going on. If it was a move against the Jedi—against their families and children—I can see why they did it that way."

She was silent a moment, a small upright line between her brows as she called back to mind the old data. Beyond the metal shutters that blocked the orchard lights from the bedroom, Leia heard the sleepy trilling of pellata birds and manolliums among the trees, making one final stakeout of their territories before nestling down for the night. Chewie, smelling as only a damp Wookiee can smell, paused in brushing out his fur and growled softly.

"A fighter wing was sent to Belsavis, interceptors mostly, fast but light," said Mara after a time. "And a whole chain of remote-trigger relay stations was set up, mostly on satellites, or hidden ground stations; completely automated, but what it was they were supposed to activate or signal I never could find out. The mission file was cut to paper dolls. I gathered there was supposed to be a linkup with something that never arrived, something heavy. But later I got copies of some of the Emperor's private invoices, and there were millions paid out about that date to an engineer named Ohran Keldor . . ."

"I know about Ohran Keldor," said Leia softly. Even after all these years her body went hot at the thought of his name, as if a thousand needles were rising up through her skin. "He was a student of Magrody's, one of the designers of the Death Star. One of the teachers at the Omwat orbital platform that produced the rest of that design." Her hands trembled involuntarily and she tightened them hard; felt Han's swift, worried glance.

"That's him," said Mara. She regarded Leia for a time, her own thoughts hidden behind the cool mask of her face, but if she understood the hatred of one who has had her world destroyed, she made no comment, and Leia herself said nothing. Could say nothing.

"Same guy?" asked Han, a little too quickly, seeking to cover. "I mean, that was, what? Twenty years before they put the Death Star together . . ."

"Twenty years isn't that long," said Mara. "And Keldor was a boy genius back then, Magrody's best. Looking at the kind of thing he designed later—military and industrial both—I'd say the Emperor paid him to design a supership of some kind. That was back when they needed a vessel the size of a city to carry the blasting power they wanted. Whatever was on Belsavis, it looks like the Emperor didn't want anything breathing when the dust settled. Logically, it has to have been an installation, because of the firepower and because of the trade that started up later in xylen chips and gold wire, salvage goods; far too much to be just the gleanings of a battlefield. But I always wondered what kind of installation was so important that they'd go to that much trouble."

Han crossed his legs and pulled the dark-patterned native sarong he wore up to cover his knees. "But somebody dropped the ball."

Mara shrugged. "That part had been pulled out of the file, but it sounds like it, yes. The supership—or whatever it was that those automated relays were designed to summon—never arrived. Most of the relays were destroyed or lost, so somebody must have guessed what they were. The interceptors got mauled by a small planetary force, pretty badly by the sound of it. The file said 'subjects departed.' The officers in charge said they strafed everything in sight and did maximum damage with the weaponry available, but most of them were cashiered when they came home. A couple of high-ranking designers of artificial intelligence constructs and automated weapons systems were reassigned to places like Kessel and Neelgaimon and Dathomir . . ."

"Real vacation spots," murmured Han, who'd visited all three.

Mara's red mouth quirked in a small, chilly smile. "There are worse places. Ohran Keldor dropped out of sight for a while."

Chewbacca growled.

"Yeah," agreed Han, "I would have, too. But it looks like somebody reinstated him."

"That was probably Moff Tarkin," said Mara. "He was a man who never lost track of so much as a paper clip. He was in charge of the Omwat orbital and that's where Keldor showed up again, trying to work himself back onto the Emperor's good side."

She shook her head again, a look on her face that was half speculation, half wonderment. "So it was the Jedi and their families. No wonder he wanted the whole planet done."

She was silent for a time, and looking at her, Leia wondered suddenly if that was what had drawn Mara to the Emperor in the first place: that Palpatine, Force-strong as he was, had been the only one who could teach Mara, the only one like herself that she knew.

Having grown up herself with the knowledge that she was somehow just slightly different, without knowing how, Leia could understand that need. The need to have someone who understood.

"Nothing in the records about where those 'subjects' went?" she asked. The bitter heat in her chest had chilled, but her own voice still sounded like a recording in her ears. "Nothing about the group itself? How big it was? How many ships they had? What direction they took off in?"

The smuggler shook her head. "The file didn't even mention who and what they were. Just that they 'departed.'"

"So you went to Belsavis to see who they'd been?"

"Not exactly. But I was curious. I filed the whole thing away in my mind, but I kept an eye out for mention of the place. For a few years there was a lot of salvage running out of there: xylen chips, gold wire, polarized crystals, the kind of thing you'd see if an old base was being tapped. Rock ivory from antigrav units. Some old jewelry. I went there once, around the time of the Battle of Hoth, but Nubblyk the Slyte had a tight grip on the locals and I couldn't stay long enough to figure things out."

"Look familiar?" Solo fished the gleaming chip from his pocket. "The Slyte was making a good living off these, but the supply pinching out wasn't why he quit. You know what happened to him?"

Mara leaned forward a little to study the chip through the Holonet's shimmering transceiver field, then sat back with a long flash of white leg. "That's the stuff. You ever do the Belsavis Run, Han? There's a spot in the southern hemisphere that's far enough from any rift or vent to be atmospherically stable about the same time every twenty-four hours. The Corridor, it's called. Because of the storms and the ionization in the upper atmosphere they can't track anyone who's not coming down a charted beam. You come in high, drop fast, and run along close to the ice to one of the pads."

"I heard about the pads out on the ice," said Han.

Chewie rumbled a comment.

"Yeah," agreed Han. "Not something I'd want to do, either. I guess there's still one or two in operation."

"There were twelve or thirteen back then," said Mara. "Most were within a few kilometers of the rifts, about half of those near Pletwell . . . Plawal, they call the place now. I could look up the coordinates for you if it would help. Nubblyk started thermoblasting the pads right after the Clone Wars, when Brathflen and Galactic first came to the planet. He'd sound out geothermal fissures below the ice, tunnel down to them, then t-blast the pads within half a kilometer of the tunnel heads. That kept the people running the goods in and out through the Corridor dependent on Nubblyk, because only Nubblyk knew where the tunnel heads were. The Jedi." She shook her head again. "I'd never have guessed that."

Chewbacca stopped brushing his fur long enough to offer a nominal sum against odds that Bran Kemple had been one of the tunnel guides, and Mara said, "Not on your life."

Leia rested her hands on Han's damp, towel-wrapped shoulders. "And Drub McKumb was one of the guys who ran the Corridor."

"Drub McKumb?" Mara's usually cold expression relaxed into a grin at the memory of the man. "Is he still around? Yes, he was one of the Corridor runners. How's he . . . ?"

She saw the stillness in Han's face, and her eyes went cold and flat. "What happened?"

Han told her, and went on to outline his and Chewie's adventures underground. "They were smugglers, Mara," he said after a long—and somewhat expensive—silence on both ends of the Holonet transmission. "Whiphids, a Twi'lek, a Carosite, a couple of Rodians . . . local Mluki. Humans. They looked like they'd been down there years. Like Drub."

Mara swore: briefly, comprehensively, and filthily. Then for a time she sat in silence again, staring into the darkness beyond memory and time.

"Does it sound like anything you know about?" asked Leia. She came around and Han made room for her on his chair. "They didn't find any drugs in him."

"No," said Mara distantly. "They didn't use drugs."

"Who didn't?"

Mara didn't answer. Leia said, still more quietly, "Vader?" Again her skin grew hot, around a core of bitter ice. Her father. Luke's father.

No, she thought. Bail Organa had been her father.

The smuggler nodded, once. "Vader and Palpatine." She brought the words out, crisp and cold and without qualification, as if she knew nothing could make it easier. "They mostly did it with semisentients: Ranats, Avogui, Zelosian Aga, cidwen. They'd use them for enclosure guards in places where they needed stormtroopers for other work. Drug them with a hallucinogen like brain-jagger or Black Hole, something that worked on the fear/rage centers of the brain. They'd use the dark side of the Force to burn it into them, make it permanent, like a constant waking nightmare. They'd hunt and kill anything that came their way. Palpatine could drive them with his mind, call them or dismiss them . . . I don't know of anyone else that could calm them down."

"Would yarrock work?" Han put an arm around Leia's waist, felt her body rigid as wood. "To calm them? The healers on Ithor seem to think it would, though I don't know how Drub would get any in the tunnels."

Mara shook her head. "I don't know."

In the silence Artoo bleeped faintly from the door, to let them know the coffee and supper Leia had put in the heater were done. Nobody said a word and the little droid, evidently reading the atmosphere of the room, did not signal again.

"Thanks, Mara," said Han at length. "I owe you dinner when we get back to Coruscant. If you can get back with me on the coordinates of those pads it might help. Sorry about waking you up . . ."

"It beats being pulled out of bed by an airstrike."

"One more thing." Leia looked up suddenly. "You say you were keeping an eye on Belsavis. Did anybody from Palpatine's Court take refuge there after Coruscant fell? Anyone you know about?"

The woman who had been the Emperor's Hand settled back into her chair, running memories, rumor, recollection through her mind like bolts of colored ribbon, seeking some flaw or slub. In time she shook her head. "Not that I know about," she said. "But Belsavis isn't that far from the Senex Sector. That's practically a little Empire itself these days—the Garonnin family and the Vandrons and their kind always wanted it to be. Who were you thinking of?"

Leia shook her head. "I don't know," she said. "I just wondered."

"You okay?"

Leia turned sharply. She'd folded back one of the metal shutters to step out onto the balcony, and the diffuse light from the orchard fell in a muzzy bar into the room behind her, picking out the hard edge of Han's arm muscle, the sharp points of collarbone and shoulder, the small scar on his forearm. The dark print of the sarong he wore was like the black-on-black mottling of a trepennit's hide, lost in the shadows of the room.

She didn't answer. She wasn't sure what she could have said, and she'd long ago learned that lying to Han was impossible. In the sticky warmth of the night his hand, dry and cool from the air-conditioning of the house, was a welcome strength on her bare arm.

"Don't worry about Keldor." His hands went from her shoulders to her hair, gathering its auburn weight against his face. "Somebody'll find him one of these days. Same—"

She felt in the very slight flinch of his hand the swift cutting off of speech and thought midsentence. As if, she thought, he believed she didn't know. Hadn't been thinking the same.

"Same way someone found Stinna Draesinge Sha?" she asked. "And Nasdra Magrody . . . and his family? The way some . . . some so-called patriot from the New Alderaan movement came to me a month ago hinting there were people ready to foot the bill if I used my 'influence' to have Qwi Xux murdered? And all the rest of the list who were just 'following orders'?"

"I don't know about Qwi," said Han softly, naming the fragile genius whose mind had been manipulated into participating in the Death Star's design. "She always seemed to me more a victim than anything else even before what she went through later . . . but I've never talked to anyone who didn't think you had every right to take a shot at the rest of them."

"No." Leia sighed, feeling as if it had been years since she'd last relaxed enough to breathe. It was good beyond words to feel his arms around her, his body pressing into her back. "No. I don't have any right. Not if I'm the Chief of State. Not if I stand for doing things in accordance with the law. Not if I stand for everything that Palpatine was not. That's what hurts, I think. That it's what I want to do—and what I cannot let myself do—and everyone thinks I did it anyway. So why not do it?"

"But you didn't," Han told her gently. "And you know that, and I know that . . . and that's what counts. What's Luke always saying? *Be what you want to seem.*"

She pulled his arms more closely around her, closing her eyes and drifting in the scents of soap, and his flesh, and the thick, slightly sulfurous murk of the night. Had it been only that afternoon they'd stood on the tower? Seen the children of the Jedi playing around the grille that covered Plett's Well? Felt the lost peace, the stillness of those other days, rising around them like the warmth of a long-forgotten sun?

Very low, she said, "I have dreams, Han; dreams where I'm hunting through all those rooms on the Death Star, running through corridors, opening doors, looking behind hatches, searching all the lockers, because there's something somewhere, some key, that will turn off the destructor beams. I dream that I'm running down the hallways with—with whatever it is—clutched in my hand, and if I can just make it to the Ignition Chamber in time, just do the right thing, I'll save them. I'll switch off the beam and be able to go home."

His grip tightened around her, holding her fast against his body. He knew she had dreams. He'd waked her up from them, and held her against his chest while she cried, too many times to count. She felt the breath of his lips move the hair at the crown of her head. "There was nothing you could have done."

"I know. But at least once a day I think: *I couldn't save them, but I can make those who did it pay.*" She turned in his arms, looking up at him in the misty apricot light. "Would you do it?"

Han grinned down at her. "Like a shot. But I'm not the Chief of State."

"Would you do it to please me?"

He laid his hand along her cheek, leaned down to kiss her lips. He said softly, "No. Not even if you asked."

He led her inside. As he stopped to close the shutters behind them, Leia paused by the room's small table, where a half dozen shallow cakes of colored wax floated in a great glass bowl of water. She flicked the switch on the long stem of the lighter, touched in turn each wick. The drifting lights painted wavery circles of amber and daffodil on the ceiling and walls. Her eyes met Han's over the floating candle flames; she let slip the shawl she'd worn over her shoulders, and held out to him her hand.

They wouldn't let her sleep.

They kept coming into the steel-walled cell, asking her questions, threatening her—telling her this person had told them this, that person had told them that. That she had been betrayed, that everything was known, that her father had been working for the Empire all along, that those she trusted had sold her out . . . that she would be lobotomized and taken to one of the barracks pleasure houses . . . tortured . . . killed. She'd tried to keep her mind on the Death Star plans, on the threat to the Senate, on the danger to hundreds of planets rather than on her own terror . . .

No, Leia whispered, trying to surface from the drowning, breathless horror of the dream. *No . . .*

Then the door of the detention cell had slipped open with its evil hissing sound, and Vader had been standing there, Vader huge and black and terrible, surrounded by stormtroopers. And behind him, darker, shinier, more evil still, the black smooth floating bulk of the Torturer . . .

"No!"

She tried to scream but could manage no more than a gasp. Nevertheless it woke her, to darkness, and the faint, sinister whirring of a droid's engine, and the moving glint of red lights in the dark.

There was another noise, thin and steady, a half-familiar whining . . .

The overload alarm on a blaster?

"Artoo?"

Leia sat up in bed, confused and panicky and wondering if it was a dream, if the terrible sense of evil was something left over from her nightmare. Across the room a faint, hissing zap sounded, and the white light of Artoo-Detoo's electric cutting beam illuminated the round, blocky form of the little droid visible beyond the foot of the bed. A second alarm began to sound. It was unnaturally dark in the room; Leia hadn't even begun to sort out why when Han flinched and turned beside her, and she heard the door of the small wall cupboard slide shut.

The sound of the blaster overload alarms grew immediately muffled.

She felt rather than saw Han reach for the holster that hung beside the bed, and at the same moment, the white glare of Artoo's cutting beam illuminated, like a tableau, the droid and the corner of the room by the cupboard as he neatly fused the lock.

"What the . . . ?"

She hit the light switch by the bed. Nothing happened. In a panic of confusion her mind reached out, groped for the candles that had illuminated the room earlier with such soft, romantic light. Luke had taught her . . .

Fire sprang to life again on the floating wicks.

"You crazy little . . ." Han strode across the room to where Artoo had definitely posted himself in front of the cupboard door. Muffled and shrill, the fast pulse beat of the alarms was rising; Leia reached for the hideout blaster where Han usually kept it under the pillow and found nothing. In the same instant, it seemed, Artoo swung around and pointed his cutting torch in Han's direction. The white bolt of electricity leaped out; Han sprang backward, barely avoiding it. In the dim saffron glow his eyes were suddenly wide.

Han and Leia both looked toward the windows. The shuttering mechanism was a fused blob of metal.

"Artoo!" cried Leia, confused and suddenly scared.

Outside the bedroom doors Chewbacca roared, and the door rattled in its sliders. With startling speed Artoo darted for the door, the electric cutter extended; Han yelled, "Let go of the handle, Chewie!" a split second before the droid put several thousand volts into the metal handle, then swung back, cutter still zapping hot, short jolts of blue-white lightning. Han, who in addition to shouting his warning had made a plunge for the cupboard, backed hastily, the droid following him for half a meter or so.

"Dammit, what the hell do you think you're doing?"

A substitution? thought Leia crazily, catching the pillows from the bed and circling in the other direction. When he'd run away from her on the way to the MuniCenter . . . ? That was insane. She *knew* it was Artoo.

Artoo backed against the cupboard again, his welding arm held out, the live end of it gleaming dangerously in the candlelight. Almost inaudible in the cupboard the blasters' double whine scaled upward, an insect-like warning of an explosion that would certainly destroy most of the house.

"Leia, put your boots on," said Han, pulling his own free of the corner and hauling them swiftly onto his feet.

She dropped her load of pillows and obeyed without question. There couldn't be more than a minute or so left. They were sealed in the room.

. . . Chewie was hammering on the outer door with something but it was clearly going to take more time than they had.

Looking a little ridiculous—he wasn't wearing much besides the boots—Han crossed the bed in two strides to her side. He turned his body, for a moment blocking the droid's view of his hand as he pointed to her the thing he wanted her to use; she understood his plan by the thing's very nature. She wanted to say, *Not Artoo . . .* but didn't.

There was something appallingly, hideously wrong, but there was no time to figure out what or how or why.

Not Artoo . . .

Han was already moving in on the little droid. He had a blanket in one hand, as if he planned to use it to smother the electric charge of the welder. The droid stood still, guarding the locked cupboard where the blasters were screaming into the final stages of overload, but fairly vibrated with deadly readiness.

Leia thought, *He hasn't made a sound . . .*

Han struck. Artoo lunged at him, lightning leaping forth, and in that instant Leia scooped the water basin, candles and all, from the table and hurled it with all the strength she could summon at the droid. Han was already leaping back with the hair-trigger reflexes of a man who has lived all his life on his nerve ends, and the vast drench of water doused and grounded the electrical discharge of Artoo's cutting tool in a sizzling, horrible spatter of blue light and spraying sparks. Smoke and lightning poured from the droid's open hatch, small threads of blue electricity leaping and twitching as Artoo gave one frantic, despairing scream. Han sprang in past him, driving one insulated boot sole through the thin wood of the cupboard door and digging out the blasters. It all seemed to happen in the space of one second and Leia thought, *If Artoo's welded the power cells into the triggers they'll blow up in his hand . . .*

A ridiculous consideration, she thought—the explosion would kill both of them and Chewie as well . . .

Han ripped the power cores out of both blasters and hurled the stripped weapons across the room onto the bed, where Leia buried them under pillows. The triggering blast—without the power that would have vaporized everything in the room—was like a violent hiccup, the kick of some huge, fierce, sullen thing under the bedding.

An instant later, with a rending crash, Chewbacca smashed his way through the bedroom door.

For a moment there was stillness, Han standing beside the cupboard, staring down at the two blaster power cores that lay hissing in the puddled water around his feet.

The room was filled with the stench of burning feathers and scorched insulation.

Chewie looked at Artoo, bowed forward, blackened by the electrical discharge, motionless and dead. Then he moaned, a long animal howl, grieving his friend.

Chapter 13

In addition to cutting all the power in the house, Artoo had fused the comlinks. Chewbacca had to venture forth into the steamy fog of the night to bring Jevax a report of what had taken place. The Chief Person returned to the house with him, concerned and shaken—he had been awake, he said, at the MuniCenter, trying to raise communication with the nearby valley of Bot-Un, whose comm center had gone out for the fifth time in six months.

"I don't understand it," the old Mluki said, looking from the ruin of fried bedding to the charred, motionless droid, upon whom Han was grimly affixing a restraining bolt. "The pump stations and the mechanical feeders, yes—we're still very much a shoestring operation in some ways, whatever the corporate brass likes to say. Most of our equipment *is* secondhand, and quite frankly pretty old. But your Artoo unit—"

"Wait a minute." Leia had removed her boots by this time and wrapped herself in a darkly patterned crimson-and-black local kimono, her hair hanging in a burnished mass down her back. She'd spent the past fifteen minutes locating every glowrod and emergency power-celled panel in the house, even retrieving the candles from the watery mess on the floor. "Are you telling me programming failures like this are common?"

"Not common." The Mluki's eyes met hers frankly under the heavy ridge of brow. "But every now and then a tree feeder will go mildly amok and wander through the streets squirting nutrient at passersby. Or one of the ice walkers will start hiking away across the glaciers, forcing its passengers to bail out and walk back to the valley. Most people who have business out on the glaciers—who're traveling to Bot-Un or Mithipsin, for instance—pack thermal suits and distress signals as a matter of course."

He spread his white-furred hands, and the silver in his ears glinted as he tilted his head. "Personally—though I'm not a mechanic—I suspect it's the result of doming the valley. It was always pretty damp here, but enclosing the valley has made it more so, and the pumping stations can't eliminate or neutralize all the corrosive gases that rise out of the vents at the bottom end of the rift. They've never reported mechanical problems like this in Bot-Un."

"But it's not a mechanical problem," argued Leia. "It's a programming fault . . ."

"Well, that's what the mechanics here say." Jevax scratched his head. "But the programmers swear it's mechanical."

They would, thought Leia late the following morning, as she watched Chewbacca poke around in Artoo-Detoo's mechanical innards in a hissing sizzle of sparks. She had yet to meet a programmer who'd admit that untoward results weren't universally attributable to either hardware failure or operator error. Even Qwi Xux honestly and sincerely believed to this day that the Death Star would have made a wonderful mining instrument.

And yes, the air in the Plawal Rift was extraordinarily damp, plastering Leia's dark linen shirt to her arms and back as she leaned on the railing of the terrace where Han and the Wookiee were working to take advantage of the daylight—Jevax's promised engineers had yet to arrive to repair power in the house and completely unstick the welded shutters. If they worked on anything like the MuniCenter's schedules, thought Leia, they wouldn't see them until the packing plants shut down for the night again.

And yes, secondhand machinery not designed specifically for work in hyperdamp climates did develop the occasional flutter.

But presumably the mechanics would install dehumidifier packs in everything—they were certainly present in all the kitchen's quaintly old-fashioned blenders and choppers. And Artoo had spent considerable time in the marshes of Dagobah without becoming homicidal, a restraint of which Leia wasn't sure *she* would be capable, after hearing Luke's account of that green, snake-ridden world.

As her old nanny had phrased it, something about it all just didn't listen right to her.

Whatever programmers said, thought Leia, perching herself on the stone rail of the balcony, a "mechanical flaw" might possibly account for Artoo's running amok and trundling off the path into the trees . . . but by no stretch of the imagination could it cause him to perform a complicated series of specific activities like closing doors, sealing locks, crossing wires within wall panels and blasters.

It was definitely Artoo: The serial numbers on his main block and motivator housing matched. Chewbacca—his arms and shoulders crisscrossed with strips shaven in his fur and synthflesh patched in beneath but otherwise little the worse for the events in the caverns last night— hadn't found any kind of relay mechanism inserted into Artoo's motivators that would have given him instructions from the outside.

And in any case, when would such a thing have been installed? He hadn't been out of Leia's sight last night for more than a few moments, and for part of that time she'd heard him moving.

"So whaddaya think?" Han wiped his fingers on an already unspeakable rag.

Chewbacca pushed back his eyeshades and groaned noncommittally. The Wookiee had reassembled the engines of the *Millennium Falcon* when they'd been in worse shape than this and the thing had flown; Leia, regarding the loose piles of wire and cable still spread around the stone flagging of the terrace, had her doubts.

Artoo rocked a little on his base and managed a faint, reassuring cheep.

"What did you think you were . . . ?" began Han, and Leia reached over to touch his shoulder, stopping further words. Artoo had to be feeling utterly wretched already.

"Can you tell us about it?" she asked gently.

Artoo rocked harder, swiveled his top, and beeped pleadingly.

"Can *he* tell us about it?" demanded Han. "*I* can tell you about it! He tried to kill us!"

The droid emitted a thin, despairing wail.

"It's all right," said Leia. She knelt beside Artoo, touched the droid on the join of base pivot and body, disregarding her husband's muttered commentary. "I'm not mad at you, and I won't let anything happen to you." She glanced over her shoulder at Han and Chewie, a sinister-enough-looking pair, she supposed, leaned against the stone railing with their arms full of drills and grippers. "What happened?"

All Artoo's lights went out.

Leia turned back to Chewie, who had pushed his welding goggles back onto his high forehead. "Are you sure you got his wiring back the way it's supposed to be?"

"Hey, he works, doesn't he?" retorted Han.

Leia stepped back while Chewbacca knelt and went to work again. Though not much of a mechanic—Luke had taught her to break and reassemble a standard X-wing engine in a pinch, and on a good day she could even identify portions of the *Falcon*'s drive system—Leia had the impression the Wookiee was redoing some of the repairs he'd done half an hour ago. But Han and Chewie, like Luke, were mechanics, and thought in terms of mechanical failure.

She found herself wondering if there was a way of getting in touch with Cray Mingla.

It occurred to her that she had heard nothing from Luke or any of his party in days.

Something moved in the orchard below. A bright-yellow manollium burst out of the ferns like a startled flower and went winging away through the trees, and Leia—who had never lost the watchfulness of those years on the run between the battles of Yavin and Endor—looked automatically for what had startled it.

She didn't see much, but it was enough. A ghostlike impression of movement faded at once into the mist, but there was no mistaking the white gown, the night-black tail of hair. From the balcony behind her Han's voice said, "I never asked you last night, Leia—you find anything in the city records?"

"Yes," said Leia briefly, swinging herself over the balcony rail and dropping lightly the meter and a half to the thick ferns below. "I'll be back. . . ."

In the mist it was impossible to see more than a few meters clearly. Tree stems, vines, beds of shrub and fern made dim, one-dimensional cutouts in the glassy grayness. Half closing her eyes, Leia reached out with her senses, as Luke had been teaching her to do, and picked up the

subliminal stir of fabric among leaves, the squish of wet foliage underfoot
. . . the trace of perfume.

Her hand moved automatically to check for the blaster usually hol-
stered at her side, even as she moved in pursuit. Nothing there, of course.
Still she didn't turn back. Not swiftly, but steadily, she worked to keep up
with the woman whose face she'd seen under the lamplight of the path
through the orchard last night.

She remembered now where she'd seen her before.

She'd been eighteen, newly elected the youngest member of the Imperial Senate. It was customary among the old Houses to bring their daughters to Coruscant when they emerged from finishing school at seventeen—
or sixteen, if their parents were ambitious to start the long and elaborate
jockeying for a good match at Court. Her aunts, she remembered, had
been horrified when she'd refused, doubly appalled when her father had
backed her up in her decision not to be presented to the Emperor until
she could do so as a Senator in her own right, not simply as a young girl in
the Court marriage market . . .

She wondered what they'd think now, those aunts, if they could see
her married to a man who'd started life as a smuggler, whose parents had
been nobody-knew-who. If they could see her as Chief of State, after years
of dodging around the galaxy in the company of a ragged gang of idealis-
tic warriors with a price on her head.

She honestly didn't know whether they would have been aghast or
proud. When she was eighteen, she hadn't known them well; hadn't
known them as an adult knows other adults.

And they had all died before she could.

She stepped from among the trees of the orchard. The white dress
was at the far end of Old Orchard Street, moving swiftly. Heading for the
market square, Leia thought.

For a long time she'd tried not to know whether it had been day or
evening in the capital of Alderaan when the Death Star had appeared in
the sky. Somebody had eventually told her that it had been a warm
evening late in the spring. Aunt Rouge had undoubtedly been having her
hair dressed for dinner in front of that gilt-framed mirror in her boudoir;
Aunt Celly would have been lying down indulging in her daily bout of
hypochondria, and Aunt Tia would have been reading aloud to her or
talking baby talk to the pittins. Leia even remembered the pittins' names:
Taffy, Winkie, Fluffy, and AT-AV—"All-Terrain Attack Vehicle." She'd

named that last one. It had been pale candy pink and small enough to fit in her cupped hands.

The pittins had all died, too, when somebody had pulled that lever on the Death Star.

And everything else had died as well.

Everything else.

Leia gritted her teeth as she moved along the steep slant of the street, keeping close to the jumble of old walls and prefab shops, fighting the sting behind her eyes and the dreadful tightness of her throat. Her aunts had made her girlhood an intermittent burden, but they'd deserved better than that.

It had been her father who had presented her to the Emperor—in the Senate rotunda, as junior representative of Alderaan. She remembered as if it were yesterday the evil dark eyes peering like a lizard's from that desiccated face in the black hood's shadow. But her aunts were the ones who had insisted on taking her to the levee at the palace that night.

That was where she'd seen this woman—this girl.

She herself had been eighteen, clothed in the spare, formal white of Senatorial office, as her father had been. There had been few other Senators there, and the crowd in the pillared hall had been an autumnal flower bed of dull golds and bronzes, plum and dark green. Among the usual courtiers, the sons and daughters of Governors and moffs and the scions of the ancient, aristocratic Houses, whose parents were trying to arrange alliances, Leia had noticed a half dozen women of truly startling beauty, exquisitely gowned and jeweled like princesses, who did not seem to belong with either the bureaucrats' wives or the more elite groups of the old Houses and their vassals. She'd asked Aunt Rouge about them and had gotten a very superior, "Whom the Emperor wishes to invite is of course his business, Leia dear; but one is not obligated to speak with them."

Leia had realized they were the Emperor's concubines.

This woman—this girl—had been one of them.

Leia was catching her up. The woman glanced behind her as she threaded swiftly through the barrows of vegetables, jewelry, cosmetics, and scarves in the market square, like a small fish hoping to lose a larger one among bright-colored rocks. She began to run, and Leia ran after her, dodging vendors and shoppers and the occasional lines of antigrav wagons on their way in from the orchards. The woman—who must be only a few years older than she, Leia thought—ducked down an alley, and Leia ran on past its mouth, then doubled down the narrow lane beyond. The houses around the marketplace were old, built on the sunken foundations and lower stories of the original dwellings of the town; Leia descended a short flight of steps at a silent run, dodged through the squat pillars of what had once been a hot-spring hall and was now a sort of open cellar under the gleaming white prefab of the upper house, knee-deep in swirling ground mist and smelling faintly of sulfur and kretch. At the far side she sprang up into the alley again.

The woman had concealed herself behind a stack of packing crates and was watching the mouth of the alley to see if Leia was going to come back that way. She was still slender and small, almost childlike, as she had been eleven years ago. Her exquisite oval face was unlined, her slanted black eyes unmarred by wrinkles—Leia remembered inconsequentially Cray's vast catalog of such products as Slootheberry Wrinkle Creme and Distilled Water of Moltokian Camba-Fruit designed to preserve such perfection. The black hair that hung down her back in a heavy tail ringed with bronze—the hair that had been piled into the elaborate, masklike headpiece at the Emperor's levee—was untouched by gray.

All the way from the house in the orchard, Leia had been trying to recall the woman's name, and as she stepped from between the lava pillars and up into the alley she finally did. "Roganda," she said, and the woman spun, her hand going to her lips in shock. In the drifting, shadowless mists it was hard to see her eyes, but after a moment the woman Roganda Ismaren stepped forward and sank into a deep curtsy at Leia's feet.

"Your Highness."

Leia hadn't heard her voice before. Aunt Rouge had seen to that. It was soft, and pitched rather high, with a lisping, childish sweetness.

"I beg of you, Highness, don't betray me."

"To whom?" asked Leia practically, and gestured for her to rise. The old hand movement, drilled into her by her aunts' deportment teachers, came easily, a whisper from the dead past.

Roganda Ismaren wasn't the only one in danger of betrayal here. Leia and Han would probably find themselves far less able to pursue their investigations—if there was in fact anything to investigate—were it known who they were.

Roganda got to her feet, the hem of her gown stirring the mists that drifted up from the old house foundations, the lower end of the moss-grown street. "Them." She nodded toward the bustling noises of the market, half invisible in the fog, and her gesture took in the stone foundations of the houses around them, the patched-in white cubes with their terraces, their trellises, their steps. Her every movement still retained the implicit beauty of a trained dancer's. Like Leia, she had been well taught how to carry herself.

"Anyone in this town. The Empire laid it to the ground not too long ago, and even those who came in afterward have cause to hate even the unwilling servants of the Emperor."

Leia relaxed a little. The woman was unarmed, unless she had a dagger or an extremely small blaster under that simple white linen gown, and the liquid drape of the fabric made even that unlikely. As Palpatine's concubine, Roganda would have found herself very much in the crossfire between the Emperor's enemies and his friends. Leia wondered how she'd gotten out of Coruscant.

"This place has been my refuge, my safety, for seven years now," Roganda continued softly. She clasped her hands in a gesture of pleading. "Don't force me out, to seek another home."

"No," said Leia, embarrassed, "of course not. Why did you pick this place to come to?"

She was thinking only of the Emperor's levee, of the jeweled headpiece Roganda had worn, massy gold and layered with a galactic dazzle of topaz, ruby, citrine; remembering the elaborate bunches of shimmersilk skirts, held in swags and volutes with gemmed plaques the size of her palm; the chains of jewels, fine as embroidery thread, dangling row on row from the curved golden splendor of her concubine collar. Roganda's hair had been augmented and amplified by swags of lace, swatches of silk in every shade of gold and crimson, her small white hands a glory of scintillant rings.

But Roganda hesitated, seemed to draw back. "Why do you ask?" Then, quickly, "It was out of the way. . . . No one knew of it, no one would look for me here. Neither the Rebels from whom I fled when I left Coruscant, nor the warlords who tried to take it back. I wanted only peace."

She gave a shy smile. "Since you've come this far, will you come to my rooms?" Roganda gestured back along the alley. "They aren't elegant—

you can't pay for much elegance on a fruit packer's wages—but I do pride myself on my coffee. The one remnant of earlier glories."

The coffee served at the Emperor's levee was one of the things that had stayed in Leia's mind. The Emperor had had special farms on a number of suitable worlds to provide the beans solely for the use of his Court, including several that produced vine-coffee, a variety notoriously hard to rear. The transition to this provincial town among its orchards couldn't have been an easy one.

"Another time," she said, shaking her head. "Surely there were other places you could have gone?"

"Few as out of the way as this." Roganda half smiled, and brushed aside the tendrils of dark hair that trailed across her brow. Her complexion was the clear, pallorous white of those who live without sunlight, on starships, or underground, or on worlds like this where the only thin sunlight that leaked down through the mists had to be magnified by the crystal of the dome.

"Even smugglers rarely bother anymore. I knew I wasn't going to be welcomed in the Republic—*his* name was too hated, and those who haven't been . . . coerced, as he could coerce . . . would not understand that there was no question of refusing him."

Leia remembered what Luke had told her of his days serving the Emperor's clone, and shuddered.

"And as for going to the worlds, the cities, still under the rule of the Governors and the new warlords, or the worlds where the old Houses still hold sway . . ."

She shivered, as if chill winds blew down the alley instead of the dense warmth of the drifting fogs. "He lent me to too many of them . . . as a gift. All I wanted to do was . . . forget."

"What were you doing outside the house?"

"Waiting for you," said Roganda simply. "For a chance to speak to you alone. I recognized you last night, when your droid malfunctioned. . . . I hope you got it back to the path without mishap? I almost came down to help you, but . . . on other worlds where I thought to take refuge, I've had bad experiences with those who remembered me from the Emperor's Court. And I admit I was . . . unhappy enough to do some foolish things in those days."

She averted her face, twisting on her finger the small topaz ring that was probably the only jewel she had left of those days. Maybe, thought Leia, the only thing left unsold after her passage here had been paid. Her hand was still white and small and fragile as a cage-reared bird.

"I lost my nerve," she concluded, not meeting Leia's eyes. "Then last night I began to fear that you had recognized me. That you might speak of it to your husband, and he to others here. I . . . I made up my mind to come to you in private. To beg for your silence."

A bright drift of music keened from the market as the jugglers started setting up their pitches. A busker cried, "Step right up, ladies'an'gennelmens . . . three turns and turn 'em over . . ." Somewhere Leia heard the dim, skeletal clatter of a mechanical tree feeder being walked out of a repair shop back to the orchards, and a musical Ithorian voice sang, "Fresh tarts! Fresh tarts! Podon and brandifert, sweetest in town . . ." while high overhead the vast, flower-decked gondolas of the silk and coffee beds glided along their tracks, lifting and lowering, silent as birds beneath the crystal of the dome.

"But you didn't."

Roganda looked down at her hands again, turning her ring. "No," she said. Her long black lashes trembled. "I can't . . . explain, exactly. I've been so afraid for so long. It's hard to explain to someone who hasn't been through what I've been through."

She raised pleading eyes to Leia's, darkness and old memories shimmering in them like unshed tears. "Sometimes it seems I'll never cease being afraid. The way it seems some nights that I'll never cease having nightmares about *him,* for as long as I live."

"It's all right." Leia's voice sounded gruff and awkward in her own ears, shaky with the memory of her own nightmares. "I promise I won't betray you to those who live here."

"Thank you." Her voice was barely a whisper. Then she smiled tremulously. "You're sure you won't have coffee with me? I make it rather well."

Leia shook her head. "Thank you," she said, and smiled back. "Han will be wondering where I've gone." She started back for the market square, then turned, remembering something else. Something her aunt Celly had whispered to her in a corner when Aunt Rouge was over lecturing the head of the House Elegin about the proper deportment of its scions . . .

"Roganda . . . didn't you have a son?"

Roganda looked quickly away. Her voice was almost inaudible under the musical chatter of the market. "He died."

Turning swiftly, she vanished into the mist, the white swirl of it absorbing her like a white-robed ghost.

Silent in the narrow alleyway, Leia recalled the day the Rebels had taken Coruscant. The Emperor's palace—that endless, gorgeous maze of crystal roofs, hanging gardens, pyramids of green and blue marble shining with gold . . . summer quarters, winter quarters, treasuries, pavilions, music rooms, prisons, halls . . . grace-and-favor residences for concubines, ministers, and trained assassins—had been shelled hard and partially looted already, Rebel partisans having killed whichever members of the Court they could catch. These had included, if Leia remembered correctly, not only the President of the Bureau of Punishments and the head of the Emperor's School of Torturers, but the court clothing designer and any number of minor and completely innocent servants of all ages, species, and sexes whose names had never even been reported.

As Leia walked back across the market square she thought, *No wonder she was twisting her hands in fear.*

And stopped, to be cursed at by the driver of a puttering mechanized barrow of cheap shoe kits from Jerijador, but she hardly noticed. She was seeing, suddenly, the topaz ring on Roganda's hand—a hand smaller even than her own, childlike, *and completely innocent of either bandages, small cuts, or purple stains.*

"You can't pay for much elegance on a fruit packer's wages . . ."

Oso Nim's old pal Chatty had had at least three bandages on his fingers. So had half the clientele of the Smoking Jets and most of the people she passed in the market. Bandages on their fingers, and purple hands—or red, or yellow, depending on whether they were packing bowvine, brandifert, lipana, or vine-coffee . . . And podon and slochan were sturdy enough to be packed by droids.

Leia found herself wondering, as she walked quickly back toward the house on Old Orchard Street, what would have happened to her if she'd gone with Roganda to her rooms for coffee.

Chapter 14

Who are you?

The words glowed in amber silence in the almost-darkness of the quartermaster's office on Deck 12. Somewhere in the distance a sweet, complex humming echoed in the labyrinth of corridors and rooms: the Talz singing in their hidden enclave of junior officers' staterooms. Threepio, before he'd shut down, had tried to tap into the Will on this terminal and had reported that though power still functioned in some of its circuits, cable-greedy Jawas had torn out the computer connections somewhere up the trunk line.

Perhaps, thought Luke, that was one reason he felt instinctively safe here.

The far-off wailing halted, then resumed with transmuted rhythm. Even the air circulators were silent. The rooms smelled of Jawas, Talz, the vanilla whiff of the Kitonaks clumped like podgy mushrooms at the end of the corridor, chatting endlessly in their soft, squeaking voices. Luke gazed into the onyx well of the screen and felt suddenly tired unto death.

Who are you?

He felt that he already knew.

The word swam up out of the depth, whole, not letter by letter—as if it had existed there for a long time.

>Callista<

His breath paused. He hadn't actually thought this would work.

Then, >She's all right. They haven't harmed her. Not beyond what she'd take in a rough training session<

Relief was a flood of sensation so violent it was almost like a headache, release bordering on physical pain.

Thank you, typed Luke. He was struck by the absolute bald inadequacy of the words on the screen; something you'd say to someone who moved a chair out of your way when your hands were full. Nothing to do with the interrogator droids in the Detention Area; nothing to do with the bruises on Cray's face, or the dead, bitter look in her eyes. Nothing to do with the Gamorreans holding the screaming Jawa over the shredder.

"Thank you," he whispered aloud, to the no-longer-quite-empty darkness of the room. "Thank you."

>They're on Deck 19, in the starboard maintenance hangar. They've dismantled half a dozen TIEs to make their village—or Mugshub has, anyway. It's the sows who do all the work<

There was a pause.

>Fortunate, since the boars are about as smart as the average cement extruder and aren't good for much besides getting into fights and making little Gamorreans<

Can you get me up there?

>I can take you to the cargo lift shaft they're using as a communications tunnel. They've got it booby-trapped and guarded. Can you levitate?<

Yes. I've been—

>You don't have to keyboard, you know. Internal Surveillance had every room and corridor on this ship wired. Charming people<

"I've been using perigen for my leg," said Luke, still looking at the screen, as if it were a wall or a blacked-out window behind which she dwelled. "It's beginning to interfere a little with my concentration, but I can manage." Even as he said it he shivered. In addition to the painkiller's eventual side effect of reduced concentration, fatigue, exhaustion, and the slow grind of constant pain were eroding still more his ability to manipulate the Force. The thought of self-levitating over a lift shaft hundreds of meters deep was an unnerving one.

Again he asked, meaning it differently, "Who are you?"

She didn't reply. After a very long time, more amber words appeared on the screen.

>The droid with her, the droid with the living eyes—What is he? What is this? Is this a new sort of creature Palpatine thinks he can use? What is this, that's happening between them?<

"Palpatine's dead." Laser light showing up the Emperor's bones within his flesh . . . The pain in his own bones, his own flesh, destroying him. Darth Vader's voice . . .

He pushed the images from his mind. "The Empire has broken into six, maybe ten major fragments, ruled by warlords and Governors. The Senate's in control of Coruscant and most of the Inner Rim. A New Republic has been established and is growing strong."

The screen wiped dark for a moment. Then, spreading and flashing across it, a growing design, a dancing spiral geometry of outflung joy. Her joy, Luke realized. The essence, the heart of what he himself had felt in that tree village on Endor's green moon, when he knew that the first terrible hurdle had been cleared.

Music by someone who no longer had a voice.

The joy-dance of the bodiless.

Triumphal delight and utter thanks.

We won, we won! I died but we won!

If she had been here, he knew, she would have flung herself into his arms.

Like Triv Pothman, she'd been waiting a long time.

What she said was, >You have made this worth it for me<

The designs whirled themselves across every screen in the room and then away, like a ring of dancing waves moving outward.

Luke said softly, "Almost."

Another long pause. >98%<

He knew it was half jesting, and he laughed.

>You're Master Luke? Is Calrissian your real name?<

"Skywalker," he said. "Luke Skywalker."

He was conscious of the silence implicit in the suddenly black screen.

"Anakin's son," he added quietly. "It was Anakin who killed Palpatine."

There was nothing on the screen still, but as if he looked into another person's eyes, he sensed the changing tides of her thought, the wondering contemplation of the vagaries of time.

>Tell me<

"Another time," said Luke. "What happened to this vessel? This mission? What started it again? How long do we have?"

>How long we have I don't know. I am . . . side by side with the Will, but there are things of the Will that I do not and cannot touch. Thirty years I have existed so. I managed to cripple the receptors, and before coming here, damaged or destroyed most of the slaved autoactivation relays that would have triggered the computer's core from a distance. The components of the relay were crashed, shattered, destroyed; no one could have found them to activate this station by that means, but there still remained the danger the station could have been activated manually. That's why I . . . stayed<

"Then I was right." Luke felt his scalp prickle. "I knew it, sensed it . . . those guns weren't fired by a mechanical. On a ship this size—"

>No. I was the one firing the guns. That's where I've been all these years. In the gunnery computers. I was sure you were the Empire's agent. Before you came on board there was no one, nor is there anyone on board save yourself, and the aliens the landers brought in after the Will was activated again<

"I don't understand," said Luke. "If no one came on until the Will was activated . . ."

>It was the Force. I felt it, sensed it . . . The broken activation relays were set off, all of these years later, by the use of the Force<

Luke was shocked silent, the neat amber letters like a hammer blow hitting him over the heart.

"The *Force*?" He leaned closer, as if to touch her arm, her hand . . . "That's impossible."

>Yes, I know it is<

"The Force can't affect droids and mechanicals."

>No, it can't<

Luke thought about that for a time, about what it meant or could mean. Ithor came back to him, and the cold flood of dread as he'd sat in semitrance at Nichos's side, the sense of something terribly wrong. The wave of darkness spreading outward, reaching, searching . . . The random numbers that had led him here—the dream of some terrible attack creeping stealthily through the desert night.

"But why? Why bomb Belsavis now? There's nothing there."

Nothing except Han and Leia and Chewie and Artoo. Nothing except thousands of innocent people—and the usual handful of the not-so-innocent. And Han and Leia hadn't arrived there yet, when he'd felt that first dark surge. To his knowledge nobody had known they were going.

"All personnel, report to your section lounge." The computer's voder contralto broke abruptly into his thoughts. "All personnel, report to your section lounge. Abstention or avoidance will be construed as . . ."

>Better go< flashed the orange letters on the screen.

>Can't let your actions be construed as sympathetic to the ill intent of the etcetera. Watch your back<

For that moment he could almost see her grin.

- The Imperial Military Code Section 12-C classifies as capital offenses, among others: Incitement to mutiny against duly constituted authority; participation in mutiny; concealing known or suspected mutineers from central authority of the vessel; concealing evidence of planned or executed acts of mutiny or sabotage from chain of command, physical plant, or automatic self-checking devices on board any Fleet vessel
- After examination of all evidence, the defendant has been found guilty of mutiny against the central authority of this vessel, and of inciting by her participation further mutiny and acts of sabotage by persons unknown

"What, are they blaming the Jawas on Cray now?" murmured Luke to Threepio, who had switched on again to accompany him to the section lounge. They stood in the portside doorway, half hidden by the Kitonaks who had been brought yesterday to observe Cray's trial and had remained there, chatting, ever since.

Closer to the screen, the Gakfedd tribe squealed and snarled and yelled, "So it's *her* fault, the witch!" and *"She*'s the one behind the festerin' Rebels!"

• Despite the excellent record of the accused, it is the decision of the Will that Trooper Cray Mingla be executed by laser enclision at 1600 hours tomorrow. All personnel are to report to their section lounges . . .

"Luke . . ." Cray raised her voice above the voder monotone of the Justice Station. Her face was gray and haggard under the bruises, her dark eyes exhausted and sick with inner pain. "Luke, get me out of here! Please get me out! We're on Deck Nineteen, Starboard Front Sector, Maintenance Bay Seven, we came up Lift Shaft Twenty-one, it's guarded and booby-trapped—"

The Gakfedds hooted and yelled, and in the Justice Chamber the nearest Klagg guard snapped, "Zip it, skag-face," and Cray flinched— Cray, who despite her makeup and stylishness had never, to Luke's knowledge, shown physical fear in her life. Hot rage flooded him, blotting the pain in his leg.

But she went on, fast, as the guards seized her arms, dragged her to the door, "Lift Twenty-one! Ten guards, they ricochet blaster bolts down the shaft to hit the lower doors, there's a booby-trap ten meters down the corridor—"

"Yeah, tell us about it, Rebel tramp!" "Blow this laser enclision, steam her!" "Dump her in the shredder!" "Throw her in the enzyme tanks!" "Hey, toss her to the garbage worms . . ."

"Sixteen hundred hours tomorrow," whispered Luke, icy chill fighting the red rage in his veins. "We can—"

"Hey! You."

Ugbuz, Krok, and three or four other boars stood before him, heavy arms folded, yellow eyes glittering evilly in the reflected glow of the emergency lights that were at this point the only illumination in most of the sector. As more and more systems failed, the ship was growing dark. Since the Jawas were stealing power cells out of the emergency lamps, and any glowrods they could find, someone had set burning wicks in red plastic bowls of cooking oil all around the lounge—there'd already been one fire in a nearby rec room from the same source. The MSEs and SP-80s were still cleaning up the sodden mess left by the overhead sprinklers—

when Luke had passed on the way to the section lounge, he'd seen Jawas, like myrmins at a picnic, carrying away several MSEs and looting the power cells out of the larger droids.

The whole section smelled now of Gamorreans and smoke.

"I put your name through Central Computer, Calrissian." Ugbuz planted himself between Luke and the doorway.

Exhausted as he was, Luke found it a strain even to focus the Force on Ugbuz's mind. "I'm not Major Calrissian."

"That's what the computer says, pal," snarled Krok. "So who are you and what're you doin' on this ship?"

"We know what he's doin' . . ."

"You're thinking of someone else." But Luke felt the cold shadow of something else in their minds, the ugly certainty of the Will.

Turning to the nearest Kitonak, Threepio reeled off an endless chain of whistles, buzzes, and glottal stops, to which all the Kitonaks listened intently while Ugbuz growled, "There's somethin' funny goin' on here since you first came on board, mister. And I think you and I need to have us a little talk about it."

The Gamorreans closed in around Luke at the same moment that the Kitonaks, with a sudden burbling ripple of interest, closed in and as one entity seized the Gamorreans, each Kitonak grasping a Gamorrean's arm in huge, stubby hands. And they began to talk.

Luke darted between them—"Grab him!" yelled Ugbuz between the two portly mushrooms that held him in a grip like stone. He tugged furiously at their hold, but he might as well have tried to un-embed his hand from fast-set concrete. The Kitonaks, having found an audience for whatever it was they had to say, were not letting go. "And somebody get these stinkin' yazbos off me!"

Two ersatz troopers were already trying to free their compatriots with axes—as he ducked through the lounge door, yanking Threepio after him, Luke saw the ax blades bounce harmlessly off the Kitonaks' rubbery hides. Then the door hissed down behind him with a furious snap.

>Deck 6, laundry drop< appeared on the narrow monitor plate where the door's serial combination would usually be shown.

Luke grabbed Threepio by the arm and hobbled. Behind them the door jerked in its tracks, rising half a meter or so. There was furious pounding, curses, the sizzle of blaster bolts that sang and zapped and ricocheted wildly in the section lounge and—a moment later as the

Gamorreans finally got out—in the hall. The fugitives ducked down a cross-corridor and across an office pod, hearing behind them a mellifluous treble outcry of "After them! After them!"

Luke swung around, gathered all the waning strength of the Force to sweep every desk and chair in the room like the blast of some huge hurricane at the multicolored riot of Affytechans who came barreling through the door. They tripped, fell, tangling in comm cords and terminal cables—Luke's mind flashed out, transforming the cables for a moment almost into the semblance of living things, grabbing snakelike at his pursuers.

He staggered, his mind aching, and Threepio dragged him on.

"You go first," he gasped, not knowing if he could levitate Threepio down eight decks of repair tube. He fell to his knees, trembling in a sweat of exhaustion before the open panel.

"Master Luke, I can remain behind—"

"Not after that trick with the Kitonaks you can't," gasped Luke. "What'd you say to them?"

Threepio paused halfway through the panel—an incredible display of trust considering that he was not flexible enough to use the ladder rungs. "I informed them that Ugbuz had expressed an interest in their ancestors' recipe for domit pie. That's what they've been discussing all this time, you know. Exchanging recipes. And genealogies."

Luke laughed, and the laughter gave him a kind of strength. Closing his eyes, he called the Force to him, lifting the golden droid within the dark confines of the shaft. Lowering him . . . *There is no difference between that leaf and your ship,* Yoda had said to him once. Raising a single yellow-green leaf the size of Luke's thumbnail, making it dance in the warm, wet air of Dagobah. *No difference between that leaf and this world.*

Luke saw the leaf—small, light, shimmering, shiny gold—descend the blackness of the shaft.

Voices in the corridor behind him. The Gamorreans' curses and squeals, the stern soprano yammering of the rainbow Affytechans.

He dragged himself into the shaft, hung for a moment on the ladder of staples, trying to summon the strength to levitate himself down. Trying to summon even the physical strength to hang on while he shifted his good leg down one rung, then one rung more . . .

You can. He felt her, knew she was there with him. *Luke, don't give up . . .*

He couldn't levitate. In the corridor he heard Ugbuz swear, Krok yell, "That way, Captain . . ."

Feet thundered away. Rung by rung, one aching drop at a time, Luke descended, the shaft falling away bottomlessly below him. He felt the warmth of her, the awareness, beside him every agonizing meter of the way.

Deck 6 was utterly dark. The dead air stank of Jawas, of oil, of insulation, of Luke's own sweat as he dragged himself along its lightless corridors, his shadow and Threepio's lurching like drunkards in the dim flicker of the glowrods on his staff. Even those were failing—he'd have to cannibalize a power cell from somewhere and the thought of that niggling little chore made his whole aching body revolt. Ahead of him, and in all directions, he heard the squeak and scuffle of Jawa feet, saw the firebug glimmer of their eyes.

Threepio, he thought. *They'll be after Threepio if I pass out.*

Now and then he smelled, and heard, the Talz, and breathed a sigh of thanks that the Sand People, being essentially conservative, would defend their own territory rather than explore new corridors at this stage of the game.

Everywhere he saw torn-out panels, looted wiring, SPs and MSEs lying gutted and derelict along the walls. Helmets, plates, dismantled blasters and ion mortars strewed the halls—Luke checked the weapons and found that, one and all, they'd had their power cells pulled. Limping painfully down the echoing blackness, Luke had the eerie sensation of being trapped in the gut of a rotting beast, a zombie killer still bent on destruction though its body was being eaten from within.

This section of Deck 6 was dead to the Will. No wonder Callista had directed him here.

Cray. Somehow they had to rescue Cray. She'd know how to cope with the Will, know how to disable the artificial intelligence that ruled this metal microcosm.

Sixteen hundred hours. His whole body felt on the verge of collapse. Somehow he'd have to get enough rest to get up the lift shaft tomorrow.

Thirteen levels. His mind flinched from the thought. *They ricochet blaster bolts down the shaft . . .*

"Callista . . ."

But there was no reply.

I exist side by side with the Will.

She had died in the computer core. Luke had seen how the spirit of the Jedi could detach itself from the physical body, could imbue itself in other things, as Exar Kun's had imbued the stones of Yavin.

Knowing she had disabled the automatic trigger—knowing the Empire might very well send an agent to trigger the *Eye* manually—she had stayed in the gunnery computers for thirty years, guarding the entry to the machine that had taken her life, a fading ghost keeping watch on a forgotten battlefield.

"Come on, Threepio," he said, and bent to retrieve a hank of cable from the corpse of a gutted MSE. "Let's find ourselves a terminal."

>On Chad< Callista said, the letters fading in slowly as a single paragraph, as if rising whole from the depths of her recollection, >if our ark were in wystoh territory—and wystoh hunt most of the deep oceans where our ranch was—and we had to make a hull repair, or go out to the herd to help an off-season calving, we'd send out something called a foo-twitter the night before, a floater that made some kind of hooting or tweeting. Since wystoh are frantically territorial, they'd all head for the thing—which by then would be kilometers from the ark—and that would give Papa or me or Uncle Claine a chance to do what we had to do in open water and get back to safety. Would the Klaggs respond to a foo-twitter long enough for you to get up the shaft? They seem pretty territorial to me<

"If it sounded like Ugbuz and the Gakfedds, they would." Luke leaned back into the heap of blankets and thermal vests Threepio had gathered to make cushions for him in the corner of a repair shop, and considered the screen before him. It had taken most of his salvaged batteries and power cells, rigged in series, to fire up even the smallest of the portable diagnostic units in the shop. With the Jawas in control of most of the deck it would be a hard search for more. But it was a trade-off he was willing to make. Not just that he needed Callista's advice, he realized.

He wanted her company.

"Any of the bigger game systems in the lounges will have voders," he said at length. "Threepio, you know the stats on Gamorrean vocal range, don't you?"

"I can reproduce exactly the language and tonalities of over two hundred thousand sentient civilizations," replied the droid, with perhaps pardonable pride. "Gamorrean verbal tones begin at fifty herz and run up to thirteen thousand; squeals begin at—"

"So you could help me program the voder?"

"With the greatest of ease, Master Luke."

"Then what we need is a way to get the voder up to Deck Nineteen in time to pull the Klagg guards away from the shaft."

A schematic appeared on the screen. Not the precise, every-wire-and-conduit blueprint a ship's computer would display, but a more or less to scale sketch of a section of the vessel, labeled in one corner DECK 17. A bright circle flashed around a gangway. Then a window appeared in the screen.

>The gangway's wired. It leads from Recycling—the area of the ship where only the droids go—to Deck 19. If you make your foo-twitter light enough, you should be able to propel it up fast while you keep the enclision grid misfiring enough to let it through with-out too many hits<

Luke thought about it. "That's how you did it?" he asked at last. "Caused the grid to misfire?"

A long hesitation. The schematic faded from the screen. At some slight sound in the corridor, Threepio clanked his way out to check, and the whitish glow of the screen edged his golden form in threads of light as he stood listening in the utter black of the doorway square.

>It's like causing a blaster to misfire. You can't keep them all from firing—there are too many, and some of them always get through—and you can't keep all the bolts from hitting you<

Another long pause. She would, Luke thought, have avoided his eyes, as Leia sometimes did when she spoke of Bail Organa, not letting him see her grief.

>The more that hit you, the more that will. But if you case the voder in a gutted tracker droid, you can shoot it up the shaft fast enough to survive a few hits. And a mechanical can absorb a lot more hits than human flesh<

The more that hit you, thought Luke with a chill, *the more that will.* She'd climbed the shaft from the gun room, knowing she'd be hit . . . knowing the first hit would break her concentration on the Force, damage her ability to keep the grid from firing, lessen her chances to avoid the second . . . and the second hit would lessen her chances to avoid the third.

He remembered how the Klagg's blood had trickled down the steps, and the smell of burned flesh. His heart contracted within him, aching, as the silence lengthened. Very softly, he said, "I wish it hadn't happened."

Wise, powerful, comforting, he approved with bitter sarcasm. *The wisdom of a true Jedi Master.*

>It's all right<

They were silent for a time, as if they stood on either side of fathomless night, reaching across to fingers that could not touch.

"Were you from Chad?"

The screen was dark for a long time. He almost feared he'd offended her by asking, or that the batteries had failed. Then words came up, white flowers in the sunken meadow of the void.

>We had a deep-water ranch. We moved with the herds along the Algic Current, from the equator almost to the Arctic Circle. The first time I used the Force was to move pack ice one winter when I got trapped with a band of cows. Papa never understood why I couldn't stay, if I was happy<

"Were you happy?" He looked down at the lightsaber she'd made for herself, on Dagobah, perhaps, or on whatever planet she'd taken her training. She'd put a line of *tsaelke* around its handgrip, in memory of the tides of her home.

>I think more happy than I've ever been since<

Luke didn't ask, *Then why did you leave?* He knew why she'd left.

"It's funny," he said softly. "I always hated Tatooine, always hated the farm. Now in a way I think I was lucky. It cost me nothing to leave. Even if my family hadn't been killed, it would have cost me nothing to get out of there."

>The Force was like the pull of the tide. Like the deep-ocean currents that carry the herds on their backs. From the time I was a child I knew there was something there; when I learned what it was, I couldn't not seek the Jedi<

"But you also couldn't explain." Any more than he could explain to

Uncle Owen and Aunt Beru the inner tide pulling at him, almost before he knew how to speak.

"They're dead, you know," he said softly. "The Jedi."

Another long darkness, like a hollow in her heart. Then, >I know. I felt . . . the emptiness in the Force. I knew what it meant, without knowing<

He took a deep breath. "Obi-Wan Kenobi hid out for years on Tatooine; he was my first teacher. After he—was killed—I went to Dagobah, to study with Yoda. Yoda died . . . about seven years ago."

After I left him. The old grief, the old bitterness, rose in him like a faded ghost. *His last pupil . . . And I left him, only to return too late.*

He thought about Kyp Durron, his own finest student; about Streen and Clighal and the rest of the tiny group in the jungles of Yavin. About Teneniel of Dathomir, and Cray and Nichos, and Jacen and Jaina and Anakin and all he'd gone through; the hellish forge of the dark side, the Emperor's secret fortress on Wayland and all that had happened there . . . Exar Kun, and the melted Holocron, Gantoris's ashes smoking on the stones of Yavin and the destruction of worlds.

His heart was the diamond heart of a Jedi, forged and hard and powerful, but the pain he felt inside him was no less for that. Almost to himself, he whispered something he hadn't even said to Leia, who was like the other half of his soul. "Sometimes it seems like there's just such a long way to go."

"Master Luke . . ." Threepio appeared once more in the doorway. "Master Luke, it appears that the Jawas wish to speak with you." He sounded as if he disapproved in advance of whatever it was they might have to say. "They're asking what you have to trade for wire, power cells, and blasters."

"You know," said Luke, angling a palm-sized diagnostic mirror to see the delicate fastenings of the voder box as he hooked it to the tracker droid's gutted casing, "if somebody had offered me odds on which group of my fellow guests on this little tour had taken the rooms next to the transport shuttles, I'd have bet my boots and lightsaber on it being the Sand People. It *had* to be them, didn't it?"

>It's something even the Masters don't reveal about the inner nature of the secret heart of the universe<

The words appeared, minuscule, in the voder's monitor screen. Luke hadn't been aware he'd glanced there automatically for a reply.

>The deepest and darkest secret of all that the Force lets you see<

"What?"

She made a whisper by reducing the letters to the tiniest readable specks.

>The universe has a sense of humor<

Luke shuddered. "I'll have to be a *lot* higher-level Jedi than I am before I even want to *think* about that."

And he felt her rare laughter like a shimmering of the dark air.

Working on the tracker he'd gotten from the Jawas—it was the one Cray had disabled on Pzob, and at the cost of considerable pain he had used the strength of the Force to heal one of their number of the headache and nausea left over from a bad stunblast, and another of electrical burns on its hands—he'd talked: about Tatooine, and Obi-Wan, and Yoda; about the fall of the Empire and the struggles of the New Republic; about Bakura, and Gaeriel Capiston; about Leia and Han and Chewie and Artoo. About the Academy on Yavin, and the dangers to the unfledged, untried, untaught adepts whose power was growing without any sure knowledge of what to do with it or how to guide it. About Exar Kun.

About his father.

And hesitantly, a sentence or two at a time, on the tiny monitor screen or the larger diagnostic—whichever he'd been nearer at the time—Callista had been slowly drawn out: about growing up on the ranch on Chad; about the father who'd never understood and the stepmother who'd been too baffled and unhappy herself to comprehend either of them. About the moons and tides, ice and phosphorus, and the singing of the cy'een far out in the deeps. About Djinn Altis, the Jedi Master who had come to Chad, and the Jedi enclave on Bespin, floating unknown among the clouds.

>It was like riding a cy'een<

The diagnostic screen flashed a thick, long-necked fish-lizard, huge and matchlessly beautiful and shining with wild power, and Luke felt in the darkness, just for an instant, the touch of salt wind and leashed strength and heard the songs the creatures sang running free in their herds.

>Huge and fast and scary, shining like bronze in the sunlight . . . but I could do it. Barely<

"Yes," said Luke, remembering the power of the Force flowing into him as he'd battled Exar Kun for the final time, and that first moment when the lightsaber he'd called to his hand on Hoth tore itself free from the snowbank and flew into his grip. "Yes."

He told her about Cray and Nichos, and why they'd gone to Ithor to seek the help of the Healers there; about Drub McKumb's attack, and Han and Leia's mission to Belsavis. "It hasn't been that long," said Luke, sitting back and keying the foo-twitter's makeshift remote. Nothing happened. Resignedly, he undid the fasteners, angled the mirror again, and tried the second of several possible hookups to the A-size power cell. He'd stripped out all the armaments and gripper arms, and most of its memory cores, knowing he'd have to fling it up a long tunnel by effort of his mind alone. "They're still going to be there. Even if they weren't, there's a whole city on the site now, nearly thirty thousand people."

>It's hard to imagine<

The words appeared on the monitor, close beside his eyes.

>Plett's House was just a little place, though the crypts went back into the cliff, and all ways up under the glacier. But the part that was outside was just a big stone house, set in the most beautiful garden I've ever seen. I grew up without gardens—you don't have them, on the sea<

"Nor in the desert."

>I remember it was quiet, like few places I'd been or seen. Maybe night on the ark, after everyone was inside, and the stars come clear down to the edge of the world. But sweeter, because even when it's sleeping, you never can trust the sea<

"Master Luke?"

Luke sat up, aware that his back ached and his hands were trembling with fatigue. Threepio came in, yellow eyes twin moons in the almost-dark of the single glowrod's light. The smell of coffee floated around him like an exquisite sunset cloud.

"I do hope you'll find this acceptable." The golden droid set down the plast cafeteria tray and began removing dish covers. The nearest working mess room of which Callista had been aware had been the Deck 7 Officers' Lounge, and Threepio had volunteered to make the trek while Luke dismantled the tracker the Jawas had traded to him.

"Selection was rather limited, and those items for which you expressed preference were not to be found. I chose alternates with the same proportion of protein to carbohydrate, and more or less the same texture."

"No—uh—this is great." Ordinarily Luke wouldn't have touched
gukked egg, but he'd been so long without food that anything sounded
good. "Thank you, Threepio. Did you have any trouble?"

"Very little, sir. I did encounter a group of Jawas, but the Talz chased
them away. The Talz think very highly of your efforts to feed and care for
the tripods, sir."

"Are they down here, too?" The gukked eggs were absolutely horrible but Luke ate both of them and was a little surprised at how much
better he felt.

"Oh, yes, sir. Both Talz and tripods. The Talz wish me to convey their
goodwill to you and ask if they can be of service."

Luke wondered momentarily if a Talz would be any more reliable at
selecting edible food for human consumption than a droid, then dismissed the thought. By the time he needed another meal he'd be long out
of here.

>Good job there are two transports< remarked Callista, when
Luke returned to work.

>You couldn't take the Klaggs and the Gakfedds off on the same
vessel<

"And which one of them gets to ride with the Sand People?"

>Lander<

"They'll never go in it," said Luke. "They hate small enclosed
spaces."

>I wondered why they keep knocking holes in walls. You'll be
lucky if they don't sever the main power trunk to the magnetic
field<

"Another reason to hurry," said Luke grimly. "This whole ship must
be driving them crazy. Not that they were ever real good company to
begin with."

>You sound like you've studied them<

Luke laughed. "You could say they were my next-door neighbors
growing up. Them and the Jawas. Everybody who lives on Tatooine has to
learn enough about the Sand People to stay out of their way."

He leaned back and flicked the remote. A harsh, guttural voice
boomed, "Very well, men, fan out and remain quiet. We are going to
massacre those smelly Klagg Rebel saboteurs."

Luke sighed, and shook his head. "Threepio? Little change in the script here . . ."

>My, what a grammatical stormtrooper< commented Callista, where the protocol droid couldn't see.

Luke grinned as he hooked up the cable. "Edit that to, 'Okay, men, fan out and keep quiet. We're gonna kill them stinkin' Klagg Rebel saboteurs.' "

>You forgot to say "sir"<

Luke started to make the gesture of elbowing her in the arm, as he did when Leia made a smartmouth remark, but stopped. He couldn't.

Her arms were dust and bone on the gun deck floor.

Yet she had no more question than he did himself that somehow, all the *Eye*'s captives—Sand People and Gamorreans as well as the Talz, the Jawas, the Affytechans and Kitonaks and the baffled, helpless tripods—had to somehow be taken to safety. It wasn't their fault, or their wanting, that they were here, he thought, angling the mirror to affix the voder's fasteners once again. Savage, violent, destructive as they were, like himself they were captives.

He moved the mirror, seeking the fasteners, and for a moment saw in it his own reflection, and a sliver of the room behind him: Threepio like a grimed and dented golden statue in the feeble glare of the worklight, compulsively tidying up the abandoned tray.

And close beside him, visible clearly over his shoulder, the pale oval face within its dark cloud of hair, the gray eyes from which sorrow had faded a little, replaced by caring, by interest, by renewed life.

Luke's heart turned over within his ribs, and knowledge fell on him—knowledge, horror, and grief like inevitable night.

Chapter 15

"She might have had other reasons for lying."

"Like what?" Leia folded her legs up tailor fashion on the bed and sipped the glass of podon cider she'd picked up on her way through the kitchen. The craftsmen Jevax had promised had made their appearance while Leia was out. The metal shutters, armed with a formidable new lock, were nearly out of sight in their wall sockets on either side of the tall windows, and a new bedroom door was folded into its proper slot. Even the cupboard had been fixed. Sitting on the other end of the bed, Han was checking both blasters.

"Like she might be working at Madame Lota's House of Flowers down on Spaceport Row."

Leia wondered why it hadn't crossed her mind before. "Dressed like that?"

He gave her his crooked grin. "I suppose you're dressed for your job?"

She brushed a dismissive hand over the plain dark linen of her shirt, the knockabout cotton fatigue pants, and high-laced boots. "She wouldn't have been on the path by the MuniCenter last night if she were working the bars." The pile of hardcopy Artoo had made for them that first day strewed the bed between them. Nowhere was Roganda Ismaren listed on any employer record of any packing plant in Plawal.

"And if she'd followed me there from the marketplace, for instance, she wouldn't have been dressed like that at that hour."

While she was speaking, Han rose and walked out to the balcony, took aim at a small clump of ferns a few meters away in the orchard, and fired. The ferns sizzled into oblivion. He flipped the safety back on and tossed the weapon to Leia. "Good as new. So what did you find in the town records?"

It seemed like a thousand years ago. Returning last night·to find a soaked and exhausted Han patching Chewie's cuts had driven from her mind the web of speculation fed by the records themselves, and after Mara's subspace call, her mind had been on other things.

"Not . . . what I was looking for," said Leia slowly. "No mention of the Jedi, or of Plett himself, though it's obvious they were behind the different kinds of plants growing here and that they set up the archiving programs—the Municipal Records time-shares off the Brathflen/Galactic/ Imperial Fruits computer, but all the archiving programs look like they were originally designed for some kind of four-sixty model, which puts it back to the date the Jedi were here. Naturally, nobody knows where that original computer went to but my guess is it got sold for chips and wire to Nubblyk when the new one was put in."

"Good guess," muttered Han. "Not what I want to hear, but a good guess. Any record of what happened to Nubblyk?"

She shook her head. "He just disappeared one night about seven years ago. His nightclub was taken over by his 'associate' Bran Kemple, who also took over his import and export business on Pandowirtin Lane. Slyte's on the record as having bailed out Drub McKumb twice from charges of running stuff in through the Corridor. Kemple never bailed out McKumb at all. After Kemple took over, McKumb is listed as having been bailed out once by Mubbin the Whiphid—this was right after Slyte disappeared—though at no time is McKumb ever listed as having legally landed a ship at the port. Now the interesting thing is . . ."

Chewbacca appeared in the doorway with an interrogatory growl, and gestured out into the front room, where a signal was coming in on the subspace.

The code was for Leia, and the image was scrambled.

Leia punched in the unscrambler sequence, and the dazzling buzz of green, brown, and white pixels resolved itself suddenly into the image of Admiral Ackbar.

"This may not mean anything, Princess," said the Calamarian in his soft, rather sibilant voice. "Still, I thought you ought to know about it. I've received reports from operatives in the Senex Sector and the adjoining portions of the Juvex Sector. They say that the heads of six or seven of the old Houses—the ones who've been lying low, staying out of the border fighting and not committing to the warlords of the Empire—have all gone 'on vacation' . . . without taking their families *or their mistresses.*"

"Oh, yeah?" Han raised his brows. "Now, *that's* serious."

The admiral folded his squamous hands, a ghostly image in the subspace holo, like a statue wrought of mist in the receiver cubicle. "This is curious enough, but it coincides almost exactly with the 'vacations' taken by the uncommitted ex-governors of Veron and Mussubir Three, and with representatives of the Seinar Corporation and a high-up member of the Mekuun family. Drost Elegin—the head of House Elegin—evidently took his family but left them on Eriadu."

"That's a sort of epidemic of rudeness all of a sudden," remarked Han, standing behind Leia with folded arms. "Any troop movement?"

"None so far." The Calamarian touched the slim stack of report wafers on the desk just visible at his side. "Nothing from the larger warlords, but our operatives on Spuma seem to think there's increasing recruitment in basic trooper levels into Admiral Harrsk's fleet, and sources within the Seinar Corporation say there's some kind of major funding in the wind—Seinar is ordering new equipment to produce energy cells and stepping up thermal fabric production. But nothing concrete. Still, considering how close Belsavis lies to the Senex Sector, Your Excellency, you may want to consider coming into a more protected area."

"Thank you, Admiral," said Leia slowly. "We're . . . almost finished here." She brought the words out reluctantly. Her chief of staff was right, she knew. If the self-styled Lord High Admiral Harrsk was moving or about to move, she was in a desperately exposed position on Belsavis, and something about the assassination of Stinna Draesinge Sha triggered warning sirens in the back of her mind.

But she sensed some darker riddle, some deeper and deadlier puzzle, than she'd first come seeking on this world of fire and ice.

The Jedi and their children had been here.

Roganda Ismaren, once the Emperor's concubine, had come here . . . Why?

And why did something snag in her mind just now, some trace of something she had heard?

Drub McKumb had worked his way desperately, through blinding nightmares of agony and confusion, halfway across the galaxy to warn her and Han about something.

And someone here had thought it worthwhile to murder them while they slept.

Admiral Ackbar was still watching her face anxiously through the wavery light of the subspace transmission, so she said, "We'll be returning soon."

"Will we?" asked Han as the admiral's image faded.

"I don't . . . I don't know," said Leia softly. "If there's some kind of trouble brewing among the old Houses of the Senex Sector I think we'll have to. They've kept quiet . . . even under Palpatine all they wanted was to be left alone, to rule the so-called natives on their planets however they wanted to . . ."

"I've heard that before," said Han grimly. "The big corporations just *love* governments like that."

Leia sniffed. "*Ask us no questions and we'll hand you no responsibilities.* Yes." She folded her arms uneasily, prowled past Chewie and Artoo's quest game and back into the bedroom, to stand with one shoulder against the window jamb, staring out into the mists of the orchard where that morning she'd seen Roganda Ismaren, nearly invisible among the trees. Of course the woman had every right to take refuge here, beyond the frontiers of the New Republic.

The fact that it was "close" to the Senex Sector meant little. It was close only in interstellar terms. It wasn't anyplace any of those ancient aristocrats, those cold-eyed and elegantly groomed descendants of ancient starfaring conquerors, would come. She remembered Drost Elegin from her days at Court, and tried to picture that disdainful dandy in this provincial world of fruit pickers and backwater smugglers. They'd even considered Coruscant déclassé . . . "So many *bureaucrats,* my dear," Aunt Rouge had said.

A white-sleeved arm reached around from behind with her abandoned cider glass.

"So what was the other interesting thing?"

"Oh," said Leia, startled. Han leaned against the frame next to her,
looking down with quizzical hazel eyes.

"Yes," said Leia, remembering. "All along, there's something about
this business of droids going haywire that's bothered me."

"Bothered *you*?" Han jerked his head in the direction of the living
room, where Artoo's holographic geofigures were rapidly burying
Chewbacca's enraged Hero. "He tried to—"

"But *why* did he try to?" Leia asked. "Yes, I know colonies frequently
operate with substandard machinery, but in the records I found literally
dozens of unexplained malfunctions a year. Even a rough count shows the
number has increased dramatically over the past several years." She gestured back toward the bed, with its scattered counterpane of Artoo's
readouts. "Last night, before Artoo's attack on us, when I was looking at
the records up at the MuniCenter I wasn't connecting it with anything. I
think I'd like to recheck the causes of those malfunctions. If it was a
function of the climate, that would have been constant, not increasing."

"Not necessarily, if their stuff's wearing out."

"Maybe," agreed Leia. "But they're listed on Artoo's readouts as
'unexplained.' That means they checked for the obvious things, like age
and dampness."

A few years ago Han would have dismissed it as coincidence. Now he
said, "So what do you think it was?"

"I don't know." Leia ducked under his arm, crossed to the bed, and
fetched her blaster and its holster. "But I think I'd like to talk to the head
mechanic at Brathflen and see whether those malfunctions were just a
fried wire, or whether they involved chains of specific, unexpected actions."

"Like welding the windows shut and putting blasters on overload."

"Yeah," said Leia softly. She gathered the readouts, stowed them in
the cupboard. "Like that. Want to come?"

Han hesitated, then said, "If we're getting out of here soon, I think
I'm going down to the Jungle Lust"—he made a suggestive wiggle with
his hips—"and have a couple words with Bran Kemple. You want to
come, Chewie?" There was more behind the request than friendly com-
panionship—the last time Artoo had beaten Chewbacca at quest, the

game console had ended up hurled through the nearest window, and Artoo seemed well on his way to another victory now.

"He may know something about how and when and mostly why Nubblyk made tracks out of here, and if he took a ship with him when he left. You're not taking him with you, are you?" he added, as Leia, following him into the living room, crossed to touch Artoo's domed top.

Leia hesitated. She had had it in mind as a matter of course, but then, it hadn't been *her* scantly covered anatomy Artoo had been firing bolts of electricity at not twelve hours ago.

"Whatever his problem was last night, we don't know if we've solved it yet." Han was checking his blaster as he spoke, in spite of the fact that he'd tested and retested it not half an hour before. "If Goldenrod was here he might get some sense out of him, but since he isn't, I say leave him here with that restraining bolt on him till we can get him checked out by somebody better than the local toaster repairman."

Chewbacca snarled and aimed a swat at him with one enormous paw, and Han threw up his hands and grinned. "All right, all right. You did a swell job on him, Chewie; he'll make point five past lightspeed now and can outmaneuver Imperial patrols . . ."

They descended the ramp together: Han, Leia, and the Wookiee. Han gave Leia a quick, hard kiss at the foot of the ramp, and she waved to them as they disappeared into the shifting rainbows of the fog. But when they were out of sight Leia turned back, climbed again to the house, and walked over to the little astromech droid sitting beside the deactivated quest console.

"Artoo?"

The droid bobbed forward, extending his front "leg," and gave a timid whistle. His top swiveled to regard her with the round red eye of the visual receptor.

Leia often wondered what she looked like through it, and how the shape that was her—the shapes that were Luke and Han and Chewie and the kids—appeared to the astromech's digitalized consciousness.

"You can't tell me what happened?"

A wretched whistle, begging for understanding.

"Did someone tell you to do it?" she asked. "Program you somehow?"

His cap swung wildly and he rocked a little on his base.

"All right." Leia touched his cap again. "All right. We'll be out of this

place pretty quick. And I'll ask the mechanic about what happened to
you. Look . . ." She hesitated. Yes, Artoo was only a droid, but she knew
he'd been hurt by Han's mistrust. "I'll be back . . ."

No! No! No!

His desperate whistling and rocking stopped her halfway to the door.

Trust your feelings, Luke had said to her many times since she had
submitted to his greater wisdom as a teacher. Raised to trust her brain,
her intellect—raised to trust information and systems—Leia found this
difficult sometimes, when things looked wrong but felt right. She could
almost hear her brother's voice, see him standing beside the little droid.

Trust your feelings, Leia.

Artoo had tried to kill both her and Han not twelve hours ago.

Han would choke.

But then, she thought, her love for Han was the greatest triumph
she'd ever seen of "looks wrong, feels right." So he didn't have any room
to talk.

She fetched a bolt extractor from Chewbacca's toolkit in the next
room and removed the restraining bolt from Artoo's casing. "Let's go.
This way the mechanic won't have to come back here to have a look at
you."

She added to herself, *I hope I don't regret this.*

Due to vague uneasiness about taking the less traveled roadways
through the orchards again, she turned her steps to the slightly longer
route through the town market. The fog was thinner here and the proximity of the buskers, hucksters, and shoppers reassuring. As she climbed
toward the bench from this direction, the oddly patchwork structures of
the older part of town fell behind her. Only the white prefabs remained,
crammed together here into apartment blocks for the packers and ship-
pers, the clerks and mechanics, though lichen, ferns, trailing vines, and
even small trees grew out of every chance projection and ledge offered by
an uneven fit of the plastene blocks.

She wondered what the place had been like, when the Mluki had
inhabited their massive stone houses clustered against the bottom of the
bench, farming their small crops and occasionally going up to hunt on the
ice.

Not so foggy, certainly, without the dome, and not so hot, though the
jungly rift held the heat well. The orchards wouldn't have extended as far
as they did now. There would have been clumps of dense jungle around

the warm springs, nothing at all down at the bottom of the valley, where the mudflats, caldera, and steaming gas vents of the rift's true bottom poured forth more minerals than unengineered plants were capable of digesting.

Exactly the sort of place a heat-loving, plant-loving, beauty-loving Ho'Din would seek out.

She remembered her vision of Plett, tall and willowy, his flowerlike cluster of headstalks faded nearly white. A gentle face, with that look in his eyes Luke had had when he'd come back from servitude to the Emperor's vile clone.

Was this a refuge he had chosen, a place to repair, to rest? How had he learned about it, for that matter? The galaxy was filled with planets, worlds, star systems still unexplored, and unless a system was on someone's computer, it didn't exist. Roganda might possibly have heard of the place at Court . . .

Although now that she thought about it, that troubled Leia, too.

And how had Plett liked having the peace of his experiments disrupted by the influx of . . .

How many?

Nichos had spoken as if there was a fair-sized gang of children.

Leia had had almost a year of raising two enterprising Jedi babies . . . with Anakin just arrived to provide his own variety of mayhem. After years of quiet meditation, how had the aged reptiloid coped with a swarm of them, of all ages, running up and down the tunnels of his crypts, following their own leaders even where their parents had warned them not to go because of the kretch . . .

She stopped in her tracks, Nichos's deep voice sounding in her ears. *The older kids . . . Lagan Ismaren and Hoddas Umgil . . .*

Lagan Ismaren . . .

Roganda Ismaren's . . . brother? Her age was certainly right. A few years older than Leia—a few years younger than Nichos—she would be old enough to remember the world where she had lived.

That meant that Roganda Ismaren—Palpatine's concubine and member in good standing of his Court—had come from the blood and the heritage of the Jedi Knights.

The Emperor had been hideously strong in the Force. He couldn't have been unaware.

Anger flushed through Leia like the shock of a burn.

She lied.

Leia had suspected the other woman had been lying about something, but she realized with sudden clarity that it had *all* been an act—all of it, down to the sweet, frightened tones of her voice. An act calculated to play on her pity.

If Roganda was Force-strong the Emperor might have used her, certainly, might have coerced her . . . but he'd never have simply passed her around to his guests.

She came here seven years ago, thought Leia, quickly turning her steps back toward town. She wasn't sure what she should do now—certainly not go anywhere near the woman herself, and she was gladder than ever she'd turned down that invitation to coffee—but she wanted at least to find Han, to send word to Ackbar, to look again through the records Artoo had run out to see if they included port arrivals in the year of Palpatine's death . . .

But as she crossed through the small square at the head of Roganda's narrow street, she saw something that hit her in the pit of the stomach like a club.

Emerging from between the dark foundations, the white plastic buildings, she saw, across the street and quite clearly, Lord Drost Elegin walking with Dr. Ohran Keldor.

Leia looked aside at once, as if studying the small stand of sweetberry that someone had planted in the waste space between two buildings. But as Luke had taught her—had tried to teach her, in her hectic intervals between trying to be a mother, trying to be a diplomat, trying to keep the New Republic from falling to pieces and her children from dismantling poor See-Threepio—she extended her senses, identifying footfalls, breathing, voices . . . the sense and essence of what people were . . .

Ohran Keldor and Drost Elegin.

Here.

They vanished into the fog almost at once. She crossed the narrow street, Artoo trundling behind, followed the sound of the feet, the sense of their presence, cutting ahead through an alley and watching as they passed across its mouth.

There was no chance of mistake.

Drost Elegin's hair had grayed a little from the days when he'd been one of the most notorious playboys of the Emperor's Court, in and out of the *Court Gazette* for scandals about gambling, dueling, amorous affairs—

he'd mockingly called her Madame Senator and Little Miss Inalienable Rights. Only his brother's position in the Imperial navy had saved him from severe reprisals after the last of his major scandals—that, and the power his family wielded. The flesh of that hawk face had begun to sag, but the tall, gawky-graceful form and beaky features were unmistakable to anyone who'd ever seen them.

Ohran Keldor . . .

She felt as if her skin had been stuffed with red-hot pins.

She'd studied his holos until she could see his face in her dreams. His face, lit from below by the glow of the Death Star's activation consoles.

Ohran Keldor. Nasdra Magrody. Bevel Lemelisk. Qwi Xux, though Qwi Xux had been only their dupe . . .

So there was more here—far more—than just a woman hiding out.

Fog cloaked the two men as they took the paths that led through the orchards, where the rushing of water and the faint click and whirr of the tree feeders covered Artoo's soft, steady rumble. Now and then one of those huge, arachniform mechanicals would loom from the mists, picking its way across the path in front of her, intent on its tedious ministrations, and Leia wondered with a sort of chill viciousness if the droids belonging to the primary designer of the Death Star's autosystems ever malfunctioned.

Somehow she didn't think so.

The ground began to rise in a long, steady ramp. The mists thickened, darkened before them, solidifying into the dripping, vine-festooned monolith of the valley wall. Leia fell back, stepping into the lipana thickets at the bottom of the ramp, Artoo following gingerly onto the spongy ground. From here they were definitely committed: They were going to the lift shaft that led to the hangars, from which vehicles could be taken out onto the ice. She heard their voices fading away as they climbed . . .

"It seems a long, cold way to go around," she heard Drost Elegin say, in that bronze-and-velvet voice that every girl and woman at Court had seemed to believe when it said the words, *I love only you . . .* "If the tunnels connect with this smuggler pad . . ."

"The fewer people who know the way in from here the better. Even you, my lord." There was a world of implied offense on Keldor's part in the hasty addition of that last sentence. "And at this point, with Organa showing up as she has, we don't know who may be watching."

Whhish-kunk. Distantly the vapors stirred around the closing of the door.

Leia and Artoo stepped back on the path, climbed the ramp to the small curved bunker of quick-set permacrete molded into the cliff itself, the plain green sturdiplast door. Sturdiplast was a material designed only to keep minor fauna out of the bunker and the air-conditioning in. She listened through it with only minimal concentration until she heard the characteristic *ping* of the lift's arrival, and, tiny behind the thickness of the door, Elegin's voice asking, "Is it far out?" The last words were cut off, presumably by the lift doors.

Leia still counted out two minutes before inserting her card.

To her utter relief—despite the sound of the lift, for many years with the Rebel Alliance had turned Leia into a confirmed pessimist about things that could go wrong—the small lobby in the bunker was empty. She touched the summoning switch and looked swiftly around her.

A small metal door proved to be a locker, filled with gray mechanics' coveralls. She picked the smallest human-fit she could find, dug around in the pockets of the others until she located a billed cap, which she crammed on her head, shoving her hair up underneath.

Is it far out? If Elegin was asking, then Keldor knew . . . which meant Keldor had been here longer.

How much longer? And Elegin—meeting someone? Someone else who'd "gone on vacation" with wife and children and then dropped them off at a fashionable resort in order to take a fast ship elsewhere?

The lift doors opened. Leia stepped in, keyed to the hangar, the only possible destination. While the lift was ascending she flipped open Artoo's front hatch. Usually the droid was kept spotless, but Chewbacca's rough-and-ready engineering had resulted in a great deal of soot and grease, which she smeared on her face. After a moment's thought she transferred her blaster from her belt to the coverall's copious pocket. She hoped she could carry off the impersonation of an inconspicuous mechanic when she reached the hangar, but if she couldn't . . .

Elegin and Keldor, as she feared they might be, were just pulling on protective thermal suits preparatory to climbing into the smallest of the available ice walkers, a low-slung vehicle built along much the same lines of a tree feeder, whose dozen long legs were capable of both climbing over the rugged glacial terrain and spreading out to anchor in the face of the brutal winds. They'd heard the lift ascending and were watching as

Leia came out, but the sight of the slight, shuffling figure in an unbelted gray coverall trailed by an astromech droid was apparently a reassuring one, because they climbed into the ice walker and slammed shut the cowl.

A moment later the bay doors cranked open. Leia shuffled over to the crew lockers at the far end of the hangar and pretended to canvass her pockets for keys until the walker moved into the bay.

The moment the doors shut behind it she pulled a pair of wires out of her inner pocket and flipped open Artoo's hatch again, hooking the bare ends in as Han had showed her once. "Okay, Artoo," she said grimly. "Let's see how good a burglar you'd make."

They opened four lockers before they found a t-suit that fit her; the gloves in its pocket were clearly intended for a Bith. She reset the oxygen and temperature controls for human levels and checked the seals as she pulled it on. There were a couple of Ikas-Adno speederbikes of various models in the hangar but Leia regretfully passed them up. Antigrav vehicles moved fast, but in a high-wind environment like the glacier they were worse than useless. Instead she chose a very old Mobquet Crawler, mostly for its low profile and small engine, which would probably fail to register on a detector if Keldor was watching his trail. She dragged a couple of oil-stained planks over to make a ramp for Artoo, up the back between the high trapezoids of the treads.

"You set back there?" She climbed in, shot the canopy into place, and hit the latches. The inner bay door creaked open, warm air swirling the powder snow and ice crystals that still strewed the dirty concrete floor.

Artoo tweeped an affirmative.

"So let's see what's actually going on on this ball of ice."

The outer door opened. Bleak winds howled across the wilderness of rock and ice: bitter, vile, toothbreakingly cold, a Hell-winter that had already lasted for five thousand years.

Leia set homing coordinates, glanced back to make sure Artoo had hooked himself into the guidance computer, and set out across the frozen landscape in the distant ice walker's wake.

Chapter 16

In a way, you, Princess, are responsible for our choice of target . . .

She could see him still. A tall man, pale as bleached bone, a skull face above the olive-green uniform, and behind him the blue-green jewel of Alderaan burning like a dream against the velvet darkness beyond the viewscreen.

Ice spattered on the triple plex of the crawler's bubble, wind rocking the low-slung vehicle like the paw of a huge pittin batting at a slow-moving sludbug crawling across some hellishly vast kitchen floor. Leia, though her attention was focused on every shudder of the control bar, every fluctuation of the gauges—on the bobbing pattern of yellow lights that marked the ice walker's gawky, arachnoid limbs, far out ahead of her in the wind-torn desolation of the ice—was in the deeper part of her mind scarcely aware of it.

Her consciousness was back on the Death Star, on Moff Tarkin's colorless eyes.

"You, Princess, are responsible . . ."

. . . you are responsible . . .

Had she been?

She knew Tarkin. She knew he despised Bail Organa and she knew he was aware of the opposition centered on Alderaan. She knew that under his self-satisfied efficiency he had a spiteful streak the width of the Spiral Arm and loved to tell people that his—or the Emperor's—most frightful retaliations were actually the fault of the victims.

Of the Atravis Sector massacres, he'd said, "They have only themselves to blame."

She knew, too, that as a military man he'd been dying to try his new weapon, to see it in action . . . to describe its performance to the Emperor and hear that pale cold voice whisper like dead leaves on stone, "It is well."

In her heart, she knew he'd intended Alderaan as his target all along.

But in her dreams she was responsible, just as he said.

The lights were far out ahead of her on the ice, reeling and dodging among themselves with the motion of the walker's legs, like a pack of drunken firebugs. Away from the hot thermals that rose off the Plawal dome and cleared the dense roil of clouds, storm winds and blowing sleet covered the glacier, cutting visibility and darkening the already feeble daylight to a whirling, cindery gloom. Black bones and spines of rock, scoured bald by the winds, thrust like dead islands through narrow rivers of ice; drifts of snow packed high in places like wind-sculpted desert dunes, and in others the violence of storms had carved the ice underfoot into toothed, ridgy masses, like the waves of an ocean flash-frozen in the midst of storm.

Twice crevasses loomed before them, ghostly sapphire depths falling farther than her eye could easily judge in the shadowless twilight. The walker's longer legs had taken them in stride, and Leia cursed as she trundled the crawler along the rim for hundreds of meters, looking for a place where the chasms narrowed sufficiently to make the heart-stopping jolt over the emptiness. Rumbling back along the rim to pick up the choppy trail again, she prayed the wind-blown ice hadn't eradicated the walker's marks.

Ohran Keldor was aboard that walker. Ohran Keldor, who had helped design the Death Star.

Ohran Keldor had been aboard it, watching when Alderaan was destroyed.

Leia had more or less forgiven Qwi Xux, the Death Star's primary designer, when they had finally met, seeing the woman's stricken horror at what her abilities had wrought. It was a little hard to appreciate how anyone could be naive enough to believe Moff Tarkin's assurances that the Death Star was a mining implement, but she understood that the Omwat woman had been raised in a carefully constructed maze of ignorance, coercion, and lies.

And when she had seen the truth, she had had the courage to follow where it led her—not something everyone did.

But Ohran Keldor—and Bevel Lemelisk, and others whose names the Alderaan Alliance of survivors had collected—had known precisely what they were doing. After the destruction of Alderaan, they'd all been dropped at Carida, when the Death Star started its final voyage to destroy the Yavin base. But all of them had wanted to see the first test of their theories.

And Keldor was here.

And so was Drost Elegin, she thought, and in all probability the heads of those other old Houses, those planetary rulers who headed up the human—or humanoid—populations of planets settled long ago, rulers who'd hated the Senate's interference with their local power and who hated the Republic more. Those rulers who had only supported Palpatine because he could be bribed to a "gentleman's agreement" to let them run things as they pleased.

They are gathering . . .

Gathering around Roganda Ismaren, former concubine of the Emperor and child of the Jedi, and who knew what besides?

Out in the sooty maelstrom another light glowed briefly blue. It blinked away almost instantly, but Leia saw the moving tangle of the walker's leg markers turn in that direction. "Got that, Artoo?" she yelled into the com, and barely heard the reassuring affirmative chirp. Course bearings flashed green on her readouts, and the wind slapped hard as she steered the crawler out from behind a twisted cliff of ice, like some impossible marble monolith thrown up by the restlessness of the volcanic line far beneath.

Her hands were shaking, and she was weirdly conscious of the heat of the blood in her veins.

In a way, it surprised Leia that nobody had mapped the location of the smuggler pads. Because of the intensive ion storms, high-altitude scans were out of the question, but a ground-level geothermic trace would have been possible. Possible, but not easy, she reflected, fighting the control bar as the crawler heaved up over a talus slope of rotting ice under the feet of another, older cliff. And probably not worth anybody's while.

The wind nearly took her off her feet when she climbed out of the crawler in the lee of the scoured black rocks that sheltered the pad. The t-suit was certified below the freezing point of alcohol, and still she felt the cold creep through it as she fought her way up the knife-edge crest of drift and rock to get her first clear look at her goal.

It wasn't a pad anymore.

Where a sort of bunker had been—precast permacrete and designed for little more than an inconspicuous staging point beside a clear space thermoblasted into the rock-hard glacier—Leia saw through the screaming sleet the low black walls of what the military referred to as a permanent temporary hangar, snow frizzing wildly away from a magnetic field that was clearly both new and extremely powerful. The old permacrete bunker had been added to by others, mostly perm-temps, low-built structures whose black walls blended with the rock of the ridge against which they backed. Were it not for the magnetics they would have been buried by drifts in hours.

Leia muttered a word she'd picked up from the boys in the old Rogue squadron and edged her way down to the walls, slipping in the heavy pack snow, with Artoo's treads squeaking sharply in her wake.

The ice walker was gone. That didn't mean the hangar was deserted —Leia could see by the melt patterns that something had landed on the ice and been taken into the hangar less than three hours ago, and at a guess they'd have left crew. Above the battering howl of the wind it was difficult to extend her senses into the main shed, but the door to the smaller buildings adjacent to it was on the lee side, and those smaller buildings were empty, anyway. It was a matter of moments, even with gloved fingers in the deepening cold, to have Artoo hotwire the locks. The stillness when the door slid shut behind them was almost painful.

She pulled off her helmet, shook out her hair. The small annex's heating system was a relief, but she could still see her breath in the dim gleam that fell through the connecting passage to the main hangar itself.

The ship in the hangar was a Mekuun Tikiar model, sleek and dark and curiously reminiscent of the avian hunter for whom the model was named. Tikiars were a favorite, she knew, among the aristocratic Houses both in the Senex Sector and elsewhere.

Two crew. She leaned against the doorjamb, listening deeply, focusing her mind through the hazy brightness of the Force. Relaxed . . . watching a smashball game—illegally—on the subspace net.

The Dreadnaughts were getting pasted again.

Reassured, she surveyed the annex room behind her.

It was filled with packing crates. Stacks of them, piled around the lift doors, dark anonymous green plastene bare of destination but emblazoned with corporation logos and serial numbers.

Mekuun-made DEMP guns and heavy laser carbines. Seinar ion cannons. Scale-50 power cells, sized for the smaller, older TIEs and Blastboats; smaller cells, Cs and Bs and Scale-20s by the dozen. Blaster size.

We've lost contact with Bot-Un again, she heard Jevax say.

That's where they're bringing in the men. The realization came to her, complete and logical. *Bring them down the Corridor, come in high, drop fast, run along above the ice . . .*

Communications between the rifts failed so frequently that it might be a week before anyone took an ice walker out across the glaciers to check. Or more.

"You getting all this, Artoo?" She pulled her helmet back on, braced herself as they slipped out to the frozen nightmare outside. She had to cling to the droid for support as they struggled back to the crawler, picked up the trail of the walker's huge grippers across the ice.

The astromech tweeped assent.

Ohran Keldor, last of the Emperor's fleet designers . . .

Designing something new? She shook her head. Only with an effort now could she see the almost obliterated tracks. Too expensive, beyond even the capacity of a coalition of the Senex lords, and the corporations they dealt with would be wary of backing them on major construction. Keldor had more probably been called in as a consultant on some older apparatus, maybe the very Jedi equipment Nubblyk and Drub had been looting and smuggling out all those years ago.

But her instincts whispered, *No. Something bigger.*

Something else.

Something they'd assassinated Stinna Draesinge Sha over, lest she hear something that would ring familiar from her own studies and notify the Republic of their danger.

The black rock outcroppings of the main ridge formed a wind trap east of the hangar itself. No one, thought Leia, grimly hanging on to the crawler's control bar, would have been able to track the site of the tunnel from the air. The pale sun's light barely penetrated the scudding clouds and only faint scuffs remained of the walker's tracks. She only saw the cave where they left the craft, and the permacrete pillbox that covered the shaft head itself, because of the puckery masses of dimples fast fading in the blowing snow.

New military structures at the landing pad but no improvements on the shaft head, thought Leia, maneuvering the crawler behind the last spur of rock out of sight of the walker in its cave. *And bringing Elegin in the long, cold way around. Don't trust the Senex lords, do we?*

Snow squeaked under Leia's boots as she crossed to the pillbox, and the hot air rushing out around her as the shaft head doors opened to Artoo's breaker program made her gasp. She stepped inside quickly, the droid at her heels, and the door slid shut once more. More crates filled the shaft head, bearing all the logos and labels she'd seen before: Mekuun, Seinar, Kuat Drive Yards, Pravaat—the massive consortium in the Cela-non System that manufactured and sold uniforms to whoever cared to pay for them. The pale strings of battery-run glowpanels threaded around the room showed the floor scratched with fresh drag marks and spotted with oil leaked from secondhand droids.

Han. I've got to let Han know.

Kill you all, Drub McKumb had said. *They're gathering. They're there.*

Five sets of tracks marked the powdered snow that lay all over the cement floor, ending at the doors of the lift. Four humans and the broad, short, slightly rounded prints of what might have been a Sullustan or a Rodian. Leia recalled that many of the executive board of Seinar were of the rotund, flat-nosed Sullustan race.

She recalled other things as well.

"Artoo," she said softly, "I want to see how this tunnel links up with the smuggler tunnels under Plawal itself. But if we get into any trouble, your default command is to head back to the crawler and get Han." While she spoke she broke the seals on three of the crates, helped herself to a flamethrower, a semiauto blaster carbine, and a forcepike, which she assembled swiftly, deftly, as the boys in the Hoth dugout had taught her when it looked as if they weren't going to get out before the Imperials came in.

"Give him coordinates, information, everything. Don't stay to defend me. All right?"

The droid beeped and trailed her onto the lift.

The smuggler tunnel would surface somewhere in Plawal, she knew. But from Han's description of the lava caves and the well in its circle of standing stones—from the fact that Roganda Ismaren had spent a part of her childhood here—she guessed they connected with the crypts under Plett's House as well. What she was concealing there, and how she had managed to thwart sensor probes after people started disappearing, Leia couldn't imagine, but it was clear to her now what had become of Drub McKumb and Nubbyk the Slyte . . . and who knew how many more besides?

Vader . . . and Palpatine, Mara had said.

And, evidently, Palpatine's concubine . . . though the woman hadn't struck Leia as particularly strong in the Force. Certainly not imbued with that aura of eerie strength, that silence that even as a cocky teenage Senator she had felt emanating from the Emperor.

What, then?

Leia slung her weaponry straps over her shoulders, and stepped out warily into the dark.

For a long distance the smuggler tunnel was simply raw stone, chewed out of the bedrock of the planet under five thousand years' worth of glacier, which ran occasionally through the widened beds of what had once been underground streams. The floor had been smoothed to permit the passage of cargo droids: ramps built, roofs heightened, crevasses bridged. It was easy to follow; all she had to do was move as silently as she could.

Later, when the way branched, or cross-tunnels were cut in the rock, or when they passed through caves stifling with fumes and smotheringly hot from sullen craters of steaming mud, she listened, stretching out her senses, feeling in the Force for the touch, the essence of the five people who led her on. Painted Door Street—the narrow lane on which Roganda had said she lived—backed onto the vine-curtained bench on which Plett's House stood. Before the dome was built, the rift had been periodically subject to storms. Of course the Mluki would tunnel . . . and of course the smugglers would find at least some of the tunnels in the foundations of those ancient houses.

Not all the dwellings on Painted Door Street were built over the older dwellings, of course . . . but Leia was willing to bet Roganda's was. She had lived here. She had known this place. And she had come back, when Palpatine died in the seething heart of his second attempt to cow the galaxy by terror.

Why?

Leia sensed the swift scramble of claws, the snuffling pant of animal breath, even before Artoo whistled his nearly soundless warning. They were far off but coming close fast, their direction almost impossible to determine in the maze of cross-tunnels, caves, carved-out rooms, ramps and stairways ascending and descending.

"They're probably tracking us by scent," she said softly. "So let's have some light, Artoo."

The droid barely had time to brighten all his panel lights when the things were on them.

Rodian, human, and two Mluki—or what had been those races once. Leia identified them even as she cut with the forcepike—not as clean or as strong as a lightsaber, but in trained hands potentially deadly. It had the advantage of keeping more than one at bay at a time, without danger of ricochets, and as they fell screaming on her, Leia struck at her attackers, cold, scared, and furious. She slashed a Mluki halfway through the neck and swung immediately to the Rodian, whose broken metal club gashed open her sleeve and the flesh of her arm. The weight of them nearly overpowered her. There was nothing in them she could warn to keep back, nothing that realized they were in danger. When one of the humans ripped the forcepike away from her she barely brought the flamethrower up in time, searing at them, blasting them, and they attacked her, still burning, as she caught up the pike again to finish the job.

They had hardly fallen when the kretch appeared, slithering out of the darkness to feed on the corpses and the blood.

From the depths of the tunnels—behind her, around her, in a dozen directions—the second Mluki's final cry was echoed by a chorus of screams.

Kill you all. Kill you all . . .

She fled down a tunnel, Artoo's beam flashing ahead of her to the archway of an artificial entrance in the rock. She ducked through, to an area of cut stone, hewn chambers, ramps of desiccated and kretch-gnawed wood covering steps and changes of level. A bridge crossed a fast-running stream whose water steamed thinly in the hot air. A tunnel where she sensed an echo of the Force whispering, *Don't come down here . . .*

Dead glowpanels, small trunk beds in corners . . .

Something huge and hair-matted and stinking fell upon her from a doorway, and Leia slashed without thinking, blood splattering her t-suit as the thing collapsed shrieking at her feet. She sprang over it, Artoo nudging past the body, and the air around them seemed to breathe with foul, snuffling, guttural snarls and what might have been stammered, mind-blasted words.

Refuge. She sensed it, felt a curious lightness, the sudden impulse of safety. A sense of what she'd long been seeking.

It lay to her left, calling her, it seemed, through a dark triple arch.

An open hall, wide and dark with soda-straw stalactites and thin curtains of mineral deposits forming through cracks in the roof. A stream divided the wide room in two, planks thrown across it, but no sign of a bridge. Right, left, and center, three open, arched doorways led out of the room on the far side of the water, and as Leia crossed the plank, the center one called.

Distantly, as Artoo shined his spotlight into the room beyond the center arch, Leia felt as she had felt looking down from the tower, as if she saw and heard things not of her own time.

Children's voices.

The bone-deep awareness of the presence of the Force.

She stepped through the arch, and Artoo brightened his lights again. Chips and threads of metal winked at her all the length of the long, barrel-vaulted room.

A glass tank a few centimeters thick, empty save for a thin layer of yellow sand.

A glass cylinder a meter tall, hermetically sealed and containing only the withered skeleton of a leaf. Beside it on the table lay a ball of black volcanic glass, a gold ring, and a crude doll wrought of rag and twigs.

The whole back wall of the room was taken up by an exquisitely balanced apparatus of suspended spheres, rings, rods, and pulleys, glistening in enigmatic welcome. Two other machines of shafts and buckets and polished steel balls seemed to beckon, tempt, and tease the mind with a monumental silliness of potential chain reactions.

There was a glass sphere filled with dull pinky-gold liquid that seemed to stir, colors coalescing briefly at the vibration of her stride.

The children were here, thought Leia.

The joy and fascination they'd felt seemed to have soaked into the stone of the walls.

She might not have found their names, Leia thought . . . but she'd found their toys.

She reached tentatively, touched the sphere of liquid, and where her fingers contacted the glass, molecules of red separated themselves from the pink suspension, hung like dissipating clouds in the fluid atmosphere of the ball. Uncertainly—because Luke had taught her nothing of this, though it seemed ridiculously easy once she tried—she prodded with her mind, and the liquid separated itself, golden on the top, crimson on the bottom. Something in the color of the crimson made Leia look deeper, summon the Force . . . In the blood-colored molecules were hidden enough of a third color to form between the existing zones a narrow band of cobalt blue.

Jacen and Jaina need these, she thought. Anakin, when he grew older.

There were other things, maddeningly simple things she could not understand.

Why a circle of empty bowls, straight-sided and of varying size? What went in them? Leia could see nothing on the black tabletop except gray stains like watermarks . . . Was the composition of the table part of the riddle? Dense and shiny, it looked like lacquer until she touched it, but under her fingertips it clearly said, *Wood.*

What were all those weirdly heavy metal spheres, lined up according to size in a rack?

The bars, ropes, hanging beams of the ceiling were self-explanatory . . . or were they?

Luke has to see this.

None of this was mentioned in the Holocron, or in the records Luke had salvaged from the wreck of the Jedi ship *Chu'unthor. Maybe they didn't think it worth recording, as we don't think to mention the alphabet when we write literary criticism. Or stop to explain the human enzyme system at the start of a love story.*

Or the human need for oxygen, for that matter.

Perhaps it was premonition, some dark tension in the air that keyed and stretched Leia's senses. But amid the shadows of levers and pulleys of that great toy on the wall she caught sight of something half familiar and, stepping forward, pulled it from where it had been tucked almost out of sight. It was a small packet of black plastene, powdered with a dirty residue whose smell brought back to her the dim blue-green grotto of the *Cloud-Mother*'s Healing House; Tomla El's soft voice saying, *Yarrock.*

New, she thought. Not anything the Jedi would have left here. But who?

By the doorway, Artoo whistled a warning.

Leia froze, not breathing, reaching with her mind into the dark.

The shrieks and snuffles of the mind-stripped guardians of the tunnels were mute.

But the air itself seemed to thicken, coalescing, sinking in on itself.

The Force. An enormous darkness, masquerading as the silence of nothing there.

Then from the darkness she heard a very faint, chitinous scratching.

Some shift of pressure, a change of the deep, hot atmosphere of the caves, brought her the smell, like the vast exhalation of rotting sugarcane or the decaying debris of the fruit-packing plants, a chemical dirtiness that lifted the hair on her nape.

"Let's get out of here, Artoo." She slid the packet back where she had found it, crossed quickly to the door, and Artoo flashed the beam of his spotlight past her, to the ebon silk of the water flowing down the center of the room, and the stretch of floor beyond it.

The floor moved. Glistening shapes heaved over one another like a lake of black jewels amid a vast, filthy scratching of claws.

"I wouldn't advise it, Your Highness."

Roganda Ismaren, small and pale and fragile-looking in her white gown, stood framed in the narrow archway to Leia's right. Beside her stood a dark-clothed boy, like her slim and raven-haired, like her small, with a suggestion about him of wiry grace.

Ohran Keldor, Drost Elegin, and another man—stocky, hard-faced, fifty, in black—stood grouped behind.

"Artoo, go!" ordered Leia. "Now—"

Roganda only gestured. Elegin and the third man strode to cut Artoo off before he reached the bridge and Leia brought up the flamethrower. The dark-haired boy snickered derisively and said, "Oh, *please!*" and Leia, warned by some instinct, flung the weapon from her as the tank glowed and ruptured in a burst of fire. She shucked her carbine and caught up the forcepike, feeling the yank of the boy's mind on it, forcing her own mind against his like a resistant wall as she sprang between the men and Artoo. Elegin fired his blaster at her but she was already dodging, moving in on him, driving him back. The other man yelled, "Put it away, idiot!" as the bolt hissed and zinged against walls, floor, ceiling in shattering ricochets. Leia couldn't probe with her mind to strike the weapon out of his hand but she could at least keep it from being done to her.

At Roganda's side, the boy said, "Don't waste your time, Elegin, Garonnin. You . . ."

He fixed his wide eyes, like cobalt glass, on Artoo. "Back here. Now."

Artoo, who had crossed the plank bridge and was a few meters from the arch leading away into the dark maze of passageways, came to a stop. Kretch crawled and squirmed wildly over his slick sides in a way that turned Leia sick, but the little droid took no apparent notice. It was the boy who had stopped him, the boy's voice . . .

"Back here," the boy repeated calmly. "You aren't going anywhere."

"Artoo, go!" Leia shifted sideways, forcepike raised, keeping a wary eye on Elegin and the man called Garonnin—surely not a member of the House Garonnin?

"Oh, really, Leia," said the boy impertinently. "If I could make him almost blow up the house you were sleeping in, you don't think he's going to disobey me now?" He sniggered again, his face twisting in an unpleasant grin. "I'll make him run into the water and short himself out."

He turned those glass-cold eyes on the droid. "Come on. Open all your repair ports and back this way, one point five meters left and parallel to your original course."

"Artoo!" She couldn't look, keeping an eye on the men.

The astromech droid rocked on his base and emitted a desperate whistle.

"Come on," ordered the boy.

"Irek, just send the kretch away and Garonnin will—"

"No!" said the boy furiously. The black wings of his brows plunged together over an ivory curve of nose. "I told him to come back and he won't. Back here. One point five meters left and parallel course—"

"Artoo, get out of here!"

Artoo ran a pace back, a pace left, kretch twisting like a net of filth over him and crunching stickily under his treads.

"Come back here!" ordered the boy, all calm suddenly gone from his voice. "One point five meters . . ."

Artoo wheeled in a tight circle and headed for the door into the tunnels.

"Send away the kretch, Lord!" Garonnin made a feint toward the bridge, Leia stepping to block, vibroblade raised. "Once he gets into the tunnels we won't be able to track him!"

"Obey me!" yelled Irek, pale face twisting, ignoring the older man completely. "Come back!"

"Picture the schematic . . . ," began Roganda evenly, and Irek turned upon her like a wildcat.

"I know what I'm supposed to do! It worked before . . ."

Artoo vanished into the tunnels in a brown smear of mashed kretch. Irek stared after him, panting with rage and disbelief, and Leia felt the vicious fury, the concentration of the Force, flung after him . . .

And remembered, vividly, Chewbacca amid a tangle of wire and solder on the terrace, patching the droid back together.

"Send the kretch—"

"Don't bother me!" screamed Irek, and strode toward the bridge, shoving Garonnin aside.

Leia stepped in front of him, vibroblade raised in her hand. The boy stopped, staring at her in astonishment that anyone would thwart his will. Leia felt the tug and jerk of the Force against her grip on the pike haft and tightened her grip, bringing all her mind, all her concentration, to bear on keeping him back.

The blue eyes widened in stark fury and he whipped a black-hilted lightsaber from his side. At the same moment Leia felt her breath choke off, had to fight with all her strength to draw past it . . . She could see he didn't handle the laser weapon properly, using instead the stance and grip of formal blade-dueling, totally inappropriate for the two-handed weapon's balance. In a duel Luke would make strip steak of him . . .

The blade slashed at the forcepike and Leia feinted upward with it, ducked aside, and nearly took off his feet at the ankles. Battling for even a thread of air, she faced him off, and with a yell of fury he came at her . . .

"*Irek!*" shouted Roganda.

The kretch had begun to swarm across the bridge.

Leia felt the bitter grip on her windpipe relax, saw the swarming anthropods halt in the middle of the planks and begin to mill, as if an invisible barrier prevented them from coming further. Closer to the door, there was a turmoil among them as they devoured the bodies of those Artoo had crushed.

"Mother, she's doing something!" cried Irek angrily. "It isn't working. That droid should come back. That doddering old scumbag said—"

"Irek, be silent!"

Leia saw the look Roganda gave her son, and saw, too, the concubine's swift wary glance at Garonnin and Elegin.

She's keeping something from them . . .

"Lord Garonnin, Lord Elegin," said Roganda in her sweet, reasonable voice—that same sweet voice, with just a touch of helpless deference, thought Leia, that she had used to speak to Leia herself in the market. "Step back this way. We seem to be in a rather simple impasse. Irek, remember not to lose your temper and always take the easiest way out. Your Highness . . ." She stepped a little aside in the doorway, to let the two aristocrats past her. Irek remained where he was, just out of range of Leia's forcepike, sullen blue eyes flickering from Leia to the kretch.

"Right," said Irek softly. And he grinned. "You put it down, Princess, or I let the kretch come all the way across the bridge. Maybe I should do it anyway." He tittered, and stepped back a pace; the kretch flooded across, pouring onto the near side of the floor like a seethe of bloody mud.

"Irek!" commanded Roganda furiously.

The kretch stopped, milling again; Leia had backed a few paces but knew at the speed they ran she'd never make it to safety even if she knew in which direction it might lie. Particularly not, she thought, if Elegin had his blaster trained on her.

"Well, why not do it now?" demanded Irek sullenly. "Without her the Republic would crumble."

"Without her the Republic would simply elect another Chief of State," replied Lord Garonnin quietly, a twinge of disgusted contempt in his voice.

He stepped around Roganda and walked across the room toward Leia and the kretch. Leia, fighting not to run headlong from the filthy things, wasn't sure she could have done that. The light of the single glowpanel in the doorway behind Roganda made a stiff gold fuzz, like a metal halo, of the elderly man's short-cropped hair.

"Surrender your weapon, Your Highness. That's the only hope you have to come out of this alive."

Some hope, thought Leia bitterly, as she switched off the vibroblade and slid the forcepike to him across the stone of the floor.

Chapter 17

When Nichos had been diagnosed with Quannot's Syndrome, Cray had said, *There's got to be something I can do.*

Trembling and panting for breath, Luke leaned on the wall of the fifth or sixth gangway Callista had shown him, his leg a cylinder of red pain that spread upward to devour his body in spite of the double dose of perigen he'd plugged into it. He remembered Cray's face that day, the brown eyes blank with shock and refusal to give up hope.

There's got to be something, she'd said.

He closed his eyes, the wall cold against his temple.

There had to be something.

And Cray would be the one to do it.

The *Eye of Palpatine* would be jumping to hyperspace soon. Even the most intricate of waiting games came to an end at last. It had waked, and it would fulfill its mission, and something told Luke that this wasn't simply a matter of laying waste a planet that thirty years ago had sheltered the Emperor's foes.

Something wanted the ship. Something that could use the Force to affect droids and mechanicals. Something had called out to it, commanded the long-sleeping Will.

Whatever it was, he couldn't risk letting it wield this kind of fire-power, this kind of influence.

Not even for Callista's life.

But everything within him turned away from the thought, unable to bear the understanding that he wouldn't get to know her. That he wouldn't have her always somewhere in his life.

It was worse than the pain of his crippled leg, worse than having his hand cut off . . . worse than the pain of realizing who his father was.

He literally didn't know if he'd be able to do it.

He leaned his weight on the gangway railing to support himself while he stepped up the next riser with his good leg, and straightened his body again. Lean, step, straighten. Lean, step, straighten, and every muscle of his shoulders and back cried out with the days of unaccustomed labor. The few perigen patches Threepio had been able to scrounge for him from emergency kits around the ship were nearly gone, and the droid had covered all of Decks 9 through 14. When he'd lost his hand he'd had a mechanical within hours, and he would have fought, or traded, or sold almost anything he could think of for a working medlab and a 2-1B unit.

The foo-twitter floated at his back.

By the chronometer on his wrist it was just after 1000 hours. Threepio should already have located the main communications trunk and isolated the line that controlled the Deck 19 intercoms. It was information classi-fied to the Will, but the Will couldn't prevent Callista from whistling a trace note from one side of the deck to the other, loud enough for the protocol droid's sensitive receptors to detect. Failure of the line would be attributed to the Jawas, in their guise as Rebel saboteurs, or just possibly —when the guards on Lift Shaft 21 heard the Gakfedd voices—to some plot by the Gakfedds themselves. With luck, Luke could get up the shaft and get Cray out of her cell before they were even aware they'd been tricked.

Abyssal darkness and faint, ghostly clankings lay at the bottom of the gangway beyond the open doorway labeled 17. This was one of the ship's recycling centers, cut off from the crew decks or any realm of human activity. The droids who occupied themselves with the reconstitution of food, water, and oxygen needed no lights to work. The glow of Luke's staff picked out moving angles, blocky SP-80s going about their monoto-nous business in company with apparatus not intended to interface with humans at all, MMDs of all sizes, scooting RIs and MSEs, and a midsize Magnobore that bumped Luke's calves like a mammoth turtle. He'd disconnected the gauge lights on the altered tracker to delay as long as possible the moment when the Klaggs realized they'd been duped, and it drifted forlornly behind him, like a rather dirty balloon attached by an invisible line to the trackball in his pocket.

Right turn, then second left, Luke repeated to himself. A wall panel in one of the recycling chambers, a narrow shaft at a forty-five-degree angle . . . He settled his mind, collecting about himself, in spite of the pain and the slow numbing of the overdoses of perigen, the mental focus, the inner quiet, that was the strength of the Force. For the dozenth—or hundredth—time since that particular side effect had begun to make itself felt, he wondered if he'd be able to work better with an infection-induced fever and the constant stress of pain.

It had to work, he thought. It had to.

He turned a corner, and stopped.

A dead Jawa lay in the corridor.

It had a handful of cables wound around one shoulder, a satchel open beside its hand. Luke limped to the body, eased himself down to kneel beside it, and touched the skinny black claw of wrist. A charred pit of blaster fire gaped in its side.

Batteries and power cells lay strewn around the open satchel. Luke scooped them back into the leather pouch, slung the strap over his shoulder. Faint whirring made him look up, to face two small droids of a kind he'd never seen before. Gyroscopically balanced on single wheels, they reminded him of some of the older models of interrogation droids, but instead of pincer arms they had long, silvery tentacles, jointed like snakes. Small round sensors, like cold eyes, triangulated on him at the end of prehensile stalks.

The two droids were barely taller than Artoo-Detoo but there was a curiously insectile menace to them that made Luke back slowly away.

The tentacles extruded with a whippy hiss, encircled and lifted the Jawa's tattered little carcass. The droids swiveled and shot away. Luke followed to the door of a cavern lit only by the sickish glow of gauge lights and readouts. The smell of the place was like walking into a wall of muck: ammoniac, organic, and vile. Steam frothed thinly from beneath the covers of the three round, well-like vats whose metal curbs rose scarcely half a meter above the bare durasteel of the deck. As the snake-eyed droids approached the nearest tank its cover dilated open. The stench redoubled as steam poured forth, knee-high ground fog that swirled to the farthest corners of the room.

The droids raised the Jawa corpse high and dropped it into the vat with a viscous *ploop*. The cover dilated shut.

A sharp rattle at Luke's side made him jump. A slotted hatchway popped open in the wall, and a tumble of belt buckles, boot latches, a stormtrooper helmet, and some half-dissolved bones clattered into the catchbin under the hatch, everything dripping brownish enzymatic acid.

The skull of a Gamorrean grinned up at Luke from the bin.

Luke stepped quickly back. Though he knew that full recycling from enzymatic breakdown products didn't kick in until the second or third week of deepspace missions, still he found himself queasy at the memory of that gukked egg.

The foo-twitter waited for him in the corridor. Luke led the way through another door, past backup enzyme tanks locked up cold and closed, to the far wall. At the touch of the lights on his staff the three SP-80s ranked in a corner swiveled their cubical upper bodies, the wide-range sensor squares casting dim blue glare. A small MMF rolled out of the darkness and rattled its three arms at him like a bare mechanical tree. It halted beside Luke as he knelt to pop the panel hatches, reached to take the hatch cover from him with the surprising, irresistible strength of droids. Luke leaned around the back and hit the pause button. The MMF froze, panel still raised in its grippers.

Within the shaft, the enclision grid's lattices grinned at him like broken, icy teeth, fading out of sight into the dark chimney above.

Very carefully, Luke leaned into the shaft. It ascended two levels at a steep slant, climbable at a pinch, but not by a man with a useless leg. The square, cold patchwork of the walls seemed to whisper, *Try it. Go ahead.*

It's like causing a blaster to misfire, Callista had said.

And, *The more that hit you, the more that will.*

He thumbed the trackball in his pocket, and the silvery tracker drifted close.

He'd examined the latches that dogged panels shut from behind, so it was an easy matter to reach through with his mind—as he had reached behind the panel leading into the shaft—and twist the latches aside at the top. More difficult was blowing the panel clear, for it was hard to concentrate through fatigue and pain. He felt the hatch cover give, two levels up, and dimly heard the clang of it striking the floor.

Air flowed gently down the shaft against his face.

Two levels. Eight meters at a slant, though the darkness was too dense for his eyes to penetrate.

"Okay, pal," he whispered to the foo-twitter. "Do your stuff."

He thumbed the trackball to edge the tracker to within centimeters of the enclision field. Focused his mind, gathered his thoughts, put aside pain, weariness, and growing anxiety. Each square of the grid came to his mind, flawed, delayed, molecules not quite meeting, synapses not quite touching—momentary shifts in atmospheric pressure, conductivity, reaction time . . . And beside that, kinetic force building up like lightning, dense and waiting, aiming like a sited cannon upward into the dark.

It was like shouting a word, but there was no word. Only the silent explosion of the foo-twitter's speed, rocketing upward, ripping air as if fired from a slugthrower, and the spattering hiss of lightning. Few, spidery, too late, the blue bolts zapped and fizzled from the opal squares around the metal casing, sparking where one hit, two . . .

Then he felt it in air, and the grid fell silent again.

Luke checked the monitor on the trackball.

The foo-twitter was still transmitting.

Shakily, he leaned his forehead on the jamb of the panel, thanked the Force and all the Powers of the universe . . .

And turned, to see what, for that first moment, he thought was another foo-twitter hanging in the dark behind him.

The next second his reflexes took over and he flung himself sideways, barely in time to avoid the scorching zap of blaster fire. *Tracker* flashed through his mind as he rolled behind the disused tank, jerking his bad leg out of the way of a bolt that burned a chunk out of the heel of his boot. He remembered the charred hole in the Jawa's side. Evidently the floating, silver trackers were equipped to do more than just stun and fetch.

He grabbed for his staff where it lay in the open and whipped his hand to safety—empty—only just in time. Another bolt hissed wildly off the decking and he dodged a second tracker that swam up out of the darkness.

In the meadow on Pzob he'd watched these silvery, gleaming spheres in action, and knew the few instants' whirring shift and refocus of the antennalike nest of sensors—rolled, ducked, changing direction. The central vision ports shifted and the second droid splatted fire, not at him, but in a line of quick bursts on the floor in a raking pattern, driving him toward the open panel of the shaft and the enclision grid within.

"Oh, clever," muttered Luke, crawling back, gauging his timing for a leap. More by instinct than anything else he flung himself through an opening in the pattern of bolts, rolled up to his knees, and whipped the diagnostic mirror from his pocket as the trackers swiveled in his direction again. He caught the bolt of the first one on the angled glass, clean and vicious and perfectly aimed. It struck the second tracker in the instant before it fired. The tracker burst in a shattering rain of shrapnel that clawed Luke's face like thorns, but it gave him the second or so he needed to reangle the mirror as the first tracker tried again—and zapped itself into noisy oblivion with its own reflected bolt.

Luke lay on the floor, gasping, the warmth of the blood trickling down his face contrasting sharply with the cold of drying sweat. One dead tracker lay like a squashed spider on the floor a meter from his side. The second still hung fifty or so centimeters above the floor, broken grippers trailing, turning disjointedly here and there. Luke got his hands under him preparatory to crawling for his staff.

With a faint whirring, the three SP-80s in the corner came to life.

Luke dove for the door as they whipped toward him, moving faster than he'd have given those tractor treads credit for. He held out his hand, calling his staff to it, as the MMF came to life again and shot out a gripper. Luke rolled out the doorway, wondering if he could get as far as the gangway in time, and skidded to a halt as two more SPs and the biggest Tredwell he'd ever seen—a 500 or 600 at least, a massively armored furnace stoker—loomed out of the hall's darkness, reaching for him with inexorable arms.

The lightsaber whined to life in his hand as snaky silver tentacles caught his wrist from behind. He struck at one of the snake-eye droids, the other jabbing at him with a long, jointed rod, and the jolt of the electrical shock knocked him breathless. He flipped the lightsaber to his left hand, as he could when he had to, cut at the snake-droid's sensors. Something struck him from behind, wrenching strength grabbing his arms, lifting him bodily from the floor. He cut again, sparks exploding as the glowing blade severed a G-40's servocable, but, unlike human oppo-nents, the droids didn't know enough to back off, and were incapable of going into shock. They surrounded him, gripping with an impossible strength, and when he slashed through sensor wires, joints, servotransmitters, there were always more.

The Tredwell's case-hardened arms resisted even the cut of the laser. It was made to work in the heart of an antimatter furnace, and though the lightsaber hissed and slashed, the searing violence of the blows reverberated up Luke's arms as if it would shatter the bones. Arms dangling, eyestalks dangling, such droids as were still operable followed the stoker as it bore Luke through the doorway, and the mephitic stink of the enzyme chamber's darkness engulfed them. Luke hammered, twisted, slashed at the pinchers that held his arms and ankles, but couldn't so much as make them flinch. The stink redoubled as the enzyme vat irised wide. Steam boiled up around him like thin foam, the smell as much as the heat of the dark red-brown liquid that bubbled beneath him making him dizzy.

Luke went limp. The lightsaber's blade retracted. *A leaf on the wind,* he thought. *A leaf on the wind.*

The Tredwell let him drop. Relaxed, almost as if he could sleep, Luke summoned the Force as he fell, light and true as if he drifted above the steam. From some abstract distance he was aware of his own body rolling lightly sideways above the seething filth in the vat, away from the droids, levitating effortlessly to the far rim.

Just beyond the rim he fell, and hit the floor hard. His crippled leg gave beneath him as he tried to stand, stumbled and plunged for the door, crawling desperately as the droids clanked and ground in pursuit. They weren't as fast as the trackers had been—he had the coverplate off the manual door release when they were still a meter behind him, and ran his lightsaber into the works to fuse them once the door was down between him and the droids.

He managed to crawl a considerable distance before he passed out.

"Callista, we can do it." The man's voice held a thin veneer of patience and confidence over a core of rough irritation. He put his big, calloused hands through the back of his belt and looked from her to the blackness framed by the faintly glowing rectangle of the magnetic field.

Luke recognized the hangar, though it seemed less cavernous in the clear cold lighting of the glowpanels than it had been when he'd stood there by the shorn, chalky light of the stars. The Moonflower Nebula's drifting banks of light could be seen outside, speckled with the darker chunks of asteroids, an eerie field of glow and lancing shadow. The Y-wing stood where he'd seen it, scars and holes glaring in the brightness. On the marks that had been empty stood a Skipray Blastboat, crowding the smaller craft.

"The station lays its defensive fire in a double ellipse pattern, that's all. We got in, didn't we?" The man's eyes were bright blue in a hatchet-jawed, amiable face grubby with three days' rust-colored beard. He had a gold ring in one ear.

"The Force was with us or we'd never have made it." It was the first time Luke had seen her clearly, but it was as if he'd always known that she was tall, slim, long-boned without the smallest trace of lankiness. The lightsaber with its rim of bronze cetaceans hung at her belt. Like her companion she was filthy, a universe of heavy brown hair unwashed and trailing from a knot the size of his two fists at her nape, gray eyes light against the soot and oil that stained her face. Shrapnel or shattering glass had opened a three-inch cut on her forehead; the way it was scabbed, it would leave a hell of a scar. Her voice was like smoke and silver.

She was beautiful. Luke had never seen a woman so beautiful.

"I'd like to think I had something to do with that." The man's long mouth twisted.

"You did." Callista looked taken aback that he'd feel offended. "Of course you did, Geith. The Force—"

"I know." He made a gesture, a slight pushing of the air, as if against something heard before for which he had no time. "The point is, there's other ways of doing this than getting ourselves killed."

There was silence between them, and Luke saw, in the way she stood, in her diffidence, her concern that he would be angry at her. She started to say something, visibly checked, and after a moment changed it to, "Geith, if there was any way for me to go up that shaft, you know I—"

By the flare in his eyes Luke saw he'd read her words as an accusation of cowardice. "And I'm telling you neither of us has to do it, Callie." Anger in his voice; Luke saw that no lightsaber hung beside the blaster at his waist. Was that between them, too?

"It's not going to take us that long to get clear of the Nebula's interference and back to where we can signal for help. Help in dealing with this hunk of junk"—his expansive wave took in the chill gray-walled labyrinths of the silent *Eye*—"and at least let Plett know what's coming at him. As it is, if we try to be heroes and fail, they won't know zip until they catch a lapful of smoking plasma."

"They won't know if we make a run for it and get nailed, either."

Her voice was low. His rose. "It's a double ellipse with one randomized turn. I've got it scoped, Callie. It'll be tougher in that tub than in the Y-wing but it can be done."

She drew breath again and he put a hand on her shoulder, a finger on her lips; a lover's gesture of intimacy, but still meant to silence her.

"You don't have to be such a hero, baby. There's always ways of doing things without getting killed."

Luke thought, *He doesn't want to climb up that shaft. He's told himself there's another way—and he probably even believes it—but at bottom, he doesn't want to be the one who climbs through the grid while she's using the Force to make it misfire.*

And he saw this understanding, too, in Callista's gray eyes.

"Geith," she said softly, and in her hesitation Luke heard the echo of his previous rages. "Sometimes there's not."

He threw up his hands. "Now you're starting to sound like old Djinn!"

"That doesn't make what I'm saying less true."

"The old boy's too damn ready to tell other people how they should die for a guy who hasn't been off that festering gasball of his for a hundred years! Callie, I've been around. I know what I'm talking about."

"And I know that we have no idea how long we've got until this thing goes into hyperspace." She still didn't raise her voice, but something in its level softness stopped him from cutting in again. "None. If we destroy it, it's gone. Dead. If we leave it, run for it—"

"There's nothing wrong with jumping clear and getting help!"

"Except that it'll lose us our one sure chance."

"It'll lose us our chance of getting the hell blown up along with this thing, you mean!"

"Yes," said Callista. "That's what I mean. Will you help me or not?"

He put his hands on his hips, looked down at her, for he was a tall man. "You stubborn fish rider." Affection glinted in his smile.

Her voice flawed, just slightly, as she looked up into his face. "Don't leave me, Geith. I can't do it alone."

And Luke saw something change, just slightly, in Geith's blue eyes. Pain came back to him, shredding away the scene in the hangar. He opened his eyes, felt under him the slight, smooth jostle of movement. Thin dark lines passed like scanner wires above his head, traveling from head to feet . . . ceiling joins.

Moving his head, he saw that he lay on a small antigrav sled, beyond whose rim See-Threepio's grimed and dented metal head and shoulders were visible as the droid guided the sled along a hall. There was a sound somewhere ahead and Threepio froze into the perfect immobility of a mechanical. The yellow reflection of a tracker droid's dim lights passed over the metal mask of Threepio's face, glinted very faintly on the perfect, intricate shape of his hand where it rested on the sled's rim.

The yellow light passed on. Threepio moved forward again, footfalls hollow in the empty corridor. Luke slid back toward darkness.

The foo-twitter, he thought. He'd misfired the enclision grid and thrust the silvery globe up ten meters of shaft, but it had been hit anyway —four, maybe five times. He'd heard the shrill zing of ricochets against the metal. Threepio had cut the comm trunk, Cray was in danger, he couldn't lie here . . .

The more that hit you, the more that will.

He saw her in the gun room.

The lights were on there, too.

She was alone. All the monitors were dead, blank black idiot faces, holes into the Will's malignancy—she was sitting very still on the corner of a console, but he knew she listened. Head bowed, long hands folded loose over her thigh, he could see the tension in the way she breathed, in the slight angle of movement. Listening.

Once she looked at the chronometer above the door.

"Don't do this to me, Geith." Her voice was barely audible. "Don't do this."

After long, long, grinding silence like years of cold illness, though absolutely nothing changed in the room, Luke saw when she understood at last. She got to her feet, crossed to a console, and tapped in commands: a tall girl whose gray flight suit hung baggy over the long-limbed fighter's frame, whose lightsaber with its line of dancing sea clowns gleamed against her flank. She called a screen to life, and Luke saw past her shoulder the hangar, with the ruined Y-wing and the empty meters of concrete floor where the Blastboat used to be.

She toggled in a line of readings, then, as if they weren't enough to convince her, tapped VISUAL REPLAY.

Luke's eyes were the eyes of the pickup camera concealed among the craters of the dreadnaught's irregular hull. There was no question that Geith was one hellskinner of a pilot. Blastboats were landing craft, not fighters; clumsy to handle, though in a crisis they had the speed to outrun, if not outmaneuver, most pursuit. And Geith had been right—half by observation, half by instinct, Luke saw/felt the pattern of the shots the Will laid down, a complex double ellipse with a couple of random twitches.

A couple, not the one that Geith had said.

Dodging, dropping, veering among the sheets of light-filled dust, the half-hidden chunks of tumbling rock, Geith handled the Blastboat as if it were a TIE, flipping through the white streaks of death with breathtaking speed. He was almost out of range when a random bolt that shouldn't have been there holed his stabilizer.

The more that hit you, the more that will.

He must have got the craft in hand somehow, spinning crazily but keeping his trajectory. An asteroid swam out of the dust and took off one of his power units, dragged him around . . .

And it was over.

Luke saw the white blast of the final explosion as a reflection from the replay screen cast up on Callista's face.

She closed her eyes. Tears traced a line in the grime. She had the look of a woman who hadn't slept or eaten in days, exhausted, skating the edge. Maybe the Will had tricks for dealing with those who entered by other means than the landers with their indoctrination bays. Maybe if Geith had been 100 percent alert, 100 percent sharp, he'd have done as he'd meant, and gotten out to fetch help.

She turned her head, and looked up at the dark shaft, like an upside-down well into the night above the ceiling. The enclision grid had the look of pale, dementedly regular stars. She drew her breath without change of expression, and let it go.

He woke again, or thought he woke, to utter blackness, and she was there, lying against his back. Her body curved around his, her hip spooned behind his, her thigh touching the back of his leg—his leg didn't hurt, he realized, nothing hurt—her arm lying over his side and her cheek resting against his shoulder blade, like an animal that has crept stealthily to a human's side, seeking reassurance and warmth. The tension of her muscles frightened him, the pent-up bitter grief.

Grief at dreaming the dream that he'd seen. At remembering the one who'd betrayed her. At having to do it alone.

Gently, fearing that if he moved at all she'd flee, he turned and gathered her into his arms.

As she had in the gun room, she breathed once, hanging on to something for as long as she could, then let it go.

For a long time she wept, silently and without fuss or apology, the hot damp of her tears soaking into his ragged jumpsuit, her body shaking with the draw and release of her breath.

"It's all right," said Luke quietly. Her hair, thick and rough-textured as it appeared, was startlingly fine to his touch, springy where gathered into his hands, filling them and overflowing. "It's all right."

After a long time she said, "He thought I'd never try it myself. He meant to save my life. I know that. He knew I'd know."

"But he still made it his decision, not yours."

Against his chest he felt her small, wry smile. "Well, it was *his* decision, so it had to be right, didn't it? I'm sorry. That sounds bitter—a lot of his decisions *were* right. He was a demon of a fighter. But this . . . I felt it. I knew there would be no getting back in, once we were away. I was angry for a long time."

"*I'm* angry at him."

He remembered the faint, attenuated sense of her, less than a ghost even, in the gun room. Hidden, eroded, worn by exhaustion almost to nothing.

"I'm surprised you helped me at all."

"I wasn't going to," she said. He felt her move her arm, push the hair from her face. "Not out of hate, really, but . . . It all seemed so distant. So unreal. Like watching morrts scurry around the bones of the ship."

"Yet you stayed," said Luke, even as he spoke understanding that he was dreaming; understanding that the warmth of her body, the long bones and soft fine hair and the cheek resting on his shoulder were her memories of her body, her recollection of what it had been like, long buried and nearly forgotten. "You used the last of your strength, the last of the Force, to put yourself into the gunnery computer, to keep anyone else from taking the ship. For all you knew, forever."

Against his shoulder, he felt her sigh. "I couldn't . . . let anyone come aboard."

"All those years . . ."

"It wasn't . . . so bad, after a time. Djinn had taught us, had theoretically walked us through, the techniques of projecting the mind into something else, something that would be receptive, to hold the intelligence as well as the consciousness, but he seemed to regard it as cowardly. As being afraid or unwilling to go on to the next step, to cross over to the other side. Once I was in the computer . . ."

She shook her head, and he felt the gesture of her hand, trying to speak of some experience beyond his ken. "After a time it began to seem that it had been my entire life. That what came before—Chad, and the sea, and Papa; Djinn's teaching, the platform on Bespin, and . . . and Geith—they turned into a sort of dream. But the tripods . . . they're a little like the treems back home, sweet and harmless and well-intentioned. I wanted to help them. I was so glad when you did. That was the first time I really . . . really saw you. And even the Jawas . . ."

She sighed again, and tightened her hold on him, her arm around his rib cage sending a shock of awareness through him, as if its shape and strength and the pressure of her hand had somehow a meaning and a truth to which all other things in his life were tied. He understood for the first time how his friend Wedge could write poems about Qwi Xux's pale, feathery hair. The fact that it was Qwi's made all the difference.

She said, "Luke . . ." and he brought her face to his, and kissed her lips.

Chapter 18

In the throbbing indigo darkness, Framjem Spathen rolled back his head so that the long electric ropes of his glowing hair brushed the floor, raised arms glistening with cutaneous diamonds to flash in the bloody light, and screamed. The scream seemed to lift him onto his toes, rippling through that hard-muscled body in wave after wave of sound and pain and ecstasy as he rolled his head, heaved his hips, stretched his fingers to the utmost . . .

"Were those muscles all really his?" wondered Bran Kemple, drawing on a hookah that smelled like old laundry steeped in alcohol and regarding the holo—an extremely old one, Han had seen it in dozens of cheap clubs from here to Stars' End—with half-shut eyes.

"Sure they were," said Han. "He paid about two hundred credits per ounce for 'em, plus installation, but after that they were his, all right."

The dancers on either side of Framjen's holo were real; a boneless Twi'lek boy and a massively breasted Gamorrean female, undulating under the red glare of lights for the edification of half a dozen seedy customers. It would have been hard to picture anything less conducive to lust, Jungle or otherwise. The day-shift hustlers of various races and sexes were working the floor hard, chatting up the patrons and drinking glass after glass of watered liquor at prices that should have brought 100 percent Breath of Heaven. Even they looked tired.

Han supposed that having to listen to a fifteen-year-old Framjen Spathen holo for eight hours would tire anyone.

Bran Kemple sighed heavily. "Nubblyk the Slyte. Now there was a hustler who could run things. Things was all different in his day."

Han sipped his drink. Even the beer was watered. "Pretty lively, hunh?"

"Lively? Pheew!" Kemple made a kiss-your-hand motion toward the ceiling, presumably a signal to the Slyte's departed spirit. "Wasn't even the word. Half a dozen flights in a week that never made it on the port manifests, people appearin' and disappearin' through the tunnels out under the ice . . . Decent drinks and decent girls. Hey, Sadie!" he yelled, gesturing to the one-eyed Abyssin barkeep. "Get my friend here a decent drink, fer pity's sakes! Festerin' barkeep can't tell the festerin' difference between a mark and somebody in the trade, fester it."

He shook his head again, and mopped at his broad, pale-green brow with a square of soiled linen he'd dragged from the depths of his yellow polyfibe suit. His curly brown hair was surrendering to its destiny, and he'd picked up a couple of extra chins in the years since Han had last seen him as a two-bit gunrunner in the Juvex Systems.

"So what happened?"

"What happened?" Kemple blinked at him through the gloom. "Place got cleaned out. He'd been strippin' old machinery, droids and computers and lab stuff, down under the ruins. Some kind of old laboratories, they musta been, and there were rooms full of 'em, Nubblyk said. I will say for Nubblyk . . ."

The Abyssin brought Han a drink that would have flattened a rancor, and Kemple, evidently forgetting for whom he'd ordered it, polished it off, his long, prehensile tongue questing around the bottom of the glass for stray drops.

"I will say for Nubblyk, he kept a strong hand on the loot, played it out and kept anybody else from hornin' in. It was his show, nobody else's, and he didn't trust a soul. And why should he, hey? Business is business. He never even told *me* how he was gettin' into the tunnels."

"D'ja look for the way in, after he left?"

" 'Course I did!" Kemple's vertical pupils flexed open and shut indignantly. "Think I'm stupid or somethin'?" Two new dancers climbed up to an even older—and scratchier—holo of Pekkie Blu and the Starboys. Han winced. "We checked the cellar of this joint, and that house he had in Painted Door Street, and finally ran a deep-rock sensor scan of the ruins themselves." He shrugged. "Double zeros. Not enough gold or xylen under there to register. We couldn't even pay the rental on the scanner. He musta cleaned the place out before—"

He stopped himself.

Solo raised his eyebrows. "Cleaned the place out before he went where?"

"We don't know." He lowered his voice and glanced nervously over at the Abyssin barkeep, who was pouring out a drink for a tall black girl and listening to a long tale of the last mark's perfidy. "That woman who rents the house in Painted Door Street says the credit house where she sends the money every month changes a couple times a year, so it sounds like he's on the run. But before he left he said . . ."

He leaned forward to whisper. "He said something about the Emperor's Hand."

Mara Jade. Solo's eyebrows quirked up. She'd neglected to mention this in last night's discussion. "Oh, yeah?"

Kemple nodded. Solo recalled that the man never could keep that enormous mouth of his shut. "He said the Emperor's Hand was on the planet; that his life was in danger." He leaned close enough for Solo to be able to tell the composition of his last three drinks by the smell of his breath and sweat. "I'm thinkin' he cleared out and ran."

"Could he have cleared out that much loot?"

"How much?" Kemple straightened up and reached for his hookah again. "It must have been playin' out, anyway, for him to take it all with him. Believe me, we ran sensor scans up, down, backwards, and sideways of the ruins and this place and his house, and you don't get *that* many sensor malfunctions."

Oh, don't you? thought Solo, remembering Leia's questions about unexplained flutters in the behaviors of droids.

"Mubbin didn't buy it."

Han looked sharply around at the new voice. It was one of the hustlers, a childlike Omwat like a little blue fairy, with eyes a thousand years old.

"Mubbin the Whiphid," he explained. "Another of the Slyte's runners. He always said there were shipfuls of stuff still down there—"

"Mubbin didn't know what he was talkin' about," said the city boss quickly, a gleam of guilty nervousness in his eyes. He looked back at Han. "Yeah, I heard Mubbin go on about how much stuff there still was . . ."

"He was Drub McKumb's pal, wasn't he?" Solo addressed the question to the hustler, not Kemple. He remembered the Whiphid Chewie had killed, thin and starved and screaming in the dark.

The boy nodded. "One of my pals was with Drub when he went down that well in the ruins and ran a scan, looking for Mubbin. Drub was convinced he'd gone down looking for the stuff and never came out." He glanced at Kemple. "Some people around here refused to give him a hand when he said he'd go looking himself."

"Those scans found absolutély zip," pointed out Kemple hastily. "Zero. A lot of zero. If that wasn't good enough for Drub, then—"

"Wait a minute," said Han. "They ran a *life scan* down there?"

"From the room at the wellhead," said the Omwat. Like most of his race he had a high, sweetly flutelike voice. "My pal was a treasure hunter. She had a Speizoc g-2000 she'd got off an Imperial Carillion ship and that thing could pick up a Gamorrean morrt in a square kilometer of permacrete."

"And there was nothing down there but kretch and pit-molds." Kemple blew a thin cloud of steam. "Drub ran two or three scans—one for the Whiphid and one for xylen and gold. Did the same from the house on Painted Door Street, lookin' for a tunnel entrance there."

"What'd he tell the woman renting the place?"

"Miss Roganda?" The boy grinned. "That they'd had reports of 'malignant insect infestation' and were inspecting every old Mluki foundation in town. She got all helpful and offered 'em tea."

"Roganda?" Han felt the hair lift on the back of his neck. "You mean she's the one who's renting Nubblyk's old house?"

"Sure," said Kemple, turning his attention back to the dancers. "Nice lady—darned pretty woman, too. She could work at this place like a shot, not that this place, or anyplace in town, has that kind of class anymore. Got *somebody* keepin' her in high style, anyway. Showed up a month or two after the Slyte disappeared and said she'd made arrangements to rent the place. She seemed to know him." He gave Han a wink that was supposed to be slyly sophisticated and succeeded only in looking puerile. "Roganda Ismaren."

The room where they put Leia was a large one, hewn out of rock and equipped—startlingly—with a window of three wide casements, through which wan daylight filtered even before Lord Garonnin slapped the wall switch to activate the glowpanels of the ceiling. "By all means try to break it if it will amuse you, Your Highness," he said, observing the immediate direction of Leia's interest. "It was put in long before the dome, and the locks are made to withstand almost anything."

She walked over to it, leaving Lord Garonnin, Irek, and Roganda in the doorway. The window was in a sort of bay, whose jut from the rock of the cliff hid any sign of it from below. A more massive jut overhung it from above, like every irregularity of the cliffs bearded with curtains of vines, so that light from the window could not be seen from anywhere in the rift at night. Through the dangling creepers Leia could see, ten or twelve meters below her and to the right, the topmost courses of the ruined tower.

She remembered seeing this vine-grown overhang from the tower, one of many in the cliff wall behind Plett's House. How many of those, she wondered now, hid the windows of this warren of tunnels and rooms? If she angled her head, she could see down into the stone enclosure where she'd glimpsed the echoes of Jedi children playing. Beyond, the rift was a lake of mist and treetops above which the hanging gardens floated like an armada of flower-bedecked airships. Leia could see the feeders—mostly of the nimbler races, like Chadra-Fan or Verpine, since mechanicals were out of the question under the circumstances—scrambling along the ropes and catwalks that stretched from bed to bed, or from the beds to the supply station, clinging amid its own luxuriant cascades of sweetberry to the cliff wall.

"I still say we should put her in one of the lower rooms," insisted Irek. He shook back his long hair: shoulder-length, black as a winter midnight, and curlier than his mother's. Like hers, his skin was slightly golden, but pallid with the pallor of life lived mostly underground. Like her, he dressed simply but carried himself with the cocky arrogance of one who believes himself to be the center around which all the universe turns.

Leia was familiar with that posture from her days in the marriage mart of the Emperor's Court. A lot of the young men had had it, knowing the universe revolved around them and them alone.

"If we keep her at all," he added, and gave her a look, up and down, calculated to be an insult.

Lord Garonnin replied quietly, "Whatever her position in the Republic, Lord Irek, Her Highness deserves the consideration due to the daughter of one of the Great Houses."

Irek opened his mouth to snap a reply and Drost Elegin's lip curled slightly with something close to smugness, as if his opinion about the boy and his mother had been borne out to their discredit. Roganda put her hand quickly on her son's shoulder and added, "And for the time being, my son, she is our guest. And this is what we owe to our guests." It might have been Aunt Rouge speaking—Leia could see Roganda's eyes on Elegin as she brought out the words, and guessed they were more to impress him with her knowledge of how Things Should Be Done than from any true concern for Leia's comfort.

"But . . ." Irek glanced from his mother's face, to Garonnin's, to Leia's, and subsided. But the full lips were sullen, the blue eyes smoldering with a secret discontent.

"It is time we looked to our other guests."

Irek threw a cocky glance back to Leia and said, with deliberate malice, "I suppose we can always kill her later, can't we?" He transferred his gaze to Garonnin and added, "Have you caught that droid of hers yet?"

"The men are searching the tunnels between here and the pad," said Lord Garonnin. "It won't get far."

"It better not."

The boy turned and strode out, followed by Roganda in a whisper of silk.

Garonnin turned back to Leia. "They are parvenus," he said, his matter-of-fact tone containing, by its sheer lack of apology, something abyssally deeper than contempt for those not of the Ancient Houses. "But such people have their uses. With him as our spearhead, we will be able to negotiate from a position of power with the military hierarchies that fight for control of the remains of Palpatine's New Order. I trust you will be comfortable, Your Highness."

Chief of State of the New Republic and architect of the Rebellion she might be, but Leia could see that she remained, in his eyes, Bail Organa's daughter . . . and the last surviving member of House Organa. The last Princess of Alderaan.

"Thank you," she said, biting back the annoyance she had always felt at the old Senex aristocracy and speaking to him aristocrat to aristocrat, sensing in him a potentially weak link in the chains that bound her. "I appreciate your kindness, my lord. Am I to be killed?" She fought to keep sarcasm out of her voice, to replace it with that dignified combination of martyrdom and noblesse oblige with which, she had been taught, aristocratic ladies surmounted every adversity from genocide to spotty tableware at tea.

He hesitated. "In my opinion, Your Highness, you would be of far more use as a hostage than as an example."

She inclined her head, veiling her eyes with her lashes. Lord Garonnin came of the class that did not kill hostages.

Whether the same could be said for Roganda and her son was another matter.

"Thank you, my lord."

And thank you, *Aunt Rouge,* she added silently, as the burly aristocrat bowed to her and closed the door behind him.

The bolts hadn't even finished clanking over as Leia began her search of the room.

There was, unfortunately, little enough to search. Though large, the chamber contained almost no furniture: a bed built of squared ampohr logs and equipped with an old-fashioned stuffed mattress and one foam pillow so old that the foam was starting to yellow; a worktable, also of ampohr logs, beautifully put together but whose drawers contained nothing; a lightweight plastic chair of a truly repellent lavender. A screened-off cubicle contained sanitary facilities; a curtainless rod with pegs embedded in the wall behind it indicated where someone had once hung clothes.

Leia noted automatically that all the furniture was human proportioned, the plumbing fitted for human requirements.

The room had been cut out of stone, accurately but roughly, the walls smoothed after a fashion but not finished. The door was metal, and fairly new. Marks of other hinges indicated it had replaced one probably less substantial. This high above the hot springs that warmed the caves, without her t-suit it would have been unpleasantly cold.

Leia touched the places where the older set of hinges had been, and thought, *They changed this place over to be a prison . . . When?* She wished she knew offhand the decay rate of foam pillows. It might tell her something.

And for whom?

The door latches clicked.

She felt, at the same moment, a thick, weighted buzzing in her head, a heavy sleepiness, and for an instant nothing mattered to her but going over to the bed and lying down . . .

The Force. A trick of the Force.

She shoved it off—with a certain amount of difficulty—and retreated from the door as far as she could, knowing who would come in.

"You're still awake." Irek sounded surprised.

He had a blaster and a lightsaber. Leia kept to the vicinity of the window, knowing better than to bolt for the door. "You're not the only one around here who can use the Force."

He looked her up and down again, contempt in his blue eyes. He was, she guessed, fourteen or fifteen years old. She wondered if he'd made the lightsaber that hung at his side, or had gotten it from somewhere—someone—else. "You call that *using* the Force?" He turned and regarded a place on the rock of the wall slightly to the right of the bed. She felt what he did with his mind, with the Force; felt, as she had in the tunnels, the trained power of his will and the dark taint that stained its every usage.

Where there had been only the dark reddish stone, there was now a hole about half a meter square.

He giggled, childishly shrill. "Never seen anything like that before, have you?" He crossed to the place, but Leia still felt him watching her. His hand was close to his blaster and she remembered his words in the hall of the stream.

With her dead, the Republic will crumble.

He hadn't liked being contradicted and, what's more, didn't believe he was wrong. She suspected he didn't believe he *could* be wrong.

He would have loved to shoot her while trying to escape.

He took a black plastene pouch from the hole, and at his nod, the stone reappeared as it had been. He gave her his cocky, charming grin. "Even my mother doesn't know about that one," he said, pleased with himself. "And she wouldn't know how to open it if she did." He tossed the pouch lightly in his hand. Leia recognized it—the twin of the one

she'd found hidden in the old toy room, and of the one Tomla El had
taken from Drub's pocket.

"She doesn't know as much as she thinks she does. She thinks I can't
handle this, either; thinks I can't use the Force to turn it into another
source of power."

The blue eyes glittered. "But with the Force on my side, *everything* is
a source of power. As they'll all find out."

Leia watched him, saying nothing, as he crossed to the door. Then he
turned back, his face suddenly clouded.

"Why didn't your droid stop?" he asked. "Why didn't it obey me?"

"What made you think it would?" she returned, folding her arms.

"Because I have the Force. I have the power."

She tilted her head a little to one side, considering him in silence. Not
needing to say, *You obviously don't all the time.*

And he couldn't tell her she was wrong, she thought, without telling
her how he had acquired that power in the first place.

After a moment he hissed at her, "Sow!" and stormed out the door,
slamming and locking it behind him.

It took Leia fifteen sweating, aching minutes to open the hole in the
wall once more. She had sensed, quite clearly, what he did—the compartment in the wall was built with a segment of the rock that covered it keyed
to be literally shifted into another dimension by the power of the Force. It
was old, she sensed, designed and built by a Jedi of vast power, and even
so small a quantity of shift required a control and a strength almost
beyond her capacity. By the time the shift took place she felt drained, as if
she'd worked out with the sword for an hour, or run for miles. Her hands
were shaking as she reached inside.

There was a little cream-colored yarrock powder spilled on the bottom.

Easily obtainable enough in any spaceport, of course. If Irek was
anything like some of the more self-destructive spirits at the Alderaan
Select Academy for Young Ladies, he had packets of the stuff cached
everywhere. It would explain how Drub McKumb had come by it, and
obtained the temporary sanity it brought.

There were other things in the compartment, shoved farther in. Bundles of flimsiplast notes. Tiny skeins of wire. A couple of small soldering
guns. A handful of xylen chips.

A gold ring that, when brought to the light and rubbed, proved to be the mark of an honorary degree at the University of Coruscant.

A small gold plaque commemorating the dedication of the Magrody Institute of Programmable Intelligence.

A woman's gold-meshed glove.

Leia opened the notes, and at the bottom of the last page a signature caught her eye.

Nasdra Magrody.

To this day I don't know if Palpatine knew.

Curled up in the window seat, Leia read the words with a strange sense of almost-grief, of pity for the man who had written them in this room, not all that many years ago. The heavy black lines of the chip schematics traced on the other side bled through the pale-green plast a little, giving the effect of a palimpsest, like an allegory of tragedy. Calm scientific fact and the dreadful usages to which it had been put. In his way, Magrody had been as naive as the Death Star's hermetically sheltered designer, Qwi Xux.

She wondered if he'd written this on the back of his notes because it was the only writing material he was allowed.

Probably, she thought, considering the marginless edges, the way the bold calligraphy cramped at top and bottom. *Probably.*

> *I should have suspected, or known, or guessed. Why would an Imperial concubine, with all the pleasures and privileges available to those who have nothing to do but care for their own beauty, have sought out the bookish middle-aged wife of a robotics professor, if not for some kind of intrigue? I never paid attention to the affairs of the Palace, the constant jockeying for position among the Emperor's ministers and the more vicious, behind-the-scenes power plays engaged in by wives and mistresses each intent on being the mother of Palpatine's eventual heir.*
>
> *I thought such matters beneath the concern of scholarship.*
>
> *I paid a high price for my absentminded ignorance.*
>
> *I only pray that Elizie, and our daughter, Shenna, will not be required to pay as well.*

Leia closed her eyes. All the reports she had received after the destruction
of Alderaan and the demolition of the Death Star had assumed Magrody
had disappeared willingly, probably into the Emperor's infamous think
tank, in flight from retribution by the Rebellion for what he had done.
Those reports, that is, that didn't assume that Leia herself had been
behind the distinguished scientist's sudden absence. Many attributed
work on the Sun Crusher to him. *Took his wife and daughter and went into
seclusion someplace . . .*

Would her father have traded his ideals, gone to work for the Emperor, to save her?

It had been her biggest fear on board Vader's Star Destroyer, and
later on the Death Star itself—that Bail Organa would yield to threats to
do her harm.

She still didn't know. He'd never been offered the choice.

*Mon Mothma will laugh, I suppose, at the ease with which I
was lured to the place where they picked me up. And well she
might, should circumstance ever permit her to laugh at anything
connected with the evils that I have been required to perform. I
thought all I had to do was some single service—they'd let Elizie
and Shenna free, perhaps put me down on some deserted planet,
where I'd eventually be found . . .*

A frightening annoyance, but finite.

Dear gods of my people, finite.

*Roganda Ismaren told me it was all in the Emperor's name.
She had a small collection of bullyboys around her, military types
but none in uniform. I suppose she could have bribed them with
money juggled from Treasury funds, or deceived them as she
deceived me. She was herself clever enough with finances—and
blackmail—to obtain whatever she wanted. There seemed to be far
more money than personnel in evidence:* [Leia had noticed this
herself] *the finest, newest, most exquisite equipment available, cut-
ting-edge programs and facilities, but the same ten or twelve guards.*

*Though she told me—and the guards—that all was by his
command, I never received one scrap of empirical or circumstantial
evidence that Palpatine was in any way involved.*

It didn't matter.

*I didn't even know what planet they took me to, or where
Elizie and Shenna were, after the one time I saw them.*

Leia shivered, though the window seat where she read was the warmest
spot in the room, and looked out into the eerie rainbows of the atmosphere under the dome. She remembered, the night before the Time of
Meeting, sitting beside one of the fountains in the rooftop gardens of the
Ithorian guest house while Han pointed out to Jaina and Jacen which star
was Coruscant's sun. On Coruscant itself—the Scintillant Planet, old
songs called it—the flaming veils of its nightly auroras prevented amateur
astronomy, but Ithor was without even the lights of cities. The sky there
seemed to breathe stars.

Most of those stars had worlds of some kind circling them, though
they might be no more than bare balls of rock or ice or frozen gas
habitable only after prohibitively expensive bioforming. Fewer than
twenty percent had been mapped. Before the day of Drub McKumb's
attack, Leia had never even heard of Belsavis.

Worlds were large.

And life appallingly short.

*What they wanted was simple, they told me. My talents—
unsuspected, I thought, by any—had led me to study the records of
the old Jedi, to experiment with the mental effects attributable by
them to the energy field referred to as the Force.*

Talents? thought Leia, startled. *Magrody was Force-strong?*

It was something she hadn't known, something Cray had never mentioned, probably hadn't known either. Considering the Emperor's attitude toward the Jedi—in which he had never been alone—it was hardly
surprising the man had kept it hidden.

*I thought I had been successful in concealing, in my experi-
ments, my own abilities to influence this energy field by means of
thought wave concentrations, an ability that I believe to be hereditary and not limited to the human species. Perhaps Roganda Ismaren, or the Emperor himself, had deduced from my articles in the*

Journal of Energy Physics *that I knew more about directed thought waves than I ought.*

In any case, for my sins, I had reflected on the tradition, or legend, that the Jedi were unable to affect machinery or droids by means of the "Force." In the light of the nature of subelectronic synapses, I speculated about the possibility of an implanted subelectronic converter, to be surgically inserted in the brain of one who possessed such hereditary ability to concentrate thought waves, enabling him or her, with proper training, to influence artificial intelligences of varying complexities at the individual synaptic level.

This was what they wanted me to do.

Irek, thought Leia. Perhaps the boy actually was the Emperor's son, though given Palpatine's age at the probable time of Irek's conception—and given Roganda's coolly unscrupulous talents as a planner—the odds were good that he wasn't.

And if Roganda was his mother, there was no need for Palpatine's seed to guarantee that Irek would be himself strong in the Force.

Given the atmosphere of Palpatine's Court, the pervasive use of fear and threat, the infighting of factions and pretenders to power, Leia could only guess at what attempts might have been made on Roganda's life before Irek was born.

No wonder Roganda was a liar, a chameleon, an adept manipulator of emotions and situations and behind-the-scenes power. If she hadn't been she'd have been killed.

It was quite clear from the timing of events that Roganda, a child of the Jedi herself, had set out almost at once to better the hand she had been dealt at Irek's birth.

Irek had been implanted at the age of five, before the debris from Alderaan had even settled into its permanent, ragged orbit around what had been that planet's sun.

Had she planned it herself in her most malicious daydreams, Leia could have evolved no more wretched vengeance upon the man who had taught the Death Star's designers.

Nasdra Magrody had been kept, drugged with mild doses of antidepressant just sufficient to rob him of any will to leave, in a comfortable villa on a planet so inhospitable, so dangerous, so teeming with bizarre insect-borne viruses, that to step outside the magnetic field that surrounded the gardens would have resulted, within hours, in his death.

I can only be thankful I had already been soothed with Telezan before they demonstrated this fact to me [he wrote sadly]. *I still don't know the name of the man they tied up outside the boundaries of the field, or his crime, if he'd committed one—the commander in charge assured me he had, but of course that could have been a lie. The bullyboys who took him out there wore t-suits, which they then cut to pieces in front of me. The man himself lasted two hours before he began to swell up; his decomposing flesh didn't begin to slough until nearly sunset, and he died shortly before dawn. If it hadn't been for the drug I don't think I'd have slept at all, either that night, or any night in the four years that I remained there.*

They supplied me regularly with holos of my wife. I was comfortable, and studied, and perfected the techniques by which subelectronic synapses could be controlled. I think that in spite of the drugs I was aware that in those two years there was no alteration of Elizie's face—nor of the length of her hair—in the holos. Of Shenna, who would have grown from girl to woman in that time, they never sent me anything at all. I did my best not to think about what that meant. The drugs made that easy.

When Irek was seven, his training began. It was obvious to Leia, from what Magrody said, that the boy had already had training in the use of the Force, the swift and easy simplicities of the dark side. With the less punitive accelerated learning procedures Magrody had developed for the Omwat orbital station, he learned enough, by the age of twelve, to qualify for an advanced degree in subelectron physics or a position as a droid motivator technician—at what cost Leia, recalling Cray's desperate measures to accelerate learning, could only guess.

Every now and then a tree feeder will go mildly amok and wander through the streets of the town squirting nutrient at passersby . . .

Bizarre enough when Jevax had told her of it last night, but clear as daylight, Leia realized, when she understood that a twelve- or thirteen-year-old boy was developing his powers to alter the behavior of droids.

Visualize the schematic, Roganda had said . . .

Leia thought about the mechanical intelligences behind every ship in the Republic's fleet, and shivered again.

Chewbacca had repaired Artoo, obviously not rewiring in the same fashion . . . and Irek had lost his power over the droid.

Han, she thought desperately. Like Drub McKumb, even if she lost her own life, she had to get word out to them of the danger they faced, and how to circumvent the boy Irek's powers. *They're there . . . they're gathering . . .*

Going to kill you all.

More of that night at the Emperor's reception returned to her. Aunt Celly, plump and pink-faced with her fading fair hair looped into the sort of lacquered confection of twirls, pearls, and artificial swags popular twenty-five years previously, had taken her aside and whispered conspiratorially, "It's a hotbed of intrigue, dear; just terrible." She'd glanced across at the slender exquisite concubines. "I'm told they're all at daggers-drawing, my dear. Because of course, whoever can provide him with a child, that child is going to be his heir."

Leia particularly remembered Roganda, like an enameled image of crimson and gold, moving from dignitary to dignitary with that same air of vulnerable shyness . . .

At that time, Leia realized, Irek had to have been at least four years old, and Roganda already gathering her own power base, laying her plans. From things Magrody said, she must already have been training her son in the ways of the dark side of the Force.

There was no way Palpatine would have let such power exist without using it for his own ends. And having acted for him in some things, it would be easy to say, *These orders come from him.*

She wondered how Roganda had come to the old man in the first place, and whether it was he who had turned her to the dark side, as he had turned Vader and for a time turned Luke, or whether Roganda had sought him out when she saw the fate of Jedi who tried to stay free. Somehow, Leia strongly suspected the latter.

Looking back at that levee, she had the tremendous sense of seeing yet another palimpsest, one set of circumstances rising up through another in a complex jungle of double meaning, which at the time she—eighteen years old and filled with her father's Republican ideals—had been completely unaware of.

Her own response to Celly's words still made her wince at her own naïveté: She'd indignantly quoted a dozen points concerning the transfer of power from the Senate Constitution, just as if Palpatine weren't going to tear up that document later in the year.

But in fact, in the power vacuum that had succeeded Palpatine's fall, the generals, with a few notable exceptions, had mostly gone each for him- or herself. None had wanted a regent, particularly not one for an infant child.

The boy is now thirteen years old [wrote Magrody in his final paragraph]. *His control over droids and mechanicals increases daily; his use of the various artifacts of the Jedi his mother brings to him is ever more adept. He can alter sensors and sensor fields, keeping abreast of the wiring patterns of all the standard makes; he amuses himself by causing minor machinery to malfunction. His mother demands much of him, and in consequence of this I fear he has begun dabbling in substances of which she disapproves—telling himself they increase his perceptions and his abilities to use the Force, but in actual fact, I believe, simply because he knows she would disapprove.*

I see well what I have created. Mon Mothma—my friend Bail —all those who tried to enlist my support and help against the rise of Palpatine's power . . . I can only beg for your understanding, for I know that what I have done is not something that can be forgiven.

I will try to get these notes to you in some fashion. Should I not, I fear that all will believe the worst of me. I tried to make the best decisions I could . . . with what results, I pray that you will never have occasion to see.

To you I sign myself in all wretchedness,
Nasdra Magrody

Leia folded the notes together and slipped them into the pocket of her t-suit.

I fear that all will believe the worst of me . . .

With all her power, once the Emperor was dead Roganda had not joined in the immediate and general grab for power—possibly because Irek was too young to use his powers, and possibly because warlords like

High Admiral Thrawn had something against Roganda that Roganda considered insurmountable . . . a DNA comparison, for instance, between the Emperor and the child Irek that proved that the boy was not, in fact, Palpatine's son.

Possibly Thrawn simply didn't like the woman.

It was a viewpoint for which Leia had a good deal of sympathy.

Instead Roganda had come here, to her own childhood home, where she knew she could raise and train her son unnoticed—and where she knew the Jedi had left at least some training aids. Raise him and train him until he *could not* be ignored.

It occurred to her to wonder whether Roganda had been grooming and preparing her own child to replace Palpatine at all.

It sounded very much more, thought Leia uneasily, as if Roganda's intent had been to raise up not another Palpatine . . . but another Darth Vader.

Chapter 19

"Master Luke?"

It was very important.

"Master Luke?"

He had to wake up, come out of it, cross back over to the conscious world from the peaceful subsurface darkness of dreams.

"Please, Master Luke . . ."

Why?

He knew that on the other side of that fragile wall of waking lay the fire heat of nearly unbearable pain. Much better to stay unconscious. He was tired, his body desperate for rest. Without rest, all the Force he could bring to bear on self-healing was wasted, as if he were trying to fill a jar up with water before he'd patched the hole in its bottom.

His leg hurt, a raging infection and stress injuries exacerbating the original severed tendons and cracked bone. Every muscle and ligament felt stretched and torn and every centimeter of flesh ached as if he'd been pounded with hammers. The dreams had been unpleasant. Callista . . .

What could be so important on the other side that it couldn't wait?

After Callista had left—or perhaps while she still lay in his arms, her head pillowed on his shoulder in the aftermath of loving—he had drifted into deeper sleep. He had seen her far off, in the girlhood left behind on Chad, riding mermaidlike behind the sleek black-and-bronze cy'een with her brown hair slicked where the waves broke over her head, or sitting alone on an outbuoy to watch the sun drown itself in the sea. Conversation replayed in his mind: "You sound as if you've studied them." "You could say they were my next-door neighbors growing up . . ."

Only he and Callista were no longer in the dark office, orange words coming out of the black screen like stars at sunset. Rather they sat side by side in that old T-70 he'd sold for bantha feed to pay passage for Ben and himself on the *Millennium Falcon*, all those distant forevers ago.

It surprised him that he hadn't known Callista then. That she hadn't always been someone he knew.

They were on the cliffs above Beggar's Canyon, passing his old macrobinocs back and forth to watch the startlingly unobtrusive progress of a line of banthas among the rocks of the opposite rim, the clumsy beasts moving faster than one would guess from their appearance, the dry wind fluttering the sand-covered veiling of their riders and the slanting sun flashing harshly on metal and glass. "Nobody's ever figured out how to tell a hunting party from a tribe moving house," Luke said, as Callista made an adjustment to the focus. "Nobody's ever seen children or young or whatever—nobody knows whether some of those warriors are females, or even if there *are* male and female Sand People. Mostly when you see Sand People—or even hear the banthas roaring—you just head the other way as fast as you can."

"Has anyone ever tried to make friends with them?" She handed the binocs back, brushed a blowing trail of hair from her eyes. She still wore the baggy gray coverall she'd had on in some earlier dream, but her face was clean and unscarred now and she looked less strained, less exhausted, than she had. He was glad of that, glad to see her happy and at ease.

"If anyone tried, he didn't survive to talk about it." Out of sheer habit Luke scanned his own side of the canyon rim, and the rocks below. He saw no sign of the Tuskens, but then, one frequently didn't. "There was an innkeeper over at Anchorhead who had the bright idea of trying to get them on his side—I think he wanted to go into the desert pirate business. He noticed they raid pika and deb-deb orchards—those are sweet fruits they grow in some oases—and cooked up sugar water in a still to see if he could use it to bargain with them. It supposedly got them paralytically drunk and they seemed to enjoy it. He made up another batch and they came back and killed him."

Luke shrugged. "Maybe they didn't like feeling good."

She turned, her gray eyes widening, like one who has seen a revelation. "But that explains everything!" she cried. "It's a clue to where they come from!"

"What?" said Luke, startled.

"They're related to my uncle Dro. He *hated* to have a good time and didn't think anybody else should either."

Luke laughed, and all the diamond hardness, the dark-forged Jedi strength of his heart, was transfigured into light. He swung the speeder in a swooping dive away down the trail. "Wow! That means your uncle Dro is related to *my* aunt Coolie . . ."

"Which means we're long-lost cousins!"

Luke mimed a wildly exaggerated double take of recognition; they were laughing like teenagers as they sped down the trail. "C'mon," he said. "We're gonna be late—it's past noon now and we've got to be there at sixteen hundred." The speeder's shadow fluttered after them, like a blue-gray scarf dragged over the rocks.

Sixteen hundred, thought Luke. *Sixteen hundred. It's past noon now and we've got to be there at . . .*

Sixteen hundred!

He came to consciousness with a cry, as if he'd been tipped into an acid bath of pain. All the aches and stiffness of his struggle against the droids fell on him like a collapsing wall; he stifled a moan and Threepio cried, "Thank the Maker! I was afraid you were never coming around!"

Luke turned his head, though to do so felt as if he were breaking his own neck. He lay on a pile of blankets and what felt like insulation on the worktable in the fabrications lab just beyond his old headquarters in the quartermaster's office on Deck 12, illuminated by sputtering yellow emergency lights. The antigrav sled floated near the floor along the far wall. Threepio stood beside his makeshift bed with the air of one who had paced at least fifty kilometers back and forth across the four-meter room, the black box of an emergency medkit in his hands.

"What time is it?"

"It's thirteen hundred hours thirty-seven minutes, sir." He set the medkit down beside Luke and opened it. "Miss Callista informed me that you ran afoul of the ship's maintenance droids—and I must say, sir, that I'm absolutely shocked that even the Will could induce such disgraceful behavior in mechanicals—and gave me the coordinates to find you. In addition to changing the dressing on your leg, on her instructions I've administered antishock and a mild metabolic enhancer. But frankly, sir, even with proper first aid I don't consider you in any condition to fight the Gamorreans, although I can only speak from personal observation, not being a medical droid myself. How do you feel, sir?"

"Like the last third of a hundred-kilometer road race with a busted stabilizer." Luke taped shut the gash in the leg of his coverall over the last three perigen patches he or Threepio had been able to find. "I think I want one of those about the size of a blanket." He gingerly moved his shoulder, which had been all but dislocated in the struggle—the shrapnel cuts on his face smarted with disinfectant and the flesh all around them was swollen and exquisitely tender to the touch. His left hand and arm, burned by shorting wires, had been clumsily bandaged and dosed with some kind of local anesthetic, which wasn't working very well. The skin of his right hand had been cut open, bloodless, to show the glint of metal underneath.

"I don't believe they make them in that size, sir." Threepio sounded worried.

As well he might, thought Luke.

"I wonder if the foo-twitter is still up there?"

"It's fine." Her voice was in his head, clear and soft—the words might even have been actually audible, because Threepio replied, "But, Miss Callista, diversion or no diversion, Master Luke is scarcely up to taking on Gamorreans—"

"No, we've been going about this all wrong," said Luke. "If the Will can program droids to think I'm garbage that needs recycling—or can program Gamorreans to think Cray is a Rebel saboteur—it's about time we went into the programming business ourselves."

Torches were burning all around the Gakfedd village when Luke limped through the wide doors of the storage hold. The place stank of acrid smoke and a suggestion of malfunctioning waste disposal, or at the very least too few visits by the increasingly scarce MSEs. By the light of the huge bonfire in front of the central hut Bullyak was constructing a splendid mail shirt of red and blue plastic mess-room plates and engine tape. She looked up with a fierce grunt as the slender Jedi and his gleaming servant stepped into the ring of the firelight.

She said something to him and gestured to him to advance. Threepio translated, "The Lady Bullyak asks if her husbands did this to you." Another long string of guttural rumbles. "She adds her opinion that neither of them is particularly intelligent or sexually competent, though I really fail to see what bearing that has on the matter."

"Give the Lady Bullyak my compliments and tell her that I've discovered a path to allow her husbands and the other boars of the tribe to redeem themselves in truly heroic combat against worthy enemies."

The sow sat up. Her greenish eyes gleamed like evil jewels in their pockets of warty fat.

"She says that her husbands and the other boars have all become stupid and idle from looking at the computer screens too much, and have neglected their duties to their tribe and to her. She would be grateful to you if you could recall them from this stupid enslavement to the thing in the monitor screens that thinks more about catching vermin than it does about the need of boars to act like boars. She adds further detail that has no apparent connection to the matter at hand."

Luke suppressed a grin. In his mind he could almost hear Callista's snort of laughter.

"Ask her where her husbands might be found."

"Behind you, Rebel scum!"

They were actually grouped in the doorway—empty-handed, for which Luke was profoundly glad. Having paid off the Jawas with the corpse of the G-40 to cut certain power lines, he'd feared his grubby hirelings would be caught in the act.

Ugbuz shoved Threepio aside, sending the droid sprawling with a clatter. Two other boars seized Luke's arms.

"This outage is your doing, eh?" snarled the Gamorrean. "You and your Rebel saboteurs . . ."

Bullyak surged to her feet. "You can be brave warriors against a puny little cripple and a walking talk machine," translated Threepio, rather feebly, from the floor. His voice was nearly drowned by the sow's thunderstorm of shrieks. "But given the chance to meet and fight those stinking misbegotten soap-eating Klaggs, you all run away like morrts to do the bidding of something behind a screen that never even shows itself."

Ugbuz hesitated. The Gamorrean in him was clearly at war with his indoctrinated stormtrooper persona. "But it's orders," he argued at last. "It's the Will."

"It's the Will that you act like true boars," put in Luke gently. In spite of the sweat-stringy hair hanging in his eyes and the bruises all over one side of his unshaven face, his voice was the voice of a Jedi Master, reaching to touch the minds of those with little mind of their own. "Only by being true boars can you be true stormtroopers."

The big boar hesitated, almost visibly wringing his hands. Luke added, to Bullyak, "I have heard that Mugshub laughs at you for having a feeble tribe that won't fight, and calls you Piglet-Mommy."

Bullyak let out a furious squeal and, as Luke had expected, struck him hard enough to have knocked him reeling had the warriors not been holding him. He went limp and rolled with the blow; the infuriated sow kicked Threepio halfway across the hold, then started slapping Ugbuz and every boar in sight, screaming obscenities that Threepio, from his corner, dutifully translated in a startling wealth of anatomical detail.

"But it's the *Will!*" insisted Ugbuz helplessly, as if this were self-explanatory. "It's the *Will!*"

Threepio translated what, in Bullyak's opinion, Ugbuz could do with the Will, and added, "But I'm afraid that doesn't sound at all physically possible, sir."

"Perhaps the Will has changed," offered Luke in his soft voice. "Perhaps now that a way has been found for you to do your duty as fighting boars, it is consonant with the intent of the Will that you do this."

As one, Ugbuz and his men dashed into the big hut at the far end of the hold, Bullyak in high-volume pursuit. Luke picked himself up from the floor where he'd been dropped, helped Threepio to his feet, and, wiping the blood from the corner of his mouth, limped after them.

He found them clustered breathlessly around the monitor screen. In spite of the fact that all computer lines had been cut to the storage hold over an hour ago, a line of orange letters swam up into view.

- It is consonant with the intent of the Will that you ascend to Deck 19 by means of Lift 21 and annihilate those stink-

ing sons of cabbage-pickers, and their mangy little
morrts, too

They nearly trampled him barreling out the door.

"What is it?" growled Ugbuz. At Luke's signal the two stormtroopers
who'd been carrying him for the sake of speed stopped and set him on his
feet. "This ain't Lift Twenty-one." The Gamorrean's piggy yellow eyes
gleamed suspiciously in the dim flare of the emergency lights. The whole
deck was dark now, and the air felt cold, stuffy, and strange. Curious
scramblings and scufflings seemed to whisper all around them in the dark
and Luke realized it had been quite some time since he'd seen a working
SP or MSE. Only their gutted corpses, like roadkills along the walls.

Threepio stood silhouetted in the dark door of the quartermaster's
office, gleaming in the feeble reflection of the lights of Luke's staff.

"Intelligence report." Luke hobbled to the droid's side and put a
hand on the golden metal shoulder to draw him through to the storeroom
beyond the office.

The antigrav sled was there. Additional power had been jacked into it
from the cells of the G-40 and the two snake-droids Luke had killed to
raise it three meters above the floor.

"You okay in here?" he asked softly.

"Quite all right, Master Luke. As long as I remain within the perime-
ters programmed into the trackers the Jawas cannot molest me. But I
suggest that you pay off the Jawas quickly, before the power ebbs to the
point where the sled settles any further."

It had already settled a good half meter—even with the two trackers
Threepio had reprogrammed to stun Jawas, once the sled with its load of
dead robots got within two Jawa-heights of the floor—the point at which
they could stand on each other's shoulders—one way or another, they'd
find a means of helping themselves. Luke could already see the little knot
of brown-robed figures grouped in the door making their calculations,
muttering among themselves in their shrill, childlike voices.

"Any problems?"

The smallest of the Jawas scurried forward, lay down, and kissed
Luke's boots. "Master, we did our best, did our best." It got up again. It

was the one he'd rescued, whom he'd nicknamed Shorty in his mind.
Yellow eyes gleamed like firebugs in the black pit of its hood. "Went to
the places you said, tried to cut the wires you said."

It held out its hand. Luke winced. The clawlike fingers were blistered
and black with burns. Others stepped forward, stretching out their arms,
and the evidence of injury was appalling.

"It's true, Luke." Callista's voice spoke soft at his side. "The cables
feeding power to the Punishment Chamber aren't only shielded, they're
booby-trapped. One of the Jawas was killed trying to get in and two
others are badly stunned. We can't cut power to the grid."

"Something else?" queried Shorty. "Trade you six hundred meters
silver wire, fourteen size A Telgorn power cells, thirty size D Loronar cells
for drive housings, and optical circuitry of two Cybot Galactica
Gyrowheel Multifunctions."

Luke barely heard him. He felt cold, panic whispering under the
bones of his chest. Cray was due to be taken to execution in under an
hour and the grid in the Punishment Chamber was still live. His mind
raced, trying to fit new plans, new conditions . . .

"Twenty size A Telgorns," Shorty urged. "This is all we have. Without
them we will grope in the dark like blind grubs in the rock, but for you,
master, we make a special deal . . ."

"Thirty As," said Luke, recovering, knowing what he'd have to do. If
the Jawas claimed they had twenty size As it meant a stockpile of at least
forty-five. "And thirty Ds, and thirty meters of reversing shielded cable, in
trade for the Gyrowheel Multis. For the rest, you do another job for me."

"All the rest?" Half a dozen hooded heads turned—one Jawa moved
a step toward the black, floating shadow of the sled, and both trackers
swiveled in a flashing of baleful lenses. The Jawa stepped back the precise
eight centimeters required to put it beyond the tracker's range. Luke
realized he'd have to conclude his deal quickly or his currency would end
up being purloined before he even got back with Cray and Nichos. If he
got back with Cray and Nichos.

"All the rest," said Luke. "Easy job. Easy."

"At your service, master, master," whined the Jawas in chorus. They
crowded around him, waving their burned hands and arms. Some had
been bandaged with rags and strips of insulation and uniforms—Luke
wondered if it would be safe to detail Threepio to get them disinfectants
from sick bay and decided it was too risky until Cray was safe. "Do

anything," promised Shorty. "Kill all the big guards. Steal the engines. Anything."

"Okay," said Luke. "I want you to go all over the ship, everywhere, and bring me back all the tripods and put them all in one room. All in the mess hall, and keep them there. Don't hurt them, don't kill them, don't tie them up—just get them there gently, and put out water for them to drink. Okay?"

The Jawa saluted. Its robes smelled like a gondar pit. "Okay, master. All okay. Pay now?"

"Bring power cells to Lift Twenty-one and I pay half." Luke tried not to think how little time remained between the present moment and 1600 hours. Cray was going to be executed and he had to play junk broker to the Jawas . . . "And hurry."

"There already, master." The Jawas flurried away into the darkness. "There yesterday!" High above the floor, the trackers clicked and whirred and dangled their grippers in blind-brained automated disapproval.

Luke leaned on his staff. He was trembling with fatigue. "You okay here by yourself for a little longer?"

"Quite all right, sir. A stroke of brilliance, if you will permit me to say so, sir . . ."

Luke produced the sled controls from his pocket, lowered the sled itself to the floor. He was aware of the smell of Jawas strengthening in the room as he opened the tailgate, awkwardly balancing against the side of the sled as he dragged out the gutted Tredwell and the two Gyrowheel snake-droids. "Okay," he said, slamming the gate again. "It'll be tougher to guard, but I need the sled. You think the trackers can handle it?"

"For a time, sir." The droid sounded worried, peering into the impenetrable shadows, which were not quite impenetrable to those heat-sensitive optic receptors. "Though I must say, those Jawas are diabolically clever."

Callista's voice spoke from the shadows, where Luke had had, all through the conversation, the sense that she stood, just—and only just—out of sight. "Sure is lucky for our side that Luke's diabolically clever, too."

He felt her pride in him, palpable as the touch of her hand.

———

The Jawas were at Lift 21 with the power cells by the time Luke and his sweatily odoriferous forces arrived. Luke was steering the antigrav sled, thankful to be off his feet—he could feel the creep of exhaustion and pain beginning and thought, *Drat, I only put that perigen in a few hours ago!*

He glanced at the chronometer above the doors of the lift. 1520. Down the lift shaft from some floor above, a soft contralto voice floated, "All personnel are to report to observation screens in the section lounges. All personnel are to report to observation screens in the section lounges. Failure to do so will be construed as . . ."

Ugbuz and his stalwarts turned automatically around. Luke sprang from the sled, wincing as he stumbled, and caught the captain's arm. "That doesn't mean you, Captain Ugbuz. Or your men."

The boar frowned laboriously. "But failure to report will be construed as sympathy with the intent of the saboteurs."

Luke focused the Force into the small, cramped dark of that disturbed and divided mind. "You're on special assignment," he reminded him. "Your assignment is to fulfill your destiny as a boar of the Gakfedd tribe. Only thus can you truly serve the intent of the Will."

How easy, he thought bitterly as he saw relief flood the boar's eyes, *it must have been for Palpatine to maneuver men using just those words, just those thoughts.*

And how easy for anyone who did it to become addicted to that smiling rush of satisfied power, when the stormtrooper captain signaled his followers back to the open doors of the shaft.

It was the work of only minutes to link the power cells in series and hook them to the sled's lifters with the long green-and-yellow snakes of the reversing cables. From above, Luke could hear, if he stretched out his perceptions, the breaths and heartbeats of the guards at the upper levels of the shaft. The dim glow of his staff showed him the fused patches of ricochets on the shaft walls, the black scars all around the lift doors where the Klaggs had practiced their aim. In the slow rise of the antigrav sled, the Gakfedds would be sitting targets.

1525.

Luke took the foo-twitter's trackball from his pocket. As he pressed the activation toggle he reached out still farther with his senses, listened to the hollow of the shaft, praying that the enclision grid hadn't shorted the voder circuits . . .

"Nichos!"

Distant, echoing, reduced to a half-heard wailing breath, the cry still came to him, a hideous echo of terror, despair, and fury. Luke's breath caught painfully as he heard—half heard, maybe only felt—the scuffle and clang of boots, the hiss of a door. "Nichos, damn you, act like a man if you remember how!"

And closer, the sudden drift of a guard's voice, "Wot's that?"

Luke heard nothing. But after a moment someone else said, "Stinkin' pond-scum Gakfedds are up here!"

There was a rush of retreating feet.

"Now!" Luke hit the activators on the sled's motors as two Gakfedds slid it out over the edge into the lift shaft. It balanced, bobbed, like a rowboat in a well. Luke graded the power up on a slow curve as the ersatz stormtroopers piled into the sled. He was horribly aware of the dark drop of eighty meters or more beneath him. The sled sank a little under their weight, then held steady; the shaft carried few echoes, but far off, if he shut his eyes, stretched out his awareness, he could hear the Klaggs cursing as they followed the drifting foo-twitter through silent halls and storerooms lit only by the feeble penny dips of emergency lighting. Could almost hear—a breath within his mind—the reverberation of Callista's silent laughter as she maneuvered the tracker ahead of them, like a child pushing a balloon.

Then Cray's voice again, bitterly cursing the man who could not help her as they dragged her through the halls toward her death.

No, thought Luke despairingly, as he upped the slow feed of power into the repulsorlifts. *No, no, no . . .*

The engines whined a moment, desperately fighting weight twice their design capacity on a gravity column already dozens of times higher than they were intended to rise . . .

Luke shut his eyes, and drew on the strength of the Force.

It was hard to concentrate, hard to focus and funnel the glowing strength of the universe through a body crumbling with fatigue and a mind clouded with growing pain. Hard to call into jewel-clear power the lambent energies of stars and space and solar winds, of life—even the sweaty, smelly, angry, and desperately confused creatures around him. For the Force was part of them, too. Part of the tripods, the Jawas, the Sand People, Kitonaks . . . All of them had the Force, the glowing strength of Life.

Concentrating was like trying to focus light through warped and dirty glass. Luke fought to clear his mind, to put aside Cray, and Nichos, and Callista . . . to put aside himself as well.

Slowly, the sled and its burden began to rise.

Only the lift, only the rising, thought Luke. *They are the only things that exist.* No before or after. Like a glittering leaf ascending in darkness . . .

The yells of the Klaggs grew louder.

As if looking at a gauge that had nothing to do with the body or the soul of Anakin Skywalker's son, Luke observed the orange torchlit doorway sinking toward them and readied his hand on the repulsorlift controls. *The idiots are going to jump on each other's shoulders to get to the doors first . . .*

It would capsize the sled and spill them all down nearly 100 meters of shaft, but he couldn't break his concentration enough to say so. Instead he slowed his mind, sped his perceptions, trimming the sled's four lifters separately to compensate as—right on schedule—the Gamorreans leaped and grabbed and piled on each other's shoulders to be the first ones through the doorway, squealing, cursing, waving axes and shoulder cannons, heedless of Luke's execution of maneuvers that would have made a transport tech blench. The sled rocked and heaved but nobody fell. The Gakfedds, accepting the navigational near miracle as a commonplace, were all out of the sled and gone before a true commander would have let any of them stand.

Panting, shaking, sweat burning in the cuts on his face, and cold in every extremity, Luke timed the power dim precisely with their departure so that the sled wouldn't shoot up through the end of the shaft, and then steadied the much-lightened vessel into the torchlit guard lobby of Deck 19. He collected his staff and rolled over the side, too weary to open the tailgate; lay on the floor, fighting the wave of reaction, the weakness of calling on the Force far beyond his current strength.

On the wall, the chronometer read 1550.

Cray, he thought, breathing deep of the stuffy, smoke-filthy air. *Cray. And Cray will help me save Callista.*

I'll pay for this later.

He climbed to his feet.

Now.

In a way it was harder to focus the Force in his own body, to call strength from outside himself, channeling it through muscles burning with the toxins of fatigue and infection and a mind hurting for rest. But that, too, he put aside, moved forward with a warrior's light strength, barely aware of the lurch and drag of his injured leg, the awkwardness of the staff.

The corridor around him rang with the sudden cacophony of battle.

He flattened to the wall as Gamorreans fell out of the hall before him, hacking, yelling, firing almost point-blank with blasters whose shots ricocheted crazily or ripped long burns in the walls; gouging at one another with tusks and raking with stumpy claws, then screams like the rip of metal and canvas and stray gouts of blood stinking like hot copper in the air. Luke dodged, swung around the corner and into the heat of the fray, but saw no glimpse of the green uniform Cray had been wearing, no cornsilk flash of hair. A nightmare vision of Cray lying bleeding in some corridor flashed through his mind—then from the door of a through-passage Callista yelled, "Luke!" and he ran, holding himself up against the wall, barely feeling the sawing pain. "This way!"

"All personnel are to report to the section lounges," said the tannoy, clear now, and Luke thought, *This part of the ship is still alive. The Will is here.* . . .

"All personnel are to report . . ."

"Luke!"

He skidded to a stop around a corner, facing the shut black double door of what was labeled PUNISHMENT 2, over whose lintel a single small light burned amber. Nichos stood against the wall, a statue of brushed silver, the only thing alive in his face the desperate agony of his eyes.

In front of the door stood a human stormtrooper in full armor, blaster carbine ready and pointed in his hands.

"Just stay where you are, Luke," said Triv Pothman's voice. The helmet altered it, rendered it tinnily inhuman, but Luke recognized it all the same. "I know you feel loyal to her but she's a Rebel and a saboteur. If you back off now I can testify in your favor."

"Triv, she isn't a Rebel." Luke scanned the hall with his eyes and mind and detected not a fragment of loose metal, not even a gutted MSE or a mess-room plate . . . "There are no Rebels anymore. The Empire is gone, Triv. The Emperor is dead." He literally didn't think he had the strength to rip the carbine out of Pothman's grip by the Force alone.

Over the door the digital readout changed to 1556, and the amber light began to blink red. Triv hesitated, then repeated in precisely the same tones, "I know you feel loyal to her but . . ."

"That was a long time ago." Luke reached out with his mind, feeling his way to the older man's thoughts as if physically trying to penetrate the white plastic of the dog-faced helmet, the guarding darkness that armored his thoughts. Six meters separated them. Exhausted, blank, vision tunneling to grayness, he fumbled to collect the Force and couldn't, and knew he'd be shot before he covered half the distance. And he wasn't sure he had the strength for even that.

"The Empire left you alone," he said softly. "Alone to be yourself. Alone to do what you wanted, to grow a garden, to embroider flowers on your shirts." He could almost hear, in the dark of the old man's mind, the shrill voice of the Will: *The Jedi killed your family. They descended on your village in the night, they slew the men in the space among the houses, rounded up the women under the trees. . . . You fled in the darkness, stumbling in the mud and streams . . .*

"Remember your captain and the other men killing each other?" said Luke, conjuring the green shadows of the shelter, the gleam of those forty-five white helmets on a plank. The crunch of leaves underfoot and the smoky smell they produced. "Remember the camp you made, and the meadow by the stream? You lived there a long time, Triv. And the Empire disappeared."

"I know you feel loyal to her but she's a . . ."

Vines. The earth. A tiny reptile with jewel-colored feathers picking up a thrown breadcrumb in the doorway. The smell of the stream.

The reality of what had been. The years of peace.

"She's a Rebel and a saboteur . . ."

His voice trailed off.

What had really been, thought Luke. He held it out to Pothman, shining memories of place and time; memories of those things that he himself had actually seen and knew, like a slice of sunlight piercing the digitalized tape loop in Pothman's mind.

The light above the door blinked faster. 1559.

"Festering Skybolts!"

Pothman wheeled and dragged on the locking rings of the doors. Luke sprang, scrambled to help him, the rings gripping fast, refusing to budge, as if held from the other side—or from within the walls themselves, by the Will. Nichos seized them, twisted with the sudden, inexorable, mechanical strength of a droid. Air hissed as the seals broke. "It's fighting me!" yelled Nichos, dragging the door open, and indeed, the heavy steel leaf was pulling visibly at his grip. "It's trying to close . . ."

Luke's lightsaber whined to life in his hands. Cray stood manacled between two support posts, face white with shock and exhaustion in the chalk-opal sheen of the grid's strange light. She yelled, "It's too late!" as Luke limped, stumbled in, slashed at the steel that held her wrists. "It's too late, Luke!"

With the last of his strength Luke blasted at the grid with his mind—misfire, flawed connection, a crucial jump of energy not jumping . . .

A searing, single bolt of lightning pierced the calf of his bad leg like a white needle as Cray dragged him out through the door.

Chapter 20

Cray said softly, "He was there." She wrapped her arms around herself, pulling close the thermal blanket he'd brought her, bowed her head until her cheek rested on her drawn-up knees. "He was there the whole time. He kept saying he loved me, he kept saying be brave, be brave . . . but he didn't do one damn thing to stop them." With her chopped-off hair ragged and dirty and her face haggard with exhaustion and emotional ruin, she looked much younger than she had when Luke had seen her on Yavin, or in her home territory at the Institute, or in Nichos's hospital room.

In all of those places, for all of her life, she had worn her perfection like armor, he saw.

And now that, and all things else, were gone.

Smoky light wavered from the crude lamp in the corner, the only illumination in the room. The air in the cul-de-sac of the quartermaster's office and the workrooms beyond it had gotten so bad Luke wondered if he should take the time to wire the local fans to cannibalized power cells, provided he could find them . . .

If there was time.

Heart and bones, he felt there wasn't.

"He had a restraining bolt—"

"*I know he had a scum-eating motherless restraining bolt, you jerk!*" She screamed the words, spat them at him, hatred and fury a bitter fire in her eyes; and when the words were out sat staring at him in blind, helpless rage behind which Luke could see the fathomless well of defeat, and grief, and the ending of everything she had ever hoped.

Then silence, as Cray turned her face aside. The nervous thinness that had advanced on her during Nichos's illness had turned brittle, as if something had been taken, not just from her flesh, but from the marrow of her bones. Over the torn uniform, grimed with blood and oil, the blanket hung on her like a battered shroud.

She took a deep breath, and when she spoke again her voice was perfectly steady. "He was programmed not to obey anything I said. He wouldn't even get me food."

Luke knew this—Nichos had told him. The tray Threepio had brought from the mess hall was untouched.

"Don't hate him for being what he is," he said, the only thing he could think of to say. "Or for being what he's not."

The words sounded puerile in his own ears, like a half-credit computerized fortune-teller at a fair. Ben, he thought, would have had something to say, something healing . . . Yoda would have known how to deal with the wretched ruin of a friend's heart and life.

The mightiest Jedi in the universe, he reflected bitterly—that he knew of, anyway—the destroyer of the Sun Crusher, the slayer of evil, who'd defeated the recloned Emperor and the Sith Lord Exar Kun, and all he could offer someone who had been disemboweled was, *Gee, I'm sorry you're not feeling so well* . . .

Cray brought her hands up to her head, as if to press some blinding ache from her skull. "I wish I did hate him," she said. "I love him—and that's worse to the power of ten."

She looked up at him, her eyes tearless stone. "Get out of here, Luke," she said without animosity, her face like flash-frozen wax that would crack at a breath. "I want to go to sleep."

Luke hesitated, instinctively knowing that this woman shouldn't be left alone. At his side, Callista said softly, "I'll stay with her."

Nichos, Pothman, and Threepio were in the fabrication lab outside.

Threepio was explaining, "They're quite the slowest and most deliberate race in the galaxy. To the best of my knowledge all of the Kitonaks are still grouped in the section lounge exactly where the Gamorreans put them, still discussing their grandparents' recipes for domit. It's most extraordinary. And yet during their mating season—during the rains—they move with quite amazing speed . . ."

They all turned as Luke came through the office door, and Nichos stepped awkwardly forward, holding out one hand. Cray had taken the mold for it when he was in the hospital, accurate down to the birthmark where the V made by thumb and forefinger came to a point.

Accurate like the blue eyes, the mobile fold at the corner of the lips. Like the gigabytes of digitalized information on family, friends, likes and dislikes, who he was, and what he wanted . . .

"She all right?" asked Pothman into the silence.

"Come on, Nic," said Luke quietly. "Let me get that restraining bolt off you."

Nichos's eyes went past him to the shut door. "I see."

Luke drew breath to speak—though he didn't know what he was going to say, what he *could* say—but Nichos held up his hand, and shook his head. "I understand. I expect she will not want to see me ever again."

As he fetched the toolkit from the locker on the wall, and the old stormtrooper brought one of the flickering battery lights to illuminate his work, Luke honestly didn't know whether, given Cray's parting words to him, she would want to see her fiancé again or not. He took refuge in the task at hand, which was more complicated than a simple pop-on, pop-off bolt usually employed with droids. This one was dogged in with minute magnetized catches, and, Luke could see, programmed in a number of specific ways. The Will had to have instructed the Klaggs in its installation. He ran a quick integral test on it to make sure it hadn't been booby-trapped, then collimated the probe down to the smallest increment and began to pull the internal relays.

There was a certain amount of comfort to be obtained from purely mechanical tasks. He told himself to remember that for another time.

"Luke . . ."

He looked up quickly, to meet the blue glass eyes. In the shadowy gloom the face that he'd known so well was almost a stranger's, affixed monstrously to the silver cowl of the metal skull.

"*Am* I really Nichos?"

Luke said, "I don't know." He had never in his life felt so helpless, because in his heart—in the secret shadows where the truth always lay—he knew that this was a lie.

He knew.

"I was hoping you would be able to tell me," said Nichos softly. "You know me—or you knew *him.* Cray programmed me to . . . to know everything Nichos knew, to do everything Nichos did, to be everything Nichos was, and *to think that I really am Nichos.* But I don't . . . *know.*"

"What do you mean?" protested Threepio. "Of course you're Nichos. Who else would you be? That's like asking if *The Fall of the Sun* was written by Erwithat or another Corellian of the same name."

"Luke?"

Luke concentrated on pulling out the minutely programmed fiber-optic wires.

"*Am* I 'another Corellian of the same name'?"

"I'd like to tell you one way or the other," said Luke. The bolt came away from the brushed-steel chest, lay thick and heavy in Luke's hand. One hand real, one hand mechanical, but both *his.* "But I . . . I don't know. You are who you are. *You* are the being, the consciousness, that you are at this moment. That's all I can tell you." That fact, at least, was true.

The smooth face did not alter, but the blue eyes looked infinitely sad. "I had hoped that, being a Jedi, you would know."

And Luke had the uncomfortable sensation that, having been a Jedi, Nichos knew perfectly well that he was keeping something back.

"I love her." Nichos looked again toward the doorway, his face the calm face of a droid, his eyes the eyes of a desperately unhappy man. "I say that—I know that—yet I cannot tell the difference, if there is one, between the devotion, the loyalty, that Artoo and Threepio feel toward you. And I don't remember whether that's love or something else. I can't set them side by side to compare. When they were holding Cray a prisoner, when they mistreated her, struck her—forced her to go through those stupid parodies of a trial—I would have done anything to help her. Except that, since I was programmed not to interfere with them, it was literally something that I could not do. I could not make my limbs, my body, act in a fashion contrary to my programming not to interfere."

He took the restraining bolt from Luke's hand, held it between thumb and forefinger, examining it dispassionately in the jaundiced glare of the lamp on the table beside them. "The terrible thing is that I don't feel bad about it."

"Why in the universe should you?" asked Threepio, startled.

"No reason," said Nichos. "A droid cannot go against his basic programming, or restraints placed upon his programming if they do not conflict with the deepest level of motivational limiters. But I think Nichos would have."

"She's asleep now."

Luke was as aware of her entering the room as if she'd come through the shut door that separated it from the tiny office. He was alone. In the dense shadows—the batteries on the lamp had gone, finally, and the only illumination came from the emergency supply of grease, burning with makeshift wicks in two big red plastic mess-hall bowls on the worktable—he could almost trick himself into believing he saw her, tall and lanky with her brown hair hanging down her back in a tail as long and thick as his arm.

I can't let her be destroyed, he thought, and his heart twisted with despair.

"Is Nichos all right?"

Luke nodded, then caught himself, and shook his head. "Nichos . . . is a droid," he said.

"I know."

He felt her presence beside him, as if she had hiked herself up to sit next to him on the edge of the workbench, booted feet dangling, as he was sitting. The warmth of her flesh came back to him from his dream, the passionate strength with which she'd clung to him, the sweetness of her mouth under his.

"Luke," she said gently. "Sometimes there is nothing you can do."

He expelled his breath in an angry gust, fist clenched hard; but he did not, after all, speak for a time. Then it was only to say, "I know." He realized he hadn't known that, two weeks ago. In some ways, learning about Sith Lords and cloned Emperors had been easier.

He made a crooked grin. "I guess the trick is learning when those times are."

"Djinn Altis used to teach us that," said Callista softly. "*We have been for ten thousand years the guardians of peace and justice in the galaxy.* He always used to preface his stories, and his teaching, with that. *But sometimes justice is best served by knowing when to fold one's hands.* And he'd come up with some illustrative story from the archives and the oral tradition of the Jedi about some incident where what appeared to be going on wasn't actually what was going on."

He felt the rueful chuckle of her laughter.

"It used to drive me crazy. But he said, *Every student is obliged to make one thousand eighty major mistakes. The sooner you make them, the sooner you will not have to make them anymore.* I asked him for a list. He said, *Thinking there's a list is mistake number four.*"

"How long were you with him?"

"Five years. Not nearly long enough."

"No," said Luke, thinking about the few weeks he'd spent on Dagobah. He sighed again. "I just wish some of those one thousand eighty mistakes didn't involve teaching students. Teaching Jedi. Transmitting power, or the ability to use the Force. My ignorance—my own inexperience—cost one of my students his life already, and threw another one into the arms of the dark side and caused havoc in the galaxy I don't even want to think about. The whole thing—the Academy, and bringing back the skills of the Jedi—is too important for . . . for 'Learn While You Teach.' That's . . ." He hesitated, hating to say it of his teacher but knowing he had to. "That's the mistake Ben made, when he taught my father."

There was silence again, though she was as near to him as she had been in the landspeeder on the canyon rim, passing binocs back and forth while they watched for Sand People . . .

"If Ben hadn't taught your father," said Callista softly, "your father probably wouldn't have been strong enough to kill Palpatine . . . nor would he have been in a position to do so. You couldn't have done it," she added.

"Not then, no." He'd never thought of it that way.

She went on, "I'm recording everything I remember about Djinn's teaching." Her voice was very quiet, like the offer of a gift she wasn't sure would be well received. "I've been working on this, on and off, since you first told me about what you're doing. Techniques, exercises, meditations, theories—sometimes just the stories he'd tell. Everything I remember. Things that I don't think should be lost. Things that will help you. I understand that a lot of the techniques, a lot of the . . . the mental powers, the ways to use the Force . . . can't be described, can only be shown, one person to another, but . . . they may be able to help you, after you leave here."

"Callista . . . ," he began desperately, and her voice continued resolutely over his.

"I'm not a Master, and my perception of them isn't a Master's perception . . . But it's all the formal training that you didn't have the chance to receive. I'll make sure you have the wafers of as much of it as I can finish, before you leave."

"Callista, I can't . . ."

He felt her gaze on him, rain-gray and steady, as she had looked at Geith; and he couldn't go on.

"You can't let this battle station fall into the hands of whoever it is who's learned to use the Force to move electronic minds," she said. She was so real—she had come back so far along the road—that he would have sworn he felt the touch of her hand on his. "I traded my life for it thirty years ago, and I'd trade yours and Cray's and whoever else is on this battle station if I—if we—have to. Where did you send the others?"

He recognized it as a shift of topic, a deliberate looking away from the realization that he would have to destroy her; or perhaps, he thought, it was just that she knew—as he knew—that time was too short to waste words when they both knew she was right.

He took a deep breath, reorganizing his thoughts. "To the main mess hall," he said. "I've figured out how to neutralize the Sand People and get at the shuttles."

"If she's angry at *you* for only doing what you had to," said Triv Pothman, his soft bass voice echoing strangely in the utter silence of the lightless halls, "she's not going to want to even see my face. And I don't blame her!"

See-Threepio's hyperacute hearing dissected the tight shrillness of anguish in his voice, and the sensors on his left hand—which the human was clasping, since the corridor was pitch dark—registered both abnormal cold and greater than usual muscular tension, also signs of stress.

That Pothman would experience stress in the circumstances was of course understandable. Threepio had learned that total darkness created disorientation and symptoms of fear even when the human involved knew that he was in perfect safety—which was certainly not the case on this benighted vessel. But he gathered from the context of the words that the darkness, the realization that air was no longer circulating on these decks and available supplies of oxygen would be exhausted in eight months— even with the small amount of photosynthesis being produced by the Affytechans—and the knowledge that Sand People occupied the vessel, were not the main sources of the former stormtrooper's distress, though in Threepio's opinion they should have been.

"Surely she realizes that the indoctrination process rendered you no more capable of independent action than Nichos was while under the influence of the restraining bolt?" Threepio kept his voder circuits turned down to eighteen decibels, well below the hearing threshold of either Gamorreans or Sand People, and adjusted the intensity so that the sound waves would carry exactly the .75 meters that separated his speaker from Pothman's ear.

"I hit her, I . . . I insulted her . . . said things I wish I'd cut out my own tongue rather than say to a young lady . . ."

"She was indoctrinated herself, and will be familiar with the standardized secondary personality imposed by the programming."

"Threepio," said Nichos's quiet voice from the darkness behind, "sometimes that doesn't matter."

Pale light dimmed the darkness up ahead, delineating the corner of a cross-corridor, the appalling mess that littered the floor—plates, gutted MSEs and SPs, shell casings from projectile grenades, broken ax handles, and spilled food and coffee. Morrts scuttled among the filth and their sweetish stink, like dirty clothes, added to the general offensiveness of the scene. The soft murmur of air-circulating equipment became audible, if one could separate it out from the truly appalling clamor coming from the mess hall: squeals, shrieks, and drunken voices singing "Pillaging Villages One by One."

Pothman closed his eyes in a kind of embarrassed pain. Nichos remarked, "Well, I see everybody made it back from the battle."

"Awful thing is," said Pothman, "I suspect Kinfarg and his boys are doing the same thing up on Deck Nineteen. Mugshub was pretty sore at them for not doing their duty by her and getting into fights with everybody they saw."

"Really," said Threepio in prissy disapproval, "I doubt that I shall ever understand organically based thought processes."

"You'd better stay out in the corridor," whispered Nichos to Pothman. In the dim glow from the mess-hall door—the only area on Deck 12 that retained any power—the antigrav sled bobbed behind them like a dory at a wharf. The overburdening it had taken in the lift shaft had left it with a blown stabilizer, but it was still easier to tow it than to carry what Luke had instructed them to bring back to the fabrications lab.

"Threepio and I are perceived as droids—that is, something they don't have to worry about." Indeed, with the fine metal mesh that had covered his joints and neck torn away and hanging in rags to expose the linkages and servos beneath, he looked more than ever like a droid. "I don't think they'll even notice us or ask us about what we're doing. They might recognize you as a Klagg."

Pothman nodded. He was rather like a shining robot himself in the white armor of a stormtrooper, a blaster slung at his side, except for the thin dark face with its lines of age, its gentle eyes and fluff of graying hair. "I'll make sure the coast stays clear," he said, and gave a shy half smile. "You boys be careful in there."

Threepio halted in turning away, running a swift scan of possible intentions to see if the slight sensation of offense he experienced was appropriate, but Nichos, in a sudden rare flash of humanity, grinned.

In the mess hall, the celebration was going full swing. Imperial battle stations and cruisers were equipped with automatic limiters on the total amount of alcohol they could produce at any one time but the Eye's designers had reckoned without the brewing skills of Gamorrean females. Dish after brimming dish of heady potwa beer were dippered out of the giant plastic oil drum that stood in the middle of the room; the tables were strewn with stews, steaks, and fragments of sodden bread; a bowl of beer clattered off the wall beside Threepio the moment he put his head around the door, and he drew back hastily.

There were shouts in the room, "I got him!" "No, you didn't!" "Well, I'll get him this time!"

"Come on, Threepio," said Nichos resignedly. "We've got sealed circuits. We might as well get this over with."

"Really, the things I've had to put up with . . ."

Threepio braced himself visibly and stepped back through the door. Bowls of beer and plates shied discus-wise clacked and bounced off the wall beside him as he made his way toward the food slots, Nichos in his wake. The Gamorreans weren't any better with tableware than they were with blaster carbines or handguns; one bowl caught the golden droid glancingly on the back and doused him with beer, but that was the extent of it. An argument immediately developed among the Gamorreans as to whether the hit counted. It turned violent, Gakfedds hammering one another with plates, axes, and chairs, screaming and squealing, while Bullyak sat back and smiled benevolently upon the scene in utter content.

Part of the programming of a protocol droid was to understand not only the language, but the customs and biologies of the various sentient races of the galaxy. Though he understood that intense sexual competitiveness for the attention of the Alpha female underlay all the outrageous violence of Gamorrean society—though he realized that, biologically and socially, the Gamorreans had no choice but to behave, think, and feel as they did—the droid felt a momentary flash of sympathy for Dr. Mingla's irrational prejudices against individuals who behaved exactly as they were programmed to behave.

Threepio bypassed the limiters on the food slots with a few simple commands—the language was absurdly easy—and asked for twenty gallons of Scale-5 syrup. When the half-gallon containers started appearing behind the plexi shields, he drew them out and handed them to Nichos, who carried them back to the hall where Pothman waited with the sled. A large number of morrts, shaken off their hosts during the fight and evidently drawn to the sugary smell of the syrup, scurried over to investigate.

"Get away from here!" Threepio waved angrily. "Filthy things . . . shoo! Shoo!"

They sat up and regarded him with beady black eyes, tongues flicking in and out of the toothed lances of their probosci, but took no further notice of his gestures. The Gamorreans, now happily smashing one another over the head with tables, took no notice of him at all.

When Threepio had borne the last of the containers out into the darkened hallway, he found Pothman and Nichos flattened, with the sled, against the wall to let an armed column of Affytechans pass—188 of them, Threepio counted, and "armed" with brooms, fragments of dissected SPs, pieces of pipe, and blaster carbines gutted of their power cells, all held weaponlike over their shoulders.

"Riiight—*turn!* Paraaade—*march!*" Their commander's voice snapped briskly as they vanished into the utter darkness of the hall.

"Really," said the protocol droid disapprovingly, as he set the last of the syrup canisters on the sled, "though I find laudable Master Luke's desire to remove all the passengers from this vessel before destroying it, I must admit to a certain amount of doubt about whether it can be achieved."

A bowl of beer came flying through the mess-hall doors and crashed sloppily into the wall.

"There has to be an alternative to blowing up the ship."

"Not one that's foolproof. Not one that's chance-proof."

"It doesn't need to be proof," said Luke desperately. "Just . . . enough. To cripple the motivators. To disengage the guns."

"Whoever has summoned it—whoever has learned how to manipulate the Force to this extent—is going to come looking for it, Luke. And he—or she—is powerful. I can feel that. I know it."

Luke knew it, too.

"The station has to be destroyed, Luke. As soon as it can be done. It takes two people, one of them a Jedi . . . The Jedi uses the Force to interfere with the firing of the enclision grid above the gun room ceiling long enough for the other person to climb. That's how Geith and I were going to do it. I can tell you, or Cray—whichever one of you is going to do the climbing—which switches to pull, which cores to overload once you get to the top. Whoever stays at the bottom . . . there's a mission-log jettison pod in the bay at the end of the corridor by the gun room. I didn't know about it when Geith—when Geith and I . . ." Her voice hesitated over the name of the lover who had abandoned her to die. Then she went on. "Anyway, I've found it since. It can be fitted with an oxygen bottle and the person who stays at the bottom can make it to that tube, if they run."

There was silence, shaped by her presence beside him.

"It has to be that way, Luke. You know it, and I know it."

"Not right away. Eventually, yes, when I've had time—"

"There is no time."

Luke shut his eyes. Everything she said was true. He knew it, and he knew she was aware of it. At last he could only say, "Callista, I love you."

Who had he said that to? Leia, once, before he'd known . . . And he loved her still, and in pretty much the same way. This was something he'd never felt, he'd never known that he could feel. "I don't . . . want you to die."

Her mouth on his, her arms around his body . . . the dream had been real, more real than some experiences of the flesh. There had to be a way . . .

"Luke," she said gently, "I died thirty years ago. I'm just . . . I'm glad we had this time. I'm glad I stayed to . . . to know you."

"There has to be a way," he insisted. "Cray . . ."

"Cray what?"

Luke turned, sharply, at the new voice. Cray leaned wearily in the door of the office, the silver blanket that half hid her torn and dirty uniform gleaming like armor, the marks of exhaustion and bitterness and the death of hope gouged into her bruised face as if with knives.

"To turn her into what Nichos is? To cannibalize parts from the computers, wire together enough memory to digitalize her, so you can have the metal illusion around to remind you what isn't yours—and can't be yours? I can do that . . . if that's what you want."

"You said Djinn Altis showed you—taught you—to transfer your self, your consciousness, your . . . your reality—to another object. You've done it with this ship, Callista. You're really here, I know you are . . ."

"I am," she said softly. "There's enough circuitry, enough size, enough power in the central core. But a thing of metal, a thing programmed and digitalized, isn't human, and can't be human, Luke. Not the way I'm human now."

"Not the way you and I are human." Cray came over to them, her blond hair catching fire glints in the greasy light. "Not the way Nichos was human. I should never have done it, Luke," she went on. "Never have . . . tried to go up against what had to be. My motto was always 'If it doesn't work, get a bigger hammer.' Or a smaller chip. Nichos . . ."

She shook her head. "He doesn't remember dying, Luke. He doesn't remember a switchover of any kind. And as much as I love . . . Nichos . . . as much as he loves me . . . I keep coming back to that. It isn't Nichos. He isn't human. He tries to be, and he wants to be, but flesh and bone have a logic of their own, Luke, and machinery just doesn't think the same way."

Her mouth twisted, her dark eyes chill and bitter as the vacuum of space. "If you want me to I'll make you something that'll hold a digitalized version of her memories, her consciousness . . . But it won't be the consciousness that's alive on this vessel. And you'll know it, and I'll know it. And that digitalized version will know it, too."

"No," said Callista, and Luke, through a blind haze of grief, still noticed that Cray and he both looked at the same place, as if Callista were *there* . . .

And she was, indeed, all but there.

She went on. "Thank you, Cray. And don't think I'm not tempted. I love you, Luke, and I want . . . I want not to have to leave you, even if it means . . . being what I am now, forever. Or being what Nichos is now, forever. But we don't have the choice. We don't have time. And any components, any computers, you take from this ship, Cray, will have the Will in them as well. And if you disconnected the weapons, if you disabled the motivators, if you pulled the cores, to leave the *Eye* floating in the darkness of space until you could find some way to build another computer, or droid, unconnected to the Will . . . I think the Will would lie to you about being disabled. I think it would wait until your back was turned, and seek out whoever it was that called it.

"It has to be destroyed, Luke. It has to be destroyed now, while we can."

No, he was screaming inside. *No* . . .

She'd said that she loved him.

He knew she was right.

Cray went on tiredly. "I'll be the one who goes up the shaft, Luke. Your command of the Force is worlds stronger than mine," she added, as Luke started to protest, "but I don't think you can levitate that far, and I can't hold it off you long enough for you to make the climb with a bad leg. If we're going to blow off all three of our lives we can't risk you losing strength halfway."

Luke nodded. With the little rest he'd been able to get he felt stronger, but it took everything he could summon of the Force to keep the pain in his leg from utterly swamping his mind. He would probably, he thought, be able to misfire the grid, but in spite of what Yoda had taught him, levitation took a lot of energy.

"We can program the lander to take off with the Sand People in it," she went on, "if you insist on getting them off the ship."

"If it's at all possible," said Luke. "I think it will be, once Threepio and . . . and Nichos"—he hesitated to speak her lover's name to her, but though her eyes moved from his she didn't flinch—"get back here with the syrup. It can be picked up and towed back to Tatooine."

"Triv and Nichos can each pilot a shuttle. Once they're out of the ship's jamming field they can transmit distress signals, though somebody's going to have their work cut out for them deprogramming the Gamorreans . . . not to mention convincing the Affytechans they aren't stormtroopers. They're multiplying, too, you know . . ."

"I know." Luke sighed.

"How you're going to get the Kitonaks on the shuttles . . ."

"I think I've got that figured out, too," he said. It was in his mind that even as he couldn't drag his staff up the shaft with him—even as he wouldn't be able to move quickly enough among the stations at the computer core—he probably wouldn't be able to make it down the long corridor to the jettison pod before the engines blew.

But that, he understood, was a technicality.

"Callista . . ."

He didn't know what he would have said. Tried to talk her, one more time, into letting Cray try to make some kind of computerized vessel for her mind and memories, her thought and heart . . . tried to talk her into escaping . . .

But the bench on which he was sitting gave a sudden, jarring lurch, almost throwing him to the floor, and the cold sickness of gravity flux drew at his belly, dizzying . . .

Another lurch, and he caught at one of the lamp-bowls as Cray grabbed the other halfway to the floor. Far off they felt the humming vibration rising within the ship's bones, the drag of power shifting . . .

Callista said quietly, "That's it. Hyperspace."

Chapter 21

Even before he and Chewie got up the steps of the lightless house, Han had a bad feeling about things.

"I'm terribly sorry, General Solo." The Bith in charge of the MuniCenter Records Office—and of the sales, invoice, and workers' benefits archives of the three major corporations that actually owned Plawal's central computer—tilted its domed, putty-colored head in the dim shiver of the holo field and regarded with huge black oil-slick eyes the point before it where Han's holo-phone image would be. "Her Excellency does not appear to be in the building."

Han glanced out the long windows, to the black fog pierced only by the raveled blurs of the orchard lights. Chewbacca, standing beside the glass, turned his head with a sound between a growl and a moan.

"Can you tell me when she left?" It was even possible, thought Han, that she might have stopped at the Bubbling Mud—which did serve pretty decent meat pies—for dinner, though that was something she liked company for . . .

"My apologies," said the Bith politely. "Her Excellency does not appear to have been in the building all day."

"What?"

"There is no record of her access card in any of the file banks, nor has—"

"Get me Jevax!"

The Bith inclined its head. "I will endeavor to do so, sir. Will you remain at your current location?"

"Yeah, just find him and get him . . . Uh, thank you," added Han belatedly, remembering Leia's repeated admonitions. "I appreciate it. I knew it, Chewie," he added as the slight image faded, "I knew she shouldn't have gone out with Artoo!"

The Wookiee made a questioning noise and flipped in his paw the restraining bolt they'd found on the table.

"Of course she pulled it off him," said Han. "She wouldn't think any harm of that little can of bolts if he . . . Well, he *did* try to murder her, dammit!" He surged to his feet, paced like a caged Endoran vethiraptor to the table where the bolt had lain beside Chewie's open toolkit.

The Wookiee growled again.

"I know she stands by her friends! But she—"

The holo phone blipped again, and Han leaped at the pickup switch as if it were the cancel toggle on a planetwide self-destruct cycle. But instead of the green local light, the blue star of the subspace receiver flickered on. A moment later Mara Jade's slim, leather-clad form appeared in the booth.

"Got your coordinates for you." She held up a yellow plastene wafer. "What's your receiving speed?"

"Why didn't you tell us you were after Nubblyk the Slyte?" demanded Han roughly.

"Because I don't lie to my friends," replied Mara sharply. "And if that's all you've got to say—"

"I'm sorry." Han looked away, angry with himself. "But I heard . . ."

"What's the matter, Solo?" She took another look at his face and all the sarcasm sponged away like yesterday's makeup.

"Leia's disappeared. She went up to the MuniCenter this afternoon and I just found out she never made it there. She's with Artoo-Detoo . . . He went haywire last night and tried to kill us, we had him in a restraining bolt but it looks like Leia pulled it off him and took him with her . . ."

Mara made an extremely unladylike comment and Lando Calrissian appeared behind her shoulder, waxed and combed and dressed in his best purple satin for an evening out.

"What is it?"

Han told him, adding, "We're waiting on Jevax now. She talked about visiting the city repair center, so maybe she took Artoo with her to get him checked, but it's after dark already and there's been too many weird things going on lately."

"Why'd you ask about Nubblyk?" asked Mara. "Who told you I was after him? I spent all of about twelve hours on that ball of ice and I don't think I could finger Nubblyk in a lineup if he'd picked my pocket."

"He told his toady the Emperor's Hand was after him," said Solo. "The Emperor's Hand was on the planet, and he had to get out of there before she found him. Nubblyk disappeared about seven years ago—after you'd said you'd been and gone. I figured you'd come back . . ."

He fell silent, just from the change in her eyes.

For a moment she said nothing, but even through the medium of the subspace holo, her rage was tangible, like the shock wave of a thermonuclear blast.

When she spoke her tone was deceptively normal, and very calm. "That reptile," she said. Her eyes stared out unseeingly, filled with a sudden, vicious, killing hate. "That son of a slime-crawler."

"What?" Lando stepped quickly back, almost out of range of the holo. "What's . . . ?"

"He told me I was the only one," said Mara, still in that calm, almost conversational voice. "The only Hand of the Emperor. His weapon of choice, he said, when he needed a scalpel rather than a sword . . . his trusted servant." The set of her red-lipped mouth was hard, the settled rage of one whose position had been not only her pride, but her entire life.

"That lying, drooling, scum-swallowing, superannuated underhanded festering filth-sucking *parasite*! He had another Hand!" Her voice sank to a deadly whisper. "He had another Hand all along!"

She had not moved from her seat, but the fury that radiated from her was like the pressure drop before a storm. Though it was directed against a dead man it made Solo very glad he was several hundred parsecs away in another star system entirely. "He lied to me! He used me! His 'trusted servant'! Everything he told me was a lie! *Everything!*"

"Mara," said Lando uneasily, "Mara, he's dead—"

"You know what that means, don't you?" She turned, cold-eyed, upon Lando, who backed a step. Neither man had ever seen Mara this angry and the sheer intensity of it was terrifying.

"It means he had her in reserve to use against me. Or to use me against her. Or who knows who else, to keep either of us from being anything more than the pawns of his lies!"

She was almost trembling with rage, the rage that had once led her to direct all her energies toward killing Luke Skywalker for taking from her the position that had been her life. "Is she still on the planet?"

"I don't know. I . . ."

For some reason he remembered Leia telling him of the Emperor's concubine, a member of the Emperor's Court . . . A woman who claimed to be working in a place where she wasn't working. A woman who'd shown up suddenly, bare weeks after Nubblyk's disappearance, knowing exactly what house it was she wanted to rent.

"Yeah," he said. "I think so. Woman named Roganda . . ."

Mara's eyes widened as she recognized the name, then narrowed to green and glittering slits. "Oh," she said softly. "*Her.*"

The holo image reached out to where the transceiver switches would be, beyond the range of the transmitters. The image vanished.

"We simply cannot take the risk." Roganda Ismaren opened the plastene case she carried, took from it the slim silver wand of a drug infuser, and fitted an ampoule into its slot. "Hold her."

Ohran Keldor stepped warily toward Leia, who had risen from her chair at the sound of the door lock switching over; she backed to the wall, but Lord Garonnin stood in the doorway, stunpistol in hand. Keldor hesitated—though small, Leia was fit, wiry, thirty years younger than he, and quite clearly ready to fight—and Garonnin said, "If it's risk you're worried about, Madame, I'd say using that drug on her is more risk than I like to see. You don't know what it is—"

"I know that it works," retorted the concubine. "I know it will keep her quiet while our guests are here."

"We know that it works *sometimes.* On some people. In some doses. It's been in those deserted laboratories in the crypts for thirty years at least, maybe twice that. We don't know whether it's deteriorated with time, whether it's become contaminated . . . That smuggler we used it on four or five years ago died."

"He had a weak heart," said Roganda, too quickly. "Oh, Lord Garonnin," she went on, her soft voice pleading, "you know how much depends upon those who will be here tonight! You know how desperately we need backing if your cause—*our* cause!—is to succeed! You know Her Highness's reputation. We cannot risk even the chance of her somehow escaping and interfering with the reception of our guests."

The Senex Lord's flat, cold eyes rested on Leia; the muzzle of his stunpistol was unwavering. Then he nodded.

Keldor stepped forward.

He was expecting Leia to duck away, so she sprang into his advance, hooked his ankle, and shoulder-blocked him—hard—and as he fell doubled and darted for the door. She'd thought the movement would take Garonnin at least a little by surprise, enough for his first shot to go wild, to give her a chance to get past him, but it didn't. The stunblast hit her like a blow to the solar plexus, winding her at the same moment that her whole body felt as if it had been pulled inside out.

Even on mildest stun the effect was awful—perhaps worse than a heavier blast, because she didn't even lose consciousness. She just collapsed to the floor, her legs twitching with pins and needles, and Keldor and Roganda knelt by her side.

"Stupid," remarked Keldor as the infuser was pressed to the side of Leia's neck.

A blast of cold. She felt her lungs stop.

She was submerged, she thought, in an ocean of green glass a thousand kilometers deep. Because glass is a liquid it filled her lungs, her veins, her organs; it permeated the tissues of her cells. Though she was sinking, very slowly, the glass was shot through with light from above, and she could hear the voices of Roganda, Keldor, and Garonnin as they left the room.

". . . antidote as soon as the reception is over," Roganda was saying. "We simply haven't the personnel to keep her under constant guard. But the drug's effects aren't as unpredictable as you fear. Everything will be perfectly all right."

Your cause. Our cause.

Keldor. Elegin.

Irek.

She had to get out.

The Force, thought Leia. Somehow, with her body suspended in this dense, unbreathing, light-filled silence, she could feel the Force all around her, sense it within reach of her fingertips, hear it like music, a tune that she herself could easily learn.

If she touched the Force—if she drew the light of the Force into herself—she could see the room in which she lay on Nasdra Magrody's bed, one hand resting on her midriff and dark auburn hair tangled around her on the discolored pillow.

Cray's right, she thought. *I really do have to be more diligent about applying that Slootheberry Wrinkle Creme around my eyes.*

I wonder if I can get up?

She breathed experimentally, drawing the Force into her like a kind of strange, prickly light, and stood up.

Her body remained on the bed.

Panic seized her, disorienting; she called to mind some of the disciplines Luke had taught her, calming, steadying . . .

And looked around her at the room.

Everything seemed very different, seen without physical eyes. Other times, other eras were present, as if she viewed through pane after pane of projection glass. An elderly man with graying hair sat writing on the back of green flimsiplast notes at the table, and broke off to lay his head on his arms and weep. A slim blond Jedi Knight lay in the bed—which had been on the other side of the room then—reading stories to her husband, who was curled up next to her with his dark head pillowed on her thigh.

Leia looked at the door, and knew she could walk through it.

I'll get lost!

Cold panic again, the sense of being naked, unprotected.

No, she thought. She stepped back to the bed, touched the body that lay there. Her own body. The scent of her own flesh, the sound of her own heartbeat, was unmistakable. If she concentrated, she could find her way back to it, even as she'd followed the far fainter and less familiar traces of Elegin and Keldor in the tunnels.

Terror in her heart, she stepped through the door.

Immediately she was conscious of voices. This part of the passageways had been the living quarters of the Jedi, converted from Plett's endless greenhouse caverns: The dreamy consciousness of the plants and the weary, bittersweet benevolence of the old Ho'Din Master permeated the rock of the walls. She followed the voices to a long chamber illuminated not only by a ceiling full of softly radiant glowpanels, but by half a dozen windows of various sizes, thickly glazed against past storms and, like those of her own chamber, concealed in the rock and vine-curtains of the valley wall.

She recognized a good two thirds of the people present.

Some of them had aged in the eleven years since she'd seen them at the Emperor's Court. Others—like the representatives of the Mekuun Corporation and the president of the board of directors of Seinar—were of more recent acquaintance. Lady Theala Vandron, acknowledged superior among the Senex Lords by virtue of heading the oldest and noblest of the Ancient Houses, had visited the Senate quite recently, to answer charges of inhumanity and planet-stripping brought against her by the High Court: She'd seemed surprised that anyone had considered it his business if she let slavers run breeding farms on her homeworld of Karfeddion.

"Your Highness, they're only Ossan and Bilanaka," she'd said, naming those two sentient but low-cultured races as if that placed the matter beyond need of further explanation.

A heavyset, stately woman in her forties with a blandly superior stubbornness in her blue eyes, she was further expressing her views on the matter to a small group comprised of Roganda, Irek, and Garonnin. "It's simply useless to discuss these matters with people in the Senate who refuse to understand local economic conditions."

A little R-10 unit rolled up to the group with a tray of glasses, and Roganda said, "You must sample the wine, Your Highness. Celanon Semi-Dry, an exquisite vintage."

"Ah." Vandron tasted a minute quantity. "Very nice." Leia heard in her mind Aunt Rouge: *Only spaceport types go in for the Semi-Dries, my dear. You really must cultivate a more refined taste.* Every word of it was compacted into the slight lowering of the painted eyelids and the fractional deepening of the lines around Lady Vandron's mouth.

"An Algarine, perhaps?" inquired Garonnin. Algarine wines had been her father's favorite vintage, Leia recalled.

"Of course." Roganda addressed the R-10. "Decant the Algarine from the cellars; chill to fifty degrees and the glass to forty."

The cellarer droid rolled quickly away.

"It isn't as if we were kidnapping people from their homes," Lady Vandron went on indignantly. "These creatures are specifically bred for agricultural work. If it weren't for our farming they wouldn't be born at all, you know. And Karfeddion is in the midst of severe economic depression."

"Not that they care, on Coruscant." Lord Garonnin set his own glass down on the sideboard of marble and bronze, Atravian of the best period, one of the few pieces of furniture in the long, stone-floored room.

"Which is why, Your Highness," said Roganda in her low, sweet voice, "we must deal with both the warlords *and* the Senate from a position of strength, rather than one of the hat-in-hand subservience they seem to expect. We will be . . . a power to reckon with." She laid her hand on her son's shoulder, her red lips curving in a proud smile, and Irek modestly cast down his eyes.

Close to the buffet, which was laden with a collection of confections and savories clearly put together by a droid of some kind, a bioassisted Sullustan executive asked Drost Elegin, "Doesn't look much like the Emperor, does he?" in the softest of undervoices. The Sullustan glanced across the room at Irek and his mother, both conservatively clad, he in black, she in white; Irek had gone to speak to one of the Juvex Lords whom Leia recognized dimly as the head of the more militant branch of the House Sreethyn. It was clear the boy had a great deal of charm.

Elegin shrugged. "What does it matter? If he can do what she says he can do . . ." He nodded in Roganda's direction.

She was still working hard on getting Lady Vandron to unbend. Leia could have told her she might as well have tried to stuff a full-grown Hutt into her pocket. Ladies of the great Houses do not unbend to women who have been concubines, no matter whose, and no matter what their sons can do.

"Well," said the Sullustan doubtfully, and adjusted the gain on the eyepieces he wore. "If the great Houses back him . . ."

Elegin made a gesture with his eyebrows, dismissing—or almost dismissing—the dark-haired boy. "At least his manners are good," he said. "Don't worry, Naithol. When the ship arrives, we'll have the nucleus of a true fleet; more powerful than anything those scattered jarheads can command these days. And indeed," he added with a malicious grin, "once the various warlords have had it demonstrated to them exactly what Irek can do, I think they'll be most eager to ally themselves with us and listen to what we have to say."

Ship? thought Leia uneasily.

The Sullustan turned toward the buffet again and paused, the enhanced visual receptors he wore—probably to compensate for the corneal defects many Sullustans developed after the age of thirty—turned in Leia's direction.

She wasn't sure what he saw—how, or if, the psychic residue of the drug made her register on the pickup—but with a little shrug he went on toward the food. But it was enough to make her move off, drifting like a ghost among the other, fainter ghosts that flickered in this room, dim echoes of children playing obliviously on the floor between the cool aristocrats and the watchful bureaucrats, secretaries, and corporate scouts.

Irek, Leia noticed, was working the room with the adeptness of a candidate for the Senate, deferring politely to the Lords and Ladies of the great Houses, condescending with just unnoticeable noblesse oblige to the corporates and to the secretaries of the Lords. As Drost Elegin had remarked, he had beautiful manners. Since formal dueling was one of the accomplishments valued by the Lords among their own class, the boy was able to discuss this with the younger aristocrats.

"We've heard all about this ship," said Lord Vensell Picutorion, who had been one of those presented at the same time as Leia's Senatorial debut. "What is it? Where is it coming from? Are you sure it's large enough to give us the power, the armament, to create our own Allied Fleet?"

Irek inclined his head respectfully, and the other Senex Lords gathered around. "It is, quite simply, the largest and most heavily armored battlemoon still in existence from the heyday of the Imperial Fleet," he said in his clear, carrying boy's voice. "It was the prototype transition between the torpedo platforms and the original Death Star. It doesn't have the focused power of the destructor beams," he added, and Leia detected a note of apology in his voice, "but it has almost the power capacity of the Death Star . . ."

"I think we're all agreed," put in Lord Garonnin, "that planet-killer technology is wasteful, to put it mildly."

"But you must admit," said Irek, a gleeful glitter far back in his blue eyes, "it makes a wonderful deterrent."

"In fact, it doesn't," said His Lordship bluntly. "As events leading to the breakup of the Empire can attest." And, when Irek opened his mouth to protest, he went on. "But be that as it may." He turned to the other Lords. "The battlemoon *Eye of Palpatine* was originally constructed for a mission thirty years ago," he said. "It was built and armed in absolute secrecy, so that when the mission itself was aborted unfulfilled, almost no one knew of the battlemoon itself, and all record of its hiding place—in an asteroid field in the Moonflower Nebula—was lost."

"Careless of them," commented a younger Lady, whose tanned muscles spoke of a lifetime in the hunting field.

Several laughed.

Garonnin looked annoyed, but Roganda said smoothly, "Anyone who's dealt with a really large ancestral library will know that one small defect in the computer can result in the disappearance of, for instance, an entire set of wafers, or a good-size book . . . and the size ratio between one book and, say, four or five rooms is much smaller than between even the largest battlemoon and twenty parsecs of the Outer Rim."

She would know, thought Leia, remembering Nasdra Magrody's despairing words.

A battlemoon!

"And it's on its way here?" asked Lord Picutorion.

Irek smiled, smug. "On its way here," he said. "And at our service."

Roganda put her hand on his shoulder and smiled again, that proud smile. "Our guests are thirsty, my son," she said in her soft voice. "Would you go see what's become of that R-Ten?"

A nice personal touch, thought Leia, observing the approval on the faces of Lady Vandron and Lord Picutorion. Irek suppressed a wicked grin and said, "Certainly, Mother."

There was a soft murmur at the back of the group about how well brought up and malleable he was as the slender boy strode from the room. Leia followed, uncertain but not quite liking the look in his eyes.

The R-10 unit was trundling up the corridor, small and square, about a meter tall and rimmed around its flat top with a decorative brass railing. The top itself was black marble electronically charged to grip drinks, glasses, and anything else set on it; Leia had watched almost without consciously noticing the slight rotation with which everyone in the room took up his or her glass from it—she barely noticed herself when she did it back home. It was second nature to anyone with a modern R-10.

It bore on its surface now the appointed bottle—a twelve-year-old Algarine dry, suitably dusty—and a frosted glass, solitary tribute to the importance of Lady Vandron, as Roganda intended.

Irek folded his arms and stood in the middle of the corridor with that same evil grin. "Stop," he said.

The R-10 whirred to a halt.

"Pick up the glass."

It extruded one of its long, multijointed arms with their slightly sticky velvet pads and obligingly picked up the chilled wineglass.

"Throw it on the floor."

The droid froze in midmotion. Breaking glasses—breaking *any* sort of dish or utensil—was part of the black-box code hardwired into any household droid.

Irek's grin widened and he fastened his gaze on the R-10. Leia felt the shiver of the Force in the air, reaching into, digging at, the droid's programming, forcing it synapse by synapse to rearrange its actions in spite of multilayered restraints against it.

The droid reacted with great distress. It backed, rocked, turned in a circle . . .

"Come on," said Irek softly. "Throw it on the floor."

While his mind, as Roganda had instructed no doubt—as Magrody had taught him—formed the subelectronic commands necessary for the implementation of the act.

Jerkily, with a flailing movement, the droid hurled the glass down. Then it immediately extruded a brush-tipped arm from its base and a vacuum hose to clean up the broken glass.

"Not yet."

The implements stopped.

"Now take the bottle and pour it out."

The droid rocked with wretchedness, fighting the most absolute of its programming not to ever, ever, *ever* spill *anything* . . . Irek was clearly reveling in its confusion. His blue eyes did not waver, bending his concentration on the Force, channeling it through the implanted chip in its mind . . .

Then his head turned, suddenly, and Leia felt his concentration leave the droid as if the boy had simply dropped a toy he'd been playing with.

The droid replaced the wine bottle on its top and bolted for the party as fast as its wheels would carry it, but Irek did not even notice.

He was turning his head slowly, scanning the corridor. Listening. Sniffing.

"You're here," he said softly. "You're here somewhere. I can feel you."

She felt him gather the strength of the Force around him, like a terrible shadow; saw him with changed eyes, like a wraith of mist and coals.

"I'll find you . . ."

Leia turned and fled. Behind her she was aware of him striding two paces to one of the small red wall buttons that were mounted at intervals on the dark stone of the corridor walls, heard him slap it, and then heard the stride of heavy boots, and Garonnin's voice, "What is it, my lord?"

"Get my mother. And fetch the smallest steel ball from the toy room to the Princess's prison . . ."

Leia bolted down the corridors, twisting, weaving through the maze. She felt Irek's mind invading them, searching for her, reaching like vast wings of smoke to fill the ill-lit passageways with shadows she knew could not be real but which terrified her anyway. It was hard to sense in which direction her body lay, hard to hear the distant heartbeat she followed . . .

She skidded to a stop in horror as the floating black ball of the interrogator droid drifted out from around a corner, lights flashing, flickering . . . Not real, not real, but even knowing this she turned aside. Down another corridor the huge, heavy, stinking shape of a Hutt reached for her with a quivering prehensile tongue, copper eyes dilating and contracting with ugly lusts.

She turned aside from it, sobbing, trying to find some way around, and in her mind she heard Irek's voice whispering, Irek's shrill boy's laugh. *I'll trap you. I'll find you and trap you. You'll never get out . . .*

The drug, she thought. The drug they'd given her must have left a psychic residue he could track. . . .

She couldn't let him catch her. Couldn't let him overtake her. Blocks and slabs of darkness loomed in front of her, walls of stench overpowering her ability to track where she should go. The smell of kretch, of roses, of filth. Great, howling waves of power jerked and dragged at her, pulling her back, washing her sideways. In the back of her consciousness she was aware of Irek running lightly, skipping and hopping down the corridors with the sheer delight of trying to find her, trying to track her, trying to block her from the room where her body lay.

Luke, she thought desperately, *Luke, help me . . .*

And like a mocking playground echo, Irek mimicked jeeringly, *Oh, Lukie, help me . . .*

There. That corridor there. She knew it, recognized it, flung herself around the corner . . .

And he was standing in front of the door.

The towering black shape, the glister of pallid light on the black helmet, the evil gleam of lights within the shadows of his great cloak, and the thick, indrawn breath.

Vader.

Vader was standing before the door.

She swung around in terror. Irek stood in the passageway behind her, the dark radiance that surrounded him seeming to pulse with lightning. In his hand he held one of the steel balls that had so puzzled her in the toy room, but now, with her disembodied consciousness, she saw that there were entrances to it, entrances invisible to eyes limited by the electromagnetic spectrum.

Entrances that did not serve as exits.

And within the ball itself, maze after maze of concentric, ever tinier labyrinth balls.

He smiled. "You're here. I can tell you're here."

Leia turned. Vader still stood before the door. She could not pass him. She *could not.*

"Mother can't stop me," said Irek. "She won't even know."

He held up the ball, and his mind seemed to reach out into the corridor like a vast net, drawing at her. Leia felt herself dissolving like a smoke wraith, an unskilled illusion; drawn as if by a vacuum toward the steel ball; dissipating into the power of the dark side.

There had to be a way to use the Force to protect herself, she thought . . . to get past the dark terror that stood before the door. But she didn't know what it was.

The boy puckered his lips and inhaled, pulling her in with his breath. "Irek!"

Roganda appeared in the corridor behind her son, her white dress gathered up in her hand as if she'd been running.

"Irek, come at once!"

He swung around, his concentration broken. The shadow of Vader vanished. Leia flung herself at the door, through the door, hurled herself to the sleeping form on the bed . . .

With human perceptions once again she barely heard the voices through the door, but she recognized, nevertheless, Ohran Keldor's voice.

"Lord Irek, we've picked it up on the scanners! It's here! The *Eye of Palpatine.*"

Chapter 22

"Master Luke, are you quite certain this is going to work?"

"You got me." The logistics of managing a staff and the rope with which Luke was towing the small pump salvaged from a laundry room were not the best in the world, but at this point Luke was simply delighted to have located a pump that still worked. Very little on the *Eye of Palpatine* still worked.

Except the guns, he thought. *Except the guns.*

"How much time will it give us?" inquired Nichos, striding silently along under his load of two oil drums filled with sugar water. "Provided it works at all."

"Maybe an hour clear." The lights on his staff were failing, too, and the service corridor, with its low ceilings and bundles of conduit lines, was beginning to take on the appearance, dampness, and smell of some cavern far below ground level. Here and there water dripped down the walls. Luke examined the places and nodded with satisfaction. They were certainly on the line of the main water trunk for this section of the ship.

"That isn't much, to check the lander and the two shuttles," remarked Triv Pothman.

Luke shook his head. Every step was like having pieces of bone ripped out of his thigh. "It'll have to do." The last of the perigen was long gone—the Force alone kept him from going into shock, kept the fever of internal infection at bay.

Cray, walking behind them with a five-gallon bucket of sugar water in each hand, said nothing; had said nothing while Luke outlined his plans for getting the ship cleared, and very little more during the process of cutting into the main sensors for a reading of their position and an estimate of how much time before the shelling of Belsavis would begin. Only when Callista said, "That's too much time," at the display of twelve hours, thirty minutes, had Cray spoken.

"It's what the file says."

"It's what the Will says the file says. Don't you see?" Callista had gone on. "The Will's going to do whatever it can, use whatever it can, to delay us and fulfill its mission. Mission Control would never have left a delay of twelve and a half hours after coming out of hyperspace. Not with Jedi on the planet. Not with the fleet of Y-wings they have . . . had."

"She's right," Luke had said, glancing over at Cray. He'd expected an argument, since Cray had never believed that computers could or would lie.

But since leaving the security of her laboratory, Cray had been through trial by the Will, and her only reaction was a slight, bitter tightening of her lips. She had watched in silence when Luke and the others had mixed the syrup with water to produce a thick, hypersweet mixture, had taken her share of it when the antigrav sled had proven too large to enter the service corridor vent. She moved as if every step, every intake of breath, was a chore she had to get through, and she would not, Luke saw, meet Nichos's eyes.

"Thank the Maker," exulted Threepio, as they turned a corner and dim worklights gleamed along the ceiling overhead. "I was beginning to fear this quadrant of the ship around the shuttle bays was without power as well."

"Jawa're probably too scared of the Sand People to get close enough to raid it." Luke turned down a side corridor, following the main conduit.

"Yet," remarked Callista, her voice coming from beside him, as if she walked close by.

"I like a cheery girl."

She sang two lines of an old nursery song, *"Let's everybody be happy, let's everybody be happy . . ."* and Luke, in spite of the agony in his leg, laughed.

"It must be driving them crazy," Callista went on after a moment. "The Sand People. If they're as . . . as rigidly bound to tradition as you describe, they must hate the fact that everything is different here, with no day and no night, and only walls and corridors to hunt in."

"As time goes by I'm less and less thrilled about it myself." The door to the main pump room was locked. Threepio convinced the lock program that a key had been inserted and the door whooshed open.

"Break the mechanism, Nichos," said Luke quietly. "You're right, Callista. I don't trust the Will any farther than I can throw this ship, uphill and against the wind."

"Funny," said Pothman, looking around him at the oily black root system of pipes and vents, as Luke hooked the small portable pump into the main mechanism. "I never thought about it while I was a trooper. But now, looking back, I think I never could get used to living in corridors and rooms and ships and installations. I mean, it seemed normal at the time. Only after I was living in the forest on Pzob I realized how much I loved it, how much I'd missed the woods and the trees of Chandrila. You miss the oceans, Miss Callista?"

"Every day."

Cray, standing in the doorway, only leaned her forehead against the jamb and said nothing, watching while Luke hooked the makeshift power cables into the main outlets, pressed the switch. The dry, whirring rasp of the motor fired up, small and shrill against the deeper, calmer throb of the main pump that half filled the room before them. Luke breathed a sigh of gratitude and unshipped the small pump's hose.

"Here goes."

He plunged the hose into the first of the sugar-water drums, watching the connection between the small pump surge and stiffen with the pressure of the stuff, then, a moment later, the line between the small pump and the large.

Callista called up, softly, to the oblivious Sand People inhabiting the regions above the pump room, "Here's looking at you, kids."

They pumped, in all, close to twenty gallons of concentrated sugar water into the Sand People's water supply.

"Leave it," said Luke, as Nichos turned back from the door to fetch the portable pump or tidy the buckets. "We're not coming back."

"Ah," said Nichos, remembering that everything was going to be ion vapor this time tomorrow, and shook his head deprecatingly. "Perhaps a touch too much tidiness programmed in." The next moment he glanced sidelong at Cray, realizing that the jest might have been construed as a criticism—or simply as a reminder that he was, in fact, a collection of programs—but she managed a smile, and for the first time met his eyes.

"I knew I shouldn't have cribbed that part out of one of those SP Eighty wall washers."

They stood looking at each other for a moment, startled and not quite certain how to deal with her admission of having programmed him, of his being a droid . . . then she reached out and touched his hand.

"Think they'll mind if we crash their party?" whispered Callista when they reached the top of the gangway. The noise from the shuttle hangar the Sand People had taken for their headquarters was tremendous: groaning, grunting, howling; whoops and clatters as machinery or weapons— gaffe sticks? rifles?—were hurled here and there. Every now and then they'd all begin to yowl together, hair-raising ululations that rose and fell in volume and pitch and then died away into raucous shrieks and crashes.

"Let's sit this one out." Luke leaned back against the wall, aware that he was trembling and that sweat rolled down the sides of his face, glittering in the chill of the corridor lights. He wanted to sit down, but knew that if he did he'd probably never get up. He was burningly aware of Callista beside him, close by him, as if she were merely invisible and would become visible again later . . .

He pushed the thought away.

Triv hunkered down, listening but coiled to spring up again, his blaster in his hand. Threepio stood a meter or so away down the corridor to their backs, auditory sensors turned up to highest gain. Awkwardly, Cray and Nichos stood together, as if not certain what to say.

Cray asked, "Will you be okay, Luke?" and Luke nodded.

"This shouldn't take too long."

"A bunch of deep-water cy'een herders'd have these boys under the table before they'd even warmed up their elbows," commented Callista.

More whoops.

"Maybe that's why they killed that storekeeper."

The riot subsided. A few broken grunts and shouts, then silence. Someone yelled his opinion about something to his by now oblivious fellow tribesmen, and then there was a clatter, as if of a dropped metal drinking vessel.

"Right," said Luke."Let's go. We don't have much time. Threepio, get the Talz."

"Certainly, Master Luke." The droid creaked off briskly into the darkness.

The shuttle hangar was carpeted in somnolent Sand People. Sugar water was spilled everywhere, soaking into the dirt-colored robes and head wrappings, and several bore dark, harsh-smelling stains on their robes, as if of ichor or blood. A small, square service hatch on one wall was scratched and dented as if hacked at by maniacs—gaffe sticks and spears strewn like jackstraws all around it amply indicated that someone had thought it a useful target to demonstrate everyone's skill. The wall around the square hatch bore considerably more damage than the hatch itself.

"Swell party," commented Luke, and scrambled painfully up the ramp into the first of the shuttlecraft while Triv and Nichos prudently collected every weapon in sight. The gauges looked all right—under Cray's expert cutting the on-board computer woke up without reference to its passwords and expressed itself ready for action.

"Doesn't seem to be hooked into the Will at all," she commented.

"About time something went our way."

"I warn you," said Triv Pothman worriedly from the door, "I was never trained to run one of these things. And those readouts of the surface you're getting aren't making me feel any better about learning."

"I'll slave this shuttle to the other so Nichos can control them both." Cray settled into the pilot's chair, ran her hands through her hair with the old gesture of tucking aside stray tendrils—and winced a little at the touch of the sawed-off bristle—then called up the core program and began tapping instructions in. The gesture of tidying her hair filled Luke with an odd sense of relief, of gladness. Whatever she'd been through, its darkness in her was lightening. She was returning to herself.

"Nichos isn't a hotshot jet jockey like Luke," she went on, "but he can take both in even through that mess, if somebody on the ground can talk him down. A lot of the stabilization's preprogrammed for the planet, of course. And believe me, when the main ship blows, there'll be somebody out here to investigate."

"Cray," said Luke, "I need to talk to you about that."

She didn't so much as spare him a glance. "Later," she said. "First let's hear your plan for getting those Kitonaks down here and into a shuttle in something under two weeks."

Outside there was a groaning clamor, a bellowing war cry. Luke and Cray, stumbling to the door of the lander, were just in time to see a Tusken Raider launch itself at Triv Pothman, swinging its gaffe stick in such a fashion as to present considerably more danger to itself than to the former stormtrooper. Nichos leaped over two intervening slumberers and caught the Tusken's arm, pulling the weapon from its fumbling hand. Triv was saying, "Hey, hey, hey, my friend, just relax, okay? Have another little shot . . ."

The Raider accepted the silver cup half full of sugar water from the trooper's hand, downed it in a gulp, and subsided once again to the floor.

"Master Luke . . ." Threepio appeared in the doorway of the hangar, followed by a half dozen fluffy white Talz.

"Great!" Luke scrambled down from the shuttlecraft, stumbling as his leg gave under him with a shocking blast of pain. Cray caught his arm and three of the Talz were immediately at his side, steadying him and crooning worriedly.

"Thank them," said Luke, struggling to control his breath, to fight off the pain that threatened to blot his consciousness. "Thank you," he added, speaking directly to the tall creatures, as Threepio produced a succession of hoons and hums. "Tell them that without their help I could not possibly hope to save all those here who need to be saved."

Threepio relayed Luke's message to the Talz, who replied with snufflings, hoots, and heavy, patting hugs. Then without further ado the Talz began to pick up Sand People and carry them out of the hold, heading for the lander on Deck 10.

"You know that even with my reprogramming that lander won't do anything but head out a couple of kilometers and hang there," Cray said, watching them go. "It can't be steered."

"That'll do," said Luke. "I'll leave instructions with Triv and Threepio that nobody's supposed to open the thing till it gets to Tatooine anyway."

"You really think anybody'll tow it to safety, once they know what's inside?" She put one fist on her hip, turned to look at him sidelong, weary and bitter.

"I don't know," said Luke quietly. "If I make it out . . ." He hesitated. "Or if you make it out, please see to it that someone does."

Her face softened with the wisp of a smile. "You never give up," she said, "do you, Luke?"

He shook his head.

"Funny," Cray said, as they walked up the ramp into the second shuttle. "You'd think that since we appeared in this sector somebody'd be out from Belsavis to check on who we are anyway. But there's not a thing."

"I've never seen anything like it." Jevax flicked through another series of screens, the two technicians—another Mluki and a glum-looking Durosian—leaning over his shoulders. None of the three looked up as Han and Chewbacca thrust their way through the door and into the port's central control.

The Durosian shook his head. "It has to be a malfunction somewhere in the slave relay to the bay gates themselves," he said. "The program tests positive. All the gates couldn't malfunction mechanically at the same time." His earth-colored brow furrowed down over opalescent orange eyes, and he rubbed the hard beak of his mouth.

"What's going on?"

Jevax looked up, seeing Solo and the Wookiee for the first time, and got to his feet. "I hope you're not coming for takeoff clearance," he said in a tone of voice half jocular, half puzzled—nobody in his right mind would take off into the nightly inferno of Belsavis's winds. "Did Her Excellency find what she needed in the MuniCenter records? I'm afraid I wasn't able to—"

"Leia never got to the MuniCenter at all," said Han.

The Mluki's eyes widened with shock, then flickered to the chronometer on the wall.

"There's a woman living on Painted Door Street, in the house Nubblyk the Slyte used to own—Roganda Ismaren. Came here about seven years ago . . ."

"Ahh," said Jevax thoughtfully. "Roganda Ismaren. Woman so

high . . ." He gestured to someone about Leia's small height. "Black hair, dark eyes . . ."

"I don't know. I've never seen her. She used to be one of the Emperor's concubines so she's probably beautiful . . ."

"The human males who come into port treat her as if she's beautiful," said Jevax with a small smile. "When she's seen, which is rarely. We're a small town, General Solo, and everyone ends up knowing a great deal about everyone else's business . . . and though it's none of *my* business, I admit I have always nursed a deep curiosity about Roganda Ismaren."

"You know where her house is?"

Jevax nodded.

At the Chief Person's suggestion they stopped at a small apartment block, to include in their party Stusjevsky, a meter-tall, dark-furred Chadra-Fan who worked in the vine-coffee gardens as a sniffer. "Some things you just can't explain to supervisors," sighed the little creature as he bid a quick good-bye to the group of convivial friends who'd gathered in his apartment for a wine-and-grooming party. He trotted down the outside stair at Jevax's side, big, clawed hands making quick work of the complicated latches on the silk vest he was donning. "The new girl keeps asking why the beans shouldn't be harvested yet—'They're the right color,' she says. Right color my left ear!"

As if called upon for corroborative evidence, his left ear twitched.

"They're more or less the right color outside, but they smell green inside. Well, she'll learn . . . What can I do for you, Chief?"

Black fog shut them in, huge moths and glowbugs dancing around the blurred yellow wool of streetlamps and windows. Overhead the lights on the hanging gardens twinkled dimly through the mists, like alien galaxies of flowering stars.

Jevax gave him a swift and bowdlerized version of the problem, ending with, "We have reason to believe the house itself is wired with alarms. Before we go in—before we tip anyone off as to our presence—we'd like to know whether anyone's home or not. Can you do that?"

"Humans?" The Chadra-Fan's huge ears cocked forward, and he glanced from Han to Chewie.

Jevax nodded.

Stusjevsky gave him the circle-finger sign universal among those races with opposable thumbs: No Problem. They turned to cross the market square, all lights retreating into dim smudges in the hot, eerie dark. "So what's this I hear about the landing silos being locked up?"

The Chief Person gestured helplessly. "We think it's a malfunction in the programming of the central servo between the computer and the doors over the silos. It looks like it fired and locked at once, and ground the main gear to pieces."

Chewie turned his head sharply, with a long, rumbling growl.

"We don't know," said Jevax. "That's what's driving the tech crew crazy. It shouldn't have happened. *None* of the cutouts operated. They're going to have to go in and pull the whole mechanism and open the gates manually—which means I hope you like the food here, General Solo, because it'll be at least twenty-four hours—"

"Wait a minute," said Solo, pausing at the foot of the steep slope of Painted Door Street. "You're telling me that there's been *another* case of . . . of a fairly complicated, freak malfunction? Like our astromech droid trying to murder us? That's two in twenty-four hours."

Jevax's snowy brow ridge folded upward in the middle as he considered the matter in that light. Then he said, "Three. The comm system's down again . . . But that happens so often . . ."

There was momentary silence as they regarded each other in the heavy gloom. Then Solo said softly, "I've got a bad feeling about this."

In swift silence, they felt their way from pillar to pillar of the foundations of an old building, following the course of the street.

It was a neighborhood of ancient houses, prefabs rising out of the bomb damage like white ships stranded on high rocks. Vines growing over the old lava blocks rustled wetly as the party passed along them, and somewhere a warm spring welling up from an old foundation bubbled in the dark. The higher altitude, on the bench beneath the Citadel ruins, thinned the fog a little, and when they stopped at the turning at the top of the street, Solo could even see the house Jevax pointed out.

Han felt a cold snake of uneasiness corkscrew down his backbone. If Roganda Ismaren was the Emperor's Hand, it meant she was Force-strong . . . not something he wanted to go up against.

But if she'd hurt so much as a hair on Leia's head, he'd . . .

"That's hers." Jevax looked down at Stusjevsky. "Anyone home?"

The Chadra-Fan closed his huge dark eyes, flared his four large nostrils, and stood, breathing and listening to the night. Solo couldn't see how the little creature could be sifting out the odors of a single house from all others, for the night was redolent of greenery, wet stone, the faintly sulfurous pong of the hot springs, and the overpowering sweetness that hung in the air near the packing plants . . .

But Stusjevsky opened his eyes after a moment and said, "Nobody home, Chief."

Chewie grumbled a little and checked the pockets of his utility belt for his wire-bridging kit, preparatory to making an assault on whatever security system the house might have.

"I'll tell you this, though," said the Chadra-Fan. "Somebody in that place has been wearing *awfully* expensive perfume—Whisper or Lake of Dreams—which I know for a fact nobody sells on this entire planet."

With startling suddenness, the door at the top of the steps whooshed open.

"I thought you said there was nobody home!" hissed Han as the four of them flattened into the shadows of a shell-ravaged old colonnade.

"Nobody human," retorted the Chadra-Fan. "I can smell . . ."

There was a faint whirring in the shadows of the vines that half masked the doorway, and the movement of something pale.

Then a small form appeared at the top of the steps and paused as if intensely weary, or considering what to do next.

Battered, dented, covered with filth and slime, it was Artoo-Detoo.

Chapter 23

"Commander," announced the stormtrooper with a sharp salute, "emergency orders have arrived from the Grand Moff of the entire Imperial Battlefleet! Priority one, sir!"

The commander straightened up from grim concentration on the blacked-out control screen of a library reader and returned the salute with the three long and gaudily blossomed yellow pellicules on its right side. Several officers engaged in manning the gunnery and navigation consoles at the dead readers and vids along the library wall turned in their chairs; stems, stamens, and clusters of flowers swiveled in the direction of their commander. They were all a little pale from lack of sunlight, but still very much on the alert.

Luke, leaning in the doorway watching the scene being played out by the dim glow of his staff—the Affytechans had been engaged in their imaginary space battle in total darkness before his and Pothman's arrival —wondered for the hundredth time exactly how sentient these beings were.

The Klaggs and the Gakfedds had remained Gamorreans, albeit convinced most of the time that they were stormtroopers. They had been aware of the slow destruction of the *Eye of Palpatine,* though they had attributed it, under the instructions of the Will, to the Rebel saboteurs familiar to them from their programming. Ugbuz had remained Ugbuz, and though his aim continued to be truly dreadful he understood the difference between a charged blaster and an empty one.

To the Affytechans, their programming seemed to be so thorough that what they were programmed to believe took precedence over the actual structure of the ship itself. If they had possessed any individual personalities before induction in the lander, those had been completely subsumed . . . And, Luke noticed, those Affytechans who had sprouted on board—and he'd come across at least five nurseries, mostly in lesser mess rooms rigged with emergency lighting—seemed to believe themselves to be Imperial troopers with the same utter absorption as their seniors.

Triv Pothman, resplendent in his white armor, stepped across to the dead control screen in front of the yellow-and-black captain. "With your permission, sir." He touched a switch.

• Fleet Communications •
Urgent and Priority One
It is the intent of the Will that all ship's personnel evacuate to the shuttlecraft on Deck 16 immediately. All personnel currently in sick bays and other locations to be moved with necessary life support. The bearer of these orders will serve as director of the evacuation and pilot the shuttlecraft during and after launch.

"Not bad," approved Luke softly.

"Are you kidding?" returned Callista's voice in his ear. "For thirty years the Will is the only thing I've gotten when I tried to break into the computer. You bet I know how to do an imitation. You should see me do Pekkie Blu and the Starboys."

Luke had never heard of Pekkie Blu and the Starboys, but he would have crossed the Dune Sea on foot to hear her do an imitation of anybody.

"Is this . . . it, trooper?" The captain's voice was grave.

Neither Pothman nor Luke knew precisely what it was, but the former trooper nodded. "We have our orders," he said.

The captain returned the nod, grave and manly despite the huge coronal fluff of white tassels. "All right, men," he said. "This is it. Pack it up. Move it out."

In the Deck 12 Portside Section Lounge, and the corridor adjacent, the Kitonaks were still talking.

"They're still exchanging recipes, most of them," explained Threepio, when Luke appeared. "Although that group in the corridor has begun telling one another about last summer's run of Chooba slugs . . . an experience that all of them, apparently, shared."

"They're all here," said Callista. "Forty-eight of them."

A group of Affytechans passed them, marching in brisk military fashion, nearly seventy strong including a whole squad of seedlings less than a meter high. "Riiight square turn!" barked the sharp voice of the lieutenant in charge, and they vanished around a corner. Luke shook his head.

"Somebody's gonna have a job deprogramming them."

Her yelp of laughter rippled in the air. "Yikes, I hadn't even thought of that! Okay. Corridors are clear between here and the shuttle bay. Gangways are open. That one elevator shaft they'll have to climb is roped . . . Can they *climb* an elevator shaft?"

"Oh, yes." Luke took a deep breath. He was achingly conscious of the fact that every fragment of his strength that he expended on other matters meant that much less for the final effort, the final exertion . . .

"Threepio, you ready?"

"I believe my grasp of the Kitonak language to be sufficient for the needs of the moment."

"Yeah," said Luke, "but you better get out of that doorway."

The droid stepped hastily aside. He knew what was coming.

"Okay," said Luke. "Here goes nothin'."

Closing his eyes, he concentrated on the heat sensors of the fire prevention system of the lounge and the corridors around it. It was the simplest of all Jedi powers—directed against the most basic system in the ship—and the result was utterly galvanic.

The sprinkler system burst into gushing life.

A rainstorm of water poured down over Luke, Threepio, and every squatty, mushroom-shaped, putty-colored Kitonak in the section.

"Deck Sixteen!" cried Threepio in the Kitonak tongue. "Deck Sixteen! The water is in the shuttlecraft!" And he sprang back, dragging his master to safety as the thundering tide of Kitonaks not only slammed through the door, but broke down the walls on either side of the entryway and went lumbering and slipping up the corridor in the direction of the shuttle decks.

Luke cast his mind ahead, visualizing every carefully memorized foot of the corridors, gangway, elevator shaft between the Portside Section Lounge and the Deck 16 shuttle-hangar, superheating the thin layer of air at the top of the hallways to fire the sprinklers along the way.

Kitonaks mate in water.

Rain, to them, is the trigger for startling and enthusiastic speed.

"You think Cray and Nichos'll be able to handle getting them in the shuttle?"

"Should be no problem," said Callista. "I'll go along, but I don't think it's anything a well-bred person should see. I'll be back with you by the time we need to convince the Klaggs and the Gakfedds to go on board."

I can't do it, thought Luke, watching the ghostly flicker in the whirling rain retreat along the corridor in the wake of the lubricated and lust-crazed mob. *I can't . . . not save her.*

He stood with the water coursing down his hair and face, trying not to think about not ever speaking with her again.

"Master Luke?" Threepio's voice was diffident.

With an almost physical effort he shook himself free of that grief, the sense that there was nothing in him, body or soul, that did not consist entirely of blinding pain. First things first. "Yeah," he said softly. "Let's go get the Jawas and move the tripods out."

Roganda and her son were forging an alliance with the Senex Lords.

Leia struggled, trying desperately to return to consciousness, but her mind felt as if she had been frozen in that gelid green ocean. She was aware of the room around her—still dimly aware of the shadows of others who had occupied that room—but could neither sink back into her original coma nor rise to wakefulness.

And she had to wake up. She had to get out.

They were creating a power base, to give them position with the warlords Harrsk and Teradoc and the other remaining branches of the Imperial Fleet.

And around that power base, the Imperial Fleet might very well coalesce once more.

And that coalition would be armed with the wealth of the Senex Lords, and the massive weaponry of the *Eye of Palpatine,* drawn from the darkness of the past by a fifteen-year-old boy whose powers could cripple the Republic's unprepared defenses. To gain the *Eye,* and Irek, as secret weapons, a man like High Admiral Harrsk might surrender power that he would not have given over to a child's regent a few years ago.

She had to get out.

Or get a message out, even if it cost her her life.

Han Solo. Ithor. Time of Meeting. Once he'd stumbled onto some cache of Irek's yarrock hidden in the tunnels, once his mind had been cleared a little by the counterreaction of the drug, Drub had done everything in his power to warn his friend . . . to help the Republic that he knew was Han's new allegiance. He, too, knew they had to be warned.

She wondered at what point they'd gotten rid of Nasdra Magrody. Probably as soon as Irek was capable of controlling and directing his ability to influence mechanicals—Magrody knew far too much to be allowed to live.

Like his pupil, she thought. She remembered the report of Stinna Draesinge Sha's murder: Her room had been gone through, her papers destroyed. Magrody must have worked on the initial phases of the implanted brain chip with her, or talked to her about them.

And hadn't there been some other physicist, some other student of Magrody's, who'd died under mysterious circumstances a few years ago?

Leia didn't remember. That had been back before she'd met Cray. Magrody's other star pupil, Qwi Xux, had probably had her life saved when the renegade adept Kyp Durron had wiped out her memory.

And Ohran Keldor had been Magrody's pupil as well.

The door hissed open, and Leia felt the sharp blast of the warmer corridor air on her face. Though her eyes were closed she could "see" Lord Garonnin and Drost Elegin come inside, the stocky security chief carrying an infuser.

The metal of the infuser was cold against her throat; she felt the rush of chemical, of warming wakefulness, stir her veins.

The sensation of green glass around her vanished. So did the ghosts, and even the memories of the ghosts, of others in the room. Her head ached as if her brain had been stuffed with desiccant.

"Your Highness?"

Leia tried to reply and discovered that her tongue had turned into a three-kilo sack of sand. "Unnnh . . ."

Her eyes were still shut, but she saw Garonnin and Elegin exchange a look. "Another one," said Elegin, and the security chief frowned.

"We don't want to harm her. Idiots."

He loaded another ampoule into the infuser and put the metal to Leia's throat again.

Her mind cleared with a snap, her heart pounding as if she'd been waked in panic by a loud noise; she flinched, sat up, aware that her hands were shaking.

"Your Highness?" Garonnin sketched a military bow and replaced the infuser in his pocket. "Madame Roganda wishes your presence."

He didn't sound happy about it, though it was difficult to tell what emotions passed behind those wet-stone eyes. *Madame* Roganda was a title of courtesy . . . Roganda was certainly not a person qualified to demand that the last Princess of the House Organa come to *her*. Leia slowed her breathing, raised her eyebrows slightly, as if she had not expected *that* humiliating a slight, but with an air of gracious martyrdom rose, followed the men into the corridor. She had to call on all the physical training of the Jedi not to stumble, but managed to walk with what her aunts would have called "queenly grace."

Like Palpatine, the men of the Ancient Houses preferred resigned obedience to defiance, and until she found some way in which to actively escape Leia guessed her best course would be to rack up all the points with these people she could.

They were quite heavily armed, with stunguns as well as blasters.

She still felt shaky, strange, and a little dizzy, though moving helped. Having no desire for a guaranteed three hours' worth of headaches and nausea, Leia decided to bide her time.

Roganda, Irek, and Ohran Keldor occupied a small chamber one level up, cold despite the heating unit placed discreetly in a corner. The walls were draped with black; Leia had the momentary impression of the sort of meditation chamber used by some Dathomir sects, which used silence, dimness, and a single-point source of firelight to concentrate the mind.

A cluster of candles was grouped on the polished wooden table at which Irek and his mother sat. With such discretion as to constitute almost an apology, a quarto-size terminal was set up on a bench just within the range of Irek's peripheral vision, where Ohran Keldor was keying rapidly through a series of calculations and what looked like sensor reports. There were four glass balls of the type Leia had seen in several places in the crypts, set on stands in the corners of the room so that Irek's chair was directly where lines drawn between them would cross.

Irek raised his head, stared at her with arrogant, furious blue eyes. "I've had enough trouble from you," he said, his juvenile voice cold, and Leia was aware of Lord Garonnin's angry frown at the rudeness and lèse-majesté. "Now you will tell me. Why wouldn't your droid obey me in the crypts? What had you done to it?"

"You're dismissed," said Roganda quickly, signing to Garonnin and Elegin—Leia saw the look that passed between them as they left.

True, Roganda was in a hurry—but as a child Leia had had it impressed upon her that *no* person of breeding was *ever* in such a hurry as to speak brusquely to a social superior.

Inferiors, of course—and those whom circumstance had placed in the power of a Lord—were jolly well on their own.

She turned to face Roganda, her eyes cold. "What guarantees can you give me that I'll be returned to Coruscant safe and sound?"

"You *dare* ask for guarantees!" yelled Irek, slamming his fist on the table, and Roganda held up her hand.

"I can guarantee you that unless you tell us what you did to your droid that enabled it to escape my son's influence," she said, with quiet viciousness, "you're going to be blasted out of existence in very short order, along with every living thing in Plawal. Because the *Eye of Palpatine* is not responding to my son's commands."

"Not responding?" said Leia, startled. "I thought your son commanded it to come here."

"I did," said Irek sullenly.

"Not . . . exactly," corrected Keldor. The little man looked harried, his bald head shining with sweat in the glow of the console lights. "We knew that part of the original activation signal relay to trigger the *Eye of Palpatine* had been destroyed somewhere in the vicinity of Belsavis. By tapping into the strength of the Force, Lord Irek was able to reactivate the relay and bring the battlemoon here, where it will be close enough for him to control its on-board programming directly."

He cleared his throat uneasily, and avoided both Roganda's eyes and

Leia's. "The thing is, Princess, the *Eye of Palpatine*—a fully automated ship, one of the few designed with a completely automatic mission control in order to obviate security leaks—was originally programmed to destroy all life on the planet Belsavis. Shell out of existence anything that resembled a settlement."

"Because the Jedi were here," said Leia steadily.

Keldor's eyes avoided hers. "The Emperor took whatever steps he felt necessary to reduce the risk of civil war. Whatever else can be said about them, the Jedi were potential insurgents who he felt could not be trusted with power."

"And he could be, I suppose?" Leia looked across at Roganda. "You were one of the children here, weren't you?" she asked. "It was your family they were attacking."

"We change with the times, Princess." Roganda folded her delicate hands, the topaz of her ring a sulfurous star in the candle's light. Away from her chief of staff, and the Senex Lords whom she sought to impress, all semblance of that shy defenselessness was gone. In its place was a cool vituperative scorn, the power-loving contempt that Leia guessed sprang from envy of those who had looked down on her, and desire to get her own back.

"If I'd followed the strictest traditions of my family I'd have been destroyed, as they and my older brother Lagan were destroyed. As it was, I adapted those traditions."

"You followed the dark side, you mean."

That stung her. The winglike brows lifted. "What is the 'dark side,' Princess?" There was a good deal of Irek in her chilly voice. Here was another one, thought Leia, who could not conceive of the possibility of being wrong. "Some of us think that fanatic adherence to every jot and quibble of an antiquated code is, if not dark precisely, at least stupid. And from all I've heard, the 'dark side' seems to be anything that disagrees with the hidebound, divisive, every-tree-and-bush-is-sacred teachings that shackled the Jedi gifts—and shackled every political body that had anything to do with the Jedi, whether they agreed with them or not—like an iron chain."

She gestured, with the small hand that had never done any work in the woman's life, as if summoning the spirit of the clammy old man in the black robe whose pale eyes still sometimes stared at Leia in her dreams.

"Palpatine was a pragmatist. As am I."

"And you don't think that pragmatism—as you call that form of selfishness—isn't exactly what the dark side is?"

"Madame," said Keldor—leaving it unstated whom he was addressing—"to be strictly pragmatic . . . we have very little time. The *Eye of Palpatine* will be in range of this rift, its principal target, in a matter of forty minutes." His cold colorless eyes fastened on Leia's face, gauging her.

Like Moff Tarkin, she thought. Trying to figure out what would cause her to break.

"Now, it's very possible that you will escape the destruction by virtue of concealment in these tunnels. But I assure you"—and that flicker of spitefulness crept into her voice again—"everyone in the valley will die. That presumably includes your husband. And in every other valley on this planet. What did you do to your droid?"

"I didn't do anything," said Leia quietly. "After his attempt on our lives last night he had to be rewired."

"You changed its schematic!" Irek was shocked. "But a droid can't run if you change its schematic!" He looked in horror from his mother to Keldor, as if for confirmation of this fact. "Old Man Magrody said that every droid has a standard schematic, and—"

"Professor Magrody," said Leia, "obviously didn't hang around much with spaceport mechanics."

"But that can't be the reason!" Irek slewed in his chair to face Keldor again. "Nobody rewired the *Eye*—"

"That we know about." The chubby little man glanced once more at his sensor screen, and in the shadowy fragments of light his face looked suddenly fallen in, as if someone had let the air out of him. Leia could almost hear his battle against panic in his voice. "But the fact is, my lord Irek, we don't know if the damage to the activation relays was the *only* reason the *Eye of Palpatine* didn't rendezvous with the assault wing here thirty years ago. It's just possible that enemies of the New Order *did* learn what the relays were supposed to summon, and *did* get a saboteur on board. If part of the computer core was damaged, for instance, in an attempt to overload the reactors—"

"Can you fix it?" Roganda put a hand on her son's wrist, to forestall whatever he was getting ready to say with his intaken breath. "Take a ship up there and disable the mission command center?"

Keldor's eyes shifted. Leia could almost hear him estimating the possible strength of the rock above and around them, measuring it against the
firepower of the *Eye*'s torpedoes . . .

"Of course I can."

"And if you can't," Leia snapped sarcastically, "I suppose you figure
you'll be safer up on the ship than down here?"

Roganda's eyes met Irek's.

"I blew out the central servo on the landing silos," said the boy.
Then, defensively, "You told me to!"

"Theala Vandron's ship is still on the ice pad." Roganda got to her
feet, nodded to the portable terminal in the corner. "Bring that," she said.
She paused, considering Leia for a moment, then said, "Bring her. If you
can't get that battlemoon disarmed we're going to need a hostage."

Irek's lightsaber flashed out, flame-colored in the darkness of the
black-draped room. He stepped close to Leia, the cold cautery of the
blade hissing faintly as he brought it toward her face. "And you'd better
not try anything," he said, a glitter of evil glee in his smile. "Because I
don't think we need a hostage that badly."

The corridor outside was empty.

Garonnin, thought Leia desperately, pushing aside the last traces of
the drug's breathless dizziness. *There has to be some way to alert Garonnin
that he's being betrayed . . .*

She cast a swift look toward the red alarm buttons every dozen meters
or so along the wall, wondering if Irek's reflexes were up to slicing her in
two if she lunged for one.

She rather suspected that they were.

"I warn you, Madame," panted Keldor, hurrying at Roganda's side
with his portable terminal bundled up under his arm and straps hanging
in every direction. "The gunnery computer was a semi-independent entity
from the central mission control computer—the Will. If there's been a
problem with the Will itself, it may not even let us on board, much less
permit us into the central core."

"You mean we may not be able to stop the *Eye, or* control it after-
wards?" Her obsidian-black eyes glittered like a snake's, furious at the
stupidity that dared to unravel her plans.

Keldor flinched. "There is that possibility."

"Then wait here." Roganda ducked through a nearby door in a swirl
of white skirts, and Irek stepped closer to Leia and lifted his lightsaber

threateningly. The concubine reappeared a moment later with a heavy
black box slung over one shoulder by a carrying strap. Her scornful eyes
flicked to Leia. "More pragmatism," she said dryly. "If there's one thing I
learned in getting out of Coruscant ahead of the Rebels, it was: Never be
without money."

The spite was back in her voice, clearer now; spite and a world of
unspoken resentment, the resentment of a woman who has known what it
is to be poor. Just as if, thought Leia, she herself hadn't run ragged
through the stars with a price on her head.

But Roganda wasn't seeing that. Roganda was seeing the Emperor's
levee, too; seeing the last Princess of Alderaan, privileged and pampered,
whose aunts wouldn't deign to speak to her: the scion of all those Ancient
Houses who looked down their noses at her choice of wine . . .

And Leia raised her head in just the attitude she herself had hated in
every spoiled rich brat she'd gone to school with, and summoned every
ounce of their whiny jeers into her voice.

"You'll need it," she sneered, "if your witless incompetence at this
stage gets the heads of all the Ancient Houses killed."

Roganda slapped her. The blow wasn't hard, but Leia grabbed the
little concubine's wrist, shoved her between herself and Irek, and flung
herself the two or three meters down the corridor that separated her from
one of the red alarm buttons on the wall. She smacked it hard with the
heel of her palm and whirled, raising her hands as Keldor brought up his
blaster . . .

And before Keldor had the chance to rethink his automatic response
of not shooting in the event of surrender, Lord Garonnin appeared down
the corridor at a run, blaster in hand.

"My lady? What . . . ?"

"They're deserting you!" yelled Leia. "Running out! That battlemoon's going to blow the daylights out of this place and they're taking
off in the last ship!" And, whirling, she aimed a single hard lance of the
Force at the latch of Roganda's black box.

Panic, lack of training, and the exhaustion and disorientation of the
drugs caused her aim to misfire slightly, but the result was the same. The
strap snapped and the box—which Leia could tell was extremely heavy—
crashed to the floor, the latch sprang open . . .

And gems, currency, and negotiable securities spilled across the floor
between Roganda and her aristocratic security chief.

After an endless second of staring into Roganda's white face, Garon-nin said softly, "You faithless drab," and, with his free hand, brought up his comlink.

It was the last conscious movement he made. Irek stepped forward with preternatural lightness and severed him, right shoulder to left hip, the lightsaber cutting and cauterizing flesh and bone like a hot wire passing through clay.

Leia stretched out her hand, Garonnin's blaster flying free of his dying grasp and into her palm. Even as it did so she flung herself to the floor in a long roll, Keldor's blaster bolt spattering viciously against the rock where a moment ago she'd been standing; then she plunged down the nearest corridor, heard Irek yelling, "Kill her! She'll tell the others!" and the clatter of pursuing feet.

Leia took a flight of stairs two steps at a time, fled down a corri-dor, past deserted rooms or sealed doorways, musty and lit by the in-termittent radiance of glowpanels faded with age. She ducked through what she thought was another passageway and found herself in a long room whose single bay window looked out into the lamp-twinkling outer darkness—fleeing to the embrasure, beyond the heavy plex she saw the jut of rocky overhang, the dense curtain of vines . . . and a hanging bed of vine-coffee plants, gleaming with worklights, not three meters away.

Hanging beds. The supply platform. An emergency ladder to the bottom of the rift.

She was prepared to shoot out the window latches but it wasn't necessary; they were stiff, but not locked. Shouts, running feet out-side . . . Her breath was still short and uneven from the stimulants they'd given her but she knew she had no choice. Leia squirmed her way through the narrow opening to the minimal rock of the sill—being very careful not to look down—grabbed a handful of vine, and swung.

The vine jerked and gave half a meter under her weight, but somehow the huge steel basket of the bed was safely, easily under her. She grabbed a support cable and clung, releasing the vine, gasping and trembling all over. Lights glowed above her, below her, and all around, illuminating the other beds in the dark. Leia looked up to the dark mazes of tracks, the rags of fog drifting among the cable-and-pulley arrangements that held up the gondolas of the beds and above it all the cold white fragments of wind-thrashed ice skating across the plex of the dome itself. She knew she shouldn't look down but did . . . a swirling sea of fog, broken by dark trees and the fragile lamps of a sunken city.

A tremendously long way down.

Lightly, she ran along the duckboard that stretched the length of the bed.

The supply station affixed to the cliff wall itself, with its own thick beds festooned in vines, seemed impossibly far away.

The steel gondolas that supported the hanging beds were ten or twelve meters by six, filled with earth and overflowing with the heavy, thick-leaved coffee- or silk-vines. This was a coffee bed, tight clusters of dark beans half hidden among the striped leaves, the bittersweet smell of the foliage thick in her lungs. Narrow catwalks ran between the beds, little more than chain ladders wound on reels that extended or contracted as the beds were raised and lowered, or could be unhooked and drawn in completely if a bed was brought laterally around to one of the supply stations on the rift wall. The thought of crossing one turned Leia absolutely cold, but it was the only means of making her way from bed to bed until she reached the station . . .

The bed jarred, shook, swayed. Turning, she saw that Irek had swung from the window as she had, and was running lightly down the duckboards to her, lightsaber shining redly in his hand.

Leia fired her blaster and missed, the boy ducking nimbly and vanishing among the vines. Rather than face him—not knowing exactly what she'd have to face—she fled, ducking and scrambling across the first of the spider-strand catwalks, clinging to the safety line that formed a spindly railing for the bridge. She half expected Irek to cut the bridge behind her and try to spill her off, but he didn't, probably knowing she could hang on to the ladder and climb. She felt his weight on the catwalk behind her but didn't dare stop and turn until she had the next bed swinging and rocking beneath her feet; then she turned, in time to see him spring off the catwalk and into the vines.

She fired again but the blaster jerked in her hand, almost loosening her grip, and she ducked the whining slash of the blade close enough that she could feel its cold. The coffee vines tangled her feet but she moved lightly, ducking his cuts, weaving and springing away. She dodged again, as behind her two of the heavy stakes that held the vines uprooted themselves and slashed at her head like thrown clubs—he was attempting to drive her over the edge. Her second shot missed, and she could feel the pressure of his mind on hers; her lungs laboring, her throat tightening. Consciously she relaxed them, opened them, thrust aside what he was trying to do to her . . .

A blaster bolt whined, took a piece out of the steel rim of the basket, and left a mass of acridly smoking vines between them. Irek startled back and looked around; Leia fired from a distance of less than two meters and only at the last second did his mind try to rip the blaster again from her hand. The bolt seared a smoking rent in the shoulder of his coat, and at the same moment Keldor's voice yelled, "I've got her! I've—"

Irek lunged at Leia in response, driving her toward the edge, and then there was a shattering crack from the plex overhead and the pane cracked, frigid air pouring down through the hole the blaster had made and turning instantly to a swirling column of fog in which snow fragments sparkled viciously in the starry lights.

Leia ducked through the momentary screen of the fog to the next catwalk, raced and scrambled along it headfirst, though it was pointing slightly downward to a silk bed a few meters below and nearly ten meters away . . .

This time Irek did cut the catwalk. Leia dropped the blaster and grabbed hard and tight as the chain ladder plunged sickeningly down. The lurch, the jerk of it reaching the bottom of its arc was terrifying, jolting her belly and freezing her heart. The ladder jerked and swung and it took all her courage to release her deathgrip enough to begin climbing, but she knew she was a sitting target. A bolt burned the ends of the vines to her left.

"I've got her!" she heard Keldor yell again. Leia dragged herself over the edge of the steel cage and fell into the fusty-smelling masses of the vines. She tore up one of the heavy vine-stakes, knowing it would be almost useless against either lightsaber or blaster, but it was the only weapon to hand. At the same moment the bed lurched and began to move, rumbling along its track on the ceiling, swaying with the momentum of its speed. Leia flattened, digging her hands hard into the vines as the bed lurched and jerked against the other catwalks that connected it to the beds around it, then swayed sickeningly as the thin steel ladders broke off.

Don't look down, she told herself grimly, but, looking up, saw where the tracks crossed . . .

Another bed swept down the crossing track out of nowhere, vines trailing, whizzing along like an out-of-control freighter. Leia crushed herself flat again, and the gondola slashed by half a meter over her head, cables whining as the whole bed dipped toward her in an attempt to sweep her off. Then the bed she was on was moving faster and faster, swaying wildly as it swooped around corners, raising and lowering—

Another searing whine of the blaster, as a whipping turn brought her clear of the pouring fog and into what Keldor considered his range.

"Here! Over here!"

The moving bed lurched, stopped, and reversed its direction.

She could see Irek standing up on another bed, slightly above her, backlit in the swirling fog, lightsaber burning like amber flame in his hands.

Fog was everywhere, spewing streams of it mixed with snow as the cold air poured down through the crack in the dome. Another silk bed swept toward her on a collision course; Leia gauged the possibility of a jump to that one but lost her nerve, ducked flat, and clung as it slammed heavily into the side of her bed, nearly hurling her out, then swept away as it had come. One instant she was swaying over a sickening view of trees and clouds and tiny lights below, the next lost in dark swirls of mist through which the lights on her bed glowed like jewels.

Something huge and dark loomed out of the mist above her and she felt the jolt of someone landing on the bed. A heavy rustle of feet in the vines, then: "Don't move, Princess. I'm not very good with this but at this range I'm not going to miss again."

The silk bed lurched out of the fog. Ohran Keldor, blaster in hand, stood at the other end.

The bed slowed, but continued a constant, even course back to the bed where Irek stood like a slender black god.

In a sudden squeal of cables another garden rose from below them, missing them by less than a meter, and from its rim Han Solo launched himself into the vines at Keldor's side. At the same moment both that bed and the one Han had ridden over to them swung in another direction, heading along the track toward the vine-festooned supply station on the rift wall, where Leia could see Jevax and Chewbacca, standing at the controls.

Irek yelled, "No!" and Han, who had twisted the blaster out of the astonished Keldor's fist, shouted, "Run for it, Leia!"—instead she strode over through the vines and delivered a smashing blow with the vine-stake to the back of Keldor's head as he struggled with Han on the edge of the bed.

Keldor staggered, reeling. Han jerked him back from the edge and thrust him toward the leading end of the bed, which was now closing in on the supply station. Jevax waded through the deep vines, reaching out with a long pole to steady the incoming bed. Irek shouted something else, Leia didn't hear exactly what . . .

And the pulleys that held the bed to the trolley overhead let go with a snap.

Leia flung herself at the hanging jungle of the supply station's vines, Han leaping after . . . she thought he wouldn't make it, reached out with the Force, but didn't afterward know whether it was his own agility or some added energy of hers that let him grab the bottom ends of that trailing green beard.

But in any case Ohran Keldor, architect of the Death Star and sole surviving technician of the *Eye of Palpatine,* had neither the Force nor the trained muscle of a rough-and-tumble smuggler to help him.

And if Irek was capable of levitating him out of the falling ruin of the silk bed, he didn't react quickly enough or didn't try. The scientist's scream of terror echoed in the ghostly broil of fog still streaming down through the cracked dome, and when Leia and Han gained the safety of the platform, all trace of Irek was gone.

Chapter 24

With the closing of the shuttlecraft door behind the last contingent of the Gakfedds, the hangar seemed profoundly silent. Beyond the magnetic seal, the blue-white curve of Belsavis flung back a cold glory of light, a bony radiance that bleached Cray's features to a haggard shadow and turned Nichos's to silvery marble.

"There it is," said Callista softly. "There, where the clouds rise up in columns over the heat of the thermal vent."

Even from here, Luke could see the star-silvered night side chaos where the Plawal Rift lay.

Leaning like a tired old man on his staff, he remembered the young Jedi who'd come to him a year ago, bringing the tall, elegant blond woman—*the most brilliant AI programmer at the Magrody Institute—and strong in the Force as well.*

She'd stepped forward, he remembered, to shake his hand, taking charge of the situation so that it wouldn't take charge of her.

I'm sorry, he wanted to say to them, not knowing quite why.

For life.

For this.

For everything.

"The lander's going to be launched first, on automatic," he said, forcing his mind back to the matter at hand. Time was, he knew, now very short. "Once it gets clear of the magnetic field, Blue Shuttle will go . . ." He gestured to the massive pale block of the Telgorn; it rocked, very slightly, and a muffled thumping could be heard within. He felt a momentary rush of gratitude that the control cabin was completely separate from the passenger hull.

"Triv . . ."

The elderly stormtrooper stepped forward from the shadows where he'd been standing with Threepio. He'd shed his white armor, and wore again the faded, flower-embroidered makeshifts he'd had on when he'd come on board. His dark face was calm, but there was an infinity of sorrow in his eyes.

"I'm putting you in charge of Blue Shuttle in case there are any problems, but the controls are slaved to Red Shuttle's console—Nichos will pilot both crafts from there."

Luke drew a deep, shaky breath. "Cray . . ."

She raised her eyes. Silence had been growing around her, like a sea creature manufacturing a shell of its armor; a double shell, this time, enfolding them both.

It was the first time he'd seen Cray and Nichos so comfortable together, so close, since the days on Yavin before Nichos's hands had started to go numb, his vision to blur. With the various small camouflages gone—the steel mesh and the ornamental housings covering wrist joints and neck—he was more than ever a droid, but something in the way they stood, something in their silence, was as if the past eight nightmare months had not taken place.

"There's an escape pod at the end of the corridor outside the gunnery deck," he said quietly. "Once I make it to the top of the shaft, I'll yell down to you and you get to that pod and get the hell out of here. I think there'll be time."

"I thought I was the one," said Cray softly, "who was going up the shaft."

He shook his head. "I could never make it to the pod. I've rested . . ." It wasn't much of a lie, he reflected. "I can use the Force to help misfire the grid, and I think I have the strength to levitate to the top. Once I'm in the central core . . ."

He took another deep breath. "Once I'm in the central core I'm going to try to cripple the guns, rather than blow up the ship. According to the readouts you got from the central computer that should be possible from there . . ."

"And what if it's not?" demanded Callista's voice.

"Then . . ." He almost couldn't say the words. "Then I'll start the reactor overload. But if it hasn't blown in ten minutes, Cray—and you'll be out of there and in the pod by then—start thinking about how we're going to get enough memory in a unit to get Callista off the ship. After that's done we'll blow it."

"No," said Callista.

"Callista, I can't—"

"*No.*"

He could see her, almost, standing in front of him, her features set and white and her smoke-colored eyes grim, as they had been in the other hangar, thirty years ago . . .

"Luke, we can't risk it. You can't risk it. Say you're right, you find a way to cripple the guns—*really* cripple them, not have the *Eye* lie to you and say they're crippled. That leaves the *Eye* in orbit until you can scrape up enough units of memory, enough circuits and synapses . . . You're never going to find that kind of thing on Belsavis. From what you've told me they're just an agricultural station, and a small one at that. So you send for them. So they take a day, two days to arrive . . . And meanwhile whoever sent for the *Eye of Palpatine* comes along . . . and every Imperial admiral who picks up word of it . . . You think the Republic's going to be able to fight off the pack of them? With a station like this one for the prize?"

Luke was silent, unable to argue. Unable to tell himself that the dark flower of knowledge, the cold dread of his dream, had been illusions.

Something had sent for the *Eye*. Something was waiting for it.

And it had it almost within its grasp.

"Blow the reactors, Luke." Her voice was low, barely to be heard in the deep silence of the shuttle deck. None of the others spoke, but Luke was conscious of Cray's eyes on his face, knowing in a way that none of the others did what he was going through.

Knowing that his decision to be the one in the shaft was based partly on the knowledge that if he destroyed the ship—if he destroyed Callista—he would be in her heart when the end came.

"Don't let the Will deceive you," Callista continued softly. "Because believe me, it knows how badly you want to deceive yourself."

"I know." He doubted any of the others heard his words, but knew that Callista heard. "I know. I love you, Callista . . ."

She whispered, "And I love you. Thank you for bringing me back this far."

He straightened up, as if some terrible burden had fallen from him.

"Nichos, Threepio, Triv . . . get ready for launch. Cray, I still want you to be the one who stays below, the one who gets out of here . . ."

He turned, in time to see her take a stungun from the holster at her side.

He had, he realized, thought of everything but that. *The Will is going to do anything . . . use anything . . .* He threw himself sideways and rolled as best he could . . .

But the killing grind of exhaustion and pain had slowed his reactions and blunted any chance he had of using the Force, and the stunblast smote him like the blow of a club, hurling him into darkness.

"Who the hell was that?"

Leia dragged Han up the final half meter or so onto the platform, Jevax and Chewie reaching down beside her to pull him to safety. Cold wind whipped and tangled her hair, fog swirled around them one moment, ice crystals stinging her cheeks, then whipped away to reveal the tossing soft lake of the rift below.

Dimly, from the open window beneath the vines away along the cliff, she could hear the clamor of alarms.

"Jevax, can you get us back there? There, under that ledge . . . And sound the alarms in the valley! All over the planet, whatever other settlements you can reach! The whole planet's going to be shelled, bombed from space, I don't know how soon, minutes maybe . . ."

"Who was that?" demanded Han. "And who killed that guy in the passageway? Artoo led us back through to the crypts, then up an elevator . . . What happened to the guardians in the tunnels?"

"Bombed?" demanded Jevax, horrified.

"Now! Go! Get everyone under shelter, into the old smuggler tunnels—use the spaceport silos for safety, it won't have been a target, it wasn't built thirty years ago . . ."

Chewie ducked back into the supply shack, emerged with a controller in his paws. A moment later a vine-coffee bed approached them like a slow, splendid, flower-caparisoned barge along its ceiling tracks.

"That supership Mara told us about, the other half of the assault on Belsavis . . . it's on its way! Irek summoned it—Roganda's son, Irek—"

"That kid?"

"He's trained in the Force, he can influence mechanicals . . . He'll make hash out of our fleet . . ." She sprang down from the platform into the thick vines of the bed. After the sickening whiplash drop on the slashed catwalk, and springing from the falling bed to the thin tangle of vines, the short jump down to something securely anchored bothered her not in the slightest.

Han swore and jumped, catching the cables for support; Chewie dropped down after.

"Warn them!" yelled Leia back, as the Wookiee swiveled the joystick on his controller; the coffee bed swung ponderously along the track, breasting through a banner of fog toward the distant overhang of the cliff, and the gaping window beneath. "Get everyone under cover!"

Jevax was already swarming onto the little service elevator that would take him down the cliffside.

Drost Elegin, Lady Theala Vandron, and a motley and vociferating gang of private guards, secretaries, and corporate representatives were assembled in the room from which Leia had jumped to the first of the vine-beds. They rushed to the window at the sight of the approaching bed, but though several were armed, Leia heard Lady Vandron snap, "Don't fire, you idiots, they could have escaped!" as the bed drew near.

Chewie flung out a coil of ladder; half a dozen hands caught it, anchored it for Han, Leia, and the Wookiee to cross.

Artoo-Detoo was between Lady Vandron and one of Roganda's thugs, rocking back and forth and tweeping excitedly. As Leia swung through the window—Drost Elegin, a gentleman to his bones, held out a hand to help her descend—Leia said, "You've been betrayed, all of you! When Irek discovered he couldn't control the *Eye of Palpatine* he ran for it, he and his mother. They're the ones who killed Lord Garonnin . . ."

They looked at one another.

"Look at his body," said Leia furiously. "Irek's the only person in this place who has a lightsaber! And if you look at the place you'll probably find a trail of jewels and negotiable bonds all the way to the elevator."

She saw the glances that were exchanged among the guards. Nobody had produced a weapon yet.

"It should be a simple matter to pursue them," said Lord Picutorion. "We have some of the fastest—"

"Not with all the silo gates of the port jammed shut, you don't," retorted Leia. She turned to Lady Vandron. "It's your ship they're taking, Your Highness . . . The *Eye of Palpatine* is going to start bombing the planet any minute, so I suggest everyone go as deep as they can and as far into the tunnels as they can."

"The creatures in the crypt—" began the athletic-looking Lady Carbinol.

"Have no direction without Irek's will," said Elegin. He glanced over at Han and Chewbacca, still standing in the embrasure of the window. "As I daresay you found out on your way in." He whipped his blaster from his side. "After you, Your Highness. We may still be able to catch them before they take off."

They encountered, in fact, two or three of the wretched ex-smugglers and ex-hustlers wandering the passageways farther from the inhabited areas, where the thermal vent ran out under the ice, but as Elegin had said, without Irek's will the things ran shrieking from the lights borne by Han, Leia, and the various infuriated aristocrats who strode in their wake. Without Irek to interfere with sensor tracking, thought Leia as she ran, they should be able to round up those miserable guardians and get them whatever kind of help could best be devised.

She wondered what the old Jedi records Luke had scraped together had to say about such abuses of the power of the Force, what might be done by those with talents as healers.

"Typical," Leia heard Lady Carbinol snap to someone at the rear of the group—a group, she noticed, made up largely of the members of the Ancient Houses, the corporate types being mostly in prudent search of the deepest defenses they could find. "I never trusted the woman . . . I don't wish to sound the snob, but breeding will tell and in this case it certainly has . . ."

Every now and then they found, on the tunnel floor, a piece of jewelry, or a credit paper, to indicate the direction of Roganda's flight.

The elevator up to the surface was jammed. "Servo's blown at the top," said Han, flipping back the coverplate on the summons button to check the monitor.

"He did that on the central servo that controls the landing silos," said Leia. "I don't know at what distance his power can operate, but it's not something I'd want to have happen if I were in an X-wing going into combat. Is there a stair?" she asked Drost Elegin, who nodded.

It was, in fact, a circular ramp, since the old smugglers had to get cargo down it. Artoo-Detoo, who had followed them stolidly along the passageways and ramps from the main mazes behind the cliff, caught up with them and trundled on ahead, his small spotlight shining on the smooth stone of the floor, the battered rock walls. The place smelled of kretch and grew colder as they ascended, Leia's breath smoking in the light of the lamps. Lady Carbinol lent Han her parka when they reached the pillbox at the top, and Han, Leia in her t-suit, and Drost Elegin—the only other member of the little group to have a parka with him—struggled, with Chewbacca and the droid, over the uneven path that wound through the sheltering backbone of the rock to the ice landing pad and its low white hangar.

The hangar door was open, the lights from within shining weirdly on the snow that blew across it, puffing back from the magnetic shield. All around the ice pad, snow was scattered in the characteristic quintuple starburst pattern of a Tikiar's lifters.

Except for Lady Vandron's two crew members, tied up with engine tape in a corner and shivering with cold, the hangar was quite empty.

Leia wrapped her arms tight around herself, shivering as the wind burned her unprotected cheeks. Chewbacca growled, his long brown fur whipped in all directions by the dying winds. Overhead the black roil of clouds had broken, showing the sky the clear, pallid slate of the Belsavis dawn.

"At least we'll be able to warn Ackbar," said Leia quietly. "Irek's power over mechanicals can be circumvented if minor changes are made in the schematics. He can do damage on any ship that hasn't been warned, but we can get the word out."

"It was a plan that worked best with surprise," agreed Drost Elegin, shaking back his graying dark hair and gazing skyward. "Though from what I know of starship mechanics, there are schematics that must be adhered to if the ship is to function at all. You must admit that the initial advantage would have been devastating. Perhaps decisive."

He looked down at Leia, his pale eyes chilly. "All we want is sufficient power to be left alone by all parties, Princess. We are perhaps repaid for our greediness in thinking that a scheming trollop and her brat could provide it for us."

He turned and moved off along the path heading back for the ramp head that would take him to the safety of underground.

Han stepped forward, to encircle Leia with his arms. "You know she was the Emperor's Hand. His *other* Hand," he added, as Leia looked quickly up, a protest on her lips. "And Mara's fried as a fish about it."

"It explains how she could do things like kidnap Nasdra Magrody, and use Imperial funds," said Leia. "She must have been planning to develop Irek's powers since she first knew he had them. Maybe since before he was born. They're out there, and they're still a danger."

She sighed, suddenly very tired, and looked, as Elegin had, into the leaden sky, as if she could see the track of the vanished spacecraft fleeing the place that had been her first, and last, true home.

"We'd better get under cover," said Han softly. "If that ship Mara talked about is going to try and finish up its mission, we don't know how far around the rift it was programmed to bomb. Let's just hope the caves are deep enough."

A burning pinpoint of white light flared suddenly in the dim sky, faded, then swelled suddenly to a monstrous glare. Han flinched, covering his eyes with his arm. Leia turned her face aside and saw their shadows— man, woman, Wookiee, droid—momentarily etched black against the blue-white meringue of the drifts among which they stood.

Han said, "What the . . . ?"

"I don't know," said Leia. "But that was way too big for a Tikiar. It has to have been the *Eye*."

"Luke, forgive me."

He rolled over, body aching from the effects of the stungun's blast. There were soft hootings in the semidark, and a white, fluffy enormity came and bent over him, urging him down with padded black paws.

Talz. They clustered around the emergency bunk where he lay, and the whole dark space of the shuttle hold smelled of their fur.

Someone was singing. "Pillaging Villages One by One."

Luke sat up, and was immediately sorry.

"Forgive me," said Callista's voice as he lay down again. Somewhere close by the Jawas chattered, yellow eyes glowing in the dark. Over the heads of the Talz he could see one end of the shuttlecraft jammed with old droid parts and stormtrooper helmets used as buckets to hold scrap metal, wire, and power cells. He remembered Callista had told both groups of Gamorreans, in her pseudomessages from the Will, that it was the Intent of the Will that they leave all their weapons outside their respective shuttlecraft.

The voice was tinny, small. Turning his head, he saw the player set next to him on the thin mattress of the bunk. The holo of her face appeared dimly above it, no more substantial than the audio.

She looked exhausted, as she had in his dream-vision of her in the gun room, her brown hair straggling from the loose braid she'd put it in, her gray eyes at peace.

"It was my idea—mine and Cray's. I was afraid—we were both afraid —that at the last minute you'd try to settle for less than complete destruction of the *Eye of Palpatine* . . . that you'd try to play for time, to take me off the ship. I'm sorry that I . . . made your decision for you."

Her image faded out, and Cray's appeared, weary and stretched-looking, but with that same exhausted peace in her eyes. "With me in the gun room using the Force against the enclision grid, I figure it's just possible for a droid to make it up the shaft . . . And a droid could take a few hits and still be able to function. Nichos agreed to this."

The pale, still features of the Jedi who for a year had been Luke's pupil appeared beside hers, oddly detached-looking in front of the metal of the cranial cowling. The hand—the precise duplicate of Nichos's hand —rested on Cray's shoulder, and she reached to touch the fingers that had been programmed to human warmth.

"Luke, you know I was never more than a substitute; a droid programmed to think, and remember, and act like someone Cray wanted very much to keep. And that might have suited me, if I hadn't loved her—truly loved her—as well. But I'm not the living Nichos, and I know I never can be. I would always be something less, something that was not."

"Nichos is on the other side, Luke," said Cray softly. "I know it, and Nichos . . ." She half smiled. "And *this* Nichos knows it. Remember us."

Their images faded.

No image replaced it, but Callista's voice said again, "Forgive me, Luke. I love you. And I will love you, always."

From the starboard portholes came a blazing burst of white.

"*No!*" Luke flung himself to his feet. He thrust through the Talz, through the Jawas clustering around the ports, the gentle tripods crowding up against the massive piles of the Jawas' junk; fell against the wall to stare out in time to see the huge white flare on the far side of the drifting asteroid fade . . .

Tiny, it was, hanging in the distance . . .

"*NO!*"

Then the explosion, like the shattering destruction of the world.

Chapter 25

Mara Jade picked them up in the *Hunter's Luck* very shortly after that.

"I came out of hyperspace almost on top of that Tikiar," she said as she and Leia helped Luke along the short, prehensile temp-lock from the Red Shuttle's lock to the *Luck*'s. Behind them in the shuttle, Chewbacca was snarling furiously at the assorted Gamorreans and Jawas seeking to follow, so loudly that he could be heard in the thin almost-vacuum. See-Threepio, who'd more or less piloted both shuttles away from the spreading cloud of ruin that had been the *Eye of Palpatine,* had remained with the Wookiee to translate, explaining in a number of languages that everything was under control and they'd all be taken care of.

"It was heading up the Corridor like it had a pack of Void Demons on its tail. If I'd known who it was I'd have taken a shot at them, but they were going so fast I probably wouldn't have got a hit. You be all right, Skywalker?" She keyed the entry to the *Luck*'s main lock, and regarded Luke worriedly as the air cycled in.

Luke nodded. There seemed no point in saying anything. He'd heal, he supposed, inwardly as well as physically. He knew that people did.

The black gulf of nothingness inside him wouldn't always be the only thing he could see.

Now he just wanted to sleep.

Leia put her arm around his waist, and he felt the touch of her mind on his. *Tell me later,* she said.

Leia, he thought, would have liked Callista.

Mara would have, too, in her cold, cautious way.

"I'll be fine," he said, knowing it was a lie.

"There's a pretty good company medcenter in Plawal," Mara was saying as she eased Luke down the short corridor to one of the small cabins. The *Hunter's Luck* was a rich kid's yacht that had fallen to pirates years before, but some of the old amenities still remained, including a self-conforming bed in a niche with a small monitor screen onto the bridge. After sleeping on heaps of blankets on the decking in corners of offices, the gentle comfort was strange.

"Who's the old duffer you got riding herd on the Blue Shuttle, kid?" Han, on the bridge, glanced up at what was clearly his own screen.

Luke smiled a little at his friend's nickname for him. "Triv Pothman. He used to be a stormtrooper, a long time ago." He leaned his head back into the pillow, barely feeling it when Leia stripped open the leg of his suit and slapped two heavy-duty gylocal patches and a massive dose of antibiotics onto the bruised, inflamed flesh.

He heard Mara swear and ask, "How long has it been like that?"

It was hard to estimate time. "Five days, six days."

She sliced off the splint Bullyak had braced it with; he barely felt her stripping away the pipe and engine tape. "The Force healed that? By the look of those cuts you should have gangrene from your quads to your toenails."

"Artoo-Detoo!" He heard Threepio's voice in the hall. Turning his head, through the door he saw the protocol droid hold out his dented arms to his stubby astromech counterpart, himself battered and smoke-stained and crusted with mud and slime. "How extremely gratifying to find you functional!"

I'll never be anything but a droid, he heard Nichos's voice in his mind. *If I didn't love her . . .*

He tried to close his mind to the hurt of memory. Five days, six days, he had said . . .

"And Your Highness," Threepio's voice continued. "I trust your mission to Belsavis went as you had hoped?"

"You could say that, Threepio," said Leia.

"If you were being kind of free with the truth," put in Han from the bridge. "Whoa, what have we got here? We got a signal in the debris field. Escape pod, it looks like."

Luke opened his eyes. "Cray." *So she decided to live after all.* Something inside him wondered why.

While Mara went off to the bridge to work the tractor beam, Luke insisted that Leia strap another splint to his leg so that he could go down to the hold when they brought the pod in. "She'll need . . . to be taken care of," he said, easing himself to a sitting position as his sister fixed the brace tight. Sitting up, he caught a glimpse of himself in the mirror on the other side of the cabin behind what had once been a bar, and was startled to see how the past week had lined and thinned his face. The blue eyes seemed very light in eye sockets discolored by fatigue and sleeplessness, and fading bruises marked jaw and cheekbone under the wicked gouges that shrapnel had left. With a ragged growth of brown stubble, he looked like some dilapidated old hermit, leaning on his staff . . .

He looked, he realized, a little like old Ben.

Leia helped him to his feet. She, too, had the appearance of someone who'd been through the mill.

"Are *you* okay?" he asked.

She nodded, brushing away his concern. "What about Cray? Did Nichos . . ." He saw her hesitate on the word "die," as she remembered that Nichos, after what Cray had done for him—to him—had been incapable of death.

"It's a long story," he said, feeling utterly weary. "I'm . . . surprised she took the escape pod. My impression was she didn't want very much to live anymore."

Over the tannoy he heard Mara say, "Got it. Bringing it in through the shield."

Leia put her shoulder under his arm, and helped him down the hall, the two droids and Chewie trailing in their wake. "Apparently Trooper Pothman has succeeded in calming the Klaggs and the Affytechans on the Blue Shuttle, Master Luke," Threepio informed him. "General Solo has already sent a subspace message to the Contacts Division of the diplomatic corps, and they're arranging a party to deal with reorientation of the *Eye*'s prisoners. They say they would like your help on that."

Luke nodded, though it was hard to think more than a few minutes ahead, a few hours ahead. He saw now why Cray had done everything in her power, had wrung her body and her mind to keep Nichos with her, to try to keep Nichos with her.

Because she could not conceive of what life would be like without him as a part of it.

He is on the other side, she had said.

As Callista, now, was on the other side.

Whatever had changed her mind, he thought, she would need him there when she came out of her chilled sleep.

The lights on the hold door cycled green and the door hissed open. The pod lay on the square of the doors, directly under the hooded, cooling eye of the quiescent tractor beam. It was barely two meters long and eighty centimeters or so wide, matte Imperial green, and icy to his touch with the cold of space.

He slid the cowling back. Under it, she lay in the comalike sleep of partial hibernation, shallow breasts barely moving under the torn and smoke-stained uniform and long hands folded over her belt buckle. Despite the bruises that still marked it, her face was so calm, so relaxed, so utterly different from the brittle, haggard features of the woman she had become that he almost didn't recognize her.

Had she looked like this, he wondered, that first day over a year ago, when Nichos had brought her to Yavin? *The most brilliant AI programmer at the Magrody Institute—and strong in the Force as well.*

The standoffish elegance she had worn as a protective cloak was gone.

She was a different woman.

A different woman . . .

Luke thought, *No . . .*

He shook his head.

No.

It wasn't Cray's face.

The features, the straight nose and delicate bones, the full, almost square shape of the lips, were the same . . .

But everything in him said, *It isn't Cray.*

No, he thought again, not wanting to believe.

For a long time the universe stood still.

Then she drew a long breath, and opened her eyes.

They were gray.

No.

He put out his hand and she raised hers, quickly, as if fearing the touch. For a few moments she simply looked at her own hands, turning them over like one marveling at the shape of palms and fingers, some unfamiliar piece of sculpture, stroking the backs of them, the fingers and the knobby, stick-out bones of the wrists. Then her eyes met his, and flooded with tears.

Very gently, afraid to touch—afraid she would vanish, evaporate, turn out to be only a dream—he helped her to sit. Her hands were warm where they touched his arms. For a time they only looked at each other . . . *This can't be real . . .*

She touched his face, the bruises and the shrapnel cuts and the beard stubble, his mouth that had pressed to hers in the dream that hadn't been a dream.

If I could ask for only one thing, one thing in my entire life . . .

He brought her gently against him, holding the long slender bones, the light sinewiness of her, pressing his face against the pale ragged hair, which he knew would turn brown in time. She was breathing. He could feel it against his cheek, under his hands, next to his heart.

Then she laughed, a soft and wondering sob, and he flung his head back and everything rose within him in a single wild whoop of triumph and joy. "Yes!" he yelled, and they were laughing and crying both, hanging on to each other, and she was saying his name, over and over again as if she still didn't believe it; couldn't believe that such things were occasionally permitted by Fate.

It was her voice, and nothing like Cray's at all.

His hands shook as they framed her face, Leia and Mara and Han and the others standing in the doorway of the hold watching all this in silence, knowing something was taking place and not quite knowing what.

But after a time Leia said, hesitantly, "That . . . that isn't Cray." There was no question in her voice.

"She stepped aside," said Luke, knowing absolutely and exactly what had happened in the last moments on board the *Eye*.

"After Nichos went up the shaft," said Callista softly. "He was hit, badly, most of his systems cut to pieces . . . He was in no pain, but he could feel himself shutting down as he set the core on overload. Cray said to me that she wanted to stay with him. To cross to the other side with him. To be with him. She was a Jedi, too, remember . . . not fully trained, but she would have been one of the best."

Tears flooded the gray eyes again. "She said if she couldn't be with the one she loved in this world, at least someone could. She said to thank you, Luke, for all you tried to do for her, and for all you did."

He kissed her, like the breath of life coming into his body after long cold, and stumbled trying to get to his feet on his bad leg. Laughing shakily, holding on to each other for support, they got to their feet and turned to the group in the doorway.

He said softly, knowing it for the truth as he knew the truth of his own bones, "Leia—Han—Mara . . . Threepio, Artoo . . . This is Callista."

Chapter 26

"Everything has to be paid for." Callista passed her hands across the surface of the glass sphere, where the pink-gold liquid glittered—unstir-ring—in the glow of the lamp. Shadows bent and flickered over the other objects in the toy room, catching angles of color, shadow, light. Outside, the stream that ran through the wide hall clucked and muttered in its stone channel, and the glowrod hissed a little in a loose socket, but there was no other sound.

"I should have known there would be a risk," she went on in that soft, slightly husky voice with the slight inflection of the Chad deep-water ranges. "I might have guessed there would be a price."

"Would you have done it," asked Leia, "if you knew?"

Callista said, "I don't know."

She crossed the room to the flat rectangular tank, with its thin layer of yellow sand, moving with an odd, graceful awkwardness. She had on the faded blue jumpsuit of a spaceport mechanic, laced down as tight as it would go in the back and still baggy over flanks and shoulders, and a mechanic's heavy boots. With her cropped hair and shy, rather quirky cast of face she had an unfledged look, like a military cadet. A lightsaber hung at her belt, a gleaming line of bronze sea creatures inlaid in its grip.

"The Masters used to call images in the tank, like forming up holos. They'd project their thoughts through the sand. I don't know what its exact composition is, but it occurs naturally on a world in the Gelviddis Cluster. The sand is what makes it easy for a child to do the same."

Leia frowned, considering the faintly glittering, daffodil-colored dust, trying to evoke Han's face, or Jacen's, by thinking through it.

"Flowers were the easiest," said Callista. "Something you're familiar with. Flowers or animals. Make them come up out of the sand."

There was silence again. Leia perched on the bench in front of the tank, relaxing and focusing her mind as Luke had taught her, seeing in every detail the little candy-pink pittin that had once played with the end of her braids. Thinking *through* the sand . . .

And in some fashion she couldn't define, the images went through the sand and appeared in the tank, not bit by bit, but with an odd sort of abrupt gradualness. AT-AV, rolling on her back to bat at starblossom petals, as if she hadn't been dead for eleven years.

"Oh, pretty!" said Callista. "Is she yours?"

"Was," said Leia. "A long time ago."

"The Masters always had a problem with the children born Jedi to non-Jedi parents, you know," Callista went on, after a silence in which Leia let the image fade. "Because it's usually passed on in families, but not always . . . and it often manifests spontaneously, in people who had no experience with it and no way of knowing how to deal with children who had it. The Masters tried to catch those as early as they could, because those were the ones at the most risk from the dark side. Those," she went on, "and the children born of Jedi parents who were only a little Force-strong, who had only a tiny bit of what their brothers and sisters and playmates had full strength. Some of those were . . . the most dangerous of all."

She stopped, and there was a very awkward pause.

Then, quickly, Callista turned away. "This is a mental maze." She tapped one of the metal spheres in their rack on the wall. Leia shrank back from it as Callista took it down, remembering Irek holding it out for her, reaching out to suck her spirit into it, to be trapped forever.

"Most people didn't go into them really," said the taller woman. "Not with their whole . . . whole being, whole spirit. And they're easy to get out of once you know how. The big ones are the simplest, and they get more complicated the smaller they get, mazes within mazes within mazes.

The juniors used to make them for fun, and try to confuse and trap each other, the way kids do."

She set the sphere on the table, spun it with her fingers, the light gleaming wetly off its whirling sides. "I wish . . . I wish I could show you."

It had been last night, when Leia, Han, and Callista had come down to the toy room, that they'd discovered that Callista was no longer able to use or touch the Force.

Luke had been taken to the Brathflen Corporation's Medcenter, to spend most of the night in the glass tank of viscous bacta fluid. It had occurred to Leia that this young woman—who despite her strong superficial physical resemblance to Cray now seemed no more like her than some distant cousin—would know the nature and uses of the toys in their room in the vaults beneath Plett's House.

Armed with tranquilizers, stunguns, and massive restraints, Jevax and Mara Jade had led parties of searchers to round up the remaining insane guardians of the crypts, so it was fairly safe to enter through the tunnels from Roganda's house on Painted Door Street. At the sight of them Mara's cold anger was revived. Many of them were people she knew.

In addition to the team from Diplomatic, a group of psychologists and healers was due to arrive tomorrow from Ithor to help deal with rehabilitation, using the techniques that, Tomla El had informed Leia over subspace, seemed at last to be working on Drub McKumb. The two shuttlecraft and the lander had been brought in safely and their occupants —with the exception of the Sand People, who were drugged and under firm restraint—were in protective custody, to be reoriented, deprogrammed, and returned to their home planets. Both Klaggs and Gakfedds had adamantly refused reorientation and were currently negotiating with Drost Elegin to be taken on as a bodyguard.

Only when Callista had attempted the first, most simple demonstrations of the toys—separating the colored fluids within the sphere, setting to motion the delicately poised levers and wheels of the Dynamitron—had the truth become clear.

She had lost all ability to use the Force.

"It wasn't something I even thought about," she said now, turning one of the mind mazes over in her hands. She did not meet Leia's eyes, shy with her and a little hesitant, not because she was the Chief of State of the New Republic, Leia guessed, but because she was Luke's sister.

"Cray had the Force in her very strongly. If she hadn't, she wouldn't have been able to . . . to leave her body the way she did. To guide me into it. To give it to me." She glanced up, her rain-colored eyes anxious. "You were her friend, weren't you?"

Leia nodded, remembering that cool, stylish, intellectual young woman whose height and natural elegance she'd so envied. "We weren't close," she said, "but yes, we were friends." She reached out and put her hand briefly over Callista's. "Close enough for me to guess months ago that she didn't want to live without Nichos."

Callista gave her fingers a quick squeeze. "He was . . . sweet. Kind," she said. "I don't want you to be angry that I'm me, and not her. She was the one who . . . who offered. Whose idea it was. We didn't even know it would work."

Leia gave a quick shake of her head. "No. It's all right. I'm glad it did."

"The Force is something that's been in me, a part of me, since I was small. Djinn—my old Master—said . . ." She hesitated, and looked away again, suddenly silent about what it was her Master had said to her, unwilling to pass it on.

"Well, anyway," she took up a moment later, "I never thought there would be a time when I . . . when it wouldn't be part of me."

Leia remembered how this young woman had fled this room last night without a word, vanishing into the lightless mazes of the geothermic caves. She herself had spent a harrowing few hours, wondering if there was anything she could or should be doing—in between a dozen subspace calls to Ithor and the Diplomatic Corps—until Han had reminded her, "She probably knows those crypts better than anyone here."

In the small hours of the morning, when Leia had gone to Luke's room at the Brathflen Medcenter, she had found Callista there, stretched out on the bed beside the sleeping Luke, her head pillowed on his arm.

"What will you do now?" Leia asked softly.

Callista shook her head. "I don't know."

Sometimes there is nothing you can do.

Leaning on the broken frame of the gateway arch, Luke remembered the words Callista had said in the darkness of the *Eye of Palpatine*.

Sometimes justice is best served by knowing when to fold one's hands.

That, too, was the wisdom of the Jedi.

Maybe the hardest wisdom he'd heard.

She sat with folded hands now, gazing out into the weird shimmer of mist and the gray shadows of trees. The crack in the dome had done strange things to the weather in the rift, and odd little currents of fidgety cool whispered through the heavy warmth of the fog.

She had known this place, he thought, before the dome had been built, before the orchards had been planted, when it had been part jungle, part volcanic barrens around acrid mudflats. She remembered it when the only settlement had been that little group of lava-rock houses clustered up against the rising benches of land at the end of the narrow valley, truly little more than a fingernail gouge in the marble wastelands of eternal ice.

She had grown up in another world, a universe separated from the present by centuries' worth of events packed into a single life span.

Like Triv Pothman—who had been enchanted with the quiet community of Plawal and was already signed up for training as a horticulturist—Callista had spent a long time as a hermit, to return to a world unfamiliar and empty of anyone she knew.

He was silent, but she turned her head as if he'd spoken her name.

It was good to walk again, without limping, without fear, without pain.

It was good to be in daylight again, and in real air.

"Are you all right?" There was quick concern in her eyes as she spoke, held out her hand to him. The tissue regeneration of the bacta therapy had left him shaky, and he knew he shouldn't be up yet.

"I should ask you that." She had been there, lying at his side, when he'd drifted to consciousness close to dawn. Later, when he'd waked fully, she'd been gone. Leia had told him what had taken place in the toy room, but it was as if Luke had known it already. He wondered if he'd been there, seen it in some now forgotten dream. Certainly when she'd wept, silently, on his shoulder in the predawn darkness, he'd known what it was she had lost.

She shook her head, not in denial, but in a kind of wonderment. "I keep thinking about Nichos," she said. "About being 'another Corellian of the same name.'" She turned her hands over, as she had when she'd waked in the *Hunter's Luck,* feeling the shape of them, their long strength and the pattern of the veins and muscles beneath the porcelain-fine skin.

Hefted in them the lightsaber she had once had the skill to make. His head close to hers, Luke could see the brown color already visible at the roots of her cornsilk hair, and knew that within a few months the whole would be that heavy, malt-colored mane he remembered from visions and dreams.

"I keep wondering if I shouldn't have stayed where I was."

"No," said Luke, meaning it, knowing it, from the bottom of his heart. "No."

She replaced the weapon at her belt. "Even if I'd known . . . this," she said softly. "Even if I'd guessed . . . been able to see into the future . . . once Cray asked me if I wanted to . . . to take her place . . . I couldn't have said no. Luke, I . . ."

He brought her into his arms, and their mouths met hard: giving, forgetting, remembering, knowing. Telling her without speech how groundless were the doubts that she didn't dare put into words.

"It isn't the Force in you that I love," he said softly, when at last they eased apart. "It's you."

She bent her head forward, rested her forehead on his shoulder; they were much of a height. "It's not going to be easy for me," she said softly. "Maybe it's not going to be easy for us. Sometimes last night, wandering in the caves, I blamed you for this. I was angry—I think I'm still angry, deep down. I don't know how you could have been responsible, but I blamed you anyway."

Luke nodded, though the words hurt. In a curious way he understood that they weren't personal, and it was better to know. "I understand."

She moved her head and looked at him with a wry quirk of smile. "Oh, good. Explain it to me?"

He kissed her again instead.

"Will you come to Yavin with me?" When she hesitated, he said, "You don't have to. And you don't have to make up your mind now. Leia tells me you've written out all the names you can remember of people who were here . . . She says you'll be welcome on Coruscant, for however long you want to stay. And I know it won't be easy to be . . . to be around students, adepts in the Force. But your knowledge of the old methods of teaching, the old ways of training, would help me . . ."

His voice fumbled with the words, and in the stillness of her face he saw her effort not to trouble him with her own pain, her own uncertainty.

Oh, the hell with it . . .

"I need you," he said softly. "I love you, and I want you with me. Forever, if we can manage it."

Her mouth moved in a smile. "Forever." The gray eyes met his, darker than the fog around them, but equally suffused with light. "I love you, Luke, but . . . it's not going to be easy. But I think . . . I feel that we're going to be in each other's lives for a long time."

"We have time," he said. "There's no hurry. But there is—and there always will be—my love for you."

They were still clinched tight in each other's arms, cheeks resting on each other's shoulders, when Han and Leia, Chewie, Threepio, and Artoo appeared in the broken gateway. Leia said softly, "Let them be for a while."

"He can kiss her on the ship," said Han good-naturedly. "Jevax has finally got the landing silos repaired, and we've got those gizmos from the toy room loaded up, and I for one want to get off this rock before something else happens."

"This would be advisable, Your Excellency," added Threepio. "Admiral Ackbar did mention concentrations of Grand Admiral Harrsk's troops in the Atravis Sector, and we have no idea where or with whom Roganda and her son have taken refuge. Given the necessity of implementing small but significant changes in the schematic of every ship in the fleet—or of finding adequate shielding where schematic change is impracticable—it would perhaps be expedient to get under way as soon as we can."

"You're right." Leia looked around her for a last time at Plett's House, or the ruin that the Empire had left of it: broken walls, shattered arches, the metal slab replaced over the well. The echoes of its ancient peace filled her, covering the pain and ruin as the exuberance of the rift's ubiquitous vines covered the scars of that ancient shelling. Somewhere she seemed to hear children's voices again, singing that old song about the forgotten Queen and her magic birds.

Callista had given her a partial list of names, all she could remember, though she herself had only visited the place briefly and didn't know most of the Jedi there. But it was a start. And she had something of those forgotten children, something of the old Jedi who had lived here, who had offered them refuge . . .

Movement flickered in the corner of her vision. *A ghost?* she thought. *Or the echo of a memory?* The shadows of two tiny children chased each other over the thick olive-tinted grass, and faded into a stray drift of fog.

Nichos? she wondered. *Roganda? One running toward the light, the other toward the dark?*

Someone whose name she did not yet know?

Or were they shadows from the future, not the children who had been there, but the children who were to come?

"Hey, kid!" yelled Han, and Leia poked him in the ribs.

"C'mon," she said. "Luke deserves a break."

It had been, for him, a long, long time.

The couple on the bench turned their heads.

"We're blowin' out of this jerkwater rock," called out Han. "Can we drop you anyplace?"

They looked at each other, their faces reflecting a curious kinship, for a moment more like brother and sister than lovers: people who have known each other for lifetimes past. Then Callista said, "Yavin. If it's on your way."

Han grinned. "I think we can manage that."

Luke and Callista crossed the grass to them hand in hand.